THE
SADDLING

Also By James Collins

Other People's Dreams
Into the Fire
You Wish!
Jason and the Sargonauts
The Judas Inheritance
Lonely House
Remotely

Symi 85600
Carry on up the Kali Strata
Village View

JamesCollinsAuthor.com
www.facebook.com/jamescollinsauthor

THE
SADDLING

JAMES COLLINS

RC Publishing

RC Publishing

First published in Great Britain in 2017
Copyright © James Collins 2017

Cover: Red Raven Book Design
Cover author photograph: Neil Gosling

Printed by CreateSpace, an Amazon.com company.

ISBN 978-1546326878

Available from Amazon.com, CreateSpace.com, and other retail outlets.
Available on Kindle and other devices.

To my friend and mentor
Nigel Edwards

Acknowledgements

I am indebted to Nigel Edwards for his advice, editing, and typesetting, and for the 1912 newspaper article, Jenine Woodhall, Neil Gosling, and Ann Butler Rowlands for their reading of early drafts (any remaining errors are all my own work), Forgotten Books for their advice on the use of *A Dictionary of the Kentish Dialect and Provincialisms*, W. D. Parish for compiling it in 1888, and Andrew Sinden for his local Romney Marsh knowledge.

James Collins
Symi, Greece, April 2017

Dialect

The dialect used by some of the characters is based on *A Dictionary of the Kentish Dialect and Provincialisms in use in the County of Kent*, by W. D. Parish, 1888. The reprint copy I have is from Forgotten Books (www.forgottenbooks.com). These are words that were in use across the whole county in the 19th century and may not necessarily be in use on the Romney Marshes. I have also used dialect I remember from growing up on the marsh, and invented some of my own.

The meaning of most dialect words should be obvious to the reader, but I have provided, below, a glossary of some of the more unusual ones. There are so many that I could have used; the language is rich with wonderful words that bring a wry smile, but I didn't want the reader to *wrongtake me nor be stounded nor put in a mizmaze*, if you take my meaning.

Below are some words used in the story which were not so easy to make obvious in the text. Some of these are my own invention.

Anting	searching for ants (behaviour of crows)
Bar-goose	a sheldrake (a kind of duck)
Barth	a cattle shelter
Beetle	a wooden mallet
Blar	to bleat
Blue bottles	wild hyacinth
Bo-boys	scarecrows
Boneless wind	the north wind
Buffle-head	stupid
Clatting	removing dirt etc. from between the hind legs of sheep
Copse bridge	a fence across a dyke
Deek	a dyke, ditch, sewer
Dole-stones	a landmark
Dowal	boundary post
Dowels	low marshes
Droke-weed	a filmy weed in standing water
Fairy sparks	phosphoric light
Falser	a liar
Fazen	a large brown eel
Felds	fields

None-so-pretty	the London Pride flower
Obediences	a bow or curtsey
Paddocks	toads
Paigle	cowslip
Pillow-beres	pillow cases
Poachy	trampled, muddy ground
Ravel bread	white-brown bread
Sparr	sparrow
Sulings	a measure of land
Swilling land	land for ploughing
Tattle	a mess
Tegs	first year sheep
Tiver	red ochre for marking sheep
Toar	long grass
Treddles	sheep dung
Willing-light	ritual candle
Wind-bibers	haws

Historical Note

The village of Saddling exists only in my imagination. The church that inspired the location is real and is there on the Romney Marshes, although I have taken some liberties with its description. You can visit it at Fairfield and, if you do, I am sure a donation towards its upkeep would be appreciated.

In the 52 years between 1236 and 1288, the Romney Marshes were hit by six bad storms which had significant impact on the landscape. The worst of these occurred in 1287; it destroyed entire villages and forced the River Rother to change its course. The same storm devastated the low-lying northwest Netherlands across the channel, causing the world's fifth worst flood in recorded history, the collapse of the Zuidersee sea wall, and the loss of over 50,000 lives.

One

The storm hit from the east. Unrelenting rain hammered through a mass of angry black cloud. Gale-force winds drove it hurtling into a sea that heaved like a lumbering monster. Waves swelled and crashed onto themselves. The unyielding rage of the storm blew them towards the shore, swamping the flat marshes and reclaiming land. Church towers fell, houses crumbled beneath the onslaught and lightning split what ground it could find.

A man in a black tunic, his head bent sideways to the stinging rain, rowed hard against the flood. His strong arms pulled back on the oars as he fought his way across the seething mass towards the only light; his church. A teenage boy lay curled in the water at his feet, his hands covering his face, sobbing.

'Bail, John, bail and pray,' the cleric, Di-Kari, shouted. The wind snatched his words and threw them overboard. The boy only responded when he was kicked and, trembling and freezing, he threw water from the boat. The faster he bailed, the faster the storm refused it. 'Keep at it, John,' Di-Kari encouraged. 'Or we die.'

A sheep carcass banged into the boat and twisted fast away. Di-Kari struggled as an oar caught beneath the water. He yanked it free, and a body rose to the surface. In a strike of cold lightning, he saw the woman's face. Stunned though he was, he held back the tears. He had seen many deaths that night.

There was no time to think of those he could not help. He had to save those he could, and the terrified boy depended on him. Di-Kari concentrated on the church on the knoll and rowed harder.

The surviving villagers sheltered in their church. Women whimpered, men did what they could to keep shutters closed and lamps alight. Some knelt on the dirt floor, others sat, wet and freezing, with their backs to the rough stone walls. The church was bare save for the stone altar. Beside it stood a tall, thin man with streaming black hair. Black robes hung from him like an unwanted skin, wet and weighty. His eyes pierced the gloom, and his mouth twisted into a sneer. He gripped the altar harder as each crash of thunder rocked the foundations beneath him.

'Enough a'your fear,' he bellowed, his voice powering through the hell outside. 'Where be 'is God now? Where's God's preacher?'

'Pray, Blacklocks, pray wi' us,' a woman, kneeling, implored.

'This be nature's own work,' Blacklocks shouted. People, attracted by his voice, left the walls and moved towards him. 'No use a-pray.'

'There's blasphemy,' a man yelled. 'Pray wi' us.'

'Our people be dying!'

'It's nature,' Blacklocks boomed. 'She be taking her wrath on us fur following 'is false teaching.'

'It be the word of God,' a man cried out.

'His God ain't always right,' he retorted. 'And who else we got a-turn to? Ten years back we lost our land a'this. Our village, our whitebacks, all drowned.' He threw up his hands, and the lamps trembled as the wind attacked them. No-one heckled. 'This be how his Creator treats His creation. Why? Our land be gone again. He takes our homes, the sea comes a-drown us all. Be this his God? No. This be the work of nature so a'her we got a-turn.'

The doors crashed open, and lightning lit the solid figure of Di-Kari dominating the entrance, the exhausted young John in his arms. Men rushed forward to shut the doors against the wind as the cleric stepped inside. When the lightning flashed, they saw floodwater foaming up the mound towards the church.

Di-Kari carried the boy to the altar, the villagers moving out if his way. He put him down, and John staggered forward.

'Here's your boy, Blacklocks,' he said, spitting out the name with contempt. 'The last of us I could save.'

'My Jeremiah?' a woman called out in hope. Her voice was swiftly joined by many others yelling names of the missing.

'Gone,' Di-Kari shouted back against the wailing of wind and women. 'If he ain't here he's dead. Drowned by the storm.' He glared at the tall man. 'Like my wife.'

The congregation fell to its knees to pray again.

'That'll do you no good,' Blacklocks laughed down at them. 'This ain't His work. We got a-call on nature 'erself a-save us from,' he pointed directly at the cleric, 'him and his bitter God.'

Di-Kari took two strides up onto the raised floor. He grabbed Blacklocks by his soaked tunic and threw him away from the altar.

'Get from my church,' he yelled.

Villagers pushed towards the safety of the east wall. Blacklocks staggered into them, and his son ran to help. He pushed the boy away.

'Fader,' John pleaded. 'We have a-save ourselves.'

Blacklocks was not listening. He stared at Di-Kari, hate flashing in his eyes. He reached into his tunic and drew out a knife.

A lightning bolt struck the ground outside. Shutters exploded inward, and the storm drove in through the devastated windows. One door flew from its shattered hinge.

'Listen a-me, Di-Kari,' he demanded. 'If this be what your God commands then I have nothing more a-hear from him.'

'Fader!' John tried to pull the knife from his father's hand.

Blacklocks was stronger. He threw him away and took a long-legged stride towards the cleric.

Di-Kari saw him coming. Amid the mayhem, his screaming flock and the nightmare of the storm, he kept a level head. His eyes focused on the blade as it flew towards him. He side-stepped it. Blacklocks lurched again but tripped on the altar step. The knife stayed tight in his hand.

'The flood!' John's voice was louder than the storm.

Outside flashed white. Di-Kari saw water enter the church. Blacklocks was on him, the knife raised, ready to strike. Di-Kari caught Blacklocks' wrist just as the wind killed the last of the lamps.

He felt the tall man on him in the darkness, smelt his sweat and wet cloth. The cleric gripped tightly as unwashed hair fell over his face and into his mouth, greasy and foul tasting. He felt the man's leg between his, his weight bending him back across the stone.

'Fader!' he heard the boy call again, closer.

'What kind a God…?' Blacklocks was silenced as Di-Kari's hand forced its way between his fingers and found its own grip on the handle.

Both men fought hard for possession, Di-Kari pulling one way, Blacklocks the other, but the cleric's hand was stronger. A burst of light lit Blacklocks' snarling face as Di-Kari wrenched the knife from him. His arm flew out wide in a long arc as he spun away. The knife met some resistance. He tripped and fell to the floor.

He knelt there with his heart pounding in his head, expecting to feel the weight of the other man on his back. He aimed the blade upwards. One thrust and he would rid the village of Blacklocks forever. He was ready.

Nothing came except a cold knowing that something had shifted.

A lamp threw gentle, yellow light on the ground as the wind died. There was no howling, no thunder, but the cleric's flock backed away from him. His hands rested on the floor. Solid earth, it was now rain-soaked mud with rivulets of water running from the altar. One little river was darker than the others. More lamps were lit, showing a channel of blood weaving its way towards the open doors. The receding floodwater washed the blade clean as the tide crept away in silence. The cloud broke up, and silver light lit the roofs of drowned houses. Dead sheep floated past. The blood ran on, the river thicker now and Di-Kari rose to look back to the altar.

Blacklocks stood with his son in his arms, John's head tipped back, his sightless eyes and wordless mouth open. Blood dripped from a wide gash across his throat.

Blacklocks stepped down and walked slowly towards the east doors. The villagers knelt or parted, crossed themselves and bowed their heads.

The cleric felt hands on his shoulders. Someone grabbed his arm. 'Murderer,' a man shouted, and other villagers took up the cry.

'No! Leave him be.' Blacklock's voice commanded silence as he reached the doors. 'Look beyond.'

The village men thrust Di-Kari forward and released him. He came and stood beside Blacklocks where he placed his hand on the boy's head and whispered a prayer.

'Don't,' the tall man said, pulling his son away.

Not knowing what else to do or say, Di-Kari obeyed. A coffin, cracked and listing, twisted in the floodwater and sank. The full moon dazzled through the parting clouds and the water, receding, lay as calm as a lake.

Blacklocks wept over his son. 'He would a-made fifteen year come Twelve-tide,' he said. 'He'll see no more winters.'

'My regret is boundless,' Di-Kari said. 'It was an accident…'

'You should a-done this afore,' Blacklocks interrupted. 'You should a-appeased nature ten year back, stopped her storm then. Maybe your mistus would be a-living now.'

'We should pray,' Di-Kari said.

'They'll be no more praying here,' Blacklocks replied. 'Your God don't live in Saddling no more.'

Two

'In Iran,' the newscaster said dispassionately into the camera, 'two homosexual youths face death by public stoning amid outrage from the international homosexual community.' The story fell on deaf ears as a slightly overweight young man with scruffy stubble passed the television, his head down over a sheet of paper. A cup of strong, black coffee sloshed and spilt from his other hand. Glancing at the floor, he kicked a pizza box out of his path and navigated an office chair across the tiles towards a cheap, laminate desk piled high with books. The chair moved in an arc, one of its wheels refusing to turn, the others only giving in after a fight. Dropping his paper to the floor and putting his coffee on the desk without regard for placement, he shifted some notebooks to reveal a computer monitor and a keyboard.

Running his fingers through his dirty blonde hair, he lowered himself into the chair, his tired eyes fixed on the wall. Small bubble-head pins marked locations on a map of Great Britain, joined by cotton threads and pulled to cork tiles at the side. Here, small index cards showed scrawled names and dates. A maniac had attacked the workspace at close range, it seemed. Papers, photos, pages from books and Post-it notes formed an arterial splatter pattern bursting out from the centre of the desk to the furthest walls. Other fragments of his research littered the floor like dead matter.

Tom realised he was at the wrong desk.

'For Christ's sake,' he muttered.

He moved sideways a couple of feet and pulled out a prefab dining chair from the well of a second table. He sat, dragged the chair in, and forgot about his coffee.

The second workstation was as chaotic as the first, if not worse. Above it, a large and extended family tree grew like a wild creeper from a central name. Fronds spread across two walls of the small room and fingered towards the ceiling. Threads connected pinned papers, bandaged with tape that overlapped more documents, hiding detailed information until lifted. As the creeper grew, so it aged from the present day back to the medieval reaches of British history. Some branches journeyed back five or six generations, others eleven or more. Family lines thickly layered with ancestors recorded a maze of names and dates. It was nonsensical and uninteresting to anyone other than the man who had constructed it; Tom Carey.

Beneath this extended tree, a lamp threw fierce light onto birth certificates, copies of marriage licences, printouts from newspaper archives and land registry documents. A second monitor stood at the side of the desk displaying a map of Kent in the south-east of England. Beside it, a mobile phone, set to silent, glowed as a call went unanswered. A missed call alert took its place in the queue with the previous twelve, and thirty unopened text messages. A battered pewter tankard held pens and, next to that, lay a particular and much-used hardcover notebook. The desk drawers were open, spewing out more fitfully doodled notes, newspapers and paperwork. Whoever had targeted the first desk had moved onto this one, and the aftermath was just as appalling.

Beside the desk stood a large cardboard box half full with crumpled papers and empty crisp packets. An old, leather-bound bible lay discarded on top.

Tom searched the desk. Moving a beer can to the edge, he dug through some papers, found his mouse and clicked it. On the screen, a page of Cornish newspaper entries immediately replaced the map of Kent. Scanning a list of headlines and editions that he had scanned many times before, he reached for a pen, knocking the beer can into the rubbish box.

'Christ!'

He reached for the can and noticed the bible. No beer had been spilt on its thick cover. He grinned at it, tipping the can to threaten the word of God with a baptism of alcohol. Remembering whose bible it was, a shiver of guilt ran through him and, instead, he drained the can, crushed it and dropped it on the floor.

Tom looked from the screen to his main notebook and squinted. Tutting, he moved the Anglepoise lamp and drew it closer to the book and a page titled, 'Carey.'

'And back to old Thomas and his boys,' he mumbled. He clicked the mouse again and the Cornish records became the map of Kent. He zoomed into an area near the coast. 'Here one minute...' He stood and took two paces to the map. From a label that read, "Thomas Carey (1899)", he traced a piece of red cotton as it migrated from Kent in the east all the way across to Cornwall in the west. 'And here the next.' His finger came to rest on a small Cornish village in the Penwith area.

Tom sat, rested his palm over the mouse and clicked on his bookmark folder. 'Once more unto the breach,' he said, selecting a free births, deaths and marriages website. 'Once more.' He typed "Thomas Carey" in the search field and selected births for all counties and a year range spanning the end of one century and the start of the next. 'Or close the wall up with our English dead. And… search.'

He had done this a thousand times without result, but still he tried, ever hopeful that someone somewhere would have added some new information in the hour since he had last searched. No-one had, and no new search results showed up. He kicked the leg of the desk in frustration, and the lamp shuddered.

Behind him, on the television, the newscaster was now interviewing a leading member of the clergy, and a discussion about the rights and wrongs of religious capital punishment was underway. Although it filled every inch of the darkened room with human sound, Tom didn't hear it. Glancing at a calendar, he confirmed the day's date and a circled note that read, "Maud calling."

He picked up his notebook. 'It's got to be here somewhere.' He flicked through the pages as the seconds ticked by.

New sounds filtered in through the background murmur of the deaths of innocents but Tom was oblivious to them. He failed to notice the rise and fall in the grumble of London traffic as someone let themselves into his ground floor flat. He didn't hear the jangle of keys, the rattle of the letterbox as the front door closed, or the footsteps that clicked closer on bare boards. The sitting room door handle moved unnoticed as the door behind him opened and light from the hallway snuck in, disturbing the cheerless room.

A woman in her early twenties stepped in. Dressed in a dark coat that reached to her ankles, a neck scarf tucked in at the lapels and a pair of black gloves, she might well have been returning from a funeral. Her thick eyeliner and the raven-black dye of her shoulder length hair suggested more Goth than burial. Her Ferrari red lips were edged in crimson and scarred her pale face. She held a pile of unopened mail in her hand and a set of house keys dangled from one finger.

Marie checked the living room, hopeful that Tom had heeded the ultimatum she had given him two days earlier. Nothing had changed. He clearly had not. The clutter persisted and grew hand in hand with his obsession. The computers remained, the phone was still unplugged (something she took personally), and the paper growth on the walls had thickened. The fireplace that she had lovingly restored when Tom first moved in was still masked by the cheap, MDF shelf unit. The smell of the room still told the same story; no windows had been opened in months.

Marie let out a long sigh; she knew what she was here for and why.

'I saw them tow your car away,' she said. Tom didn't react so she pulled the plug on the gay rights activist protesting against the Iranian stoning and said it again.

Tom stood up, his back still to Marie, and pulled aside the dark curtain. He peered into the street and, through a fog of window dirt, saw the space outside where his car had been. He'd not used it since he'd stopped going to work. He had been unable to afford the repayments months before that.

'Don't need it.'

He returned to the desk.

'I didn't try and stop them,' Marie said, but Tom made no response. Nothing had changed there either. She pocketed the keys and flipped through the mail while looking for somewhere to put the envelopes. She dropped all but one of them on the floor where many others already lay fading. Opening the one, she glanced through the letter within.

'They are going to fire you.'

'Yeah, I know,' he replied.

'The flat will be next.'

'Soon won't need it.'

'You can't be sure.'

Tom glanced at his watch, his right heel tapping fast on the floor.

Marie took the letter to the wall and, using one of the pins, skewered it hard to the only place Tom would notice it; the centre of his family tree.

'I'm getting really close, Marie,' he said, his head down over his notes. 'Look at this.'

He slid a piece of paper to the side of the desk, knocking the tankard of pens.

Marie glanced at a lot of meaningless names and dates then turned away.

'Isaac Carey, right?' Tom talked into his book. 'My great, great, uncle. He was seventeen when he died, and I know he died in Saddling. The last of us who did.'

Behind him, Marie yawned silently.

'But the thing is, after generations living in Saddling, why did his brother Thomas leave the place and move from Kent to Cornwall? And so young and on his own? What happened there in nineteen-twelve? No reason to move, no notes, letters, no results. But the answer's got to be there somewhere.'

Tom hadn't noticed Marie leaving the room. He didn't notice her return either. He was clicking through Ancestry.com, and she was carrying a small suitcase. He only looked up from his computer when Marie reached across him, disturbed some papers and removed a photo of the two of them taken in happier times.

'I'll be with you in a minute,' Tom said. 'Got to find something new before Maud calls. I'm sure I'm on the edge of a breakthrough. I've got this stuff about the Romney Marshes and Dylan's coming over to help.'

Marie backed away from the desk and stood in the centre of the room beneath the dead light bulb. Her face was half in shadow and half caught in the spill from the desk lamp.

'I have to do this,' Tom said, glued to his screen.

'Yeah.' Marie's voice was soft and edged with sadness. 'And I have to do this, Tom.'

'It's not just for the money.' He rearranged the disturbed papers with one hand and scrolled with the other. 'I'm doing it for us.'

Marie backed to the door. 'So am I,' she whispered.

'There's, like, one more missing link, one piece of information I need that will give me her answer. You know what that means?'

He realised he was alone and the room was peacefully empty. The front door clicked shut. The letterbox rattled as the set of keys clattered through. He knew she wouldn't be coming back.

Tom sighed, relieved. He was alone now and hungry for the freedom that was spread out before him like a feast.

He turned on the television. The news had ended, and a bubbly daytime personality was teaching the nation how to wrap awkwardly shaped Christmas presents in a tone somewhere between patronising and excessively patronising. Tom stretched his arms up over his head, lacing his fingers together and cracking his knuckles. A weight had been lifted, but, as he swung around in his chair and caught sight of the time, he felt another one descend.

He worked on, unaware of the dying afternoon, only aware of the minutes ticking away. He kept one eye on the Skype icon and the call he was expecting as faded faces of the gone and never-known watched him from old photographs. The manmade, blue light from his monitor stung his eyes. All around him the dead of the past taunted him in the gathering, cloying darkness, tempting him ever further back into the obscurity of his history.

Tom checked the clock. The further he searched back in time, the more it ran away from him.

Three

He stood at the cleft rail fence and thought about the dark ditch on the other side. It wasn't a barrier, and yet it was. A man could swim it or drown trying. Beyond it the marsh rolled on, marked out with random bursts of bulrushes growing thick on the deek banks. Apart from the uneven lines of hawthorn and willow that stated boundaries, the level land was constant to its vanishing point. Out there was a place he would never know. He had come far from home, to the mark where he could walk no further. He was at the edge of his world, the limit of his life.

The sky lasted forever. The texture of beryl-blue satin, grey clouds draped from it and flowed in fluid formation over his head from east to west. They rolled and fell as they grew and slipped, leading his eye towards a darkening horizon. There they faded into the approaching night, tumbling onwards, free. A breeze, smelling of earth and animals, dried his lips and stung his blue-grey eyes. The sun was low somewhere behind him, casting a brief light through the brittle air. It was enough to throw his shadow past the fence and into the forbidden land. Clouds soon smothered it, cooling what cherished warmth the dying day offered and leaving him lonely; a young figure on an ancient landscape.

He pulled his woollen coat tighter and looked inland.

The distant hill swung around in a great arc. Miles distant, it stood like a protecting battlement forged millions of years before. The forest there kept watch over the wetlands he called home. At night in the black distance, he could see tiny pricks of light from homes among the trees. Patches of grey showed where the red and orange of autumn maple and beech gave way to the starkness of winter. Only the faithful evergreens stayed on to witness the seasons change.

Over to the west, the sun threw up its last, desperate beams like the arms of a man drowning in glory. It ignited low clouds, slashing them below with blood-red streaks that dripped beneath the ominous billowing pressing down from above. A storm was fermenting out of his reach. Beyond his control, it would soon boil and overflow, bringing the solstice rains that every villager feared.

He lifted his foot onto the lower rail of the fence where moss had weathered it green and patched it with grey. He wiped away something that had gathered under his boot. It could have been mud, but it was more likely whiteback treddles. He pressed his foot into the narrow ridge of the triangular rail and the oak dug through the worn leather to massage his aching sole.

The breeze pestered his hair, flicking auburn strands across his face and into his eyes. He pulled them free and tucked them back behind his ear where they stayed briefly. The breeze always won, however, and they would soon return like the winter to sting his face.

He wiped the other boot clean and rested it on the fence. His bootshoes would clag up on the walk home for sure, they always did, no matter what the season. There was always something on the rain-soaked, tufted grass to grab and cling, something left by a wandering herd, or a molehill dampened by the dew. It had been a wet summer, and yet the crops had survived. The whitebacks had grazed freely, the hay was bailed and stored, and most of the autumn potato harvest gathered safely. He had been an all-worker on the Rolfe farm for the last six years. It was backbreaking work but rewarding. His body was in good shape. There had been wet days, spent with his hands deep in the earth, his coat soaked by day and hung to hearth-dry by night. In the morning, he had knocked off the dried mud before trudging back out to dirty his clothes again in the fields. His hands, then rough, had now had time to recover and were smooth as there was no work for him, not at this time. The recent harvest boded well for the winter, as long as the storm didn't come. The sky told him it would.

He knew he should be bound for home. It was Penit, and the Minister had called a special meeting. As one of those entitled to be chosen, he could decide not to attend but what was there to stay away from? His friends would be there, and he would find warmth in their company.

Dropping his foot to the ground with a heavy sigh, he stood up straight, pulled hair from his eyes and turned to face home. The high hill stretched on into the distance and disappeared into the west where the sun sank lower, its beam-bursts doused by rain clouds. Between him and it lay nothing but the age-old dowels, the flat marshes that were crisscrossed with deep and wide sewers draining water from land to sea. Last-light landed on them and threw up silver shimmers like brief moments of hope in daylight's certain death.

The village, a tiny dark smudge in the middle of this wild emptiness, stood out. From it rose thin trails of smoke. The evening fires had been lit against the smothering dusk that would quickly drift to night over the marsh. Some stars might shine through if the gathering cloud allowed and he knew that the moon was coming up to full. It might be enough to dissolve the cloud with its brilliance and permit some sharper days before the storm. The worst weather always took its time to tease. It delayed its inevitability until hope won out against fear and the land believed it might be spared. After twenty-two years in this life, however, he knew the certainty of the solstice storm and knew that there was only one way to avoid it.

He began his walk homeward unafraid of the gathering dark. He knew the lie of the land, the track of the deeks with their plank bridges over treacherous, muddy water, he knew where the lows lay and where the recently ploughed swilling-land would be safe to tread. There would be no danger for him; not for a few days yet.

Lazy whitebacks moved across the fields, heads down to the way-grass and, in contrast, dark shapes hopped among them where caller birds pecked for the last worms of the day. Feeding up before roosting, they jumped short distances jabbing with their greasy, black wings. Disturbed by his tall frame that was shaped and blackened by his long overcoat, one nearby bird took to the air with a warning caw. It flew fast towards him, its eyes fixed on his. His heart leapt from its stable, raced and bucked, his cold skin tingled colder and he dropped his head. Cowering, his hands dug deep into his pockets. He turned away as the caller bird flapped past. He took another path, unwilling to disturb the other birds that were now alert to his presence and considering him with treacherous eyes.

He came to a narrow drainage deek with two rotting planks as its bridge and crossed into one of the Cole farm fields. Laid in, fallow for last year, it was now planted with mangel beets and potatoes in long strips. He had helped plant them. The further fields meant the longest walk to work, but he loved the distance; the further from home, the closer to Far Field and the village boundary. There would be purple and white flowers come the spring, and then, when the time was right, there would be the harvest and the celebrations with bathtub and ale. Martin Tidy would play his home-bored flute, and Andrew his whistle. Sally Rolfe would join them on her father's accordion and sing. There would be dancing in the barn while, outside, the men would throw hay bales over a post to contest their strength. The harvest roast would be served; this year a couple of Farrow's sheep had been grudgingly promised. Barry would drink too much bathtub and make a fool of himself again, and Mark Blacklocks would sit, brood and stare at Sally until her father would come and carefully warn him away.

He stopped in his tracks, and his feet sank an inch into the soft turf. His coat blew open, and he left his hair to flap over his face like a shield. Through it, he could make out the wooden spire of the church raised up above the houses on its knoll. The chimney smoke trailed across it like marsh mist, and it faded slowly from view as the brief dusk took a firmer hold.

A caller bird croaked, reminding him that he may not see next year's harvest dance. He might not see the purple and white flowers of the potato crop or taste the earthy spice of another cup of bathtub. The village was now in Penit, and the date was nearly on them. The bird did not need to remind him of who he was, how old he was, and that he was eligible.

Daniel Vye knew full well that he might only have a few more days to live.

Four

'**W**hat you must understand is that these young men grew up within those rules, within that doctrine. They are part of a society that says, "This is wrong and if you do this, then this will happen." They knew the consequences. That was their law and that's what they must follow.'

'Surely you're not saying…'

'I am. It's simple. Keep to the law or face the consequences.'

'Even if that means they shall be barbarically and publicly stoned to death simply because they were born in the wrong place at the wrong time? How can that be right?'

'I am not saying that it is right or wrong, and it isn't wrong to the majority of people who live there, by the way. I am only saying that theirs is a very old religion.'

'So, everyone… No, please, let me in here. Everyone must be a sheep and follow the flock because that is the way it has always been? Even if that means killing your own? That's ludicrous.'

'In any kind of religion-led society, there are rules and punishments for breaking the religious law. In any civilised society, actually.'

'But they broke no rules. They were simply born different. No, they were born. That's all. And there's nothing civilised about…'

Tom switched off the television debate and saw his reflection in the darkened screen. 'Believing in God is the only sure way of going to hell,' he said and turned sideways on to check his slightly flabby belly. It reminded him that he'd not been to the gym for weeks. Choosing to ignore it, he spoke to the television. 'No unseen force rules my life.'

Using patches of clear floor like stepping stones, he picked his way across the living room and noticed a letter pinned to one of his charts. He pulled it down and read the written warning from the software design company. He must turn up for a meeting with the head of human resources on Friday at nine in the morning or else lose his job. It was only Tuesday, so that could wait. He had more important matters to see to and one of them was just about to happen.

Sitting at his desk, he opened Skype. Maud was online now and, according to the reminder, was due to call him right about…

A computerised ringtone announced his aunt, bang on cue as usual. There was no way of avoiding her. Although he needed more time to complete his search, he would have to tell her the bad news. He clicked the 'accept' symbol.

The face of his aunt appeared larger than life filling his monitor with her authority. Thin, sallow and lit poorly from the glare of her screen, she sat in a darkened room. Her eyes flicked around and then settled, looking slightly to her right. Tom angled his lamp towards his own face, chubbier but showing similar features.

'Ah, there you are,' Maud said. She sat too close to her monitor as usual. She didn't understand that she could be back from the computer and still be heard. Tom had never actually seen the room behind her. She could be calling him from anywhere.

He greeted her, but she cut him off with, 'Well? Have you found it?'

He took a deep breath. 'No,' he said. 'It's a dead end.'

'What?' Maud had a hint of anger in her brittle voice. 'But you have had three months. You promised…'

'I know, but it's proving very difficult.'

'Have you been to the village?'

'Well, I've not actually been there. But I have seen their transcripts at Maidstone.'

'Is that all you have accomplished?'

He could hear the displeasure in her voice, and it took him back to his childhood. The more he tried to lie his way out of something, the worse it was for him in the end.

'Well, no. I've also…'

'Did the family bible help?' Maud snapped back. 'It arrived?'

Tom glanced at the book and coughed slightly. 'Yes, I have it, and no, not really.' Although it contained a brief family tree, it hadn't told him anything he didn't already know. If there were other clues in it, then Maud surely would have found them already.

'What do you mean, not really?'

'Maud, I don't need the bible. Everything is online now.'

'Not everything, else you would have found something. Correct?'

She was right. 'Maybe,' he said. 'Look.' He held up his videocam and moved it around the room showing her the research papering the walls.

'What a hideous mess,' she said when the camera settled back on Tom.

'And you look fairly awful too. Shave, boy. Have you been getting fresh air? Have you been outside?'

'Not for a while. I spend every hour I can on your mystery. See here?' He held up a simple chart showing the Lawrence side of his family tree. 'Here's my mother's line, right back to fifteen-twenty-two, in Cornwall.'

'Not of relevance.'

'And now, look here.' He held up another simple, one-line chart. 'The Carey line, my father, your brother. Then my grandfather and his Cornish wife, and my great-grandfather, Thomas, and his brother Isaac, and then...'

'Tom, we know all this. What we don't know is why.'

'Yes, yes, but did you know that the Lawrence family...?'

'No.' His aunt shouted, her voice distorted through his speakers. She coughed and, once started, found it hard to stop. She turned away from the camera, struggling for breath. 'Please, don't make me do that again,' she said. 'It is very painful. Tom, we don't need to know about the rest of the family.'

Tom glanced around the room and at his months of work, dismissed in one bout of cancerous coughing.

'I am not interested in who married whom and when. I only want to know what happened to make Thomas Carey leave Saddling, alone, aged thirteen. What occurred in nineteen-twelve, Tom?'

He had no answer for that.

Maud went on. 'Why should ours, an old marsh family, suddenly abandon its home and travel three hundred miles to start again? My father never told me. I only wished I'd asked him before he passed.'

'There must be more information somewhere. It's just that there is confusion over where the recent parish records are held.'

'Recent?'

'The original, older Saddling records were stolen sometime early in the twentieth century but eventually turned up in the County Library. Those are the parish registers of births, deaths and marriages, the village accounts, rolls, that kind of thing, up to nineteen-twelve.'

'Stolen?' Maud sat back slightly from her screen, and her eyes lit up briefly. 'There is something there... Wait. A deeper mystery.' She was talking to herself.

'Well, I wouldn't say it was a mystery, it often happens. Recently the original, historical records books for the smaller, remote Kent villages were gathered in and sent to the central records office at Maidstone, as we thought. They are in the process of digitising them and…'

'Of what?'

'Basically, capturing each page on film and making a digital copy. A photo if you like. When that's done, people will be able to pay to go online and flick through them virtually. You can already do that with Essex.'

'We were from Kent. I don't give a damn about Essex,' Maud said. Tom thought he detected a smile, but if there was one it was gone in a painful flash.

'Sometimes these books held more than church records,' he explained. 'Parish notes, records of expenses, other clues about what was happening in the village at certain times, even journals and diaries if the vicar was inclined to keep them. But the available records run out in nineteen-twelve. No sign of anything since. Not yet. Maybe they'll turn up one day.'

Maud did not look impressed. 'Two things,' she said, and Tom noticed her wipe something from the corner of her mouth that might have been blood. 'I do not have enough time to wait for "one day." Secondly, and I shan't say this again, I only want to know why my grandfather Thomas left the village. You must do what you can. Do you need more money?'

'No,' Tom said without thinking.

'Good.'

He should have asked for more. She had plenty to give. He had already been through the money she had paid him to pursue her passion, a passion that had quickly become his. Being paid to research a family mystery beat his nine-to-five day job writing computer games. Maud's money quickly evaporated in searching for other ancestors and ordering books and certificates for other lines that were not part of his brief.

'You know, Tom,' Maud said. 'It is not just about your inheritance, considerable though that will be if you succeed. This is all about the family that has gone before, our Di-Kari ancestors, our Careys, the generations of those who lived the pure and straightforward life through history. It's doing what is right, for them.'

'You've told me,' Tom said, trying to hide a sigh of boredom.

'Tom, we are the last Careys. Soon you will be the very last.' She raised her thin eyebrows. 'Do you understand?'

'Yes, Aunt Maud,' he said. He understood, but he was not interested in marriage. He was not particularly interested in women, much as he wanted to be. Since Maud had given him this task, he only had time for completing it and unlocking his fortune.

He realised that she was speaking.

'I said, when can you go?'

'Go?'

'Yes. Leave that horrid room and go down to the village. That's where the book is, is it not?' The admonishing school ma'am was back.

'What book? What have you not told me?'

'The Saddling journal, it exists.'

Tom was speechless for a second.

'How long have you known this?' he said.

'It just came back to me, then, when you mentioned the theft. I'd forgotten all about it. I remember your grandfather telling me some similar story years ago. He said something about original records being taken, but that there remained a village record. A transcript of the originals. "The Ministers' Diary", he called it. Yes. He did. I'd quite forgotten that.'

'If you'd told me before...'

Tom could have slapped her. If he'd known that there was such a book for sure, he would have gone to the village weeks ago and been rich by now.

'So, now you can go and look at it. You have a car do you not?'

'Actually, not sure about that, Aunt Maud.'

'It's not far from London. What? Seventy miles to the marshes?'

'Yes, but...'

'Anyone with any sense would have gone directly there when given the money. Looked at graves, asked people. You should do it immediately. It's nearly Christmas, and the weather is not improving.'

'Yes, but...'

'But nothing. Do you want me to leave all this...' she waved her arms around at what Tom couldn't see, '...to the state? Or would you rather the Carey inheritance came to its last family member? Simple choice.'

There was no need to rub it in, Tom thought, and no reason that he could see why she just didn't will her fortune to him, full stop. Why put him through this test? He said nothing.

'I know you, Thomas,' she said, using his full name as she did when she was angry. 'If someone says sit, you stand. If someone says you can't enter, you go in. If I say to you, go to Saddling and ask questions, you will stay at home with your computers and sit on your backside. I also know that you cannot let this rest. You are stubborn and curious like all the male Careys have been.'

Another bout of coughing interrupted her speech. She recovered more slowly from each fit, and every time they came, they stayed longer and left more pain on her face. She was due for more tests in a day or two, to see how advanced the cancer was, but it didn't look good.

Tom studied the map of Kent while she composed herself. He was in North London, Kent was not that far, but there were no railway lines or roads near the empty space in the middle of the Romney Marshes where, according to old maps, Saddling was, or had been. It didn't show up on his ordnance survey map, so he doubted that the village still existed. There was only one way to find out, and that was to go there, look for this book and ask people what history they knew. He could understand her curiosity. He, too, hated to leave a mystery unsolved. They shared that family trait but her passion for ending her 'Great Matter' was overwhelming.

As if reading his mind through the screen, Maud said, 'Tom, this is crucial.' Her voice was quiet, rasping as she dabbed her lips with a handkerchief. There was no mistaking the blood this time. 'I want to die knowing what my grandfather did, and why. Was it honourable? Was it a good thing? You have to do right for the family.' Her tiny eyebrows raised in a silent greeting away from the camera. 'And now I must go,' she said, and ended the call.

Tom sat back in his chair, put his hands behind his head and stared at where his aunt had been. There were too many questions, and he could see only two ways to find her answer. One relied on hacking, and the other relied on driving to the middle of nowhere.

Thinking he would calm down with another beer, he swung his chair to the room, and leapt back in shock.

Five

A man in a scruffy parka stood two feet away holding a miniature Christmas tree. He opened his wet parka and flashed at Tom while grinning broadly and winking. His T-shirt showed a blood splatter and an over-hopeful slogan, "No More Hate."

'Jesus, Dylan!'

'I've still got the old shock magic I see, jolly good. How about this?'

'Bit naïve,' Tom said. 'And won't you get cold?'

Dylan thrust out the small Christmas tree and waved it at the family chart on the wall.

'Season's greetings to you and yours,' he said, and threw it to Tom. He dropped his coat onto the floor. 'And no, I don't feel the cold. Besides, for December it's not too bad out there.'

Tom took the Christmas tree between his thumb and forefinger and dropped it in the rubbish box.

Dylan slid into the seat at the other desk and spun himself around in the swivel chair. Tom noticed his new, slim-fit jeans and felt a twinge of jealousy. He couldn't afford new clothes, and Dylan was slim enough to wear the style. His own jeans, faded on the knees and frayed, were tight at his waist.

'Ready to go?' Dylan asked. 'I've not got long. There's a demo against the killings in an hour. You coming with?'

'What killings?'

'The kids in Iran. The gay boys.'

'What good will that do?'

'Don't get me started.'

'Besides, you're not… gay.' Tom felt his skin shiver at the word. It embarrassed him to use it.

'So? Being crushed to death by rocks hurled by an angry mob simply because you prefer chorizo to taco isn't right. Marie's coming.'

Tom turned to his monitor and opened a web browser.

'Ah,' Dylan said. 'I take it from that silence that things are not all plain sailing on the sea of dreams that was Tom and Marie.'

'No.'

'She's left you. I told you she would.'

'But moving on...'

'I mean, mate, if you're gonna have a GF you've actually got to take her out now and then, show her a good time. Maybe even introduce your chorizo to her...'

'You said you didn't have much time.'

'Hey. I'm the one doing favours here. But yeah, let's get this done. A county council, you said?'

'Kent.'

'I only asked.'

Tom almost laughed. 'Maidstone Records Office. I want to see if there's anything in there that I've not yet found online.'

'Phoned them?'

'Twice.'

'Emailed?'

'Daily.'

'Visited?'

'Don't you start.'

'Then, my lazy, PC addicted chum, all that's left to us interested family history researchers, is to hack away.'

Dylan tapped on the keyboard.

'How's the office?' Tom asked as he sat watching his friend work.

'Yeah, like you want to know. Can you imagine it, though? Being gay in a country like Iran?'

'No.'

'Can you imagine being gay? I mean, got to be odd, innit?'

Tom didn't answer. He picked up his notebook and checked some dates.

'What's worse,' Dylan went on, 'must be the knowledge that you're doomed, or possibly doomed, from an early age. I mean, there's Jude, right? Judith at the office? Oh, you are so fired by the way. They were going to write to you about it.'

'They did.'

'Jude, right? She says she's always known she was a lesbian. So, if she had the misfortune to be born in any Middle East country, more or less - no, probably - she would have grown up with the death penalty hanging over her head like these two guys we're protesting for. What must that be like? I mean how would that affect you when you were, say, a teenager? It's in Trafalgar Square. The story's gone global. Which part of Maidstone

County?'

'Kent County. Records office, it's in Maidstone.'

Dylan picked up a pencil and chewed the end of it as he mashed the keyboard.

'If we can't actually stop this barbarism,' he said, his eyes flicking up and down the screen, 'then the least we can do is shout out against it, right?'

'I guess.'

'You should never guess. Guessing causes fuck-ups. Facts only. Remember your training.'

'You sound like Professor What's-his-name.'

'Hell, he was dull. Far too stoned to know anything about the real world. By the way, you probably forgot, it's my birthday in two weeks, and I want a bloody big present for doing this.'

He typed some more, fast and accurately.

'Is it? How old?'

'Twenty-three. I told you.'

'Just checking facts.'

Tom was two years older than Dylan but nowhere near as skilled with code. Tom had no idea about how to hack a website or a data bank. He wouldn't want to. He was fearful of being caught. Being caught meant being in trouble, and that meant being told what to do by someone else; something that he had grown to loathe when at school. Tom had managed to evade the dictates of authority quite skilfully since those days. He couldn't stand to be ruled over, not by employers, the police, not even by a girlfriend. Marie had said that his fear of authority was one of his negative Aries traits. He had replied that he simply couldn't be bothered with the hassle, so he stayed out of trouble.

His foot tapped against the chair leg as he wondered what would happen if they were found hacking a local government website. He imagined the shame of a public trial and prison. Having no control over what happened to him was his biggest fear.

'You're putting me off,' the younger guy complained.

'Nothing puts you off, Dylan,' he said with a forced smile. 'How's it going?'

'You want the technical details? Well...'

'No. Just get in and see what you can find and get out before someone notices.'

Dylan took a data stick from his pocket and pushed it into the PC tower.

'No-one's gonna notice a thing with this little helper,' he said. 'It's taken me time, but I perfected it.' He clicked his mouse and sat back confidently, his hands behind his head, watching code cascade down his screen. 'Did your Aunt Moneybags have news?'

'Yes, there's less time and more pressure. Can you hurry up? There's a lot riding on this.'

'How much?'

'I'm not sure, but I remember my dad saying that the house alone was in the semi-million bracket.'

'Half a mil for a house? What else has she got?'

'I don't know, Dylan,' Tom protested. 'Are you there, yet?'

'Breaking into a government department's firewall-protected website via a machine as old and cranky as yours, over an internet connection as slow as this, takes time. I'd have thought that you, with your addiction to cyberspace, would have had a better rig than what you've got here.'

'Can't afford it.'

'Still, it's not right is it?'

'No. But when Maud goes and leaves me her cash…'

'No, stoning kids because they were born gay.'

'Jesus, you jump about. Concentrate.' There was a pause while Dylan apparently did nothing but look impressed with whatever his programme was doing. 'Anyway,' Tom finally said. 'It's an accident of birth. The Iran thing. Nothing to be done. Bored with that story now.'

'I know, man, and you've bored me enough with this goose chase. You owe me big time when I do find your… ah ha!'

'You got it?' Tom dragged his chair towards his friend and a screen busy with code. 'What you got?' he asked, catching a whiff of Dylan's scent. 'And why are you wearing perfume?'

'It's aftershave.'

'Mate, you're twenty-two, you've got a face like a black baby's arse, and you are going to a demo in the West End. You don't need aftershave.'

'Hot date,' Dylan said, his eyes fixed on the page of HTML. 'And why a black baby's arse?'

'Well, mainly because you're black.'

'Accident of birth. Ah ha!'

Strings of code flowed on the screen. Dylan tapped his pencil against the glass.

'It's all about seeing patterns,' he said and traced a line of code down the page. He found a similar one and traced that. 'See? There's nothing random in here. Marvellous, isn't it? Not like being indiscriminately picked to be executed because you grew up with an extra gene, or whatever.'

'Leave it out, will you? Saddling, nineteen-twelve. What are we looking at here?'

'Well, it's hardly FBI level security.'

'How would you know?'

Dylan said nothing but tapped a few more keys and sat back. 'There you go. You are looking at Kent County Council from the inside out. What do you want to snoop on, exactly?'

'Parish registers and records.'

'Ooh, national security breach or what?' Dylan typed some more.

'A place called Saddling…'

Dylan paused to look at his watch, said, 'I'll miss the speeches,' and then sat back. 'There.'

'Where?' Tom studied the monitor. 'I don't see anything.'

Dylan used his pencil as a pointer. 'This is a list of each parish in the county. This here looks like the place names, and here is a confirm or deny, true or false, command as to whether…' He pointed to another string of code lower down the page and read headings within less-than and greater-than symbols. 'Whether the records are on microfiche, digitally captured, transcribed, un-transcribed and awaiting processing, or missing.'

'I see that now. But Saddling?'

The pencil dragged slowly all the way down three scrolled screens.

'No such place.'

'Yes, there is. I've seen its records online.'

'No, I mean, yes. They are online. It says that, here, in the 'published' line. But nothing else is waiting to go live, no other records other than what's been put up. In other words, all Saddling records are now in the public domain.'

'No record of a village diary?'

Dylan double checked. 'Nope.'

'Are you sure?'

'Are you white?' Dylan shot back. 'Yes. No other records or books are held there with dates after… December nineteen-twelve. If you'd gone to Maidstone, you could have found that out weeks ago. Lazy bastard.'

Dylan indicated another part of the page. 'There's some references here to a place called Saddling, on Romney Marsh.'

'What references? From when?'

'Years ago.' Dylan peered closer at the code. 'Early twentieth century.'

'That's the right era. What else? Who's that?'

Among all the code and the numbers, the symbols and lines of text, one name leapt out. William Blacklocks.

'Are they taking the piss?' Dylan said.

'Who's he?'

'How should I know? You're the history freak. But it does say, if you read that line there, that you need to do what I have been telling you to do for weeks.'

Dylan pushed back from the desk, swung around to face Tom and saw how pale he had become over the past months. His eyes were pink and puffy, a sure sign of eye strain from this dark room and the false light from the PC. His chin was now nearly two, and he wondered when they had last played squash together. He felt sorry for the guy and also for their friendship. With Tom so obsessed with getting hold of his aunt's fortune, there had been no time for the friendship they used to enjoy. They'd known each other a few years, now. Tom was once punctual, funny, a good role model. But now? Now, he was a hermit, an addict with some kind of research disorder.

'Look, mate,' he said. 'I've done what I can to help. This programme has shown you what I told you all along. If you want to find out what happened to your Great Aunt Hilda, or whoever it was, you are going to have to go out there and, for a start, see if the place still exists. Secondly, see if they have any other registers, because sure as doo-dah there are no more in the county records office.'

Dylan pulled the data stick from the computer and folded his arms. 'You've got to get this obsession out of your system once and for all, or you're gonna drown in it.'

Tom's head snapped up. He glared at Dylan and his face flushed red.

'Damn,' Dylan said. 'Sorry, man, I didn't think. I didn't mean...'

'Forget it.' Tom took in a slow breath. 'But, yeah, you're right.'

'I know. Everyone knows.'

Dylan's smile showed perfectly white teeth glowing in the PC light. He winked a cheeky, round eye and said, 'So, when you going?'

'Problem.'

'No problems, only paychecks.'

'No car.'

'Take mine.' Dylan offered it without a thought. 'It's parked around the back. It's not quite dark yet, should still have its wheels.'

'I can't do that. You'll need it.'

'London Transport, can't beat it.' Dylan dismissed the objections. Tom needed a change from this room. 'In return, I'll use your machines here to do some more of my own, er, work. If that's okay?'

'If you get caught hacking on my IP address…'

'I'm a bit beyond being caught, mate, and what's an IP address? Know what I'm saying? But, I do need to get my credit rating up. So, what do you say? You go and do some spade work… I can't believe I just said that. You go do some digging down in the garden of Old Blighty, and I'll look after your…' He glanced around the room. 'I'll look after this art installation. Just be back on Friday if you want to work again. Get this whole thing out of your system and get back to being the Tom that Marie fell for, and the Tom that I used to like working with. Then, when you're loaded, let's all move on and not mention dead ancestors again. Deal?'

Tom hated to tell himself, but he knew that Dylan was right. He'd hit his head against the brick wall for long enough. He held out his hand while Dylan reached into his impossibly tight jeans and pulled out a set of car keys.

'I'll go in the morning,' Tom said. 'I'll be back the day after.'

'Good. And have a shave first, you look like shit.'

Six

Tom wondered how Dylan could afford a car like this on his salary, then remembered that his friend was, at that moment, adjusting his own credit rating somewhere in cyberspace. He smiled as he left the motorway at Ashford and followed signs for a place called Hamstreet. A roughly drawn map lay on the passenger seat beside a couple of empty Coke cans. Dylan's pristine, leather-seated, sports model was already starting to look like Tom's flat, and he'd only been in the car a couple of hours.

It felt good being out of London. 'Okay,' he thought to himself. 'You're using up the last of your overdraft on this trip which could result in nothing, but at least you've got some fresh air.' The heater blasted stuffy air and he wound the window down slightly.

'Clean air. Think positive,' Tom said. 'You're going to crack this mystery.'

He turned the power-assisted steering wheel with one finger and pressed another button on the radio. 'The thing about parenting,' a voice said, 'is that it doesn't come with an instruction manual…'

Tom switched to a station playing classical music. 'That'll do,' he said, and focused on the road ahead.

The word 'parenting' had hit a nerve, as words such as mum, dad and family always did with him. He tried to keep his mind off the subject, but it was something that refused to lie down and sleep. Even after fifteen years, the pain was still there and the nightmares still bothered him. Just when he thought his way ahead was clear and he had made it through the rubble of the past, the last sight of his parents would leap up to slap his memory and jolt his life.

Voices echoing in a high arc across tiled walls, laughs, yells, names, 'Tom!' circling from the right to the left and spiralling, fading into the distance. The way ahead was light, the tiles were white and glossy. His hand trailed along them, and his fingers bumped over the grouting at regular intervals. When he pressed his ear to the cold surface, he could hear the echoes dying away. His parents were up ahead; silhouettes against the summer daylight at the tunnel exit. His father, broad and moving slowly, held his mother's hand, their figures thinning as they approached the light.

Tom held back and let people pass him. The middle of the tunnel scared and excited him because he could sense the weight of the river above.

Fascinating drips fell from the ceiling and splashed into puddles on the concrete. He was nine, puddles were playthings.

He heard his mother calling.

'You'll get in trouble.' A stranger spoke as she passed. 'Here, come with me.'

Tom drew back. He didn't know this woman or her unfamiliar hand. Her skin was dark on the back of her hand and lighter on the palm, and she wore a ring with a large, deep-red stone. Taking the hand was wrong. He searched for his mother, but he could no longer see her.

'Thomas!' He heard her shouting.

A rumbling sound bubbled up through the voices and footsteps. The voices increased in volume, and there were more of them. People pushed past him, moving faster. The lady with the ring ran with them. Everyone was running.

'Tom. Run!'

He started to cry. The rumbling had become a vibration and the drips through the ceiling had become silver rivers pumping down the walls.

'Stay there!' His father's voice, distantly swallowed by echoes.

He felt a punch in his stomach, and suddenly he was moving away from his parents. Tucked under someone's arm, his head dangled and swayed and his tummy hurt in the too tight hold. The rumbling exploded into a crash that brought louder screams. Water splashed his face. He was thrown about as his rescuer fought against a rising tide.

'Dad?' he called, confused. No-one answered.

More rumbling vibrated in his chest. He heard his own sobs. He struggled. He saw a man's trousers, wet, wading up to his knees, the water rising fast. They climbed steps. Other people were ahead of them, the water chasing close behind. A huge crash came at the same time as a cold, dark thump that swept him away. He sank, someone pulled him up, he slipped again. He tasted cold and dirt, his throat closed up, he couldn't breathe. Feet kicked him, hard stone steps cracked into his shins. He gasped, and foul liquid tore hot in his chest. There was no way to get it out. Another arm wrapped around him and he fought back. They were going to hold him under and walk on him. Suddenly, he was being passed along a line of strangers, coughing up water and, finally, sore and bruised, his stomach empty, he felt dry grass beneath his hands.

A car horn blared, and Tom shook himself back to the road. In a flash, he expected to see himself bearing down on another vehicle and his foot shot to the brake. In fact, he had slowed right down, and the car was in danger of stalling. An angry motorist swerved by with a blast of his horn.

'Yeah, sorry, okay!'

The road was taking him downhill. He glanced at the map that he'd copied from a website after he'd given up on trying to understand Dylan's sat-nav. It worked, and he had found Romney Marsh and some villages on it but, entering 'Saddling' came up with 'location not known.' He'd looked back on old maps, found the nearest villages and drawn his own route to a nearby place called Moremarsh. After that, there didn't appear to be any new roads.

Following a sign to Brenzett and with the roads narrowing on either side, he eventually came to a roundabout. He saw a petrol station and checked his fuel gauge. He had plenty left. He took the roundabout and headed straight on, past an old Victorian school and towards Brookland. Somewhere along here, he thought, there should be a lane. The maps mentioned Moremarsh, and sure enough, there was a small, concrete and wood signpost pointing to an even narrower road. Hoping that he wouldn't scratch Dylan's paintwork, he slowed, took a right and drove carefully into a hedge-lined track that was deeply rutted in places.

He had lost count of how many miles he had crawled and bumped before the engine cut out and the car came to a dead stop.

Tom frowned at the engine with no idea what he was looking at. Finally, he thought to call someone on his mobile. He decided to start with Dylan, in case he was in some recovery scheme. Finding his coat scrunched up in the passenger's foot well, he pulled his phone from the pocket and hit the number. The signal showed one bar, but it quickly faded to none. Cursing, he held the phone over his head and moved it around.

'And what you gonna do if you do get a signal up there?' he said to himself. 'Shout up to it?'

He thought about standing on the roof of the car but then realised it was a soft-top. He noticed that the lane had widened slightly just before the entrance to a field and so, having tried to start the car again without success, he rolled it over to the verge in case anything came along; not that he had seen another vehicle since the roundabout. He remembered the garage and checked the time. The afternoon was wearing on. The best idea was to walk back and arrange for a tow.

The thought of a long walk didn't appeal to him, but hunger was starting to trouble his stomach. He'd finished his lunch of crisps and a chocolate bar well before Ashford, and it was now nearly two. It would be dark in a couple of hours. He tried the phone once more, again holding it up. He took a few paces and, still finding no signal, turned back to the car.

'That won't do you no good out 'ere.'

Tom leapt in shock, dropping the mobile.

An old, rugged man with grey eyebrows and white hair stood between him and the car. His cheeks were red. He'd either been working in fresh air or drinking heavily. He wore a rough sheepskin coat with its buttons missing. It hung open, and Tom could see a tatty white jumper beneath, stretched tightly over a round belly.

The man hooked a thumb to the car. 'That won't do you no good neither. Where d'you think you was 'eading?'

Tom bent to pick up his phone, relieved to see that it was still working.

'Saddling,' he replied. 'But, maybe I should get back to the garage first.' He noticed a flatbed truck a little way back down the lane and wondered why he'd not heard it pull up. 'Can you tow me?'

'No point. They're shit wi' engines,' the man said. 'I been fetching things out 'ere, thirty year now and they ain't never been no good wi' machinery. Only good at putting up diesel prices, ask me. Saddling, you say?'

'Yes, is it far?'

The man thought for a moment and then spoke as if he was recalling a script, his voice wooden. 'I thought it'd died. But I'll a-take you a'Moremarsh turning, if it 'elps. You can walk the sheer-way from 'ere. If you've a mind.'

'That'd be great.' Tom put on his coat and collected his bags. 'Is it a long walk?'

'Reckon on five mile, if it's still living. Not 'eard news from that place come a long time since.'

'Really?' That seemed odd to Tom. 'You must know someone from the village. My family was from there.'

He locked the car before following the man to his truck. 'The name's Carey, if you've heard of us.'

The farmer, if that's what he was, wasn't interested. He held out a hand, and Tom passed him his backpack. It contained only his notebooks and chargers. He'd not packed clothes as he hadn't expected to stay.

'Not 'eard from Saddling come a long time,' the man repeated as he yanked open a battered door. 'Climb in, nipper.'

Tom sat in the passenger seat and soon realised that his flat was nothing compared to the mess and mayhem in this farmer's truck; ripped seats, an overflowing ashtray, a gaping hole where a radio once lived and no door on the glove compartment. Empty cigarette packets and a thermos flask slid about the dashboard as the truck tipped deep into each rut. Tom clutched his laptop tightly.

The farmer slapped the dashboard and laughed for no reason.

Tom peered out and up to the sky. The sun was low, and he hoped that he would reach Saddling before dark. There was nothing right or left but hedges, ditches and sheep. A hill, presumably the one he had driven down earlier, lined the horizon. Between him and it lay endless, level fields that soaked into a misty drizzle. The vast, grey sky hung heavy overhead.

'Thing was wi' Saddling,' the farmer finally said, 'was that it were moated. Surrounded by sewers, see?'

'Sewers? Is that hygienic?'

The old man laughed again. 'No, ditches. Deeks. Them-as.'

He pointed to steep banks either side of a full, dark water channel where weeds slimed the surface. 'We calls 'em sewers in-marsh. Without 'em we'd all be back under sea tides. Saddling were an island, once as. All surrounded by its own deeks, some ten-foot wide and treach'rous. They say they was put 'ere back in 'istory, after the great storm. Kept the village safe. Others say different.'

'Is it safe, though?'

'You'll be fine, young'un. There'll be a bridge, expect. We 'ave a-be good at bridges out 'ere. Aye, there'll be a bridge if it ain't rotted-gone. Five mile on after, you'll find Saddling.'

'Five miles?'

'If it's still 'ere.'

'What if it's not?'

'Well, then, that be a question. I'd say come back this way, but careful. Don't want a-be slipping in no sewer, not this time a'year. You'll get stuck a'mud and freeze as likely.'

'And, if it is 'ere… here,' Tom corrected himself, 'does it have a pub ?'

'Maybe. If. No, I expect there'll be an inn. Whether there'll be a welcome fur ye or not, well, that's another piece of others' business.'

'Why do you say that?'

'See that?' The farmer pointed off to his right. Tom leant over to look. 'That be a lapwing.'

Was he changing the subject? 'Great, but Saddling?'

'Not far a while now.' The farmer bent forward and checked the sky. 'Storm coming. Not a'night, but soon. You can tell from them clouds, right up, see?'

They just looked like clouds to Tom.

'Prehaps,' the farmer said, 'I should take you a'Moremarsh and you can stay 'ere a night. Peg'll make you welcome at The George. Better than walking out a'Saddling this time a'day only a-find it gone.'

'I can't believe you don't know if your neighbouring village is there or not. When were you last there?'

The car lurched to a halt, and the farmer turned to face him.

'Look, son,' he said, a nervousness in his voice. 'I don't know what your business be out 'ere, but can I persuade you not a-go looking now? The night's coming in fast, see? There's a long walk after the sheep-gate, and we're coming up a'solstice. You don't want a-be out on these nights.'

'I'll be warm enough.'

Tom peered ahead. A narrow track ran from right to left and ahead was a metal five-bar gate. Another track beyond it headed off into a murky greyness.

'Bain't be the cold as is the worry,' the man said. 'Are you sure, nipper?'

'Is it that way?' Tom pointed to the gate.

The farmer didn't look. He kept his old, watery eyes on Tom and pursed his lips. He nodded, leant across and shoved opened the door. 'Walk fast,' he said. 'Straight on out that way. You'll find a wide deek wi' a bridge, least, as I 'eard. Over and on, straight line wi' sun dropping a'your left. If anyone lives there still, you'll no doubt find a Marsh welcome. Peace wi' 'e.'

Tom thanked him, grabbed his bags and slid out of the truck where he met the smell of damp leaves and manure. He closed the door as far it would allow and stepped back onto a verge thick with grass.

The truck rattled off and was soon gone. It took with it the only sound Tom could hear, and he suddenly realised how heavy silence was.

He looked both ways before crossing the track and then laughed at himself. If anything was coming, he would hear it a mile away. He hoisted his pack onto his back, checked his mobile once more but still found no signal and, with his laptop slung over one shoulder, tried to open the metal gate. It was padlocked and built on concrete posts close into a high hedge that grew on into the distance. There was no way around it so, feeling slightly guilty but being driven on by hunger, he climbed over and started walking.

'Five miles at three miles an hour,' he calculated. 'Should get me there before it gets too dark.'

Seven

After an hour of trudging, Tom stopped for a rest, wishing he'd brought water with him. Looking back the way he had come, he could see farm buildings, a silo, a distant church tower, and far, far beyond that, what must have been a power station. Electricity pylons strode out across fields with cables strung between them. He saw telegraph poles, a welcomed sight. At least the place to which he was going would have a phone.

A breeze rustled the hedgerow and he trudged on with his head down and his collar up, aware of the sounds of his breathing and the rhythm of his footsteps. The sky had been slowly changing from grey to orange and he saw clouds in broad streams of white and yellow pulled towards the sun. It was as if the huge canopy was being sucked into the night, helpless to resist.

He had the feeling that the view hadn't changed since he set off, although the light was now fading. He had passed open fields, following a long unbroken hedge that grew lower until it became little more than patches of shrub along the side of the trail. On its other side were endless fields dotted with distant sheep. Coarse grass tufted the ground between mounds and molehills and, here and there, hedges marked ditch banks.

A few birds pecked at the ground, crows mainly, and one or two lapwings. Every now and then Tom heard rustling in the hedgerows beside him. He passed gnarled and weather-beaten trees that stood out in the landscape like weird sculptures grown from nature. One, its bark mottled with yellow moss, appeared ahead like an old sentry; a sturdy trunk and two arms with a hundred sharp fingers guarding the track. Tom felt compelled to nod at it as he passed; some kind of inbuilt superstition, just like he had with single magpies. Further on he saw a twisted hag bending over a cauldron made of grass and hedgerow, her top twigs moving in the breeze. Beyond that, a small cluster of cruel witches jabbed and stabbed at a thin sapling.

A mist rose ahead and he saw the branches reaching out through it, stretching upwards for the last of the day. The closer he came to where he thought the mist was, the more it eluded him. He expected to be in it any moment, but then he would look ahead again and find it just as far distant. A glance at his watch showed him that it had stopped. He shook it, but that did no good. He reckoned that he had walked for well over an hour. His feet and thighs hurt and his chest was sore.

Suddenly, he felt that something was wrong. Although a wind moved leafless branches in bare, twisted trees, birdsong had faded, no crows cawed. Not only did the dusk rob the day of the last light, it also stole away any sound from the countryside. He stood uneasily in the unnerving silence.

A short scream cut through the stillness and sent Tom's heart racing. The cry sounded like it had come from close behind. There was nothing there, and yet it made his skin creep. Another scream was followed by a short, breathy yell.

'Hello?' he called. There was no answer, just another inhuman shriek, brief, high and chilling. 'Who's there?' This time he shouted louder. Again, there was no reply, but he saw a dark shape creeping across a field, low to the ground. Another joined it, slinking faster. It caught up with the first, and both set off, running. The foxes were gone in a second, taking their cries with them and his heart slowed.

It was then that he noticed there was no sign of the telegraph poles, no more pylons, either. He must have covered a fair distance and this gave him hope that he was almost at the bridge. He looked back and squinted to find the power station, but that was also out of view. A dog barked somewhere. The sound could have come from any direction. When he did hear noises now they were all around him. He was in the middle of each one, as if sound needed no direction on the marsh. He thought he could hear a vehicle but, straining to listen, it was only the breeze on the grass; a breeze, he noticed, which didn't affect the mist hanging above the fields.

'I wouldn't want to be lost out here,' he said to himself, and then wondered why he was whispering.

He turned to face his destination and found himself looking directly at the mist. It had crept up to him in silence and swirled around his feet, rising up to his waist. He could see across the top of it towards a black smear in the distance, barely more than a pencil dash resting on the haze. The longer he stared at the blemish on this still, silver scene, the more it came into focus until, after a minute or so, he could make out the triangle of a steeply pitched roof that stepped down onto another, and then a third. The roofs were dull amber in the setting sun and beneath them was a block of grey. He was looking at a stone church possibly two miles away, lifted above the low-lying bleakness that surrounded it. He walked on with the mist playing at his waist. It was as if he was being carried; hands with no touch and fingers without feeling lifted and floated him towards his destination with a strange and unsettling sensation.

After a short while, the mist swirled away as if it had done its job. It parted and waited all around him, showing the safe way across the deep water that the farmer had promised. The bridge was rough. Made of a few wide planks, it rested on the muddy ground on either side of the sewer. It had no handrail, and the wood looked rotten.

Something not too far distant caught his eye. A tall figure drifted like a ghost through the gloaming. Dying sunlight found its copper hair, and the mist swirled up around him as he moved silently towards the distant church. Too far away for him to call, Tom could only wonder who he was before he faded into the dusk.

He thought about the bridge, and his nervousness complained. 'It looks strong enough,' he said to himself, but it wasn't the bridge that worried him; it was the water on either side. Black and glass-flat like granite, it dared him to cross. He held his laptop tighter and tested the planks with one foot. They held, so, with his eyes fixed straight ahead, his body tense and ready for the bridge to give way, he made his way across. He kept memories of the past firmly from his mind by searching for that tall figure as, without looking down, he approached the other end.

Once on safer ground, he didn't look back. His belly paining him with hunger, his coat damp both outside and in, and his legs aching, he continued towards the church until he, too, was swallowed up by the gloom.

Like a tide rushing into a rock pool, the mist swirled itself keenly to where Tom had been standing. A man as thin as ice stepped out from the silence and considered the scene. A dark coat hung from his high shoulders to reach the ground without causing a ripple in the chill air that came with him. His hair streamed, black and beyond his collar. Parted in a straight line, it cleaved his head in two. He leaned on an ebony cane, clawing it with a leathery hand, his knuckles skull-grey, his fingers long. In his other fist he held a dead hare by the ears, blood dripping from the animal's head. His sheer nose cast its shadow over a thin mouth drawn tight in thought, and his midnight eyes, sunken hollows in the craggy hillside of his face, watched Tom approach Saddling. A smile cracked the man's lips, a knowing smile that stayed until he sensed a more familiar and unwelcome presence on the other side of the deek.

His head turned with a bone-creak, and he settled his eyes on a woman.

They regarded each other in stony silence until she dropped her head. Tapping a white stick before her, she drifted away to become one with the landscape.

The man slung the dead game over his shoulder and withdrew into the mist.

The blind woman reached her meagre home, the approaching darkness or dying light meaning nothing to her. She came to the table, feeling her way through the hanging hares, the grasses and herbs suspended in bunches from the low, beamed ceiling. Her fingers dragged along the table edge until she reached the end. She sat facing the door and reached for the shawl hanging on the back of the chair. She pulled it around herself, but it offered little comfort. The night had brought the cold with it, and both settled in her home.

She felt for a large bowl, pulled it to her and leant both elbows on the table. On winter nights when the bone-deep wind blew through her shack, she took comfort in the feel and memory of familiar things. She lowered her hands into the bowl. There was the round stone she had found by West Ditch, the ancient coin yielded by the earth at Far Field, letters with faint smells attached, and a finger bone found years ago when the deekers had cleared the east sewer. That was when she could see, and she had seen that it once belonged to a child. She found the drawing, now old and creased. Running her finger around the serrated edge, she smiled at the memory. She had kept it safe in her mind, but the feel of the paper connected her to it and the people the drawing depicted; a girl, eighteen years old, beside her a man not yet twenty, her husband and the father of the small, auburn-haired boy between them. The father stood strong and tall, his hair neatly cut. He wore his solstice clothes with pride that day, but he also wore a sad expression. His wife forced happiness through the tears in her eyes.

A sharp stab of anger ran through the blind woman as she placed the drawing back into the bowl, sat back and waited.

Eight

Daniel arrived at the village bench as the sun died behind him. He sat with his arms stretched out across the back. Barry leant forward next to him, his fingers joined and his thumbs circling each other, his left foot beating fast on the grass. He breathed out and watched his breath as it floated away and vanished. He huffed again.

'What you doing?' Dan asked. 'You're not counting, are you?'

'Jason says 'e's been counting breaths since the start of Penit,' Barry replied, without looking up. 'But I ain't counting.'

'Won't do you good. It'll only make it worse.'

'Aye, that's what me fader says. Fader said when it was 'is Penit 'e didn't sleep a week, didn't want a-waste the time.'

'Time's not for wasting,' Dan said. 'He's right on that.'

'Me fader's right on most things.' Barry leant back and pulled his woollen hat down over the tips of his ears.

Dan didn't move his arm even though Barry was now resting against it. His gloveless fingers felt the chill as the shadow of the church swamped the bench. The young men gazed ahead at the lope-way leading to the bridge at the southern mark. They spent many evenings on the bench staring at that path. There was little else to do come nightfall.

'Saw callers out at Far Field the other day,' Dan said. A reflected flare of last sunlight in a cottage window drew their gaze.

'You're always wandering there, Dan. Why d'you trouble yourself on it? You know there's nothing a-be done.'

'Do you ever wonder why?' Dan asked.

'What? Why you're forever there or why there's nothing you can do?'

'Both.'

Barry leant into Dan's shoulder. Dan could feel Barry's arm searching for his pipe in the pockets of his sheepskin.

'You'll have bad dreams,' he said.

'Any other sort, right now?' Barry filled his pipe and struck a match.

Dan smelt the bitter-sweet smoke as it blew past on the breeze. It had been windy that morning. The clouds had moved fast but the afternoon had calmed. The night would come chill with a long-night moon. They said that a full moon in Penit promised a storm for sure.

'Thing be,' Barry said, once his pipe was well alight, 'I know why you goes there, and I don't blame you. I been out that way meself, and a'the western mark. Like you I wonders what gives where the sky lights orange at night. I wonder what it's like over on the 'ill and why those lights wink. Then I remembers the Teaching telling me I'm better off where I be. So, I know why you go out there looking, Dan, but I don't know why you think you can't do nothing 'bout it.'

Dan let that sink in as the green around him darkened. Barry was right. There was nothing Dan could do about where he was and how things were, but that didn't stop him wondering.

A lamp was lit in a cottage, and he saw Mistus Seeming draw her curtains, leaving a gap where her candle burned. She stepped out into her porch and checked on a wreath of flowers hanging there. The sight was enough to make Dan's stomach turn over. Just off the lope-way, he saw Mistus Tidy lighting her gas lamps.

Barry nudged him and pointed his pipe towards the shop. Jason Rolfe stood in the upstairs window staring out at the church. A candle burned on the windowsill in front of him.

'Looks scared,' Barry said.

'Bain't we all?'

'True enough.'

'Is it right, Barry?'

'You can't be 'aving doubts now,' Barry said by way of an answer. 'Well, you can, I s'pose, but what would you do wi' them?'

'It's never felt so wrong before.'

'We never known it afore, is why. You don't rightly know what it means. Not 'til you come thirteen.'

'I feel sorry for Jacob Seeming. Thirteen is when you start counting.' Dan brought his hands to his lap and rubbed them together. 'At least it didn't happen in our thirteenth year. Imagine if you were…'

'Look, Dan,' Barry interrupted. 'You can't be talking like this.'

'You think the same.'

'Aye. But the Teaching. It can't be changed.'

Dan let out a sigh and warmed his hands between his knees.

Barry was keen to change the subject. 'I 'ope you be getting that 'air cut afore Friday,' he said, and gave Dan a nudge with his elbow. 'You don't look right all scruffy. Besides, Sally'll be at the festival.'

'Suppose,' Dan replied and looked back at his friend. Barry's ruddy face grew chubbier with each year, but it kept its permanent half-smile.

'You should think on taking it shorter, Dan. No, 'onest.' Barry stroked Dan's hair at the back. 'You'd look more 'andsome.'

'And you should try a shave some-an-then,' Dan said with a smile, pushing him away. 'Blacklocks don't like it like this. Your chin looks like the ersh left over after wheat-sheering.'

'I take me slip-chin twice a day. Must, on account of me dark locks.'

'You falser! You ain't done it today being as 'cos you're a yawnup.'

'I work 'ard as you.'

'You're the last to the felds and the first one off them.'

'Wolf-eyes.'

'Curly-flick.' Dan ruffled the waves of thick hair that hung randomly from under Barry's hat.

'Carrot-head.'

They sat shoulder to shoulder with only Barry's pipe smoke between them and silence returned.

At last, Barry said, 'Bain't no-one wi' a mate as good as you, Daniel Vye.'

'Don't get soppy again.'

'No, I mean it.'

'You always mean it.'

Barry took a deep breath. 'There's times I'm a-thinking that I...'

'You smoke too much, buffle-head,' Dan interrupted. He didn't want to hurt Barry's feelings, but there was one thing his friend was always keen to talk about. It was something that Dan was not comfortable to address.

'Least I ain't so lonesome as you,' Barry said.

'I like me own company.'

Barry knocked his head against Dan's, like a lamb wanting to be fed.

'Aye, and yours, you thick-thumbed crank.'

'Oi!'

'Sorry, first thing as came to mind.'

'Ah, you never need use sorry 'bout me.' Barry offered his pipe as he always did. 'Last of it your'n.'

Dan took the pipe. He could feel Barry's saliva on it as he put the damp mouthpiece to his lips. It was cold, but the bowl was warm in his hand. He sucked in one slow breath, tasting mostly the stale residue from the shank and only a little of the last embers. What there was of the smoke tasted like the smell of wet leaves, and it scratched at his throat. He held the smoke for a moment, felt a very mild rush behind his eyes and then blew it out where it mixed with the heat of his breath before ascending into nightfall. 'That's gone,' he said and tapped it out onto the ground. He blew into the bowl to clear any more ash and then polished the pipe on his coat tail. Handing it back to Barry he said, 'What you at a'morrow?'

'Same as yesterday, same as you, same as all. And there's Last Boblight.' Barry put the pipe back in his pocket before leaning forward. 'Will need a lot of this pipe a'morrow, reckon.'

Both men rested with their arms on their knees, heads up, staring at the ever-darkening lope-way.

The darkness thickened in the damp air. Dan's fingers were stiff with cold, and his ears were beginning to sting, but he was reluctant to leave this place of companionship. He knew he should help his mother at the inn, but there would be time for that later. There was precious little time for friends and silence.

He sat back, and Barry regarded him in the yellow cast of the streetlight. 'You nervous?' he asked.

'Thinking terrified more like.'

'Aye, me an' all.'

Dan put a hand on Barry's shoulder and pulled him back upright where they leant into each other. He took hold of his friend's hand and squeezed it. 'Here for you,' he said. 'With you all the way.'

'Aye.'

The presence of the old church weighed on their backs as they listened to their heartbeats. Around the small green, lamp-glow danced gracefully in windows where candles burned. The smell of wood smoke clung to the air as the dusk breathed its last. The few street lamps guttered and the uneven puddles of dim light at their bases flickered, disturbed.

They sat staring ahead into nothing until the dusk turned to night.

'What's that?' Barry said, and nodded towards the path.

A strange light appeared, blue in colour and swaying in a stable rhythm.

'No idea,' Dan said, peering into the gloom. 'Bain't no lantern. Looks more like fairy-sparks.'

A man came walking wearily on the lope-way between the Tidy house and Sam Rolfe's cottage. A blue light lit his mud-caked shoes and shadow obscured his upper body until he passed the curtain-less window at

Barry's home. He stopped under a lamp, but it was hard to make out his features in detail. He didn't look much older than Dan. Shorter, wider, not as stocky as Barry, and, from the little they could see of him, untidy.

Dan's heart pumped a faster beat. This man was not from within the village. He must have wandered in from beyond Far Field.

The stranger did something to the light and it cut out. He looked up and around, adjusting the strap on his shoulder.

'Be an out-marsher,' Barry said, whispering, and leaning so close to Dan that their cheeks touched. 'Looks like a tramp. Won't be welcome 'ere a'this time.'

'A foreigner for sure,' Dan agreed. 'And one that's not known a slip-chin, by the looks.'

'What's a foreigner wanting 'ere in Penit?'

Dan made no reply. He would find out soon enough. Any stranger arriving in Saddling had only one place to stay.

A dark mass of shadow, higher than the houses before it, stood on a mound. It was no more than a silhouette, but it was the building with the triangular roof that Tom had seen earlier. A short distance in front of it, at the bottom of the mound, he saw a bench. It was lit by one lamp which was either very grubby or had the wrong bulb in it as the light was subdued. A dirty yellow colour fell from it that barely reached the grass. This was the village green, he supposed, a wide circle of grass surrounded by a congregation of cottages facing across it to the raised church. He had been grateful to see houses at all, and now he was relieved to see a pub sign, half-lit and hanging from a building near the church.

Switching off his mobile to save the dying battery, he noticed two young guys sitting on the bench. They appeared to be holding hands.

Tom was about to walk on, his mind and stomach set on reaching the pub, when he saw two older men approach the bench. Squinting, as if that would lighten the scene, he saw the men stop, turn to face the youths and give a short, polite bow before moving on.

He was wondering what that was all about when he realised that they were staring at him. A flush of unease prompted him to hoist up his laptop and look away. He directed his attention to his destination, the path underfoot turning from earth to stone as he walked. He sensed his progress was being keenly followed from the bench. When he drew level with the young men, he thought that enough was enough. Yes, he was a stranger, but surely they'd had visitors in this out-of-the-way place before. He turned to face them, nodded and said, 'Evening.'

The one with the woollen hat was smiling and Tom smiled back. The youth replied with a brief nod. The other one stared. His head lifted slightly, and his hair glinted the colour of copper. His wide eyes studied Tom intently and, unnerved, Tom found himself doing what the others had just done. He gave a small bow and moved quickly on.

William Blacklocks, having followed the stranger at a distance, took a shortcut to his house and arrived through his back door just as Tom entered the green. Without lighting any lamps, he stood at his large picture window and scrutinised the scene. He was in time to see Andrew White and Martin Tidy bow to the young men on the bench, just as they should do. The stranger also gave a small bow to them while making his way around the far edge of the green. Walking with the steps of a scared man, he checked over his shoulder as though he expected the boys to leap up and come after him. Blacklocks knew how the stranger felt. Daniel Vye studied everyone and even he was occasionally unnerved in his presence.

Blacklocks could see the lads talking, but he was unable to hear their voices. They stood and hugged before Barry wandered away towards the inn. Daniel watched him go and then turned to face the church.

'Fader,' a voice in the dark behind Blacklocks said. 'My Willing-Light?'

Blacklocks saw a candle burning in the window of the inn, and his heart sank. He reached into the pocket of his long coat and rattled a box of matches. His son came and stood next to him, and instinctively Blacklocks put his arm around the boy's shoulder.

'You are all I have left, Mark,' he said. 'Our family and name rest with you.'

'Must be done, Fader. As you teach us, duty must be done.'

Blacklocks lit a large white candle with his trembling fingers.

'Must be seen to be done, son,' he said, placing it on the windowsill and grinning.

When he looked back up, Daniel Vye was standing on the other side of the window staring through at him, his piercing eyes sharp in the candlelight.

With his blood running cold, Blacklocks bowed and drew his curtains.

Nine

The pub sign showed a sturdy white sheep in profile with a large black crow standing on its back. The sheep was serene and rather dopey, Tom thought, but the crow had its sharp beak open and stared with menacing eyes. Behind them was a church and, beyond that, a large lake. Simple letters at the sheep's feet showed the pub's name, "The Crow and Whiteback".

'Cute,' he said.

The pub stood with its front door in the gable end, directly at the end of the path. The white painted, wooden door was slightly lopsided, suggesting that the building had subsided at some point. Tom clicked the iron latch and ducked his way inside.

Closing the door behind him, he felt the welcome warmth of a fire and saw it crackling away over on the right. The pub was empty but apparently open. It was one long room with the counter at the far end and between it and Tom stood several brown-wood tables with curve-backed chairs. The floor was stone, as was the large fireplace, and the white ceiling was supported by uneven, stained beams. The lights flickered and the smell of soot hung in the air.

The walls were lined with drawings and engravings. Farm implements hung in prominent places among horse brasses and rosettes. Tom relaxed. This made a change from London pubs with their blaring music and thumping fruit machines that flashed and never gave out. In fact, as he weaved through the bar, his eyes searching each corner, he saw there was no fruit machine, no sign of speakers and not even a jukebox. He was happy with that but not so glad that there was no-one to serve him. Looking for a bell, he saw that the counter was made of dark, polished wood and was chipped and scarred with years of use. There were no means to alert anyone, and he was just about to call out when someone appeared through the floor.

It was a woman, climbing a set of steep steps through a trap door, presumably from a cellar below. He saw her hair first. Long and golden, it was pulled back from her forehead and tied with a bow at the back. Her head was bowed, and she carried a small cask. This she put on the ground before she closed the trap door behind her. Tom wasn't sure if she'd noticed him and so gave a quiet cough.

'Right there, Mick, dreckly-minute,' the woman said with an accent Tom hadn't heard before. It sounded like a mix of West Country and Norfolk.

The woman stood up straight, her back still to him. She wore a plain, floor-length dress pulled in at the waist by her apron strings. The dress was grey and, like everything else in the pub, old fashioned. She reached for a bottle on one of the wooden shelves behind the bar and turned.

'Hearts alive!' she exclaimed when she saw Tom. She stepped back a pace, her hand on her chest.

'I'm sorry,' Tom said without thinking and then, to try and make up for surprising her, attempted to make light. 'Not who you were expecting?' She made no reply. 'Nice place, but not very Christmassy,' he added with a smile. 'Only four more shopping days to go.'

He laughed. She didn't.

Her face was pretty but lined. She was not unattractive, and Tom guessed her to be in her early forties. Her mouth turned down at the corners as she swallowed, looked across at a window and then made a quick scan of the bar.

'Lost are you?' she said when she settled her gaze back to Tom. Her blue eyes, ringed with red lines and dark shadows, were currently wide with surprise. She put the bottle on the counter and Tom noticed that there was no label.

'No, not if I am in Saddling.'

'That you are. Where was you heading?'

'Here.'

'Here?'

'Yes. Do you have a room? My car's dead. I've marched for hours, I'm wet, hungry, you know?'

She looked around the room again as if she was sure there was someone else with her. This was not the best reception he'd ever had from a landlady. She wrung her hands on her apron.

'I can pay up-front,' he said, 'if plastic is okay.'

'Plastic what?'

'O-kay.' Tom reached for his wallet but then let it alone. 'Cash works too. I just need to be here for a night. I'm doing some research, you see? I need to find your local vicar, or verger, or whoever, and have a look inside the church. Oh, and phone a recovery service.'

She showed no sign of understanding. A shiver ran over him like a stroke of icy air.

'Look,' he said, 'I'm sorry if I took you by surprise, but do you have a room?'

'A room?'

'Just for tonight. Anything will do. And do you serve food?'

'Well, thing is...' She hesitated. 'It be the time of year...'

'Christmas, yes, I know. But I assumed you weren't busy, no cars outside. You could do with some decorations, by the way, give the place a bit of a lift.' The bar was a colourless sight of brown wood, grey stone and white plaster, saved only by the fire.

'I'm not sure as we have anything.' She left small gaps between her words as though reciting them from a memory nearly forgotten.

'Sure, there's the spare room aside Dan's.'

Turning, Tom saw one of the youths who had been outside on the bench. He must have slipped in silently while Tom was talking; the cause of the cold shiver.

The barmaid moved so that she could see past Tom and addressed the youth. 'I'm not sure as Mr...'

'Sure we can 'elp a foreigner.' The boy said.

'Aye, but...'

'We can.'

'I don't think...'

'Remember your Teaching.'

'It is not that, Barry Cole,' the woman said, giving a small but distinct bow of her head. 'But you know what time it is.'

'You thinking I don't?' The young man's tone was harsh. 'You thinking me, at twenty-two, don't know what time we be in?'

'I'm sorry, of course...' She nodded towards the window. 'But it ain't possible.'

'Look,' Tom said. 'If you are fully booked then I'll call for a cab and go somewhere else. I'll come back in the morning.'

'No need a-be going,' Barry said. He was now standing next to Tom, his eyes fixing the barmaid in her place. Tom smelt smoke on him and a scent of damp clothing. 'Mistus Vye, 'e'll 'ave that room aside Dan's.'

'Barry Cole, I shan't be taking orders from a farmer's...'

The lad slammed his hand down on the bar top, and Tom jumped. His eyes were tight, and his voice was loud. 'I say 'e will 'ave that room aside Dan's.' He repeated it more slowly.

In the silence that followed, Tom decided that he should try and lighten the mood. 'I didn't want to cause a fuss,' he said to the barmaid, 'but it appears you might have a room. At least this chap thinks you do.'

'Name's Barry,' the lad said with no hint of anger. 'Saw you coming in from out-marsh. She always keeps a room.'

'We have the one,' she said with a humble curtsy. Her attitude had changed in a moment. She was quieter, and her head stayed slightly bowed. 'I'll show you.'

She lifted the bar hatch and stood aside.

'Thanks, mate,' Tom said to Barry. 'I hope I haven't caused any trouble.'

'No trouble,' Barry replied, and held out his hand. Tom saw his face in more detail now, slightly round, like his own, flushed and genial. He took the lad's hand and shook it. It felt cold and yet there was something warm about the gesture. Maybe it was the cheeky grin that greeted him.

'Tom, Tom Carey.'

The smile slipped from Barry's mouth, and his eyes widened for a second. He let go of Tom's hand.

'Might be seeing you 'bout then,' he said with a nod, and walked to the door.

'This way.'

She led him through to a narrow passage behind the bar. A door to his left was open to reveal a small kitchen. To his right, a narrow staircase ran up and back the way they had just come. An open cupboard beneath it held brooms and metal buckets. The woman climbed the stairs leaving Tom to squeeze his way behind her. His laptop case caught on the newel post and the only way up was to hold his belongings in front of him. The stairs were steep and he was soon standing in a low passageway.

'Front there's my rooms and bath, and you won't come near them,' the woman said. 'Back here's where you can be.' She led him, in a few paces, to the room at the furthest end of the building. Stopping outside it, she indicated the door opposite. 'This be a bathroom you'll share with my boy, and he has priority. This is his room aside yours. You keep away from it. You sleep in here.' She pushed open the small door and entered a dark room.

Tom followed her, feeling guilty for something he hadn't even thought about, let alone done. He was still groping for a switch when the room came slowly to light under gas lamps.

'Really?' he said, half amused and half worried. 'Is that safe?'

'You're a long way from home, mister. You only need turn it up and down there.' She showed him a brass knob on the wall fitting. 'There's matches there when needed. Turn it complete off at day, far down when not in the room at night. I'll have Daniel bring you bedding afore long. I can feed you after seven, downstairs only. If you've a mind to wander out, and I don't suggest it at night on the dowels, then you can go through the bar or the back. The doors ain't never locked.'

With that, she left the room with fast, precise steps, her long skirt swishing in rhythm behind her.

'Thank you,' Tom called, but she was already hurrying down the stairs.

A few minutes later Tom found himself standing in the dimly lit bedroom with his laptop cable in his hand. He had scanned the walls for a power outlet and found none. He had even checked under the bed where the floorboards were bare, and there were signs of mice, but there was no socket. There was a much scored, wooden desk beside the window, the type Tom had seen in classrooms in old films. It had a lid which lifted, and a stained well for ink. The window was small and had four panes of dusty glass framed by white painted wood. He moved the desk to check behind it, but there were no electrical outlets there either.

He put the cable on the bed and, from the window, saw a night blacker than he had ever known. He could just make out the church nearby and could see what looked like a porch lit by one flickering streetlamp. The bench was unoccupied now, and most of the houses that he saw had their curtains closed although candles were still visible in a couple of windows.

'At least that's vaguely Christmassy,' he said.

Hearing footsteps behind him, he turned to the open door.

A young man appeared and stood just inside the doorway, a pile of sheets and blankets in his outstretched arms.

'Ah,' said Tom. 'Thank you.'

The youth searched Tom with questioning eyes. The thin rims of his grey irises were as dark as his pupils, giving each eye three concentric circles. Tom felt himself being read like a book and it took him a few seconds to pull himself away from the gaze.

'Daniel, I guess? Saw you outside.'

Dan drifted to the bed and placed the pile of linen on one corner. He flattened the sheet at the top of the pile with one hand and checked that it was in alignment, adjusting the collection of linen to square it up with the corner of the bed. Once satisfied with the arrangement, he brushed the blue and white mattress with the palms of his hands and stood up straight. Again, he examined Tom. His face betrayed no emotion and yet there was something sad about it. His hair was long, his clothes were rough but clean, simple but without any particular shape, and he wore boots.

The two looked at each other without speaking for so long that Tom became edgy with embarrassment.

'I'm Tom,' he said, to relieve the pressure, and took a step forward, offering his hand.

The youth looked at it and then back into Tom's eyes.

'Daniel,' he said. He had an accent too, Tom could hear it even in that one word.

'Hi.' Tom smiled and took another step.

Dan didn't take his hand, so Tom backed off.

'Any chance I could charge my laptop?' he asked. 'It's old, battery's not that healthy. You know what it's like.'

Dan finally looked away from Tom and to the thin, grey computer. His eyes widened and shook his head. 'No.'

'Man of few words, eh? Fair enough. Thanks for the sheets. Might need another blanket, though.'

The room was nearly cold enough for him to see his breath and there was no carpet and no fireplace. He was still wearing his coat.

'You can have me lid if you need it more,' Dan said.

'Lid?'

'Blanket. You got pillow-beres there and sheets. But you can have me lid, happily.'

'Oh, no, I'll be fine.' That was a nice gesture. 'But thanks.'

Dan still didn't move.

'Thanks,' Tom said again, and nodded towards the door. 'Maybe see you downstairs? You've got good beer, I hope?'

'I... Prehaps... As is...' The guy glanced over his shoulder at the open door and then back to Tom. 'Prehaps I might...?'

It took Tom a moment to figure out 'prehaps.' 'Yes?' he prompted.

'No, not to think on it.' He changed his mind. 'But, aye, prehaps. Later.'

'Sure,' Tom replied, having no idea what the lad was trying to ask.

He nodded once as a way of saying goodbye, and that seemed to do the trick. Dan turned and left the room, latching the door behind him.

Tom heard his footsteps on the stairs, and then a door beneath him slammed shut. Looking from the window, he saw Dan run from the pub and disappear into the darkness behind the church. A light flickered through one of the church windows and he wondered if it wasn't too late to search out the vicar, but what he was looking at was just a reflecting streetlamp.

A woman hung a wreath of flowers in the porch of a house lit by hurricane lamps. Another came from the house next door and, as his eyes adjusted to the light, Tom saw that this building was a shop. This second woman also hung a wreath while speaking to her neighbour. Tom couldn't hear them at that distance, but he assumed it was Christmas conversation, season's greetings as they decorated their homes. Not exactly the garish, glowing Santas and red-nosed eyesores that he was used to in London but simple and earthy which, when he thought about it, was far more traditional.

After checking one last and futile time for a socket, he left the lead where it was, put the laptop on the desk and sat in the only chair in the room to work for as long as his battery lasted. He wanted to refresh his memory and update his notebook with all the Carey ancestors he had found so that, when he spoke to the vicar, he would be focused and prepared. The power icon read twenty percent. He would have to work fast, but that was not a problem. He was hungrier than ever and there would be food downstairs soon.

'No power, no lights, no WiFi,' he mumbled, after trying to find a connection. 'No wonder we moved away.'

Ten

Barry sat beside his father at a table by the fire. He glanced briefly at the pictures on the opposite wall and then shifted his chair to show his back to them. His dad put a hand on his arm and gave it a brief squeeze. Barry said nothing. His inquisitive eyes were on the bar where the stranger sat eating a looker's pie. He wiped his plate with a large chunk of Andrew White's bread and swallowed it. He said something to Susan, she shook her head and held up a beer glass. He nodded.

Barry studied the stranger's features. He stood out from all other men in the inn with his weird clothes, his growth of half-beard like an unkempt hedge, and his hunched shoulders. He quickly scanned the room, expecting to see the men disapproving and gossiping about the new arrival but there was no hostility at the tables. If anything, they were intent on ignoring him. Hadn't the minister said, only a few days back, that the village should be ready to welcome strangers should any come? The men observed his order with silence, but no-one had made the man welcome. It was his appearance, Barry reasoned. A young man in Saddling would not be respected if his chin was fleecy, especially in Penit.

Barry was as wary as the others, but he watched with fascination as the stranger accepted a jug from Susan. Her face was set and cold. Dan would be keen to learn about this man's off-marsh ways, and Barry shared some of that interest. A foreigner brought promise. He wasn't sure what of, but he knew that someone needed to offer this man some come-a-table.

'Don't bode good,' Mick Farrow said, following Barry's gaze.

The third man at Barry's table was a weathered farmer in his sixties. His hair was wild and white, his eyes dark and his mouth fixed in a permanent sneer. Barry could smell sheep treddles on him.

'Ah, Mick.' Matt Cole put down his beer. 'We've 'ad foreigners visit afore.'

'Not at this time.'

''Course we 'ave.' Cole laughed. 'You're as fright as a ram at wethering.'

'Blacklocks'll not like it,' Farrow mumbled. 'Not in Penit.'

'He said it only two day back at the meeting, 'ow we should welcome foreigners who might come in off-marsh any-time of year. Be right, Barry?'

'Aye, 'e said that, Fader. Even in Penit.'

'Which goes a-show me, Mick Farrow,' Cole said, ginning, 'just 'ow you wasn't attendin' the meet. Where were you at?'

Mick Farrow grimaced into his beer.

'You be too much a worrier,' Cole said. 'Likely won't stay 'round long, as 'appen. Nipper, where you...?'

Barry left the table and approached the bar.

'See,' Mick said, hunkering low over his ale and nodding towards Barry. 'Foreigners set the boys a-wondering, asking a'things. Your nipper'll ask questions 'imself, tell me I be wrong. You need a-hold that boy by your crook, some.'

'You're welcome a-try it, Mick,' Cole said with a sigh.

'Always asking something, your whelp.' Mick sipped from his jug glass, his eyes firmly on the out-marsher. 'You brought 'im up a-be right jawsy, and it only leads to 'em being mischeevious. See, be a-talking wi' 'im now. Just as I said it.'

Barry took some coins from his pocket and dropped them on the bar. Susan considered the money, Barry, and then the stranger. She dragged the coins into her apron and turned her attention to drying glasses as Barry brought Tom back to the table.

'Fader,' he said. 'This 'ere's Tom, from London.'

Cole touched a finger to his forehead. Mick said nothing.

'Sit down,' Barry said. 'This 'ere's Mick Farrow.' 'E farms north fields. Dad works wi' me uncle over south.'

'Hi,' Tom said, taking the empty chair. His back was to the fire, and the heat from it hit him the moment he sat. 'The name's Tom, Tom Carey.' He offered his hand to Mick, who sat back and folded his arms, and then to Cole who took it briefly.

Tom sensed he was only welcome at the table because the younger guy had invited him. He resisted the temptation to quip about the roughness of Cole's hand.

'Cold, isn't it?' he said.

'Be chillery,' Cole said, 'but there's no cobbles on the eaves, as yet.'

Barry must have seen the confusion on Tom's face as he said, 'Me fader's talking 'bout the ice we get 'anging in winter.'

'Oh, thanks.' Tom gave Barry a smile, which was nervously returned.

'Carey, you say?' Mick, his eyes still fixed on Tom, spoke with his head tilted as if he had trouble hearing.

'Yes. Tom Carey. My ancestors were from Saddling.'

'Not been a Carey 'ere in my lifetime,' Cole said. 'Not fur years, reckon.'

'Around a hundred,' Tom replied. He saw Cole take a sip of his beer and followed suit. It tasted of pure hops and he could tell it was strong. 'Not tasted anything like this before,' he said. 'I asked for a Bacardi Breezer and got offered something called bathtub.' He addressed Barry who seemed the more affable of the three. 'What's that when it's at home?'

'We don't 'ave it at 'ome.' Barry glanced to his dad. 'We only 'ave it 'ere at the inn.'

'But what is it?'

'It's not fur them as like as you.' Mick Farrow's voice was low and threatening. 'You should stick wi' ale and be quick wi' it.'

'It be like gin,' Matt Cole explained. 'We makes it. I mean, Susan makes it, and some others hereabouts try.'

'An old tradition?'

'We 'ave 'em a'plenty,' Barry said. 'Some easier a-swallow than others.'

Cole looked sharply at his son and drew in a breath. 'Careful, boy,' he warned.

'Penit,' Barry replied in a flash. Cole frowned and returned to his drink.

'Penit? Is that another one?'

'What be your name?' Mick Farrow asked, and Tom wondered if he had trouble with his memory as well as his ears.

'Thomas Carey. Tom.'

'Carey name do clang a ringer, mind,' Cole said. 'Might a-seen it on a sleeper-stone back a the church. Staying long?'

'Not as long as 'is lot, dead-abed in the ground,' Mick said, and laughed to himself. 'One 'undred year back? Leave 'em be.'

Tom smiled politely. 'No, not too long. I need to have my car fixed and get back to London the day after tomorrow.'

'Where's your car at? Prehaps Nate can see a-it,' Barry said. 'Nate's one a the Rolfe boys, good wi' engines. Fixed your old Massey summer gone, didn't 'e, Mick?'

Mick nodded, took a drink and then crossed his arms again.

'It's miles back, on the lane that leads to the junction with the road to... Somewhere. I don't know, but it was a two hour walk.'

'Nothing a-be done 'til a'morrow then,' Cole said. 'You'll 'ave a good night, and one of us'll see you back a'your engine a'morning.'

'Well, I was going to call a garage, but she said there was no phone here.'

Cole shook his head.

'Be a lot we ain't got at Saddling,' Barry said, earning another disproving glare from his father. 'Phone's one of them.'

'You're joking, right?'

'If you want, I'll show you 'round the village.'

'Barry.' Cole put his glass down heavily on the table. 'Enough now.'

Tom was aware that the boy had been staring at him since he sat down. He felt the persistence of his eyes on the side of his face. 'Might be a bit dark,' he said. 'But I'd like to see inside the church.'

Cole sat up straight in his chair and cleared his throat. 'You won't find no Careys in Saddling no more, lad.' The words were oddly placed as if the man was making sure he said them in the right order.

'I know, but I'm hoping to find out why.'

'Dead.' It was all Mick said, but it was enough to unnerve Tom.

He turned to face Barry and sure enough the boy was still staring at him, a smile of curiosity fixed on his lips, his eyebrows raised in expectation, still waiting.

'Oh, yes, okay,' Tom said to him. 'Show me around, but, maybe in the morning? I'd really like to talk to someone about the parish records. Is there someone who keeps them?'

'That'll be Minister Blacklocks,' Cole said. Mick mumbled something Tom didn't catch, but Barry clearly did because he laughed. 'Show respect, men,' his father admonished them.

'Who's Blacklocks?' Tom asked. 'Strange name.'

'Oldest name in the village,' Cole said. 'Along with Carey, as was. Blacklocks be minister and schooler. But 'e won't be disturbed, not now night's in, but 'e's early awake and I dare say you'll find him a'morrow. Lives on the green, other side, by the church.'

'Great, thanks.' Tom took a drink.

'But if you're a Carey you won't want a-meet up wi''im,' Cole added.

'I am,' Tom said. 'And it sounds like I must.'

'You watch out fur old Blacklooks.' Barry knocked his glass against Tom's.

'Boy!' His father's voice was sterner than before. 'Careful with your miswords and talk better of Mr Blacklocks. Remember what's a-'appen.'

'Can I forget?' Barry finally shifted his eyes and smiled sarcastically at his father.

'Remember 'e's the authority a-choose if the callers don't.'

Barry's shoulders fell, and he slumped back in his chair, cradling his drink.

'Choose what?' Tom was sure the men were skirting around some issue, something to do with Christmas perhaps. 'Is something happening?'

Cole drained his glass and put it down while still glaring at his son. He stood, and Tom realised how big he was. He had to bow his head beneath a beam. 'I'll say my a'night a'you, Mr Carey,' he said, walking away without looking at Tom. 'Mick.'

'Matthew.'

'Oh, Mr Carey.' Cole turned back. 'Now I think on it, there were a book kept in the crypt, some old village account and copies of parish lists. Not been used awhile now, don't think. You might 'ave luck and it still be there. Prehaps as there'll be something 'bout your dead'uns in it. If it ain't rotted. The book, I mean. A'night.' Cole ducked through the door and was gone.

'Well, that's good news for me,' Tom said, his spirits lifted.

'I was 'earing folks all over search fur their dead these days,' Mick said. 'I ask, why? Why go after who's gone afore?'

'It gives you a sense of who you are.' Tom tried to explain the bug that had crawled under his skin when Aunt Maud had first set him the task to discover their Carey history. 'It's like being a detective. You can do so much online, now, as well. You end up spending hours at the computer, searching through records and old newspapers. You're always trying to think up new ways to track down your family's history.'

The old farmer didn't look the least interested. 'Like I say, why?'

The thought of his inheritance made Tom's heart skip. Tonight he had come closer to finding something that might give him the missing link. That was, if the book dated from that far back, if the reason was worthy of note and if it had not perished. His hope drained away. There were still many 'ifs.'

'I'd give it up, son,' the white-haired man said. 'Graves be fur sleepers. Let 'em sleep on.'

'Graves are useful,' Tom said. 'You can get dates and names. But I'm actually only trying to find out why Thomas Carey left Saddling. Perhaps someone here knows.'

'From an 'undred year back? We live old in Saddling, but none suffer that long.' Mick laughed and reached out for his glass. Halfway to the handle, the laughter ended abruptly, and he turned to Barry.

Tom realised that this was the first time he'd seen Barry without a grin on his face. In fact, he looked pale with fear. Mick left his drink and stood up. He pulled a cap from his pocket and wrung it in his hands as he gave a short, stony-faced bow to Barry and a quick nod to Tom. He left the pub quickly.

'What was that about?' Tom asked.

Barry watched the old man leave and then took a long drink of his own beer, put it down, took a deep breath and turned to face Tom. His grin was back.

'Another ale fur you, Mr Carey?'

'Call me Tom, mate. And I'll get the next one.'

Barry beamed as if Tom had just awarded him the highest kudos.

Tom had three more pints with Barry and asked him many questions about Saddling. Barry returned few straight answers. Tom couldn't understand why they didn't have electricity. 'We're too far out, and the council ain't got 'round it yet.' Or why there were no phones. 'Too far from the main lines, council say.' What this thing called Penit was. 'Time a year.' And why people doffed their hats and bowed to Barry. 'That's 'cos I be the most important man in the village,' he had said. 'One of them, leastwise.' He had sighed and changed the subject to ask Tom about London. It was when Tom talked about his ancestors and what he hoped to find out, that the name William Blacklocks came up again.

'Why did you call him…? What was it? Black-books?'

'Balcklooks,' Barry corrected. 'Always a-moaning on something and watching us. Got a scowl like a ewe in lamb, and a bleat a'match. You'll see when you find 'im. Thin like a dead thing and never as cheery. Was me teacher fur ten year, never liked me, I never liked 'im. Gave out too much leather, ask me. Still got scars at me back. The Blacklocks 'ave owned swilling-land since start a village, when this 'bouts were an island. Ploughing land, I mean, and grazing. Raking it in, buying pastures, renting 'em out.'

'An island?'

'Be it. See, the church be up on the knoll.' Barry explained. 'Teaching says that it 'appened that there was 'ouses 'round it, like as now but, one time, beyond them was all water. An island, see? I mean this is back afore the great storm.'

'When was that?'

'Been many. Started twelve hundred and something. Took off many villages. Broomhill went, Winchelsea, nearly killed off Romney i'self as the river changed flow a'Rye. Big storm. Fearful it must 'ave been. I ain't keen on our storms. After then, in time, they inned the marsh and 'ere you see it. Dryer, but we still got water all 'round. Well, as like you would've seen as you come up the lope-way.'

Tom wasn't going to remember any of that. He was concentrating hard to understand Barry's accent. 'Can you tell me this again tomorrow? I'll make some notes.'

'Aye?' Barry's face lit up. 'I'd like that. Got some have-tos a-see a'morrow, but aye, after. Thank you.' He seemed genuinely pleased that Tom had taken him up on his offer and then, out of the blue, he leant forward and asked, 'You got a phone?'

Tom was surprised but reached into his pocket.

'No.' Barry put out a hand and stopped him. 'Not 'ere. A'morrow, prehaps.'

'Okay.' Tom, bemused, withdrew his hand. 'Why not here? It's only a Nokia.'

'Just not 'ere,' Barry repeated. He glanced at the other villagers. 'A'morrow.' He stood up. 'Best go. Ma'll worry. I'll give you me a'night.'

'Sure. Nice talking to you.'

He watched the young man leave. With his head down as he pulled his hat over his curly hair, he studied the floor as if to avoid eye contact with anyone else in the room. The few other drinkers, all men, Tom noticed, paid him no attention. Behind the bar, Susan stared out into space, her hands mechanically wiping the inside of a glass. Tom was sure it was the same one she had been drying when he'd last bought a drink.

He was relieved that he had found the village still in existence. Even happier now that he'd picked up a scent of the records he was after and, with his sights firmly set on solving Maud's mystery, thoughts of London withered.

His back was now uncomfortably warm, so he switched seats. The chair that the white-haired farmer had vacated was cold, the seat hard, but it meant that Tom could turn to face the fire at a comfortable distance while he relaxed into his drink.

He reached into his pocket again for his mobile but drew it out slowly, scanning the bar for disapproval. No-one was paying him any attention, but still, he hid it between his legs to check the time. With nothing else to do, no television to watch and no chance of getting into the church tonight, he decided to return to his room. He cleared the table of glasses and carried them to the bar saying a polite goodnight to Susan who nodded silently in reply.

Upstairs, the door to the barmaid's room was closed, not that he had any desire to look in there, but the door to the room beside his was slightly ajar. The gas lamp within threw out a dull light. Tom stopped as he passed. He could hear a man's sobs coming from inside.

Tom hesitated; none of his business, but should he tell Susan? Even though she had warned him away from the room, he was just about to knock and make sure Daniel was alright when the door was slowly closed from the inside. He heard the latch click into place and took the hint. Clearly, not all the youths around here were as affable as Barry.

He turned up the light in his own room, marvelling at how antiquated this system was and wondering if there was a way to stop the worrying hiss from the fitting. Deciding that gas lighting must be safe, he couldn't smell anything, after all, he sat at the small desk. It was like being back at school, except this desk was smaller than the ones he had used. Names scratched into the wood distracted him for a moment, Ollie Tidy, Martin White, Andrew someone, the name had been scored out and a date carved in beside it; "1952 - F S".

'Not only am I living in the past,' he said, 'I'm sitting on it.'

He opened his notebook and tried to recall his conversations with the men downstairs, but he couldn't block the out the memory of the sobbing. It played on his mind and disturbed him.

'Not my business,' he said. He closed his book, drew the curtains and turned his attention to making up the bed.

Cole looked up and out through the leaded glass. When he saw the upstairs lights go out at the inn, he hurried along the aisle. The dark church was opressive, but he knew the way, and he was guided by the light spilling up from the crypt. He descended the few spiral steps and entered the damp-smelling, humid underbelly of the church. Blacklocks stood at the wooden table in the centre of the room, reading his book by candlelight.

'Well?' he said as soon as Cole was at the bottom step. 'What did he say?'

'Aye, 'e's about your village record.'

'And?'

'Is all. I told 'im there might be such a book.'

'Excellent.' A smile cracked Blacklock's gaunt face. 'But he must not see it just yet. It is too early. He will need bait.'

'William, you sure 'bout this?'

The flame from the candles danced in the minister's eyes. He said nothing. There was no need.

'Sorry,' Cole said. 'I didn't mean a-question you.'

'He only needs to stay for the Saddling, Matthew, and then that will be the end of it.' Blacklocks waved him away. 'Forever.'

Eleven

Tom woke early, troubled by a lifelike dream. In it, he had awoken to find himself in an unfamiliar place lit by moonlight hanging in cold air. The curtains were open even though he had closed them before he turned in. His skin was numb, but it encased his whole body like a tomb. He was lying on his back and couldn't move. He was vulnerable and unable to remember if he was clothed but what was worse, he knew that he could do nothing about it. He had also known that he was not alone.

He could see the foot of the bed. Beyond the tangled blanket and the shape of his prone body, he saw an auburn-haired young man lit by a shaft of cold moonlight. He was facing the window. The moonbeam, like a powerful spotlight, singled him out in one impossibly pure beam of white. Tom's view of him was from behind. His body glowed, his shoulders were wide, his arms muscled, and he was naked. He stood there like a ghostly memory from the far reaches of Tom's mind, and yet he was real.

Tom tried to speak but no voice came. He could breathe, but nothing more. He tried to close his eyes to fall back to sleep and wake again, but even his eyes were paralysed, fixed on the mesmerising form. There was no sound in the room, no movement except for some dust that sparkled and settled in the moon's ray, recently disturbed as if the young man had drifted in a second before.

He felt no panic even though his heart was pumping fast in his chest. Although he could tell his flesh was cold, he was not shivering. It was as if something had established itself around him; a sense of finding something that had been lost for a long time, a feeling of coming home. He heard his heart rate slow. It quietened, too, until there was absolutely no sound in his ears. His breath escaped his mouth and he saw it rise, a fragile vapour in the icy air. The man at the window was also breathing deeply and his breath swirled away towards the glass where it misted and faded in a soporific rhythm.

Tom had no idea how long he lay there staring at the scene, but he had no recollection of falling back into sleep. When the first light of a wintry dawn woke him, he immediately sat up and looked towards the window. There was no-one there, but someone had opened the curtains.

The feeling of calm that had visited him in the dream stayed with him as he washed and dressed. His shirt was already stiff with yesterday's sweat and it smelt of smoke from the fire. Although he had a decent enough wash in lukewarm water and there had been soap, he felt dirty and regretted not bringing a change of clothes.

The pub beneath him slept on and, looking up the time on his mobile, he guessed it was too early to expect anything to eat. He decided to check out the church.

Downstairs, the bar was clean and tidy. There were no unwashed glasses on the wiped tables, and the ashes in the grate were the only sign of recent activity. The smell of stale beer and pipe smoke clung to the air. The room was lit by the rising sun, filtering in at the edges of closed curtains. Last night's candle had burned down to a hard pool of wax. Its drips hung from the windowsill, suspended in time.

The dawn had not yet finished its daily ritual when he stepped outside. The sky was a great sheet of grey stretching to meet a dusty horizon shielded by thin clouds. The grass on the green glittered with dew. The air was brittle but, despite the cold, there was no frost. He took the narrow path to where it branched off and meandered up the slight incline towards the church.

The stone and red brick building appeared to be in good condition. It stood as two joined parts both with a pitched roof as steep as an Alpine lodge. The nave, the largest part of the building, housed a third roof which grew from its west end and supported a squat tower. The nave was attached to a lower, smaller chancel at the east. There were no transepts, the church was too small, and it resembled a triptych of three oddly shaped ridges pushed together to make one staggered building. There seemed to be more roof on the structure than there were walls supporting it. The windows were small, just above head height and patterned with lead. The more he studied the structure, the less like a conventional church it appeared.

A stone porch jutted out on the south side of the nave and towards the back of the church. Tom searched for a door handle but found only a large keyhole. He pushed against the door in case the church, as the inn, was left unlocked. The wood was soft and gave a little under his touch, but the lock firmly resisted him. Deciding to come back later, he carried on to the west end and, stepping off the path, walked beneath the tower. This end of the church housed one small window and no other doors. Something odd struck him. He struggled with a mental image of the church from his youth, a place associated with carol concerts. These weren't his favourite kinds of memories. They were biting ones born out of difficult times, but he recalled processing into the church from a door at the west end.

'Probably too small,' he said to himself, 'Anyway, what does it matter?'

He walked to the corner and into a rambling graveyard.

It spread out towards the open fields and was littered with headstones, probably a couple of hundred or so. The grass sloped down to a low relic of some former boundary wall. Headstones rested up against it and someone was sitting there, leaning back on one.

It was Daniel from the dream, his hair was unmistakable. Towards the sunrise, shallow cloud drew a widening line across the horizon. A thin mist hovered, hanging silver and motionless for as far as he could see, and the ground lay grey in the half-light, growing to green as the sun rose. Tom trod gently among the graves and the wet grass dampened his jeans as he approached the wall. His face was stinging and he could see his breath but he was already perspiring under his clothes.

His eyes were on Daniel's back as he drew near and the guy gave no clue that he knew Tom was approaching. All the same, when Tom was directly behind him and about to speak, he lifted a hand and held up a warning finger.

Tom obeyed and waited.

Daniel lowered his finger to ninety degrees and pointed to the eastern horizon. At that exact moment, the sun broke through in a magnificent burst of red. The blazing rays of dawn escaped the clouds in crimson triumph, the land below caught fire and the mist drank in the colours. Shielding his eyes, Tom could make out sheep among the mist, small grey figures in unorganised groups. He saw some of those weird, twisted trees to the north, casting shadows through the haze, and he made out fences and hedges as thin sketches on a wide page of new-day light.

'Wow,' he said, and wished he'd brought a camera with him. 'Beautiful.'

'There also be death out there,' Daniel said. 'You must tread careful or be pulled in.'

'Daniel, yeah?' Tom asked as he came around to the side to look at him.

'Dan,' he replied.

'Dan, hi. Tom.' Tom held out his hand and Dan considered it.

Tom was embarrassed for having dreamt of him. When he saw his eyes, though, he felt the dream sense of calm return and managed a brief smile. Dan took his hand and gave it a firm shake.

'Morning,' Tom said, and turned back to the view. 'It looks too peaceful to be dangerous.'

Dan let his hand go and admired the sunrise.

'Aye, it does that. But when the weather's bad...' He left that hanging. 'You sitting?'

'Thanks.' Tom joined him on the low wall at a respectful distance and noticed that Dan was not wearing shoes. His long, thick coat looked warm but his feet must have been freezing. 'You're up early,' he said.

'Making the most of each hour,' Dan replied. 'And you?'

'Wanted to get a good start on the day. Want to find some information and get back to the car and home. But it looks like I'm too early for everyone but you.'

'Ma will be about afore long,' Dan said, and then carried straight on with, 'What've you come to Saddling for?'

'Hoping to solve a mystery.' Tom indicated the church.

'Mystery?' Dan smiled, and Tom saw that he had gleaming teeth like Barry's, only much straighter.

'A mission my aunt sent me on. Just hope it's not Mission Impossible.'

Dan's smiled dropped and his brow furrowed instead. 'Don't understand,' he said.

'Forget it. I'm not the best at jokes, and not at this time of day, that's for sure. Aren't you cold?'

Dan shrugged. 'Where you come from?' he asked.

'London.'

'Long way from here.' Dan leant back onto the gravestone.

Tom checked over his shoulder, but there wasn't one for him to lean on, so he remained upright.

The horizon was now a wash of yellow light with a grey-blue sky above. The red was evaporating and pockets of mist faded and died over far-away fields.

'How old are you?' Dan asked.

Tom thought that a strange question but answered honestly. 'Twenty-five,' he said. 'You?'

'Twenty-two. I should be twenty-three in a few days.'

'What do you do around here? There can't be much going on.'

'We get by,' Dan said.

'I mean, what is Saddling apart from a church and some houses? And your pub of course.'

'It's many a thing,' Dan said, gazing out. 'It be simple and kind. It be family and neighbours, care and duty. Farming and sometime feasting. It be all we'll need.'

Dan leant slightly towards Tom, smiling. Tom didn't like him being in his personal space, and the probing eyes made him uneasy at first. Slowly, however, the tranquil feeling from the dream rose in him again, and he couldn't help but smile back. 'What?' he asked, expecting a question.

'Tom.' It wasn't a question. Dan was simply saying his name.

'What?' Tom repeated, this time with a quick shake of his head.

'Why d'you come to Saddling *now?*' Dan moved towards Tom so they were almost shoulder to shoulder.

Tom drew his head back. 'Long story,' he said, his smile gone. 'My aunt wants to know something before she… She's not well. Probably only got a few weeks left to live.'

'Weeks,' Dan said, and, again, it was not a question. He watched the horizon and this time shielded his eyes from the sun. 'That's a lot of time, really,' he said, and his voice was quietly sad. 'A long time if you're lost.'

'I'm sure it is,' Tom said, not understanding what he meant. He remembered their brief talk in his room the night before and the later sound of sobbing. Perhaps the combination had been what sparked off the dream. 'Didn't see you last night,' he said. 'Is everything alright?'

Suddenly, Dan slipped from the wall and stood up, turning to face Tom. 'If you want to know more about Saddling past,' he said, ignoring Tom's enquiry, 'then you should ask her.'

Narrowing his eyes against the sun, Tom could see a lone figure a way off, walking slowly across a field.

'Who's that?' he asked.

'She bides near the bridge you'd a crossed yesterday.' Dan faced the inn and then moved around in a full arc, coming back to set his strange eyes on Tom. 'Stop by and see her on your way back. She knows everything.'

'Everything? Local history as well?'

'Expect so.'

'Who is she?'

'Me aunt. Yourn wants answer's mine might have. You got a car?'

As with Barry's request to see Tom's phone the night before, this came out of nowhere. 'Well, sure, it's a few miles away, though, in the lane to… Where was it? Brenzett.'

Dan's shoulders slumped. 'Beyond Far Field, 'course,' he said. 'Pay it no never-mind. Maybe one day I'll get to see it.' He eyed the church. 'You should find what you came for and get back to that car, Tom,' he said. 'There's a storm on its way in, they say. You don't want to be at Saddling when it's storming.'

'No, I'm sure I don't.' The last of the cloud and the mist had nearly burned away. 'How can you tell there's going to be a storm? Looks fine to me.'

'It always storms for the Saddling. Good luck to you.' With that, Dan walked away towards the back door of the inn.

Tom watched him go and then glanced at his bedroom window. Had Dan been in his room the night before? Was he a sleepwalker perhaps? Or had Tom really dreamed about a naked guy in the moonlight?

'Best not mention that to Dylan.' He laughed to himself and rubbed his hands together to warm them but his laughter felt hollow and he knew he was hiding behind it. 'Not going there right now,' he said. He swung himself from the wall and searched the marsh, but the woman was gone.

Tom was unaware that the man he was looking for, William Blacklocks, was already in the church crypt and holding the book Tom wanted so badly to find. Blacklocks took it from a hand-carved, wooden cabinet and placed it on the table. It was large and leather-bound with gold-edged pages. The leather spine and cover showed the word 'Saddling.' Blacklocks hooked a finger under a corner and opened the cover. The book was over two hundred years old, but its early entries included transcriptions of records from hundreds of years before it was bound. He kept the book in the cabinet to avoid as much damage as possible, but still, the smell of mould and damp clung to the pages, refusing to give up its historic grip. He turned the leaves carefully, reading the names of families through the centuries: Blacklocks, Cole, Farrow, Carey.

'Nineteen-twelve,' he said, stopping at one particular page. 'Thomas Carey, chosen.' He moved his finger to a note at the side of the entry. 'Unfulfilled.'

'Why?'

He addressed the woman behind him. 'Because, Susan, the Careys were cowards and thieves. That one left here without fulfilling his obligations to his ancestors and the village. Glance here.' He turned to another page.

Susan stepped up to the table and moved a candle towards the book. Blacklocks slid it away from the flame.

'Careful,' he hissed. 'This transcription is the only truthful record of our village apart from what he...' he spat the word out, unable to say the name, '...he stole from us one hundred years past. Our history would have been lost out-marsh or destroyed were it not for my kin and their work. This book is a thing to be cherished. So, careful with your candle wax.'

'What's it tell?'

'Many truths. Here...' He indicated the later part of the thick volume. 'This is my life's work. The new translation, it brings us from Domesday Book to the twentieth century. You see here?' He pointed, and Susan leant carefully closer. 'The year twelve ninety-two. The first Saddling, the first great storm remembered. And you see the names? William of the Black-Locks and Robert Di-Kari. Two of the oldest names in our part of the marshes.'

'I don't understand,' Susan said, and stepped away from the table.

'We have our last chance to right the wrong,' he said, closing the book.

'Meaning what?' Susan retreated to the shadows. She was picking at her fingers, and her breathing came in shallow breaths.

'We must draw him like an eel to a kiddle. Then, once he bites, he's in the weir.' Blacklock's eyes glowed in the gloom. His white face stood out from the dark surroundings and hung in the dank air with his thin mouth twisted into a smile. 'The further we cast, the harder they swim,' he added. 'Nothing must be too easy.'

Blacklocks turned his attention back to the book, and Susan left a pause before she spoke.

'William,' she said. 'I need to ask you.'

He made no response, simply grunted and brushed the cover with his sleeve, checking it for any blemish.

'It's my Daniel. It don't sit well that this foreigner is so close.'

'It is not for long.'

'But the only room we have is aside Dan's and, well, you know how he is.'

'Woman, I know how all the children are. I taught every one of them. Your Daniel is simply a dreamer wondering what's out there, what it will be like if he ever comes to see it. They all question and look for answers, disbelieving what is taught. We were the same, and we have seen it many times in others. Daniel is no different. He will grow away from it in time.'

'That's the thing though, ain't it?' Susan drew in a breath and left her fingers alone. Her fists clenched. 'Look, William, he'll be twenty-three in ten days. It's only ten days. I done all you asked me. Can't you...?'

Blacklocks rounded on her, slamming his hand onto the table. 'Do you know how often that has been said in this village?' The words flew from his mouth on spittle. 'Do you know how many have suffered for asking it? Why should you be different?' He stepped towards her, his hand raised, his eyes flaming.

Susan cowered, her back on the cold, crumbling wall.

'No-one is outside of the Lore,' Blacklocks said. 'And you out of all of us know the pain of that.' His hand came down to his side and his anger slid away like a lizard slithering under cover. He took a step closer and, although he held her shoulder gently, his voice was firm. 'Their debts will be paid. Our history will be honoured. Do not ask me again.'

'No,' Susan said, and pulled herself away from him. 'No, I shan't.'

'You know your part. Get to it.'

'Peace wi' 'e.' She nodded and backed into the blackness of the crypt.

Blacklocks carefully placed his Saddling history in the cabinet. 'Debts will be paid,' he repeated, and locked the door

Twelve

She stood with her white stick at the Saddling bridge, her back to the village. The sun was low and weak, yet she could feel it. In her mind, she recalled the view; the horse-track running away south, lined by hedges and hawthorn trees; the thin line of green that was the land beneath an immeasurable sky that could change its colour as quickly as its mood. Nature wrapped itself around the village like a battlement, offering safety to those who respected it, death to those who did not. It was her protection and her keeper, her life source and her gaoler.

She felt the rough wood of the planks beneath her bare feet. They marked this end of Saddling life as they crossed the moat that protected the village from all but the most inquisitive of intruders. She imagined how they had changed over the years. Her toes touched on splinters and sought out holes. If Blacklocks had his way they would be allowed to rot completely, cutting Saddling off from the world beyond. But the bridge was necessary. Even Blacklocks knew that. Those who were allowed, the fetchers, were able to cross and walk on, to find the supplies that the village could not produce for itself. Some of the community that had ostracised her were permitted to pass into whatever existed out there, but that privilege was not for Eliza Seeming. It wasn't then, and it certainly wasn't now.

She tipped her head towards the distinctive splash of a water vole paddling in the wide dyke under the bridge. 'Someone's come from its tunnelling to find food,' she thought. 'Someone has nothing to fear from what lies beyond the safety of its home.' She pictured it foraging free in the rushes and sedge along the bank. She could smell the fresh, grassy scent of the reeds further downstream and heard them rustle with a gentle hiss as a breeze passed through.

It brought with it a different scent. Someone was approaching.

Eliza listened to the unfamiliar footfall and knew it to be the stranger. Her smooth brow furrowed and she stepped back from the bridge. Taking two steps to her left, she turned an exact right angle and bent to take some marsh grass with which to weave a wreath. Digging her fingers into the soft earth, the roots of the plant wrapped around her hand in greeting and gave themselves to her willingly. Having taken only enough for what she needed, she stood once more, raised her head and followed the blackness behind her eyes. The damp field-edge and patches of mud, mole mounds and emmet-castes marked her progress towards her dwelling. The low breeze brought more scent of the stranger as he drew close and, although she suspected his purpose, she pondered his questions.

A mild flame lit hope in her heart that this man could be the one to make the difference. She could not fight Blacklocks on her own and now the time was nearing when she would have another chance. She had sensed badness brewing when she had listened to the meetings from beneath the church windows, and it was in the air when she had taken her nightly walks among the houses. Although Saddling slept, its secrets stayed alert and wakeful, there to be read. She had grown ever more suspicious of Blacklocks' fanaticism, but she dared not voice her worries. Eyesight was one thing to lose; life was another.

Tom, having found no joy or breakfast at the inn, and having had no luck finding the minister either, had decided to take Dan's advice and look for the woman who lived by the bridge. He had no intention of returning to the car just yet, not now that he had found another lead. He followed the main path out of the village, noting that the houses he had seen with burning candles now had new, unlit ones in their place, presumably ready for night time. There were more wreaths on doors than he had been aware of the night before and, looking at one more closely, he found no sign of holly, ivy, or anything that represented Christmas. They were circles of grass, some with old bulrushes, others with dying weeds and a few red or yellow berries; hardly celebratory or seasonal. Something else struck him as strange. None of the front doors had a letter box and there were no mailboxes at the end of the neatly kept paths.

In the distance, he saw a horse pulling something behind it. He knew little of the countryside but thought it too late in the year for ploughing. He took it to be a cart of some sort and men and children on the other side were busy around it. They were lifting white bundles, heavy, it seemed, and placing them on the back. Tom realised they were sheep. Large, black birds wheeled around overhead, and some swooped into the cart. One man, it might have been the old farmer from the pub, waved a long pole in an attempt to keep the birds away. Wondering where they might be taking the sheep, Tom walked on.

A small, white figure was following the line of the ditch bank, and he was pretty sure it was the same woman that Dan had pointed out to him.

A shack stood a short distance from the bridge and, if that was where she was heading, that was where Tom was going too. Rather than follow the track to the bridge and then turn at the right angle to follow her, he cut off diagonally across the field. The ground undulated in small mounds and was springy beneath his feet. Dried sheep dung lay among wide, flat thistles. He picked up his pace. The walking was keeping away the morning chill and, by the time he drew near to the shack, he had seen the woman go inside. He prepared questions in his head and collected his thoughts.

He arrived at the small building more out of breath than he thought he would have been. The ground was so low lying that he had not appreciated the distance.

The shack, for it was no bigger than a large garden shed, appeared to have been made from anything found lying around. The walls were planked, unpainted and, as far as Tom could see, unstained. The roof consisted of corrugated tin nailed to rough beams that rested on the walls of the single-story construction. Someone had gone to the effort of installing un-matching windows and adding makeshift shutters, and the door fitted unevenly into a purpose-built jam around it. There was no handle, but there was a latch. No letterbox again, he noticed, but that was hardly surprising. Perhaps this was a shepherd's hut, placed here on the outskirts of the village like a sentry. The bridge was not so far away and he wondered how he had missed this odd and out of place looking building on yesterday's walk into Saddling.

There was no sound from inside but, as he raised his hand to knock on the unpainted wooden door, a voice called out, 'Be open.'

She must have seen him through a window but the timing was still unnerving.

'Bain't going to open it for you,' she called. 'If you want a-see me then let yourself in.'

'Okay,' Tom called back. He lifted the latch and peered inside.

Far from being a shepherd's hut, this was someone's home. A ceiling of twisted beams showed the tin roof between them, and a variety of leafy, earthy items hung up there on hooks. Bunches of grasses and plants dripped down in dried formations like brittle stalactites. There were some pelts hanging. He recognised what was once a hare, and a few fox tails were gathered together on a hook near the door. He pushed these aside as he entered. The fur was soft but made him think of death.

His eyes took a while to adjust to the dimness of the room as he looked for the source of the voice. There was, at first, no sign of anyone. The walls were lined with wooden shelves, apart from one long gap on the right where a stone sink sat lopsided on a wooden base. Curtains shielded whatever was under this and, next to it, more shelves held jars and tins. A window faced the open fields that stretched on for as far as he could see. That wasn't very far as the window was filthy. Steam rose from a small, potbellied stove in the corner, filling the room with the smell of vegetables. It only made him hungrier.

In front of him stood a long, cluttered kitchen table, and, at the far end of it, he finally saw the woman.

'I won't apologise for the mess,' she said, fixing him with motionless eyes. 'Sit down.'

'Here?' Tom asked, closing the door and pulling out a chair.

'On the floor, if you fancy it, makes no never-mind a-me.' Her voice was deep, and she had the same accent as the men in the pub, though hers, like Dan's, was softer.

He lowered himself into the chair and found it occupied by a dead animal. He wasn't sure what to do with it. 'Is this a rabbit?' he asked, hoping she would suggest something.

'Aye, fresh.'

Its eyes were cold and staring, like hers. Its neck, when he did finally pick it up, was slack and the head dropped heavy to one side as he placed it on the table. Worrying about fleas and infections, he brushed the chair, wiped his hands on his coat and then slid into the seat.

'Done?' the woman asked.

'Yes, thank you,' he replied. 'I hope you don't mind, but Daniel said you were his aunt and that I might ask you some questions.'

'You might ask me,' she replied, still staring directly at him and stroking long, blonde hair that fell and framed her face.

'Thank you.' He glanced around the room, trying to look impressed. He wanted to make small talk before launching into his questions, but this was hardly the kind of home one would praise to its owner. A drawing that stood beside the sink caught his eyes. It was out of place among the jars and cooking implements. He recognised the young man in the picture. 'Oh, is that…?'

'No, it be Daniel's parents,' she explained. 'My sister, Susan, and her late husband.'

'A remarkable resemblance,' he said, and looked back at her. As far as he could tell she had not moved. How did she know where he was looking? 'Yes, anyway. Dan said I should ask...'

'I know.'

'You do?'

'You told me, just.'

'Right.' Tom shuffled in his seat. He felt foolish for a reason he couldn't place.

'You sit uneasy,' she said. 'Unsettled. There's things unresolved in you, and you have much needs asking. The next one is unnecessary, Tom.'

'Well, the thing is...' He drew up short. 'How did you know my name?' She was still fixing her eyes on him, and he was sure he'd not seen her blink. 'Ah, very funny,' he said, and forced a smile. 'I guess everyone knows everyone's business around here. Yes, Tom, Tom Carey.'

He stood, thinking that he should offer his hand but she simply stared.

The stick, the gawping eyes that didn't move, he suddenly realised that she was blind. He sat again, glad that she couldn't see that he was blushing. He'd only talked to one blind person before and that was back at boarding school. He'd been given the job of taking the piano tuner across the main road to the bus stop. He'd been embarrassed to be seen with an Albino man wearing sunglasses in winter. He'd forgotten to warn him about the kerb and the poor chap had tripped head-first into the bus stop.

'D'you understand what you're searching out?' the woman asked, jolting Tom's thoughts back into the cramped, strange-smelling room.

'Right, yes. The village journal. You see, Dan said...'

'No, what you're really searching for. What is it?'

The woman had still not moved. Her head was motionless, her thin, pale lips moved but a fraction, and her expression was unchanging. She wore a simple dress, like a robe and Tom wondered how she managed for heat. The shack, which was no more than a kitchen, was cold, despite the stove. The chill breeze had followed him in and played impishly around his ankles.

'Ancestors,' he replied, pulling his coat together at his waist and covering his thighs for warmth. 'It's a long story, won't go into it, but Dan thought you could help. Local history and all that?'

'And all what?'

'Sorry?'

'Sorry is a waste of emotion. Local history and what, specifically?'

'Well, Dan said…'

'How well d'you know him?'

'Not at all, but I am staying at the inn. Then, I guess you know that too.'

'What's he said?' Finally, she sat forward. She dipped her fingers into a bowl where they hunted through a collection of oddments.

'Can I help you with that?' he asked, half rising from his seat.

'You're here for me to help you,' she said. 'What's my nephew told you 'bout Saddling?'

'Well, nothing really. We didn't talk for long. I was hungry, and he was… distracted.'

'They've a lot on their minds, the boys. Aye, they're brown-deep and nohow settled. Prehaps a resolute lad here and there a one, but not many and not Daniel.' She failed to explain what she meant. 'You mention his name much.'

'Who, Dan?'

'There be the sixth one since you come in, and you no doubt thought it more.' She took a piece of bone from the bowl, put it to her nose and then dropped it back.

Tom adjusted his collar. Sweat ran uncomfortably beneath his shirt. He changed the subject. 'I'm trying to find something out, and no-one seems to have any answers for me.'

'Why should they have?'

'Well, I was hoping for some civility at least.'

Suddenly the woman threw back her head and laughed. The sound, rich and resonant, hit the ceiling and ricocheted around the shack. As her hair fell back, she tucked it behind her ears and revealed a deep scar running from one temple to the other across the bridge of her nose. Otherwise, her face was unlined, though her skin had a greyness of age about it. She dropped her head down again, and her laughter snapped off. 'What d'you really want a-know, Tom?'

Tom explained again about wanting to know why his ancestors had left the village. He put it simply, hoping to avoid any of her sideways questioning.

'You must deal with Blacklocks,' she said, and returned to rummaging in the bowl.

'Apparently, but I haven't found him yet. Bit early in the day perhaps. But still, I'll talk to anyone as long as I can get to the history.'

'You'll not be dissuaded?'

'Why should I be?'

'This… thing, this knowledge, it's so important to you?'

Tom nodded and then stopped. 'I was nodding my head, sorry.'

'I know.' She left the bowl alone and tapped her fingers along the table to the edge. Measuring out a short distance with her span, she reached down into a large jar that stood among many others on the floor. Tom leant to look and saw a row of storage pots, some open, some stoppered, all lined up at measured intervals parallel with the edge of the table.

The woman sat up straight, now holding a small, leather pouch tied with a lace. She threw it, unexpectedly, and it landed on the table in a clear patch between the dead rabbit and a plate of bulbs. Tom wondered if she was blind at all, but the track of her scar, which seemed to deepen each time he caught sight of it, removed all doubt.

'What's this?' he asked, as much to take his mind off the wound as to keep the conversation going.

'There's a lot can be learned at Saddling,' the woman said. 'And not only from books.'

Tom opened the pouch and peered inside. 'Flour?'

'My nephew and his sway, Barry, keep me supplied with what nature and village don't provide. Keep it.'

Not sure what to say or do, Tom put the flour in his coat pocket. 'What do you mean, sway?' he asked.

'Sway, best man, a marker we call 'em also. Each the boys have one.'

'Nice, thanks. You've got an interesting dialect.'

'You ain't here for chat. Ask on.'

'Oh, yes. So, tell me, why don't you live in the village?' he asked.

'As you say, long story.'

One that he clearly was not going to hear today as she said no more. 'So,' he prompted, 'this book?'

'In church, I expect,' she said with a tip of her head.

'So it exists? You've seen it?'

She left a pause long enough for him to realise what he had said and feel bad for it.

'Not everything's seen easy,' she said. 'Tom, remember this. Sometimes you have to cover things over so as to find them. Understand?'

He did not.

'You have to understand the old story 'bout the village,' she went on. 'See, the legend goes back to...'

'Sorry, stop you there,' he cut in. 'I don't deal in legends. I just need a few facts, a bit of real proof about something that happened.'

She sat back in her chair and shook her head. 'A-find facts,' she said. 'A-find proof only? You can't accept a thing without seeing it? Are you short on faith, Tom?'

This sounded like it was going to develop into some religious lecture. She already had him unnerved, and now she was wasting his time.

'Thanks, Miss... But that kind of discussion isn't what I came for. No offence. This whole set-up here is a bit strange, and I can see you've not got the answer I was looking for. So, if you don't mind, I won't keep you any longer.' He stood, but the woman slapped her stick down hard on the edge of the table. Tom froze mid-stand, and then, when she rose and stepped confidently towards him, he sank back in his chair. Memories of Aunt Maud's discipline came back to him and he sweated some more.

'You can't leave now, Tom.' Her voice was gentle, but there was authority behind it. 'You're not aware of what you started.'

'Sorry?'

'Blacklocks knows you're here. A foreigner in his village. He'll find you when he wants and when he does, you... the real you, best be ready.'

'What for?'

'For him. If you want your facts and your proof, then you'll only find 'em in the book. Aye, it existed. He'll hold it. There'll be nothing remarkable 'tween its covers.'

'Oh, really?'

'No, only truth.'

'Then, that's fine. That's all I want. Thanks.'

'Let me ask you, Tom. You sure 'bout this?'

'Yes, of course.'

'And you're ready a-see it through, willing?'

'That's why I came here. Okay, thanks, I'll go and speak to this Blacklocks character.'

She put a hand on his shoulder, her body too close to his. She smelt of earth, and he saw that she had dirt under her nails.

'You be strong,' she said, and squeezed. 'You've a passion, but in my experience passion sparks trouble. Look a-your name, Tom Carey, and trust in what can't be proved.'

'Okay, now this is getting too theatrical.'

As if to validate his words, an unannounced gust of wind threw open the shack door.

'It's all there, Tom,' she said, holding the door back for him. 'You just must a-see it.'

'Fine, well, thanks anyway,' he said, and stepped out into the field. 'And thanks for the, er, bag of flour.'

'On the way,' she added, pointing out with her cane. 'You're better a-taking the lyste-way on the side of the field and, after, the lope into the village. Don't cut across.'

'Ah, that old "Stick to the path" line, eh?'

'Don't get your meaning there, but you'll find less whiteback treddles at the edge, fewer places a-trip. You're not after an accident, not here.'

The door swung shut and the latch fell.

Taking her advice, he took the bank at the edge of the field, following it to the bridge, all the time pondering over what she had told him. When he thought about it, he realised that all she had done was question him about his motives. They were clear enough to him and they were quite reasonable, yet he couldn't help but feel that she was getting at something else, digging too deep, stirring something up inside that he would rather leave unprovoked. At least she had confirmed the existence of the book. After several paces, he realised that he had not asked her specifically about the events of nineteen-twelve and was no closer to finding out why Thomas Carey left the village.

He thought about returning to the shack but decided against it. He doubted that he would get anything more from her other than rhetoric and uncomfortable questions. Instead, he walked on and came to the bridge.

There was something worryingly familiar lying on the far side.

'What on earth...?' He stepped onto the planks, feeling them bow beneath his weight and looked closer. 'What the...?'

He ran to the other side. His shoulder bag lay with leads spilling from it like entrails. The laptop was beside it, half on the planks and half on the muddy bank. Dropping to his knees, he saw that the screen was cracked and the computer ruined.

Stabbed more by insult than rage, he leapt up and searched for the culprit. He had not been in that shack more than ten minutes. No-one had followed him here, he'd heard no vehicles. The field workers were still way off, but, other than that, there was not another living soul in sight.

Just the circling crows cawing overhead.

Thirteen

Barry leant his back against the gravestone and lit his pipe. He threw the match to the ground where the wet grass extinguished the flame immediately. He followed Dan's gaze to the circling crows.

'Gathering early,' he said. 'Don't mean nothing.'

'You know they have memories,' Dan said, his head tilted back to look up to the church roof.

'I 'eard it said.'

'One came at me the other day. It looked in my eyes. It'll remember me.'

'I've seen many and been seen by them. Tell you, means nothing.'

'There was a group of them out at Far Field. They were anting, then one flies up and straight at me.'

'It's close. Your mind be on it.'

'How can it be on anything else?'

Barry put a hand on his friend's shoulder and gave a light tug. Dan turned back to face the marsh.

'Keep 'em at our backs,' Barry said. 'There be nothing can be done.'

A pair of ink-black crows perched on the ridge tiles of the church roof and tilted their heads as if they were trying to catch the conversation below. One shuffled sideways in short, fast steps. The other followed, and they inched further along until they were both directly behind the two friends. Their claws gripped and their scaly, grey legs held them steady.

Barry felt Dan's shoulder against his as they shared the gravestone as a resting post. He drew in on his pipe. Today, the leaves tasted bitter. It was not the same rich flavour as it had been the night before and yet it was all from the same pouch. There was something else that was fouling Barry's mouth, and he knew exactly what it was. He offered the pipe across, but Dan declined.

'Aaron says he stepped past the dowel at North Grazing,' Dan said, nodding towards the distance. 'Went beyond Saddling land.'

'The daft falser also said 'e gave Judith Fetcher something a-remember 'im by,' Barry replied, and then laughed. 'And I reckon that's as likely as any of them nasty black things calling you.'

'I can't think about tomorrow.'

'That be the only way a-get through it.'

Dan drew in a deep breath and let it out slowly. 'Barry,' he said, 'have you ever…?'

Barry knew what he was asking. 'No, mate. Much as I wanted. I've stood by the dowels at North Grazing, the markers at West Ditch, and the dole-stones at Far Field. I've stood with blind Eliza at the bridge, looking out, and I've trodden the poachy foot-walk from uncle's farm a'the fetcher's trap-shed. I even stood on the sheep gate at East Sewer once and leant over. The air smells the same on that side as on this.'

'Never? I mean, not even a footstep?'

'Why would I dare?'

'But you want to, right?'

Barry took a deeper draw, but he wasn't enjoying the flavour. He blew the smoke out and tapped the pipe on the wall. Dan took it and cleaned it for him as they gazed out across the fields to the high hill miles beyond.

'Dan,' Barry said, 'can I ask you something I shouldn't?'

Dan's attention was on the pipe. He wiped the bowl with grass he ripped up from by his boots. He polished the whole thing on the inside of his coat and then handed it back.

'You're always asking me things you shouldn't, buffle-boy. And you don't normally ask to ask me.' He said it with a laugh.

Barry took the pipe and held it. 'If I did,' he said, 'step over the other side, I mean, would you come wi' me?'

A loud caw made both boys duck. The crows swooped down from the church roof and flew close overhead, their metallic voices croaking like laughter. Barry felt his heart leap and his skin turned icy.

'It be dangerous against the Teaching. It wouldn't be right,' Dan said, following the birds with his eyes.

'None of this be right.' Barry leant in closer to Dan. Slowly, his heart rate returned to its regular, reliable rhythm. 'Can't be, can it?'

'I know your feelings, Barry, but you should be careful what you say.'

'I trust you.' Barry gave him a nudge and put his pipe away. There were suddenly tears behind his eyes. He closed them, thought of his parents and his friends. He thought of Dan and pictured the two of them in later life as fetchers, bringing in goods from one of the towns that lay beyond the Saddling reaches. 'If I can't trust you with me thoughts who can I leave 'em wi'?'

'There for you,' Dan said, and Barry said the same thing in reply.

There was silence. They had nothing they needed to say to each other. Barry looked at his marker. Dan hadn't shaved but then it was hard to tell, the hair on his face was so light. Barry felt his own chin, shaved that morning. Come evening there would be stubble, and he would look untidy. He didn't care about that, but his family would expect him clean shaven in Penit.

'So, 'ow you spending a'night?' he asked.

Dan pushed stray locks of hair away from his face. 'There's only one way to spend the last night of Penit,' he said, his words measured and without inflexion. 'A quart of Old Tickle by a roaring blazer and Sally Rolfe singing to me.'

'Sally…?' Barry laughed, and punched Dan on the arm. 'You got an aching-tooth for 'er, we know, but you do talk some mire, Daniel Vye.'

'Just like they teach us, friend.'

'Ah, that they do.'

'He does.'

'Aye, 'e. But 'e did. It's not "does" no more. We're out of that schoolroom now, this way or that.'

'They won't call for you,' Dan said. 'Not when they've got Aaron and Mark, and the others.'

'Bain't so much the calling, though, is it? That be just tradition. We must all be called, us eight. It's the whitebacks and the choosing.'

Barry felt Dan's hand search out his own and hold it. The crows were gone. The marsh was quiet and still, and the breeze died away.

'Something's got a-change,' Barry said. 'If I be chosen, will you see it does?'

'And if they choose me?'

'With you all the way, mate.' Barry squeezed his friend's hand. 'Let's hope fur Mark Blacklocks, eh? He don't put nothing into the village as it is.'

'Careful, Barry,' Dan rebuked. He let go of Barry's hand to turn to face him. 'There still be things you shouldn't think on, things we shouldn't say. Remember your Teaching.'

'If you want me thoughts on that, Mr Vye, you can have 'em. But you've 'ad 'em afore, and I know you don't like 'earing 'em. That time, we was just into fifteen years, I told you what I thought on the festival, 'ow it ain't nothing but a mire-pit dug out 'undreds years back. You said you'd go tell Blacklocks. Well, you didn't 'cos you're me marker, and we're too close for betraying. But I feel the same now as then, same as Fader, and I don't care if you do go and tell 'im now. The Teaching's too old, and the whole thing's there a-make us behave when we're growing. Keeps us a-feared and away from questioning.'

'Shush, Barry.'

'Ah, you feel the same an' all, I know it.' Barry's voice rose in anger. 'There'll be time fur staying quiet a'morrow when they choose. When whoever it be takes 'is place. When Blacklocks comes out in 'is caller-robes, with 'is rook eyes and that skeleton grin…'

'Barry!' Dan stood.

'Let 'im listen.' Barry shouted. 'Let 'im 'ear and do what? Lock me in 'is cellar with no food gone three days? I'd go. Least then I'd be away from those devil-birds and their calling.' Barry's face flushed red, and he stood to face his friend. 'No, Dan, I'm sorry, and I ain't disrespecting you and what you believe, no matter 'ow much you fight 'gainst it in your silence. I know you wants to 'old the Teaching dear, but I can't no more. It's all wrong, ain't it? Plain wrong.'

'You're talking this way 'cos you're scared. It's been as it is for…' Dan stopped. 'Barry, you're crying.'

'I'm angry.'

Dan wiped his friend's face with his sleeve. 'Then don't think about it no more. Be like me. Let it happen if it happens. It's going to happen somehow, and there's nothing to be done. Don't spend your last day of Penit so afeared and worried. Spend it with me. We'll have a flagon of Old Tickle and Sally can sit on our knees, both.'

Barry took hold of Dan's hand and pressed it to his stubbled cheek. 'I can think of other things I'd like to do on my last Penit night.' He winked.

Dan pulled his hand away and took a step back, his face pale.

'I didn't mean that.' Barry gave an unconvincing laugh, but it was lost in the widening silence. 'Oh, give over, Daniel Vye. You think too much a yourself.'

Dan studied Barry's brown eyes, his face slowly falling into a distorted smile. He gave Barry a push. 'You think too much of me,' he said.

'Well, that ain't possible.'

Dan was keen to fill the uncharted distance between them that was threatening to push them too far apart. 'Leave it be and tell me, what's happening with our stranger?' he said, sitting. 'What d'you find out?'

Barry also sat, and the two of them leant into each other at the shoulder, as was their way. 'Be no 'arm, is Tom,' Barry said. 'Be gone afore we know it. Be a shame, mind. I want a-ask 'im everything 'bout out-marsh. We was talking last night after 'e walked in from beyond the bridge, but me fader was at the table, and Mick Farrow, and it didn't feel right asking 'im, even after they'd left us lonesome.'

'The Teaching roots deep.'

'That it does. You spoke wi' 'im? Seeing as 'e's at your inn.'

'He's still here?' Dan asked by way of a reply. 'He wasn't in his room back a while, though someone else was. Blacklocks I reckon.'

'Nosey old Blacklooks. I'm in 'opes Tom's still 'bout. There's plenty to ask 'im if I could only risk it.'

'I know how you're thinking, but you be careful, Barry. You'll have Blacklocks down on you like that time when he caught you driving your fader's tractor.'

'What were wrong there? I was eight. Us Coles learn a-drive when we're boys.'

'Some as think we still are boys.'

'Not after a'morrow. Anyways, I don't care what Blacklooks thinks of me, and neither does me…' He stopped abruptly. He trusted Dan with his life, they had been brought up that way, but it was not his place to share someone else's thoughts on the village minister. 'Make no never-mind, mate,' he said. 'Still, though, I hope Tom don't go.'

'Your tooth starting to ache like mine, is it?'

'Don't be a clag.' Barry tried a laugh again, to cover his reddening cheeks, but there was no getting anything past Dan. 'Promised I'd show 'im the village sometime, be all. If I'm still 'ere.'

Dan's whole body sagged. 'Please,' he said. 'Can we not dwell on what can't be changed? We'll not be going away. We'll be here Saturday, both of us, and we'll play spikers in the inn after festival's over. And then, you know what we'll have?'

'Poor guts if we're drinking your ma's bathtub.'

'We'll have sore guts for the rest of our lives, Barry Cole. Together. That's how it is.'

Barry knew Dan was right. He had to accept how things were, just as he had been taught.

'Come on, Mr Cole,' Dan said. 'Stop wearing out that graver with your back and let's walk. We should go and see Farrow's flock. See if they've

95

brought them in yet and see how the whitebacks are setting up for the morning.'

'Aye, Dan,' Barry said. 'I'm wi' ye.'

Barry stood and followed his friend through the collection of headstones.

A crow landed where he had been sitting as if it had been waiting for that spot all morning. It was a solo, male bird and it pecked at the weathered gravestone impatiently.

Fourteen

Tom's heart was pumping hard in his chest by the time he reached the first of the village houses. His mind was churning over everything he was going to say and sentences were fully formed. He had organised his anger but had not figured out at whom this anger should be aimed. Someone was to blame. Someone had tried to give him a message, and the message was clear; leave. He could find no sense in it, and that angered him more.

Who could have done this? Not the blind woman in the shack, she had been there ahead of him. Anyway, why her? To him, she was clearly eccentric, living out there in no more than a tin shed among her weird plants and dead rabbits, talking in riddles and knowing about things she couldn't see.

Reaching the village green, he saw Dan and Barry walking towards him on the path. Matt Cole stood a few feet away in his front garden and was accepting a wicker basket from a middle-aged woman whose head was covered in a scarf; a rural scene that might otherwise have been charming had Tom not been fuming.

He held up his laptop and waved it towards Cole. 'Did you do this?' His voice splintered the brittle stillness of the morning.

The woman jumped, shocked at the outburst.

'What's 'at?' Cole called back.

'Did you do this?' Tom had reached the front gate now.

Cole shook his head. The woman gave him a small curtsy and then hurried away, sidling past Tom and crossing over to a house opposite.

'What's up, Tom?' Barry came running. Dan followed at a slower pace.

'Some… someone's cracked it. Ruined the bloody thing.'

'What strange thing be that?' Cole said, taking a step closer.

Tom backed away from him. He was angry for sure, but he realised that he was in an unfamiliar place with people he didn't know and Cole was big. His coat was laying over the gate and he wore only a shirt in the chill morning, but that gave Tom the chance to see his thick arms, strong from years of field work. His hands were huge, too, and the basket hanging from one of them was like a child's toy in comparison.

'What's 'appning?' Barry asked. He stood in front of Tom and tried to take the laptop case from him. Tom snatched it away.

'Keep off it.' Tom held it out towards Cole again. 'Why would someone do this?' Dan arrived at Barry's shoulder. 'Was it you?'

'Please,' Cole said, stepping right up to Tom and putting one of his bear-like hands on his arm. Tom could feel the force of his touch and he wasn't even gripping. 'Please don't speak at the boys so, not a'day. It wouldn't a-been any a young'uns.'

'Well, it was someone,' Tom said, pulling his arm away and moving back towards the path.

'Master Vye!' The middle-aged woman was back, hurrying across the gap between the houses and bearing another basket. She waved to Dan, stopped in front of him, bowed, and then held out the basket. 'For ye,' she said.

'You're all raving mad,' Tom muttered, and left them to it.

'Tom!' Barry trotted to catch up with him. 'Slow down. What's 'app'ning?'

'Leave it,' Tom snapped, his pulse still ringing in his ears.

'Who'd a-done that?' Barry kept pace with him, and Tom found his presence strangely settling.

'That's what I want to find out.'

'Tom, best not start trouble, not 'ere a'day.'

'Why not? What's today?'

'Be the last day of Penit,' Barry said, as if that explained everything.

'You're just as crazy as the rest of them.'

'Oi! I'm wanting a-make you feel welcome...'

'Yeah? Like someone else just did? Smashing my computer.'

'Weren't me. Would never be me.'

'I hate to think what's left of my room. Someone bust my mobile, too, have they?'

'I don't know what you're saying.' Barry held back.

Tom hurried on a few paces, but his speed was draining away with his anger.

'I wanted a-show you the village,' Barry called. 'You want a-walk wi' me?'

'I've seen enough of your village, thank you.'

'You leaving?'

'Not until I've sorted this out.'

Tom had reached the inn and spent the last of his anger on the latch, gripping it hard and forcing it down with a satisfying snap.

He stepped in and threw the door shut behind him. Susan was wiping a table. She stood up straight at the sound of the door and, when she saw Tom, moved behind the table for protection.

'I laid out bread and jams for you in the back kitchen,' she said. 'And there be tea on the stove keeping warm. Milk in the pantry on the coldshelf...'

'Not hungry,' Tom barked, and kept on towards the bar. She was one of his suspects, but he doubted she would be fit enough to stalk him unseen out to the bridge and then run back here without being seen.

Tom stopped with his hand on the hatch and turned to her. 'Perhaps I should call the police,' he said, the plan only just forming in his mind.

'We have no...'

'What, no phone?'

'Aye, and no police,' she replied, moving so that she was now on the other side of the table and facing him.

'It just gets better and better,' Tom said. He lifted the hatch and it banged against the wall. He was through the door and into the back passage when it struck him, and he spun to face the woman. 'Really? No police?'

'No need.' She shook her head and put on a faint smile of sympathy. Tom growled and headed up to his room.

Susan put both hands on the table and dropped her head. She heard the stranger stamping his way up the stairs towards the back where the door was slammed shut. 'I can't do this,' she said.

'You have no choice.'

She looked up to see William Blacklocks ascending from the cellar in one long, graceful movement. He moved darkly from behind the bar and approached her, his cane tapping with each step. He placed the cane on the table between them and stood over her, looking down his long nose with his raven eyes.

'William, he's a boy like the others. I don't know how to...'

A stinging slap to the side of her face took the words from her.

'You make it too easy, woman,' Blacklocks spat. 'More resistance.'

Susan, one hand on the red welt on her cheek, tears in her eyes, nodded silently and curtseyed.

Tom surveyed his room. Nothing was out of place. His books were on the chair by the desk, his backpack was by the bed and, having had a root through it, he found nothing was missing. His mobile was in the side pocket and he took it to the window where he held it up towards the ceiling, but still no signal.

'This is bloody ludicrous,' he fumed. 'How am I supposed to find out anything without...?' He threw the phone onto the bed where it gave a 'low battery' beep by way of protest. 'Right, that's enough.'

He scooped up his books, shoved them into his backpack, threw his phone in on top, hoisted the pack onto his back and picked up the useless laptop from where he had dropped it. With no computer, no internet, no phone and no car, the only thing he could think to do was to walk back to the main road and thumb a lift to the garage. That would take him a few hours and the sooner he started out, the better. He gave the room one last check and then stepped out into the landing.

Tom stopped in his tracks. Some great black crow was coming up the stairs, turning into the passageway, its head bowed against the low ceiling. The thing put out a hand and gripped the banister with long fingers that curled around the wood one by one. Slowly, the whole thing twisted to face him, and he saw it was a man, tall but stooping, its face searching the corridor from under a huge mane of black hair. The eyes were small but captivating, and they slowly rose from the ground to Tom's head, taking in his whole body and settling on his face. Tom immediately felt apprehensive at being studied. He had done something wrong and here was the headmaster come with his cane in hand to punish him.

Strangely, when the man spoke, his voice was soft and any shock or remaining anger left Tom instantly.

'I have not yet welcomed you and already you leave us?' The man asked it in such a way that Tom blushed with embarrassment for even thinking of leaving. 'If this is your wish then it can only be for the best.'

At first, Tom didn't know what to say or how to address him. 'Well, yes, maybe. Sorry.' He cleared his throat. He was way shorter than the bent blackness that dominated the corridor, but at least he was standing up straight. This gave him the advantage, and he squared up. 'Who are you?'

'William Blacklocks.' He gave a small bow. 'I heard you were leaving, sir. I can show you the way.'

'How? I mean, who told you...? What?' Tom stumbled on his words. Their confused clumsiness mirrored the manner of his thoughts.

'Saddling in winter is no place for guests,' the man said. He gripped the banister and showed no signs of moving, or showing Tom the way out.

The eyes were wrong, Tom thought. They were too small, and yet the sockets were large around them, and the brows were great arches of grey. The hair was too black and too young for a face with so many lines. It was long but well kept. The jaw was strong, the chin pointed, and high cheekbones threw shadows over the sunken skin below. A presence seeped from the man and radiated calmness like an anaesthetic. Tom's breathing slowed, his back relaxed, muscles unwound, but still something twisted in his gut. Something was telling him to stay. He realised what it was.

'Blacklocks?' he said. 'Ah, so you are the vicar?'

Blacklocks smiled and closed his eyes briefly, giving Tom momentary respite from their searching. 'Not exactly, but I am responsible for the church.'

'So you know where this blessed book is?'

'Blessed book?' Blacklocks turned the words over in his mouth like boiled sweets.

'Your church records, the village diary?'

Blacklocks shrugged his shoulders, and they nearly touched the ceiling. 'I imagine it is close at hand.'

'You must know, surely?'

His eyes flicked to the stairwell. Tom could see he was not comfortable in this cramped space and again he felt the advantage.

'Then I reckon I'll hang around a little bit longer,' he said. 'If you can find it for me I can take a look and be off before lunchtime.'

'You will stay so long?'

'It's only a couple of hours. Why? You keen for me to go too?'

'Not at all, not if you do not want to.' Blacklocks took a step backwards on the stairs to free his bent neck and spoke across the banister. 'But I thought you unhappy. Mistus Vye talked of an accident with some machine? I imagine you need it repaired as soon as you can and, as you may imagine, we have no suitable facilities here. If you follow me, I will put you on the right path to the bridge.'

'I know the way,' Tom replied. 'No, if you've got that book, I don't need the laptop.'

'I am sorry,' the tall man said, his voice still employing the same calming tone. 'I am not sure I entirely appreciate your intentions. You will now stay?'

'Until I've seen the book.'

'Well, then, we must do all we can to make you welcome until it is located. I shall see what I can do.'

Blacklocks turned and made his way slowly downwards, the tails of his floor-length coat pouring after him like an oil slick.

'Right, thanks.' Tom called. 'When can I see...?' Blacklocks had gone. 'Catch you later, then.'

He returned to his room, his anger now completely evaporated. Putting his laptop bag behind the door out of the way, a new spark of hope ignited in his chest. He wondered how long he might have to wait for the man to return to him with the records and glanced out through the window. The sight of the church brought a renewed confidence and he expected to see the strange, twisted man hurrying there.

Instead, he saw Mick Farrow at the bottom of the slope in front of the church porch. He was leaning on a spade, watching two other hefty men as they built a scaffold. The sound of hammering drifted up in an uneven rhythm. One of the men turned to look up at Tom, saw him at the window and doffed his cap.

Tom couldn't throw off the uneasy feeling that what they were building had something to do with him.

Fifteen

Tom's flat was tidier without him even though Dylan had done nothing but shift a few things from the floor so that he could more easily reach the desk. He found some music files on the spare PC but nothing that appealed to his taste. Instead, he navigated to an online rap channel and let it boom out its jumble of anger and percussion while he pottered around inside a few credit agency websites. Yesterday's hacking hadn't gone to plan and he had been forced to hang out in some dubious chatrooms to find advice on a new way to change his rating. He was waiting for a user to get back to him as he clicked through Tom's favourites file to see what he had been browsing recently.

They were all sites to do with finding birth records, marriages, deaths, and gravestone inscriptions. None of them took Dylan's interest at first but then he remembered a family mystery of his own. He had been brought up with the story that his grandfather was born during a sea crossing from Jamaica to Britain but no-one had been able to confirm the facts. It was a romantic story and one he had always wanted to have verified. After few minutes in one of Tom's sites he found his parents' marriage and his grandfather's death. Inspired, he was just about to look for more information on a site run by the Mormons when the PC sang out to him. A few short notes repeated over again told him that Tom had a Skype call coming in. He clicked to accept it.

He recognised the face immediately. Tom's aunt sat close to the camera and bore down on the screen as if he was being examined in minute detail from afar. It was a deathly white face, drawn and thin, and was lent no sympathy from the harsh lighting thrown back at it from the monitor. She had dark lines under her eyes and her lips were as pale as her withered skin. Dylan winced and hoped she hadn't noticed. She hadn't; she was reaching for something and looking away. When Maud stared back into the screen her chicken's foot hand was holding an oxygen mask to her face. She took a few breaths and then passed the equipment to someone standing beside her. Dylan saw a younger male hand take it. She shooed that person away and narrowed her eyes as she leaned right into the camera.

'Ah, the black one. Dylan,' she said, and sat back slightly.

'Hi.' He had spoken with Aunt Maud before over Tom's shoulder and only out of politeness. He was not sure how to greet her.

'Is Tom with you?' the old lady asked, her head moving as she tried to look behind him.

'No, Miss Carey,' he replied. 'He went to Saddling yesterday.'

'Excellent news. How is he getting on?'

'I can't tell you. Sorry. Not heard from him.'

'No news at all?'

'No. Perhaps he'll call later, or I could ring, if you like?'

'Yes, would you?' She held up a hand for him to wait and he watched as she took a slow, deep in-breath. The mask was offered again but she waved it away and nodded, a sign that she was alright. 'If you can,' she said, her voice quieter. 'And ask him to let me know how he is getting on. Thank you.'

'I can try him again now if you want to wait,' he said, wondering why she hadn't tried to call him herself or at least have her assistant do it for her.

'No, presently is acceptable, thank you, but today. And tell him the date. Things have picked up pace.'

Dylan shook his head; he didn't understand.

'The doctors have been at me again. Last night, I took a turn. Bloody meddling about with scans and tests.'

'Everything okay?' He knew it was a dumb question. He could see through the screen that things were far from alright and, from what Tom had said about his aunt's health, things were never going to improve.

Maud chose to ignore the question. 'I do feel sorry for that boy, you know?' she said. She was looking off screen again, but not at anyone; she was thinking. 'Losing his parents in that way, having no-one else apart from me and, let's face it, I'm not exactly maternal.' She squinted into the camera and Dylan saw the faintest twitch of a smile. 'God, no, not maternal at all.' She cleared her throat. 'You look after him, don't you, Dylan?'

The question caught him off guard. 'Well, we're mates,' he said. 'He was good to me when I joined the company and I try and keep him out of trouble.'

'I am sure you do,' she said. It looked like she was writing something down. 'He needs looking after. He's a quiet boy, too introverted, like his father was. He would sit and do nothing all day if you let him. He needs a focus, you understand?'

'Ah, so is that why you set him this task?' Dylan waved his hand at the collection of notes and papers, the charts on the walls.

'Christ, no. That's not for Tom's benefit,' she said, but the words turned to coughing as she laughed. Within seconds the mask was back over her face. The youthful hand held it there and she struggled for a moment as if she was being suffocated. Once the oxygen had taken effect she relaxed and after a minute gently pushed the hand away. She nodded to whoever was in her room, passed him a note, and then, finally, came back to Dylan. 'Forgive me,' she said. 'This bloody thing won't even let me enjoy mirth. It's hard to walk unless Philip here is by me.' She tipped her head to the person Dylan couldn't see. 'I should have done this years ago, I suppose, but the date was wrong.'

He wasn't sure what she meant at first but then realised. 'It was harder to do the research back then,' he said. 'From what Tom says it's much easier, now, with everything online.'

'Yes, yes.' She spoke to the person off screen and then back to Dylan. 'I must go. We are on the move. Please call Tom and tell him that time is running out. Ask him to telephone me with news.'

'Will do.'

'What?' She was talking to her assistant. 'Oh, yes,' and then back to Dylan. 'I must travel, and thus Philip here has arranged a portable phone. I will give you the number.'

She dictated it and he wrote it down.

'Use that and tell him to contact me,' she said. 'I am desperate to hear our story. Oh, did he take the bible?'

Dylan saw a large book in a box of rubbish and picked it up. It was heavy, hard-covered and had brass corners, one of which cut his finger as he lifted it. Definitely a bible. 'No,' he said. 'It's here.'

'Damn it! There's more in there than he realises. I hope he paid it enough attention.' She coughed again but managed to keep it at bay just long enough to say, 'Desperate,' before her image cut from the screen.

'Oh, bye, then,' Dylan said, but she was gone.

He rested the bible on his lap and pulled back the brass clasp. Sucking on his cut finger, he let the solid cover fall open, releasing the smell of old paper. After a few pages of publisher's text, he came to the first page of a family tree. The printed parts of the yellowing pages were ornate, showing creeping vines, their leaves crowding the four corners. The initial letter F of Family was gloriously florid. It had, at some time, been damp; there were signs of mildew and the names and dates filled out in ink were smudged.

The ink had once been black but now it bruised the pages with green and fading blue as family names grew from neat letters into diffused colours.

'More in here than he realises?' He wondered about Maud's words as he studied the page.

None of the names made much sense to him though the majority were Carey. He closed it and returned to the PC monitor. Clicking the mouse, he could see that his anonymous contact in the chat room had still not replied, so he reached for his mobile and clicked speed dial one for Tom. As he waited for the call to connect he idly opened another of Tom's ancestry favourites, one headed "Known Saddling Burials." It showed a long list of names and dates. 'This guy is obsessed,' he said as he scrolled down. The phone had still not connected.

Half-way down the page something caught his eye and he scrolled back up to the top to read the list more carefully. Pressing speaker on the mobile, he put it to one side and scrolled again, this time paying more attention.

'Saddling,' he said, and then repeated the name, this time quietly.

Curiosity aroused his mind with a gentle whisper at first but then it spoke aggressively. He used the pointer invisibly to underline a name and date on the screen and then opened the bible at the family tree pages. 'Well, what are the chances…?' He turned to another page and moved to another entry on the web page. 'It's all about patterns,' he said, and leant in closer.

Something dropped from the back pages of the book and, beside him on the desk, the telephone repeatedly announced that his call could not be connected.

Sixteen

Tom had a new plan, one quickly formed over fresh bread and homemade jam. The cloth cover tied with string and the shape of the jar were exactly the same as he had seen when he was younger. They reminded Tom of the time he spent at his aunt's house after his parents had died.

Maud had been homely in those days and she always served homemade jam for breakfast. She had never made it herself and had never actually served him personally; she had a live-in housekeeper who did that. Tom remembered rattling around in a huge house out in the Cornish countryside. As soon as she had secured him a place at boarding school, though, Maud packed him off and moved away. He visited her new home during holidays when she was unable to find him an educational camp to attend or failed to send him on some Adventure Scout trip.

Her second house that he remembered had been a large bungalow sitting on a hill in the folded countryside of Devon. The same housekeeper cared for Tom while Maud spent her time doing some kind of research in what she called her study, a conservatory that faced sloping, lush fields dotted with cows. The house, for all its views and homemade jams, was a dull place; no neighbours, no friends to play with, only the old housekeeper, to whom Tom referred in his diary as Mrs Chips because she always smelt of cooking oil. Mrs Chips had her chips when Tom was fifteen. The funeral was a quiet, simple affair and the first time he had noticed his aunt looking unwell. She had been on a downhill slope since then, her demise as gentle as the hill with the cows but not as pretty.

The bitter taste of long-stewed tea brought him back from his daydreams. Blacklocks had not returned with news on the book. Checking around for the time but not finding a clock, he decided he should seek out the man in black and hurry him along.

Walking through the closed pub was a sad affair. It was clean, tidy, and the curtains were open, but loneliness hung in the room. This was a place that only saw life in the evening when the sun had gone and there was nowhere else for the villagers to go but home; a few hours of activity and then back to silence. The morning-after smell and silence suggested happier times and missed opportunities.

The place was getting to him. A village with no electricity (how was that even possible in this day and age?), a community where people bowed to each other, gave gifts, hung wreaths of dead things on their houses, had no phones; how remote were they? At every turn and with every thought he was not surprised that his ancestors had decided to leave. Who would want to live in a forgotten place like Saddling? It was another mystery he felt compelled to explore.

He clicked open the door and ducked outside. The cold winter air hit him immediately and brought him to the summit of alertness. There was a lead to follow and information to discover. He buttoned up his coat and looked across the green. Two young men sat talking on the single bench, their backs to him. He could immediately tell that neither of them was Daniel. He approached slowly and overheard their voices as they floated through the quiet of the late morning.

'I don't see as 'ow you can stay calm, Mark,' Barry was saying.

'I was brought up welcoming the Teaching, Barry Cole. While others had to be taught not to be cowards.' His voice was thin and reedy, almost whining, and his accent was clearer than Barry's. Even sitting down, Tom could see that this boy was tall. His hair was down below his shoulders, jet black and straight. Tom guessed that he must be related to Blacklocks; he was a smaller version of the man.

'Bain't right, though, is it?' Barry was saying.

'It is as it is.'

Tom had nearly reached the bench when they heard him coming. Both boys turned, saw him, and stood up.

'It weren't me, Tom, 'onest. I wouldn't 'ave done nothing like that.' Barry sounded sincere.

'Yeah, okay,' Tom said. 'I know. It doesn't matter now, anyhow. Dylan will fix it when I get home. Unless you've got a spare laptop I can use?'

Barry looked at his friend and then back at Tom. He said nothing.

'Thought not. Pretty useless without power or WiFi anyway.'

The younger boy spoke up, his brow furrowed and his dark eyebrows coming together, hooding his eyes. 'You didn't address,' he said, glaring at Tom. 'You're supposed to address.'

'Tom be an out-marsher, Mark. A guest.'

'Still should address.'

'I'm not sure what you mean,' Tom said. The boy gave him the creeps.

'You shouldn't be here.' Mark fixed him with his eyes and his hands curled into fists.

'Look, mate,' Tom said, pushing his chest out. 'I got the message about not being welcome.' This piece of work was right up there on the top of Tom's list of suspects and he'd only just met him. 'But let's cut the bumpkin bollocks, shall we?'

Barry laughed and Mark transferred his glare to him. 'Barry Cole,' he chided.

'I have no idea what you're on about with addressing and all this bowing. I kind of understand the wreaths on doors and stuff, considering the season, and I can see you've got trouble out here with your electricity, but it's nearly Christmas. Where's the festive spirit?'

Mark's smooth face flashed back to Tom. 'You mustn't go making fun, not in Penit.'

'And that's another thing...'

'Tom,' Barry said, and stepped between the two of them. 'What says I shows you 'round like I promised?'

'Don't ask questions, Mister.' Mark stepped to the side so that his eyes could bore into Tom again.

Tom was tiring of this lad. 'That'd be good, Barry, thanks. But I need to check out Blacklocks and his book first.'

'That'll be Minister Blacklocks, stranger.'

'If there's a pecking order to strange,' Tom said with a wink at Barry, 'then I reckon you're stranger than most.'

'Don't interfere,' the boy threatened.

'Bain't interfering, Mark, 'e's just...'

Tom's attention was drawn to a movement across the green. Daniel had appeared from behind the church and was walking, floating almost, towards the shop. His hands were hidden in the pockets of his sheepskin coat. His head was upright and his eyes were fixed straight ahead. He took no notice of Tom and his lack of acknowledgement stung in Tom's chest.

'What?' he said, aware that one of the lads had spoken. He could tell that Mark had also been watching Dan. His head slowly turned and Tom realised that he hadn't been watching Dan so much as seeing who Tom had been looking at. Mark's expression changed. It was less aggressive but more suspicious.

'Don't interfere,' the boy repeated.

'That's what I do best,' Tom replied with a hint of scorn, and couldn't help but look towards Dan again. He caught a glimpse of his back as he turned between two houses and disappeared.

'He shouldn't be here, Cole.' Mark walked away.

'Where you 'eaded?' Barry called after him.

'Fader needs to know something.'

'He's a bundle of joy, isn't he,' Tom quipped when the boy was at a distance. 'Who's his father? No, don't tell me...'

'Blacklocks. Aye, 'e's all our fader.'

'What?'

'No, not really.' Barry sat.

'Hang on. How old is he?'

'Mark? Be just fifteen.' Barry leant back on the bench and dug his pink hands into his pockets.

Tom sat next to him, turning slightly to face across him in case Dan should reappear. 'And how old is Blacklocks?'

'Sixty-something, we reckon.'

'Married late?'

'Married twice. His first mistus died, sudden like, after 'e found out she couldn't give 'im no nipper, know what I'm saying?' Barry tapped the side of his nose. 'So 'e went 'round again. Trouble is, 'e went 'round wi' me aunt, so it makes me and Mark cousins. But no point you knowing all that. Reckon I take you out North Pasture and show you the felds our whitebacks graze at. If you want.'

'I've seen sheep before.'

'Ah, but...' Barry fell silent and glanced over his shoulder. Blacklocks had come from the house by the church and was talking with his son. Barry turned to face Tom, his soft eyes edged with concern. 'Tom, prehaps you should be away 'ome. This winter ain't a good time a-be 'ere.'

'Too much at stake to turn around now,' Tom said. 'And I can't imagine any time of year is good in this place.' He gave a short laugh.

'Sir, please...' Barry's face fell, edged with hurt. 'Please don't say that 'bout Saddling. It's where we live. It's got its ways, fur sure. Where ain't? But fur all it's 'ardships and... things, it be me 'ome.'

'Yes, I'm sorry,' Tom said. 'It's a nervous reaction. I don't mean anything by it.'

Barry glanced over his shoulder again. Blacklocks and Mark were still talking and throwing looks their way. 'Prehaps I best go find Dan,' he said as he stood. 'I'll show you our felds another time. Will you still be 'ere?'

'Yeah, well, that depends on your old Blacklooks, doesn't it? But we'll swap email addresses or something.'

Barry puffed air through his lips and shook his head. 'The things you know,' he said. He walked away but stopped after a few paces and came back. 'Feels I must be a-saying something a-you.' His eyes flicked to Blacklocks and back again. 'You might think 'bout shaving, and tidy up your locks. If you're a-staying awhile, I means. Just that our minister don't like us lads weather-rough 'bout the face.'

Tom rolled his eyes. 'Ridiculous. Anyway, I didn't bring anything with me.'

'I'm in 'opes I sees you after and staying a time,' Barry said, looking away to the ground. 'And, if I do, then I'll see what I got fur your shaving. And your 'air. Leave it longer and you'll be needing a shearing.'

Tom laughed.

'If you want a-get 'elp from Blacklocks, you'll 'ave a-tidy up and fit in,' Barry said. 'Take me words. I don't much say wise ones so make use of them when I does... Still, best go.'

Tom watched him trudge towards the fields and admired his sheepskin coat. It was a dark tan colour with a thick lining, white fleece showing at the collar. He'd pay a fortune for that back in London. Maybe he could pick one up cheap here, assuming it was made locally. It was an idea, but he reminded himself that they didn't use credit cards in Saddling.

'Ah, well,' he said to himself, pressing his palms on his knees and standing. 'I'll soon have the cash. Back to the...'

'Mr Carey.'

'Jesus!' Tom ducked when he heard the voice right in his ear. He felt breath on the back of his neck as he stood. Blacklocks was bearing down on him, leaning over the bench, his mane falling either side of his face.

'My apologies. I thought you had heard my approach.'

'No.'

'Now, then,' Blacklocks stood straight and, without the confines of the inn ceiling, Tom saw just how tall he was. He guessed at least six foot five. He had to tip his head back to look up at him. 'I have asked about your... the incident,' he went on. 'Your machine. So far, no culprit, but not to fear, all will be questioned and dealt with. We have strict expectations within the village and none of us here tolerate vandalism.'

'Oh, it's fine,' Tom said. 'Don't go to any trouble, really. I'm over it now.'

'How gracious of you.' Blacklocks bowed slightly and Tom felt compelled to do the same.

'So,' he said instead, 'the book. Any news?'

'You want to learn about your forefathers.' Blacklocks nodded. 'I quite understand. Our own are most important to us. Today you find us in preparation for our festival.' He waved his long arm towards the half-constructed platform. 'You might consider staying for it.'

'Don't think I'm the most wanted of guests.'

'I am sure you are.' The corners of Blacklock's lips curled up to meet the hollows of his cheeks. The smile was so insincere that Tom nearly laughed. 'Tomorrow's festival is a great occasion for our village. It is held only once every ten years.'

'Charming, but I have to be back in London.'

'Oh, how sad.'

'So, if I could see this book? I won't need it for long.'

'Ah.' Blacklocks swept out his arm to show the way. It was more like a wing with his voluminous coat opening to reveal folds of material like a professor's gown. 'Perhaps you would do me the courtesy of walking with me to the chapel?'

Tom didn't want to be near him. He felt as though the acres of cloth might suffocate him but, if the church was where the book was, then that was where his inheritance might lie. 'Sure,' he said, and came around the bench, noticing as he did so that the weasel, Mark, was now watching them from within his house.

'Might I indulge you in a story?' Blacklocks asked as they began the short walk up the slope to the church door. 'It will be of interest to you. It is about Saddling history.'

'At last,' Tom said. 'I'm interested in learning all I can about our family. It's for my aunt. You see…'

'Did you know,' Blacklocks interrupted, 'that our church was founded because of sheep and crows?'

'Hence the name of the pub?'

'And there is far more to learn, Mr Carey. Lend me five minutes, and I shall tell you the full story.'

Seventeen

December 29th, 1170

With the earth like slush beneath the hooves, the smell of stagnant water in the salterns all around and the sky brewing up for more rain, the marshes offered a treacherous welcome on a cold, December morning.

The cleric had no choice but to be there. His instructions had been clear—to reach Canterbury and deliver the King's message to the Archbishop as urgently as possible. The parchment was safe and dry, scrolled into a cylindrical leather carrier that was slung from his baldric, and time was of the essence.

His mission had already been cursed by storms that hampered his near fatal crossing from Normandy and saw him make land miles from his intended destination. The weather had remained so foul that a land route was his only option if he was to avoid further delay.

Having recovered from the sea journey in the rain-soaked fishing village of Rye, he had ridden his horse downhill to the Guildford dowels. There a monk from the abbey led him through the reeds and rushes, all the time promising firmer land could be found beyond the marshes. The monk left him before nightfall and the cleric thanked him warmly. Finding nothing but boggy sulings until he reached Walland, he pressed on, taking what shelter he could with the eel fishers, wrapping himself for the night in borrowed, fleece cloaks. The eel-men pointed him inland and promised better ground still, but, with the rain continuing to fall and the wind now whipping up from the east, the going was worsening.

On the second day he set off in his huddle of cloak and wool, leading his horse until he thought it safe to ride again. He had, by this time, eaten the last of his abbey bread and the strips of salty fazen given him by the eel-men, and was feeling the first stabbing pangs of hunger. He thirsted for nothing as there was little around him but water and his mount fared as best it could on the coarse grass that grew in small clumps at the edge of the many fleets. Looking ahead and keeping a distant hill in its place so as not to lose his direction, he saw occasional specks of black movement in the distance. They came and went like motes of soot dancing erratically around a dying lamp. On coming closer, he saw that they were large birds, ravens he thought, but with a savage caw that cut through the hiss of the wind about his ears. His horse shied away and he fought to keep her from rearing. He had to keep to whatever trodden path he could to avoid the creeks and bogs that lay close to him. Should his mount slip her legs would soon be stuck fast in the mire and he would have no choice but to leave her to her fate and continue on foot. With massive grey clouds heading fast towards him, the coming storm was not something he could be sure to survive.

The only things that warmed his heart were the sight of a remote settlement, grazing sheep, and the knowledge that the letter he bore would help heal the rift between the King and the returned prelate. He had no idea what fate was about to befall Archbishop Becket as he prayed for him and his own safe passage.

A ripple of thunder growled out from over the far-off hill and crescendoed. The sound bounded towards him under leaden clouds and, suddenly loud and fierce, it startled a flock of crows which, until then, had been feeding at the stream-side. They flew into the air and directly towards him, panicking his horse to her hind legs. Taken by surprise, the cleric lost his grip on the reins and fell backwards, his spine arching painfully. He grabbed for the leather straps but missed and felt himself rolling sideways with horrific inevitability. His first thought was for his message and he pulled it across his chest as the saddle cloth beneath him gave way to air. He closed his eyes, expecting to feel the hard thump of ground but, instead, freezing water slapped his face. In a gasp of breath it was in his throat and as he spluttered and groped for support it invaded his lungs. His eyes snapped open but saw nothing; they only felt the grit and dirt of the ditch water. It tasted earthy in his mouth and he tried to spit it out, but, as soon as he did, more poured in. Through the sounds of his own struggle and the churning of the water he heard his horse whinny and prayed that she did not fall on top of him.

His feet made contact with the ditch silt and he pushed against it to raise himself to the surface. His head broke through and the brackish taste was washed away by torrents of rain that the storm now threw down on him. He unhooked the leather pouch from his baldric and lifted it above water, wiping his eyes with the edge of his cloak. It was now saturated and pulling him down. He tried to wade to the bank only a few feet away but each time he moved his feet became trapped more firmly by the sediment. It clawed its determined way up to his knees.

He called for help as he tried vainly to reach the bank but his only answer came from a sheep standing amid the chaos of the storm. It regarded him with curious eyes and gave a throaty baa. Each attempted step brought him closer to his death as his legs sank lower into the filth. Struggling harder, he could see that he was not going to live. He pulled back his arm and threw the leather pouch towards the bank; if he was lost then at least there was a remote chance someone would find the message and deliver it. He saw the pouch land safely. 'Thank God,' he said aloud, and then prayed in preparation for death.

The rain falling harder with each gust of wind washed the pouch down the slope, back towards the ditch. He strained his arms to reach it but his reach was short. The bag rolled into the water where it floated for a second before being swept away. It was pulled under, lost, and with it the King's message.

At this point, the cleric gave up hope of earthly life.

Just as he finished what he thought would be his last prayer a crook was offered to him; the crook of the guiding shepherd, he thought; Christ come to take me, to redeem me and deliver me to His paradise.

The shepherd on the bank was not Christ. His hair was long and black, his face narrow and his eyes eagle-like. He crouched as he held out his crook, his great black cloak settling around him like the wings of one of the birds that had frightened the horse. He called something in a tongue that the cleric did not understand but the meaning was clear and, with a last effort, he caught the wooden crook-head in his hand. With the shepherd pulling on the other end, the cleric found himself dragged slowly towards land. More shouts from his rescuer seemed to be telling him not to struggle and so he gave in and let the man, far stronger than he was, pull him from the grip of the mud and, finally, to the ditch-side. Soaking, shivering and praying thanks to his Maker for his deliverance, the cleric clawed at the sedge and scrambled to the firmer ground. There, the shepherd sheltered him beneath his cloak while he coughed the last of the water from his lungs.

The cleric thanked the man repeatedly and the shepherd appeared to understand as he smiled and nodded and held up his crook triumphantly. When the rain let up a little, the tall, black-haired man used his crook to catch the skittish horse which the cleric then calmed and petted.

The man with the black locks led him to a small coterell in the land a little way further. There, in the smallest of the shelters on the low rise, he offered the cleric the last of his food. With the man speaking slowly and with the cleric now clear of panic, he was better able to understand him, and the two of them spent some hours at the fire as their clothes dried. His mission had failed. Whatever warning Henry had tried so urgently to send to Becket was lost, but the cleric had his life, and for that he was thankful.

Once the storm had passed he surveyed the land around and saw several other small dwellings among the reeds and rushes. There was a community here, dispersed among the rivers and ditches. They were grazing sheep and some cattle on the abundance of grasses across the higher parts of the marshes. A community separated by water, living on small islands amid the wetlands, and one that needed to be brought together in Christ. It was then that the cleric, Di-Kari, decided that he would devote the rest of his life to building a church for these people and ministering to their spiritual needs.

It was some months later, when he learned of the murder of Archbishop Becket, that he knew to whom the church would be dedicated.

By the end of the following century, the settlement had grown to become a village. The Di-Kari family were still its ministers but the Black-Locks shepherds were growing impatient with their doctrine.

'Thus,' said Blacklocks as they stood at the church door, 'our village was founded, thanks to a group of crows and a sheep. We hold a festival every ten years to celebrate.'

'Murder,' Tom said.

Blacklock's face tightened up. 'I beg your pardon?'

'Murder,' Tom repeated, looking at the platform that had been built nearby. 'It's a murder of crows.' He winked at Blacklocks and saw his false smile climb back onto his lips.

'Indeed,' he said, and gave a slight tilt of his head. 'And here we are. The church.'

'Still named after Thomas Becket?' Tom looked up to the roof patched green and yellow with a cancerous moss.

'It's good of you to believe the story,' Blacklocks said, turning to face out to the green. 'Mr Di-Kari.'

'I guess it became changed over time,' Tom said. 'Names do that, along with loads of other things.'

'And yet, some things remain the same.'

'Yeah, whatever. Look, Mr Blacklocks, sorry to rush you, but I have to get away. You seem to know a lot about the history of this place. Can you tell me anything about the Careys who used to live here?'

Blacklocks thought for a moment before putting his hand on the brickwork and stroking it with his thumb. 'My grandfather helped rebuild this about a hundred years ago.' He pressed his hand flat against the wall and patted it. 'Families come and go, too,' he said. 'Things change. What do you know about your family history, sir?'

'That's the point. I know a lot about it except why my ancestor, who used to live at Saddling, left. Which is why I'd like to see your parish book.' Blacklocks appeared not to be listening. 'Soon.'

'I must admit,' the man said, 'I too harbour a temptation to delve into the past and see what I can discover about my own ancestors. But, as my family has been here since before the founding of the village, there really is not much else to know.'

Tom nodded at the small collection of houses around the green. 'Are these the only residents?' he asked. 'I mean, no offence, this is a small place. You must have ancestors from elsewhere, otherwise…'

'I think I know what you are asking. We have many more families further out towards the edges of the parish. We have strict rules on marriage to ensure that families are never, shall we say, too close? I have often wondered if I, and now my son, Mark, are indeed descended from the man who saved the messenger. The shepherd with the black locks.' He ran his fingers through his hair. 'It's something of a curse, you know. It never turns grey. My father's was black until the day he died at seventy-three, which, if such things run in families, gives me only another ten years. However, the founding legend has the saviour shepherd living until he was ninety. Can you believe such a thing?'

'I don't believe in legends,' Tom said with growing impatience. 'I'm here to find facts, even if I do have to find them in a church.'

Blacklocks became inquisitive. 'You are not a church-goer?'

Tom shook his head. 'It's not where I feel at home. But I'm happy to go in and take a look.' He tried to think how he could hint more obviously without turning the man against him. 'Which brings us back to the diary.' He widened his eyes while nodding towards the door.

'And there, young sir, is where we may have a problem.' The minister pulled a large iron key from under his gown and held it up. 'I only say "may", however, as, to be truthful, I have not had recourse to use the register for some time. There have been no births in the last three years, no marriages for a while now, though I am sure we will experience the joy again soon.' He put the key into the lock. 'I think young Barry Cole is nearing marriage if he would only put his mind to it. Daniel Vye has shown an interest in one of the Rolfe girls, and then there's Aaron. But let's not dwell.' He turned the key with ease and the single, thick door swung inwards.

Tom had no idea why, but at the mention of Dan's name he had felt a pump of adrenaline hit his chest. It was as if he had just realised that he should have done something vital but ignored the chance and now it was too late.

'Mr Carey?'

'What? Sorry.' He took two short breaths, shook himself and faced the door.

It opened into a porch with white and bare walls. Another heavy wooden door waited a few paces inside. This one had no lock and Blacklocks turned the iron handle with a clunk before dipping his head to step into the main body of the church.

Tom followed and immediately felt the damp cold penetrate his clothes and lay itself over every inch of his skin. The smell of silence and chill air entered through his nose and rose in vapour from his mouth. It was the smell of his schooling and brought back images of the church of his boarding school days, its stained-glass windows, the dazzling vestments, and the organ pipes that reached into a high, vaulted ceiling, the unforgiving wooden pews, the hard, stone floors paved with brass plaques bearing Latin inscriptions; memories in the floor that he must never stand on or else disturb the dead. Too much staying silent and not enough joy.

The most interesting thing about the Saddling Church was, as far as he could see, the ceiling. It was held aloft with arched, wooden beams on which were laid the roof tiles. The floor was stone, as he expected, but there were no lords and ladies resting hand in hand, no eternal love reflected in tombs and effigies. The only sounds were his footsteps as he inched his way around Blacklocks to stand looking along the aisle. Either side there were white box pews. Behind the last row, beneath the small west-end window, an octagonal font stood empty.

'Humble,' Blacklocks said, and Tom expected to hear an echo. There was none. His word was soaked up into the woodwork. 'A modest place.'

'Not what I was expecting,' Tom said. He realised he had lowered his voice; an old habit from years ago. There was nothing here to revere. No icons, no scrolls on the walls, not even a crucifix on the stone block at the far end which, he supposed, was an altar. The only things that told him he was in a church were the pews, the font, the pulpit standing to the left of the chancel, and an east end window of stained glass. He was unable to make out the image.

'And to our problem.' Blacklocks said.

Tom could feel eyes on the side of his neck. 'Go on,' he said, without returning the stare.

'And the problem is, ironically, what gave us the church in the first place. Water.'

'Water?'

'You see, the marshes are reclaimed land. Years ago, this was all below sea level. We still are. Not the church or the low hill our stones rest on, but all around us are fields that are only here because our ancestors found a way to drain the water to the sea. The elements fought against us, of course, they always do, but man prevailed and my forefathers, and yours, succeeded in making the Saddling parish a fertile and industrious place. When a storm comes from over the far hill, the water fills the dykes with such force that the barriers quickly overspill. The water table beneath us rises mercilessly.'

'Which has got what to do with this book?'

'At this time of year the land is very susceptible to flooding,' Blacklocks explained, his voice filling the nave. 'Full moons, high tides, heavy rain, every now and then a combination of all which can force the water table up until it fair drowns the little crypt downstairs, the place where the book is traditionally kept. And so, I believe that it was sent away for safety. Maidstone, I think.'

Tom's anger rose in an instant. Images of web page code and internet addresses, his monitor, Dylan and his hacking streamed through his mind, and all of them were out of place in this church. 'It's not in Maidstone.' He turned to face Blacklocks and tilted his head back. 'The last I was able to find out, it was still here.'

The man put up his palms in submission. 'The clerk assured me it had been sent away temporarily for safekeeping,' he said. 'As I mentioned, we have not had to use it for many years now and, with the winter storms…'

'So, why not just put it in your upstairs bedroom?' Tom blurted out. 'Is there a reason you don't want me to see this thing?' He was useless at confrontation and knew he would be no match in a row with this slippery-tongued minister, but he needed to see that book.

'I will be happy to inquire the next time I travel through Maidstone,' Blacklocks said, his sickly smile returning. 'I can't promise when that will be, but I could contact you when it is returned.'

'How? I've not seen a phone since I got here. Who is your clerk? I'll ask him myself.'

'If you wish. Matthew Cole.'

'Barry's dad?'

'His father, yes.'

'Right then.' Inwardly, Tom was telling himself to calm down. If the book really was not here and Dylan's hacked website had been wrong, then there was nothing he could do. If there was some reason Blacklocks was trying to stop him from seeing it (and he could think of no logical explanation for that), then, he was prepared to do his own digging and investigate until he had found the thing in one place or the other. 'I will double check with Mr Cole and also take a look at the graveyard, see what I can find, and…' He checked the bare walls again; there would be no clues there. 'And, well, I'll carry on asking around.' Turning back to a grinning Blacklocks he added, 'Are you sure you don't know why my last Carey ancestor left here suddenly in nineteen-twelve? And, no, he was not aboard the Titanic.'

'I too will make enquiries,' he replied with another small bow of the head. This time Tom didn't feel like repaying the courtesy.

'Yeah, thanks.'

'And now, I have some work to see to. If you will excuse me?'

Blacklocks clicked his way towards the altar pausing monetarily to call back, 'My apologies for your wasted journey. But do consider the festival. It is a rare event and I am sure it will satisfy your curiosity.'

Tom watched him go and a vision of his headmaster in his robes came back to him. The only difference here was that Blacklocks had no colour in his cowl. His gown billowed out as he moved and then settled again as he approached a small door to the right of the chancel. The man dipped through it and spiralled down until he was out of sight. The door creaked, half closing, and Tom saw a 'Private' sign above it. If that was the place that Blacklocks kept the book then that was where he needed to go. Tom considered following the minister and demanding to search the crypt. He thought again. The man was taller and stronger and, Tom suspected, had the power to throw him across the bridge as easily as someone had thrown his laptop.

No, whatever game Blacklocks was playing, Tom was prepared to play a better one.

'Private, my arse,' he whispered.

Eighteen

Tom left the chill of the church and stepped into the cold of the day. The sky was nothing but a sheet of white cloud; no definition, no colour. Convinced that Blacklocks was holding something back, he formed a new plan in his head. Perhaps another call to the Maidstone Records Office would confirm the location of the book once and for all. He took his mobile from his jacket pocket but, as expected, there was no signal. He held it aloft as he walked around the west end of the church thinking that perhaps the building was somehow blocking the signal, but still nothing registered. He put it away when he saw the man he was looking for.

Cole was kneeling by a gravestone when Tom approached him. He nodded to him and, gripping the top of the stone, pulled himself to his feet.

'I'm sorry,' Tom said. 'Can I disturb you?'

'You still wi' us, Mr Carey?' Cole asked, rather pointlessly, Tom thought. 'I 'eard you 'ad some trouble. Thought you were a-gone.'

'As soon as I can. Apparently, you're the man I need to ask about the book I'm looking for.'

'You still on that? I'd a-thought you'd a-found what you was looking fur by now.'

'Your minister— is that what I call him?—he says you sent the book up to Maidstone, maybe three years ago. But I've looked there and they didn't have it.'

Cole shuffled his feet pushing down some grass that covered the bottom of the headstone. 'If that's what the minister says.'

'What do you say?'

'I says…' The farmer gave a sigh and his eyes searched the fields ahead as if his next words lay among the water courses and sheep. 'I say, likely you never will find what you're after, Mr Carey. Time covers things over. Take this lichen.' He pointed to a decrepit, older stone a few feet away. It was weathered and mostly covered with the same yellow and green moss as the church roof. 'We tend our own long as we can, but when there ain't no family left, the stones fade a'dust, same as us all.'

Tom thought that rather sad and looked away to the grave Cole had been kneeling at. A small wreath of dried leaves and grasses leant up against it.

'Who's this?' he asked.

'Called 'im me younger brother once.'

Tom crouched to read the inscription. '"December 1982, aged thirteen."' He felt a pang of sadness. 'That's the trouble with this whole family tree stuff,' he said as he stood up. 'You come across cruel reminders of mortality. I'm sorry.'

'Was unlucky, is all,' Cole replied, nodding briefly to the headstone. 'There's no escaping it, see?'

'Escaping what? Was it some kind of illness?'

'Me ma and fader 'ad to accept it, same as us all. Impossible a-miss it if ye wants a nipper, and we all wants that.'

'I'm not with you.'

Cole blinked his glassy eyes and Tom saw the family resemblance. His face was round and his cheeks ruddy. He was an older version of his son but more weathered from years of working on the land. 'Pay it no never-mind,' he said. He moved among the graves, reaching into his trouser pockets.

'But the book?' Tom followed him down the incline towards the wall.

'Whatever William told you'll be true,' Cole said. He took some small pellets from his pockets and scattered them as he walked. Turning at the wall, he began the climb back up, throwing more pellets over ground he had not yet covered.

'Grass seed in winter?' Tom asked. He knew nothing about growing grass, apart from one failed attempt at a cannabis plant at college, but there was plenty of grass here already. 'Won't the birds eat it?'

'Whiteback pellets,' Cole explained. 'Gets 'em a-graze, saves me mowing.'

Tom turned to the wide vista of the marsh. The nearest sheep were way off, the closest field just a tufted carpet of gently undulating green.

'Oh, they'll come,' Cole said, as if reading his thoughts. 'My living brother and Farrow 'ave 'em penned fur the festival, keeping 'em short on feed. When winter's in the grass ain't so much a'their liking, though they eat what they must, as we all do. But come the festival, they'll be out and 'ungry.'

'What is this festival?'

'You question much,' Cole said over his shoulder. 'You should think on mending your car afore the weather's change. Long walk if the wind comes boneless from the north. And there'll be rain.' He looked to the sky and made a three-sixty turn. 'Not 'til a'morrow. Still, a long walk.'

'Mr Cole, please.' Tom's voice was steady but his tone had a pleading edge to it. 'I've come down here for one reason only and no-one is giving me an answer. It's vital I find this information for my aunt. She's dying.'

'She a Carey?'

'Yes, she never married.'

'Careys always die.'

That was too cryptic for Tom so he replied with, 'Well, we all do in the end. But can you help me? Do you know why there are no Careys in Saddling these days?'

Cole threw the last of his pellets wide, some bounced from gravestones before coming to rest in the grass. 'You should look a'your name, son,' he said.

That was what the blind woman had told him. Tom was about to ask what he meant and plead a little harder when Cole turned on him.

'My advice, boy...' He spoke as if he was sharing a vital secret. 'Take your trappings, walk a'the bridge, keep walking. I can send Nate Rolfe out a'your car. 'E's a fetcher, 'e can get it moving. But you go, wait there and sometime later 'e'll be along and fix you up. Don't stay 'ere.'

'I can't do that,' he replied. 'I have to know. My aunt has to know. She is very, very sick.' The real reason—that Tom was very, very poor—was the only reason he was pretending to plead.

'Well, am sorry no doubt a-learn of it, but I still say, go. You don't want a-be 'round 'ere at the Saddling wi' a name such as yourn.'

Tom was about to try bribing the man for more information but something rang a bell. 'The Saddling?' he asked. 'What's a Saddling?'

'What you don't want a-be.' Cole wrapped one of his large, calloused hands around his forehead. He looked Tom in the eye, studying him. His mouth opened slowly, and then he dropped his arm to his side. 'Just leave.' With that, he turned away.

'But... Please. Hey!'

Tom was ignored. The man had shown his back to him for a second time and now picked up his pace. Tom knew he would find no answers there. In fact, his short interview had only raised more questions and made him more determined to stay until he had answers.

His eyes fell on the graves. Finding ancestral inscriptions would at least confirm dates and names he already knew. It would also give him time to ponder who to ask next. He returned to the moss-covered stone Cole had referred to. The way he had spoken suggested that there was no family around to tend this grave. It was possible it belonged to a Carey. Maybe he would find an inscription that would give a clue to why his ancestors had left. It was unlikely, he knew, but it didn't hurt to hope.

Coming to the stone, he bent to study it. It was just possible to see some indentations where the lichen undulated with what were once words. He read "17…" but could make out no more. He tried peeling some moss away, knowing that he wasn't supposed to do that. His fellow family history researchers would not have approved; it amounted to vandalism in their books. Even with some growth removed it was still not possible to make out any more detail. The second one he tried gave the same problem but worse, the stone was just about smooth and, he guessed, it was older than the first. Searching out the untended stones from the others, he finally came across one that looked promising.

His cold fingers traced a readable script. "'Jane Carey, 1741 to 1807, loved wife and mother.'" Although there were no clues to the events of 1912, this might add a new detail to his family tree. He felt his pockets for his notebook and realised he had left it in his room. He considered running up to fetch it but then remembered the shop. Perhaps the people there might know about the Carey family. He would buy a notebook and, he decided, make enquiries at the same time. He made a mental note of where the gravestone was in relation to the others and set off around the back of the church.

A spade leant against the church wall in a space with no gravestones. He tried to imitate the stronger of the accents he'd heard since arriving. 'Prehaps preparing fur those who'll peg out afore long from the cold.' He laughed briefly, blew on his hands and walked on by.

Blacklocks stood bent over the large leather-bound ledger. One of his fingers moved up and down the gold-edged pages. In his other hand he held a hurricane lamp, its flame flickering, creating more shadows than light.

'You suggested he shouldn't stay for the festival?' he asked, without looking up.

'Aye.' Cole stood a footstep behind. 'As you said.'

'And you were vague about this?'

'Aye.'

'Good work, Matthew.'

'But, sir?'

Blacklocks raised his head. Standing at his full height his hair nearly connected with the beams holding up the chancel above. 'Go on,' he prompted.

'No, pay it no never-mind.'

'If you are concerned for your flock, Matthew, then, there is no need. Your whitebacks will be safe. You will survive and prosper another ten years.'

'Aye, sir, but at what cost?' The minister did not reply so Cole dared to voice his opinion further. 'This stranger, you think it wise 'e should be 'ere? The lad asks questions.'

'Not so much of a stranger,' Blacklocks replied, gazing down at the pages once more. 'Let him ask his questions. He will have no answers from us yet.' He left a pause. 'Will he?'

'No, sir.'

'So, a little later, and certainly if he shows signs of leaving, tell him that you were wrong.'

'Sir?'

'That the records are still here, that we have the book and the answer he so desperately seeks. Suggest that it may be here in the crypt. Of course, the book will not be available to him until tomorrow, and even then, not until after the festival.'

'Well, 'e insisted that 'is visit was urgent like.'

'So?'

'Sir?'

'What now?' Blacklocks was losing patience. 'You have your instructions.'

'That I do, sir, and I carry them out as me duty. But I still confess that... well, all this, it gives me doubts.'

'About what?'

Cole, who had been wringing his hands, gathered his courage. 'That you may be a-meddling wi' the ritual, and that, if you do...'

He had no time to finish. Blacklocks rounded on him, his face a mess of angles and anger in the lamplight. He bore down on Cole and shook the lamp. Cole's eyes flicked to it and, in that instant, Blacklocks had a hand around his throat. He pushed the farmer back until his head hit the stone wall and the wind was knocked from his lungs.

With his thin lips drawn tight and his eyes boring in, Blacklocks growled. 'I could meddle with much more, cousin.' He had spittle at the corners of his mouth; his breath smelt of rotting beet leaves. 'Do not make the mistake of forgetting who chooses should the choosers fail. And certainly, do not make the mistake of imagining I shan't use my authority. You, as I, only have the one son.' His grip tightened as Cole tried to choke against it, an action that only hurt him more. Wide-eyed, he nodded as best he could and Blacklocks released him.

Gasping for breath, Cole moved away from him along the wall towards the door. One hand went to his throat as if that would calm the pain there while the other tightened into a fist he knew he dare not use. Blacklocks followed him with his black eyes reflecting the yellow lamp flame until Cole reached the stairs. He ran from the crypt and Blacklocks heard the door slam.

He stepped up to the table once more and turned the pages of the book. 'For the love of the village,' he said, his voice as smooth and cold as marble. 'I hope I'm playing this the right way.'

Nineteen

From the outside, the shop reminded Tom of a set for a period drama. Rows of unwashed vegetables lay on sloping shelves and a few dead chickens and pigeons hung from hooks in front of a large window. Inside the window, more meat hung beside strings of onions and garlic. If the outside was theatrical, inside was like stepping back in time. The entrance was no wider than a domestic front door, there were no stickers on the windows, no advertising, no stack of plastic baskets and no music playing in the background. Two walls of the shop, which was no larger than Tom's own sitting room, were lined with shelves, one set of which was built around a door leading through into the back of the house. It struck him as unusual, but maybe not surprising in this place, that most of the groceries in the shop came without packaging.

There was nothing in the centre of the room except enough space for a couple of people to stand in front of a wooden counter at one end of which stood a pair of brass weighing scales. The centre bowed under the weight of an impressive antique till. A middle-aged woman leant behind the counter folding pieces of material. Behind her, more shelves housed trays of cakes and bread and above them stood glass jars containing confectionery. The woman's head was down and she was counting, so Tom didn't disturb her. He scanned the shop for writing materials until she was ready for him.

In the corner opposite the door, above a selection of gas bottles, matches, and cotton threads, Tom found a small pile of basic exercise books and a pottery jug holding pencils. Collecting one of the grey-covered books and one of the perfectly sharpened pencils, he turned back to the counter to find the woman staring at him.

Her face was angular as if someone had taken her nose and pulled, dragging her features forward to just the right point to give her uniqueness without making her ugly. Her top lip was thin and her bottom lip protruded slightly, but, for all that, she had a charming smile and, when she spoke, a soft voice with a gentle accent.

'You took me by surprise, young man. Are you the foreigner here for the festival?' She wiped her hands on the apron she wore and checked that the top button of her high-collar one-piece dress was fastened.

'Word travels fast,' Tom said, taking two steps and reaching the counter.

'Though, I'm not a foreigner.'

'Small village, no news,' she said, leaning across. She glanced out of the window and then back again. 'Folk like gossip but there ain't usually no news.' She put her hands on the counter and her eyes firmly on Tom's.

'I'm not staying,' he said. 'Not if I can avoid it.'

'As you will.' She smiled an encouraging smile, waiting to hear more from him. He saw her fingers tapping in a row as if they were performing a Mexican wave from hand to hand and back again; they made a continuous ripple sound across the highly polished woodwork.

'Just these,' Tom said, and put them down. 'How much?'

'Well, it's not as if I know,' the woman said. 'These are given free to the school, so I suppose they should be given free to you.'

'The council supplies free books and pencils?' Tom asked, mildly impressed. He knew his own education had cost his aunt a fortune and everything, even ink, had to be paid for.

'The village council, yes,' she said, and bent sideways to reach under the counter.

'I have money.' He was half expecting her to say they didn't accept money when she popped back up again and placed a brown paper bag on the counter.

'You keep that, Mr Carey,' she said. 'We tend not to bother much about it. As you're not from here we shan't barter today.'

'You barter? Incredible.'

'Why? What we want to spend money on, anyhow? Most of us never go nowhere, no need, so we barter what we must from those as has it, give to those who don't.'

'And that works?'

'Has done since the village was founded, so the Teaching says.' She slipped the book and pencil into the bag and then leant with one elbow on the counter where she beckoned Tom closer with a finger. He joined her, almost arm to arm. 'Say I wants some milk for the young'uns, as I do each day, and say my sister, Irene, needs some flour as she can't stomach Andrew White's bread—and, let's face it, who can? Well, we don't have flour and milk at our house.' She pointed upstairs. 'Not 'less we get it in. So, as we don't care for coins much, I make dresses of an evening and Sundays, and those I swap with my husband's brother, Michael, who keeps the cows out at West Ditch. He then gives me the milk and barters on the clothes. I also do men's shirts and...' she pointed down towards the floor and circled her finger, '...ladies' necessities, but I leave the men's to Bill Taylor because he is a tailor, or so he likes to think. I do the same with White for his flour, though he never wants clothes as his wife is a fair seamstress. Or so she imagines. And that's how it goes on. Whatever one don't want of another he swaps on or sells to the fetchers who go and sell it out-marsh, time to time, and so the pennies come in and then we does use them, but only as we must, gas and such, and it goes on thus-ways. But you didn't come in to hear me rattle on. What was it you were wanting?'

Tom, smiling, tapped the paper bag.

'So it was, and you have it.' She pushed it over to him. 'Anything else I can do for you?'

Tom shook his head. 'You know, Mrs...?'

'Rolfe, oh excuse me.' She wrung her hands on her apron again and held one out. Tom took it and shook it quickly. 'Rebecca Rolfe. Sam's the husband, Irene Cole is my sister, we're twins except we are not, though we were born on the same day and you don't need to know all that neither.' She laughed nervously.

Recalling the manners forced into him by Aunt Maud and applying all the charm he could muster, he told her what he was doing there and what he wanted. She listened, her small round eyes wide and alert, her face fixed in an interested smile. When he had finished, she stood up straight, folded her arms and screwed up her nose. She looked up to the ceiling, made a couple of clucking noises with her tongue and then dropped her gaze back to Tom.

'Well, Mr Carey, I have to say that I am not going to be able to help you today. I was only born forty-something year back. No-one has spoken about a Carey family through my life, not 'til you just did and, as far as I know, no-one is going to know why your family would have left us. Who would want to? We got it all at Saddling, all we need, and that's good enough for...well, for most. Now, I've made some cake today, ready for the festival a'morrow, but there always be spare, so how about I run and fetch you a piece.' She had left the shop before she finished her sentence, nipping out quickly through the back-wall door while still chatting on. 'Only some carrot cake, but there be icing and the sugar came in from Romney i'self. My cousin, Peter Fetcher—you might meet him a'morrow—he's now our chief fetcher, you see, he brings it in on his battered truck, and some comes to us.' She was back in the shop, now, wrapping a large piece of cake in paper towels.'And so I get some in return for mending his mistus' skirts or his boy's trousers that he is always ripping through on the hawthorn when he's out looking for paddocks in the deeks. Young'uns, eh? And here you go. Sorry I couldn't help.'

Tom was convinced she had not drawn a breath. He took the cake.'Very kind of you Mrs...' He had forgotten the name already. Maud would have whacked his knuckles for that. 'Mrs Rolfe.' It came back to him. 'Thank you for this, but are you sure you don't remember hearing anything about a Thomas Carey who left? He was the last of...'

'So you said, sir, so you said, and so I said I didn't and lying don't come natural in Saddling. You'd have to be that old rotten pear in the barrel, and that we Rolfs and Fetchers are not. And neither is my dear brother-in-law, Matthew, nor not his dear boy Barry neither, who, in my mind, eats far too much of my cake, but that's for another day. Ah, and here comes Mick Farrow, from his hay barn by the looks, and he'll be wanting his cheese for his lunch, so you'll have to excuse me, you've kept me talking far too long.'

She had vanished again, back through the door, and this time her chattering finally stopped. Between the hanging hares and a brace of pheasant, Tom saw Mick Farrow advancing on the shop. It was then that he noticed the smell of death in the place; the game in the window, he guessed. He was not going to discover any family information from this woman, not his own family at any rate, and so he left, just as Farrow arrived.

The old man's white hair was a mess. There were pieces of straw in it, it was sticking up and, even though it was not windy, it looked like he had been standing side on to a hurricane. The left side of his face was redder than the right and his clothes were crumpled. He passed Tom at the door and mumbled some kind of greeting. Tom heard Mrs Rolfe's voice from inside as he left.

'Look at you, Mick Farrow. You been sleeping in your hay barn again, ain't you? Your mistus should keep more of an eye on you...'

Her voice trailed off as Tom returned to the church to note down anything else he could find on the gravestones. He stopped to shovel down the cake, which was very tasty, and cast his eyes around the green. The small platform now had bars up and across at the back, as if someone was going to hang a curtain there. Struts supported this from behind and a set of small steps had been placed at the front. Tom remembered thinking, when he first saw it being built, that it was going to be some kind of pillory for him, as an out-marsher, but that moment of sarcasm had soon moved on and he could see it was only for speeches, probably from Minister Blacklocks. A couple of men, farm workers Tom would have guessed from their size and their clothes, were pulling weeds and trimming the grass at the edge of the green.

Tom considered staying for the festival as he finished the last mouthful of cake. It went down with as little effort and as much enthusiasm as the first. He instantly craved more but it had satisfied his hunger and he could feel it hitting the spot. There would have to be a very special reason for him to stay, he thought. Apart from the incident with the laptop, everyone had been civil enough, but, then again, if the records and the village diary were not in Saddling there was no reason for him to be here. Gravestones, on the other hand, were aplenty and, buzzing from the sugar "from Romney i'self", he headed for them, determined to write down every detail of every Carey he could find.

Entering the graveyard, he stopped to study the lie of the stones. There was no pattern to them. Some were small, others taller, all were the same shape and none stood in rows. A few had tilted downhill towards the patchy, green-grey dying grasses of the field. To his left, the wall crumbled into a row of small bushes, wild and natural, which continued towards a line of twisted trees. A track ran alongside for a distance and he assumed this was a path out towards what the woman in the shop had called West Ditch. Right out, so it was no more than a smudge, he saw a cart being pulled by a horse. It swayed as it made its slow way along the edge of the field. Someone was shepherding out in another field, approaching a flock of sheep with a dog keeping busy around his feet. There was no sound except for the occasional call of a crow and smaller birds twittering in the bushes. It was a peaceful scene and, had it not been for the cold, an idyllic one. He watched, wondering how anyone could have the time to move so slowly.

He considered his tactics as he walked down the slope. At the crumbling end of the stone wall, he took the exercise book and pencil from his pocket. He made a sweep of the uneven rows like Cole had done with his pellets, bending where necessary to read the inscriptions. The stones in this part of the cemetery were easy to read. Perhaps they had been protected from the elements by their lower position. None of them bore the Carey name. There were plenty of Rolfe, White, Seeming, and Tidy graves, mostly from the 19th century, some more modern.

His back ached with the effort of crouching and bending and, after a while, he stood and stretched.

The next stone he came to drew his attention because of the dates. "Matilda Cole, 1842 – December 1912" was simply carved above "Samuel Cole, 1840 – December 1912"; two deaths in the same year, the same month in fact. He made a quick calculation and worked out their ages; over seventy and dying together, buried together, always together. It was touching but maybe it was also relevant. It was the same year that his great-grandfather had left the village. Perhaps there had been some illness and his ancestor had left to avoid it. If there were more graves with this date then there would be more evidence for the theory.

'You think they're still there, or they gone beyond?'

Tom looked up, taken by surprise. Daniel was sitting on the wall a little further along. He'd not noticed him before and Tom had no idea how long he had been there, but he felt that short burst of adrenaline in his chest again; a jolt of excitement that he could not explain.

'Hi!' he said, closing his book and holding it to his ear. 'What?'

'Let them sleep,' Dan called across. 'We'll all be joining them at some time. Why are you still here?'

'Still not found what I came here for.'

'It's a long afternoon for almost the shortest day. Will you sit with me? Take my mind from its troubling?'

'Er, yeah, okay.' Tom rolled the book up and pushed it into his coat pocket along with the pencil and, using some gravestones for support, he approached over the uneven ground. Daniel shifted along the wall slightly and dangled his legs over the edge, his feet only a few inches from the ground on the other side.

'It's a good view from here, isn't it?' Tom said as he clambered into place, first squatting down and then dropping his legs over one at a time. They bumped shoulders as he shifted, trying to find a flat surface. 'Sorry.' The only way to be comfortable was to squeeze up so that they both shared the backrest-headstone. The touch of Dan's shoulder made Tom uncomfortable; it was too intimate, so he shuffled along a little but found the wall there sharp under his legs.

'No, you have to sit up here,' Dan said, grinning. 'That's why we do it. It's flat here. We can rest back. Come.'

His eyes smiled and he pulled his fringe away from them in what Tom thought was an effeminate way. He shuffled closer until they were touching again. He could smell Dan's coat. The collar was a band of velvet and his copper hair now barely came near it. He had had it cut since Tom last saw him.

'Settled?' Dan asked with a smile in his voice.

'Sorry,' Tom apologised again but he had no idea what for. 'Not used to this kind of thing. More used to sitting on an office chair looking at a monitor than stones looking out at, well, at that.' He waved a hand towards the low vista. 'What are those?' he asked, pointing out the twisted trees.

'Them's Mother trees,' Dan said. 'On account they can look like bent old women carrying a heavy load. Barry says there's one out at West Ditch looks like she's carrying a wether.'

'Carrying the weather?'

'No, a wether. A ram what's had its balls cut off.'

Tom felt himself blushing. Was it because he didn't know that that's what a eunuch sheep was called? Why should he? 'Never heard of that,' he said.

'We tail them when they're young tegs. We ties bands around the tail so as they grow they drop off; doesn't hurt none, stops all the dags and saves on clatting later. Used to go and collect the tails when I was a boy. Then, when they get old enough, the lookers wether them, fatten them up for slaughter. Keep some balls-an'all for breeding, 'course.'

It all sounded barbaric to Tom. 'Very rural,' he said. He didn't mean to sound sarcastic but that's how it came out, so, he quickly added, 'What's it like living out here in this kind of isolation?'

'Not known nothing else, so I can't compare.'

'But you've been places, seen films.'

Dan turned his head to look at him and Tom could see that he clearly had not. He noticed his lips, full and pinked by the cold. He wore a light dusting of fine hairs on his chin.

'You're telling me you don't even watch television?'

Dan shook his head.

'This is the twenty-first century. No television? Radio?'

'Heard said that the Tidy family kept one when there was a war, but no, not since, not here.'

'It's not natural, not these days,' Tom said. He inched away a little so that their faces were not so close. 'You lads should get on Facebook, get networking.'

'Not sure I knows what you mean.'

'Bloody hell! You could at least drive to... And that's another thing. I've not seen any cars here, there's no road. Does everyone have to walk to the bridge?'

'No, some have a trap 'n' pony. Fetchers use them to get out to the south where there's a truck kept. Never needed to think about it. No, wait! Barry's uncle's got an old car. Barry used to boast about it. Kept it out near East Sewer when there was a crossing there.'

'Great, so he could give me a lift later.'

'Don't reckon. Thing's not worked gone nine years. Nate said he would mend it, but he never did.'

'How on earth can you live like this?'

'We have all we need, Mr Carey. Food, ale, music. Mr Blacklocks is school, he teaches, we have the church-house for meetings, the land, our farms, each other. What else is needed?'

'What about medicine? Call me Tom, will you? I feel old otherwise.'

Dan beamed at him. 'Thank you, Tom.'

'What if someone needs a hospital?'

Dan shrugged. 'The lookers deliver lambs if the ewe gets troubled.'

'I meant people.'

'Any grandmother in the village'll pull the child out. Blacklocks makes medicines if anyone gets sick, but it don't happen much. Life takes its course, and people live long. Most.'

Tom couldn't decide if this information was fascinating or frightening. 'Hang on,' he said. 'What's a looker? Some kind of shepherd?'

Dan nodded. 'I'd like to be a looker.'

'I think a lot of girls would say you're a bit of a looker already,' Tom quipped, and nudged the young man.

'How d'you mean?' Dan asked, surprised.

'I mean, you're good looking.'

'Why d'you say that?'

'It's a joke,' Tom said. The fascination born from the previous night's dream had been shepherded away by the easy conversation, but now, as Dan showed no understanding of his meaning, it all came rushing back.

135

His cheeks warmed. 'I meant you are good looking and you call shepherds lookers, and... Never mind.'

'You calling me handsome?'

It was a simple question. There was nothing threatening behind it.

'Well, yes.' Tom was squirming inside.

'You attracted to me?' Dan asked.

'Look, mate,' Tom drew back to make sure they were not touching. 'I don't want you to get the wrong idea. I was just trying to make a joke.'

'Why'd you want to joke about me?'

'I'm not.'

'You think girls find me good looking?'

'Yes, I'm sure.'

'And do you?'

'I don't know.'

'You must know.'

Dan's voice remained level while Tom found himself flustering. 'Well, alright, then, yes.' It was embarrassing to say, but it was true. The dream passed through his thoughts like a ghost through a wall. It haunted him, and the emotions it had left him with clung about him in the air.

'That's what Barry says.'

'What?'

'Barry says I'm handsome an' all. But I reckon he means it in a serious way, if you gets me. I still be working on what I think about that.'

'Well, that's great,' Tom said, wishing he'd never said anything. The simple remark had brought up so many unwanted feelings.

At the back of his mind he knew he shouldn't be wasting time, but he found himself moving back to sit closer. They both fell silent.

The white sky now showed some patches of grey. Rainclouds were building up over the distant hill and the day darkened. The air was still, the birds had stopped chattering in the bushes, and the dyke water was unmoving. Only the whitebacks, a mile away, stirred. They meandered over the thin strip of land as, above them, the dull grey clouds followed.

Dan leant forward, resting his arms on his legs and lowering his head. Tom saw the tight fit of his coat over his broad shoulders and noticed a small piece of moss pressed to the back. He wanted to brush it off; it annoyed him to see a blemish on the material. Something told him not to touch, but it distracted him. He also leant forward so that he didn't have to see it. Their heads were close. He could hear Dan breathing and he could see his hands, pale, long fingers laced together, nails perfectly cut, his skin smooth but with veins on the backs raised like long-barrows snaking from his wrists to his knuckles. His coat was open, revealing dark trousers. A blade of grass had stuck to his thigh and, like the moss, it was an imperfection Tom wanted to remove. He was aware that his own breath was shallow and that his heart was beating faster.

Looking away was an effort, but Tom turned his head. He had come to look at graves. Instead, he was wasting his time watching empty fields in silence; both seemed to go on forever. A large, grey heron lifted itself up from beside one of the silver, silent ditches and flapped laboriously across the water. It landed on the other bank and vanished into a clump of tall grass.

'Be a hernshaw,' Dan said, his voice a whisper. 'Be hunting for eels.'

Tom suddenly found that he had no desire to continue looking at gravestones. For the first time in months, he felt the weight of worry lifting. There was no need to do anything but sit there, watch, and enjoy the company of calm.

'My fader died when he was nineteen,' Dan said, whispering out to the grey stillness. 'I was two.'

'Mine when I was eight.' The reply came naturally. There was no need to think; the words just happened and, for some inexplicable reason, they felt inevitable.

'Then he's a sleeper, an' all.' It was a statement.

They were sitting among the sleepers right now and Tom could think of no better place to rest.

'That'd be why we have a connection,' said Dan.

'Do we?' Again the words came with no thought.

Dan sat back up and Tom followed suit. He heard the boy sniff and glanced at him. He had tears in his eyes.

'I'm sorry,' Tom said, having no idea where this conversation had sprung from or to where it was going.

Dan said nothing but he studied Tom with his cool eyes glistening and reached out a hand. Tom didn't draw back as Dan put his hand on his shoulder and gripped. He said nothing as Dan pressed down, using Tom to steady himself as he lifted himself to his feet. Standing high on the wall, the tails of his coat brushing Tom's face, he paused for a moment and placed his bare hand on the headstone against which they had been resting. The hand gripped and then let go, brushed the top of the stone and gripped it again.

'See you soon,' Dan said, and left him alone.

Tom could not be sure if he was talking to him or the stone but, when he turned and read the inscription, he had the uneasy feeling that the lad had been talking to the grave. It read "Martin Vye – 1973 to December 21st 1992".

Twenty

The bedroom curtains were drawn, the room was in semi-darkness and no sound came from outside. There were noises downstairs, however. A chair scraped on stone, its sound distorted through the wooden floorboards and the handmade rugs that covered them. Someone said 'shush' and the word carried up the narrow staircase to the landing, reaching the bedroom as little more than a hiss. A stair creaked, long and slow at first and then ended its give-away with a sharp crack. Another 'shush!' This one was followed by a muffled complaint and a couple of gasps. Wood touched wood, a chair leg on a banister perhaps; another stair creak, closer this time.

A growing shadow thrown by the gas lamp that burned dimly on the landing crept into the doorway. A wide shadow with angular juts, it stole further into the room, lengthening across the floor and smothering a table. Beside this stood an umbrella stand, china, blue and white and cracked. The shadow grew to reach the bed, neatly made and covered with a patchwork of blue and green, hand stitched and padded. This was partly covered by a cardboard box containing saucepans and kitchen utensils. A tall glass jar was packed into one corner; it contained nothing more than small stones with a collection of empty snail shells on top.

As the shadow grew, so the sound of breathing came closer until the doorway was filled. A plump woman stood there carrying a dining chair in both hands and holding a cloth bag between her teeth. She spied an empty space near the front window. The bedroom occupied one half of the house from front to back. Living room and kitchen furniture filled most of it.

The woman's face was plain but for her nose which jutted forwards; her lips were thin but her eyes were large and welcoming. She breathed deeply as she made her way to the space where she placed the chair as if it were made of the thinnest glass. The feet touched the rug silently and her shoulders relaxed. Standing upright, she took the bag from her mouth and licked her lips to rid them of any cotton strands. She put the bag gently on the chair, making sure it didn't tip and spill its contents of small, framed drawings.

Turning, she saw her husband appear in the doorway, one dining chair carried in front and one held behind with his arm bent back over his shoulder. She reached out and took the first as he nodded towards the last remaining space where she placed the chair with as much care as the first. He then searched for somewhere else, but there was no place to leave it.

'It'll 'ave a-go in Barry's room wi' the others,' Cole said, and, carefully swinging the chair around to hold it with both hands, he left.

She followed him across the landing and into a second bedroom, smaller and untidy.

'I was in 'opes 'e'd clear this tattle,' Cole whispered.

'He's other things on his mind, as now,' his wife replied.

Cole put the dining chair down and ran his fat fingers through his hair. 'It'll 'ave a-do. What's left?'

'Nothing but the table and that's too wide to carry up. We'll take the risk.'

'If we can't save ourselves in the end we might least save your grandma's trappings,' Cole said. 'Mind, it seems little point a-move it up if we ain't going a-be 'ere.'

'I feel happier,' Irene Cole replied. 'Me sister can have it. I 'ope no-one comes calling. They'll question our faith.'

'Who comes calling in Penit?'

'We don't know. Blacklocks might get asky.'

'Quiet your worry, mistus,' Cole chided. 'Else someone'll take you up on it.'

'I can't hear no-one passing. None can hear me whisper.'

'We 'ave a-go careful.' He drew her away from the window and sat her down on Barry's unmade bed. 'We can't 'ave no callers and no-one must know or they'll wonder what we're 'bout. Can you do that? We know you keep secrets as well as Farrow keeps pigs. Old butter-'ead 'ad three die last month alone.'

'I'll not be talking. I've too much else on my mind.'

'Aye, I know. We all 'as, but that's where we 'ave a-keep it. On our mind. Course, we'll all 'ave a-sleep in 'ere a'night.'

They held hands in the sparse room. A few shelves nailed roughly to the walls held a couple of old school books. Drawings of Barry when he was younger hung on one wall. Pairs of heavy trousers lay strewn across a single, hard-back chair.

'I should wash 'em,' Irene said.

'No point.'

'Don't be saying that.'

'No,' Cole said, and squeezed her hand. 'I didn't mean as that. I meant we'll find new, in time.'

Irene's eyes fell on a second, single bed. This one was unmade, though a quilt was folded on the end of it as if ready for an unexpected guest.

Cole saw where his wife was looking. 'Wasn't meant a-be,' he said.

'Aye,' she replied. 'Too late now.'

He nudged her with his elbow. 'But it were fun, though. All that trying.'

She stifled a laugh and leant her head into his, knocking them together gently. 'You dirty sod,' she said.

They fell silent again and listened. Footsteps passed the window on the path below, slow and heavy.

'That's the nipper coming 'round the back,' Cole said. 'I'll talk plans wi' 'im nearer the time, but remember, Irene, all else outside us 'as got a-be normal. Whether 'e be chose or not, our minds are set, aye?'

'As you say, love. But you know as I that we can't cheat the choosing any more than we can cheat the flooding, if it comes.'

'It'll come. I've a worrysome feeling about a'morrow.' Cole gave her one more squeeze of a hand and then patted it. 'It's Blacklocks and 'is meddling that unsettles me. So, we needs be ready.'

Downstairs, the back door opened and closed.

'He's late for his dinner,' Irene said. 'Mind you, I got no idea where I put it.' She laughed again, but it was tense, nervous laughter. 'Oh, Matthew, do you know what you're about?'

'No, mistus,' he replied. 'But I know we're doing it fur the boy.'

Twenty-one

Tom returned to where he had left off and began walking the uneven rows of headstones. His mind was now divided and he was distracted. He was running out of time if he was to make his meeting in London the next day but he found that he was no longer too worried.

As he knelt and brushed moss from inscriptions and read names and dates from the past, he reminded himself that, if he could find what he was looking for, the job in London would cease to be an issue. He weighed up the thought of going empty handed to Maud against the thought that the answer was here among the sleepers and that he should stay and see it through, no matter the cost if he failed.

There was another cause for distraction, one which he tried hard to keep from the front of his mind; it was to do with his dream. The emotion it had aroused was still with him. He had been left feeling sad but, in his semi-sleep, as he lay there unable to move but sensing everything, he had felt something beyond sadness. The youth in the dream had been ethereal. There had been something other-worldly about the image, almost spiritual. As he peered at inscriptions, his back aching, he found the dream-state pressing deeper into his thoughts. Spiritual was not the right word. He felt for Dan. He didn't understand why as he didn't know him. Tom wanted to help but couldn't see what Dan needed help with. He was intriguing. Maybe that was the word he was looking for.

He blew on his fingers, now pink and numb from the cold, and approached the next crumbling headstone. None were intricate; there were no sorrowful angels, no weeping children and, he noticed, no crosses or any mention of God. This one, however, was taller than the others and it stood watch over its sleeper, unattended and abandoned. Lichen covered it like a skin cancer apart from one place where it appeared that someone had pulled some growth away. The letters "Care..." caught his attention and he knelt to inspect it more closely.

He picked at the moss with numb fingers. It came away easily except for where lichen had moulded to the stone and, although he could feel indentations of letters and numbers, he couldn't make them out. He tried rubbing them with his fingertips, but that was painful. He reached into his pocket thinking that the paper bag he'd stuffed there might be more abrasive, and yanked it out. It resisted, blocked by something else, and so he pulled harder, his eyes still on the faded inscription.

Suddenly, the paper was free but it brought with it another bag that popped from his pocket, hit the gravestone with a thud and exploded into a puff of white powder.

He backed away, but the flour had already blown onto his jacket.

'What the...' He was about to curse the blind woman when he noticed the headstone.

Some of the flour had landed on the faded letters and, thanks to the way it highlighted the shallow indents, he could now read the whole word, "Carey."

'Now who'd of thought...' he muttered. He picked up the pouch and took more flour from it, rubbing it onto the stone to see if it would reveal anything else.

It did. It showed him "Isaac Carey 1895 to 1912" but the name "Isaac", he noticed, was hard to read. There appeared to be a longer name chiselled in beneath it. The "I" of "Isaac" had been altered to a "T", and a letter "S" hung, half scratched out, on the end of the name, too close to the "C" of "Carey."

'Like they were expecting Thomas?' he wondered aloud, throwing on more flour and smearing it over the rest of the stone. 'There's got to be something else. Died of plague? Anything, come on.'

There were more words, but only two. Tom read them and sat back, his eyes searching the face of the stone for anything he had missed. The stone simply and cryptically read "For Saddling".

He wrote the details down in his book and checked the next grave. The thought that Maud's fortune rested on what he might find here spurred him on. A new car paid for, a new computer, his own house, a release from having to work for others, having to work at all, it was all possible. The lure of it all was too hard to resist. His hope guttered as he viewed another weathered, old grey stone, unattended and, at first, completely blank. A little more flour and he was able to make out "Jere—ah Care— 1744 to —786" and guess at the missing letters and number.

He stood to search for more of the same, now that he knew for certain the kinds of graves he was looking for. 'But actually,' he told himself, 'I now have confirmation of Thomas Carey's brother's death.' It still didn't help him determine what might have made Thomas leave. The year was right, and it matched the deaths of the old couple he'd found earlier, but apart from them, he had not seen 1912 on any other stones. 'Perhaps it wasn't an illness,' he said. 'But if not, then what?'

A flapping black movement caught his eye and, across the top of the gravestones, he saw Blacklocks at the east end of the church. He stood out against the white inn behind him and he was walking fast with something tucked under one arm. He saw Tom and waved.

'Going well, I hope?' Blacklocks called, without missing a step of his quick march.

Tom was about to call back but the man was gone. He had only caught a glimpse of what Blacklocks had been carrying but it was big enough to hold a book. His heart leapt, hopeful that it had turned up and Blacklocks was taking it back to the crypt. He brushed more flour from his clothes, put the remainder of it carefully back in his pocket and hurried around the building. He reached the porch just in time to hear the door close and lock from the inside. He banged, knowing that the minister would not yet be out of earshot but there was no reply. Moving along the side of the church he jumped to see through the window but it was too high.

'Jesus!' He hurried along the wall of the building to the small tower; there was no door there, just another small window. He hadn't seen one on either of the other two sides, either, so the porch was the only way the man could come out.

He waited a few minutes and then, frustrated, he headed back to his grave-hunting. He would keep an eye out for Blacklocks rather than waste time waiting for him. He needed to read inscriptions while there was still daylight. The sky had thickened. Although the clouds were not yet battleship grey and heavy with rain, they were soaking up the light.

There were now two spades leaning against the church wall. He wondered who was ill, and then wondered why he was bothered. He was just about to pull out the flour again when he saw Dan.

He was back at his father's grave, both hands resting on the stone. His head was down, and he was crying. There was no-one else about, no-one to comfort him, and Tom was unsure of how to react. He heard Daniel sob. The sound carried on the air and brought with it the enigmatic emotion from his dream, this time with more intensity. Unsure what he was going to do, he left his task and approached.

At the grave, he reread the inscription and remembered the drawing in the shack. The man in head-garland and smart costume was the body now rotted beneath the turf. He had died twenty years ago tomorrow, leaving his young family to mourn.

Tom realised what it was that the dream had instilled in him; compassion.

He was unaware that Blacklocks was now at Dan's bedroom window, watching.

Blacklocks drew in a deep breath as the scene played out below. He saw Tom Carey first stand behind Daniel and then move to be beside him. Neither of them spoke. After some minutes Tom placed a hand on the boy's shoulder, nervously, he thought, and Daniel turned to look at him. Blacklocks, from that short distance, could make out the boy's pale face, his newly cut hair, his soft skin. He saw him lift one of his gentle hands and place it on Tom's shoulder as if the two were about to embrace. Instead, Daniel turned back to the grave, and, slowly, Tom put his arm around his shoulder and pulled the lad to him so Daniel could rest his head.

Although his heart churned, a smile bubbled through the bile of envy and crept onto Blacklocks' grey face. 'No,' he whispered, 'this is good.'

The scent of rosewater entered the room. He felt soft hair against his own and heard a woman's gentle breathing.

'I want him gone,' Susan said. 'I want him to leave.' She too was looking down from the window. 'He's touching my Daniel.'

'Support only,' Blacklocks replied. 'As we are all taught; support and share, compassion in sadness. If his family had stayed, he could well have been Daniel's marker.'

'I still want him out.'

'You must trust me, Susan. Just as the Teaching commands. I am your minister.' Blacklocks turned to face her. She was as pretty as her boy, but she didn't offer the same mystery. She had none of Daniel's sadness, none of his thought, none of his beauty or allure, but he could always imagine. He took her by the shoulder and pulled her towards him.

Forcing his lips on hers, he held her against her struggling until she gave in. Then he turned her towards Daniel's bed and pushed her down onto her back.

Twenty-two

His elbows on his knees, head in his hands, Tom stared at the grass. He made his decision at the graveside with Dan and felt better for it. He knew he had lost his job already and the firm probably only wanted him to come in so they could make an example of him and satisfy their revenge. He no longer cared; finding the answer in return for Maud's money was the only thing that was important to him now; that, and spending time like this.

Dan, beside him, took his hands from his pockets where had had been warming them and rested them in his lap. 'There's things I want to tell you, Tom,' he said. 'But I can't.'

'Hey, mate, you don't have to say anything. You've still got your mum and you seem to have some good friends. Barry's a good mate, isn't he?'

Tom heard Dan laugh, briefly. 'Aye, Barry is Barry. He's a runagate.'

'A what?'

'A wild-one. He was naughty as a child. Been a runagate since. Everyone should have one of him.' Dan's tone changed and he became serious. 'But that ain't what I mean. You shouldn't stay for the festival.'

'Why not? If it's only every ten years, I'm not likely to get the chance again.'

'It be every ten years for a reason.'

'What's that, then? Costs too much?'

'In a way. But that ain't what I mean neither.'

Tom saw Barry approaching on the path from the bridge. 'Here he is now.'

'I got things to do,' Dan said, but made no movement.

'What happens at this festival then?' Tom asked, looking at the platform. Apart from that, there were no other signs of anything about to take place. 'Doesn't look like anything big.'

'I don't want you to see it,' Dan said. 'But that's all I can tell you.' He waved at Barry crossing the green towards them.

Tom saw lamps being lit in some houses, curtains being drawn in others and a candle being placed in the window of the inn. He wondered if any of his ancestors had lived in these same homes. They must have trod this green and attended the church.

'I've always had this thought,' he said. 'A bit fanciful, no doubt, but, what if time exists in layers and all that separates us from the past is life?'

'I don't understand,' Dan said.

'Well, what if, when you die, your life starts again and runs exactly the same course, but no-one sees it? You're invisible to the generation that comes along next. They live their life over the top of yours in the same place, but neither soul is aware of the other's existence. My ancestor who left here in nineteen-twelve could be sitting right beside us now, or walking across the green on his way home from the fields.'

He saw two men walk towards the shop where the light inside glowed warmly. Through the window, he watched the talkative woman wiping down the counter. The men approached, one with a spade over his shoulder; the other carried a couple of dead rabbits. They both wore long boots to just under their knees, short jackets that were heavy and thick, and both were wearing caps pulled tightly down covering the tops of their ears. He heard muffled voices.

'You see?' he said, pointing. 'I'm seeing *that* as Thomas Carey would have seen it, had he been sat here one hundred years ago.'

'You're daft,' Dan said.

Tom laughed. 'Aye. I mean, yes, I expect you're right.'

All the annoyances of modern life were stripped away in Saddling; they didn't exist and they were noticeable by their absence; no phone, no cables, satellite dishes or graffiti, no beeping phones or people tapping on small screens, heads down, no sirens wailing, breaks screeching, none of it. He could have slipped back into his ancestors' life and not noticed; not here where time was in no hurry to move on.

He felt the bench shift under him as Barry sat down on his other side.

'Hi,' he said.

'Never did get a-show you the village,' Barry said. 'You staying 'nother night then?'

Tom glanced back to the church. There was still no sign of Blacklocks. 'Looks like it.'

'Staying fur the festival?'

'It's his wish,' Dan said.

'It's not illegal, is it?' Tom asked, and smiled. 'I don't see what the fuss is about. You must have loads of people coming to it if it's so rare an event. Photos in the paper and all that.'

'It stays within Saddling,' Dan said.

'Now, why doesn't that surprise me? But, hey!' Tom looked from one to the other. They were both holding each other's gaze. 'I'm from here, aren't I? I mean, my bloodline is from Saddling. We go all the way back to the founding, if you believe the legends.'

'They ain't legends, and we do.' Dan said.

'Well,' Barry put in. 'They be stories, but we keep a'them.'

'Yeah, yeah,' Tom said. 'The Teaching. So, what's happening tonight? Any pre-festival music, dancing? Anything?'

'Last night of Penit,' Dan said.

'Last Boblight,' Barry added, nodding to the darkening sky.

'They'll be many more.'

'Not fur all.'

'I'm ready.'

'Can't say I be.'

'Sun'll be down afore long.'

'Aye, can't be stopped.'

'Look,' Tom leapt in. They were speaking directly to each other across him and he had no idea what they were talking about. 'I only asked if there was anything going on.'

'Lots going on, Tom,' Barry said, and finally looked his way. 'Lots a-be got ready.'

'Barry,' Dan warned.

Barry threw him a wink. 'It's fine, Daniel.' He addressed Tom. 'The women'll be getting their stalls ready a-give produce come morning. I reckon Mick Farrow and 'is lads'll get their "Polt the rat" out and give it a testing. There be plenty fur people a-be doing ahead a the day. It all comes together in the morning, you'll see.'

'I went over to see whitebacks, earlier,' Dan said. In contrast to Barry's jovial tone, his was flat and had its regular tint of sadness. 'They clatted 'em up well, taken off the dag-wool. They look good.'

'Did they come a'you?' Barry asked.

Tom saw Dan look down to the ground and he locked his fingers together before slowly fixing Barry with his penetrating eyes.

'No,' he said. 'They ran.'

'So, maybe you're not meant to be a whiteback looker,' Tom quipped. 'But let's not start that again. Hey, Barry.' He playfully slapped Barry's leg with the back of his hand. 'See how I'm using Saddling words now? Looker, whiteback... That's about as far as I got, but how about I buy you both a glass of bathtub at the inn?'

It took Barry a moment to respond. He was watching Dan who had stood up and was facing the church. 'Sure, Tom,' he said, without looking at him. 'Share a pipe, Dan?'

'Won't help.'

Barry also stood. 'Sun'll be going,' he said, checking the sky again. The clouds were already changing colour over to the west and they were breaking up. The threat of rain had lifted.

Dan wandered up the mound and around the church.

'Wait up!' Barry called after him.

'He's a bit upset today,' Tom said, standing next to Barry and also watching Dan. 'It's the anniversary of his dad's death tomorrow.'

Barry turned to face Tom and, for a second, Tom was sure he was going to hit him. Anger flashed across his face and his shoulders squared up. Barry blinked and the anger was gone as quickly as it had come. He dropped his head and shook it. 'There's so much you don't understand, Tom Carey, so very much.'

'Well, you're right there, mate,' Tom agreed. 'But then, no-one around here wants to tell me anything except riddles, so what do you expect?'

'Be a difficult time, the festival,' Barry explained. 'And if you're 'ere fur it, it'll learn you why.'

'I'll be here.'

'Aye, I think it's what Blacklocks wants.'

'Oh? He told you that? Actually, he did invite me.'

Barry nodded. 'That'll be it, then. Thing is, why? You must be special.'

'Don't think so.'

'We don't invite foreigners to the Sa... the festival, not that I been a'many. Two, it'll be, but only one I remember, but my fader told me strangers were rare. We hardly gets them out 'ere, 'ere and there a one, prehaps.' Barry was walking and Tom, although not invited to move with him, did so. 'That'll be why you caused a meddle, I reckon. Turning up in Penit and laying-in for the festival.'

'And now you see what I mean about people talking in riddles. There's something you're not telling me, isn't there?'

'Tom, I like you.' Barry stopped and faced him. His puppy eyes had mischief in them, his crooked smile was twitching. 'You're different to all else 'ere but...' A moment of quick confusion crossed his face but the playful look was soon back. 'No, I'll say it, and why not? It's what we gets taught, honest speaking. I like you much, Tom Carey, and I wants a-call you me mate. And we don't say that a'just any-a-one in Saddling. It be what the Teaching calls "trust shared".'

'Then, I am very honoured,' Tom said, half-jokingly. He smiled. Feeling both flattered and embarrassed, he put out his hand. 'And you can call me yours.'

Barry gawped at the offered hand but he didn't shake it. 'You mean it?' His eyes lit up and the cheeky grin morphed into a joyous smile.

'Sure.' Tom offered his hand further.

Instead of shaking it, Barry took hold of it and carried on walking. 'I was in 'opes you would.'

'Yeah, well, hang on. I don't mean anything like that.' Tom glanced nervously over his shoulder and tried to pull away, but Barry dragged him up the slope towards the rear of the church. He was laughing and his grip was powerful.

'You out-marsher, you're in a mizmaze,' he said. 'Bain't no puzzle in it. You ain't a girl. We mean nothing foreign by the trust wi' our mates, only friendness. Less it's said a'girl, then it gets far serious fur me. Walk on, friend Tom.'

There was no way Tom was going to be able to prise his hand away without a struggle and he didn't want to offend the guy. The feel of another man's hand in his was not something he was used to; punched-knuckle greetings, touching fists perhaps, but not this. There could be no secrets in this place. Someone was bound to be watching this unsettling display. The woman in the shop had said that folk liked gossip.

'If you're staying then you'll be needing my slip-chin. I'll see a'it,' Barry said at the back of the church.

'Your what?'

'We'll do it after.'

They came to the graves. Barry still held Tom's hand but it felt less awkward now that no-one could see them. Tom was just settling into the sensation when Barry let go.

'I got a-watch the sun go-to first,' Barry said. 'But, now you're trusted, you can come an' all.'

'Why?' Tom continued to feel the impression of rough skin on his palm;

there was something comforting about it.

'If any-a-one talks, don't answer. Leave that a'me. That's one good thing about being me age in Penit,' Barry added.

'Riddles,' Tom said.

'Sorry, friend, but there's a lot I want a-tell you and a lot more I can't. If you're staying, bringing the Carey back a'Saddling...' He laughed at this as he turned around and walked backwards down the slope. 'If you're bringing the Careys back a'where you come from, then I reckon you got a right a-join in. It'll take me mind from it all.'

'Riddles!' Tom repeated, and this time, added, 'And crazy. You been on that bath water stuff already? It's not even dark yet.'

A huge smile split Barry's face and he pointed mockingly. 'You got lot more a-learn if you're a-staying, out-marsher boy.'

'Less of the boy.'

'We're all boys 'til we're wed, and even then you stay a boy 'til there's no man left older. Only then you get a-call yourself a man. So, Carey-boy, trot on.' Barry ran down to the bottom of the slope, leapt up onto the wall and jumped over onto the other side. Tom hurried after him and stepped up carefully. The field beyond rose and fell in the same fashion that he had found on his way to the shack. He could see a water channel some way off and a small bridge crossing it. Dan was already on the other side.

Tom was uneasy and felt out of place until Barry took his hand again.

'Right, friend,' Barry said. 'You walk wi' me and if any-a-one makes a fuss you tell them you're 'onoured wi' me trusting.'

'Where are we going?'

'It be Last Boblight.'

Although the cloud was clearing on the western horizon it still lay thick and grey all the way back over Tom's head. Barry's hand no longer felt strange in his, not now they had crossed the bridge and were alone in another field. There was only Dan ahead, but his figure soon faded, becoming one with the dark distance.

The light was dying quickly. The folds of cloud, lit as if from underneath, rolled back in waves that, even as he watched them, turned from grey to orange and then a deep ochre. The horizon stood out where the cloud had parted to reveal a dazzling slash of amber. He saw a line of silhouettes, low trees, bushes, undulations of shadow that marked the edge of the earth cowering beneath the immensity of sky above it.

Tom didn't feel the need to ask any more questions, although there were many he would have liked answered. He was aware of his own footsteps, the feel of soft grass beneath his feet and the distant calls of crows angry at the vanishing light. To one side of him the field stretched off to reach another ditch where tall grasses stood still and silent. To the other side it reached as far as the gloom of a line of bushes, another dark marker; and behind, when he turned to see how far they had come, the church barely stood out against the cloud. His breath rose in vapour and he felt the cold air at the back of his throat. He put his other hand into his jacket pocket for warmth. He could have done the same with both but that would have meant letting go of the hand he was holding.

As they walked towards the sunset, the clouds thinned and slid overhead. They drifted back towards the sea leaving the sky clear in patches of weakening pink light. All the time the colours changed; orange became crimson as the solstice sun fell lower, where it burned with the yellow of flame.

Tom could no longer see Dan, but he could see something glowing in the gloom. A tiny speck of light moved erratically in front of a mass of shadow that grew larger the closer they came; mother trees, he remembered. They were twisted in the agony of growth, their bare branches warped by wind, boughs bent down to reach for the earth or up to entreat the air. Their highest branches jabbed at the golden sunset in natural disorder. In front of them, he now saw lanterns. He could hear the murmurings of voices, low and steady, and he was able to make out shapes in the gloaming.

Barry squeezed his hand and then let it go. Once more Tom felt it there even after it had gone.

Barry quickened his pace. Tom followed and, a minute later, found himself faced with a group of boys. Several were holding lanterns. Someone was crying and the smell of pipe smoke drifted in the air.

'Who's this?'

Tom recognised the shrill insistence of Mark Blacklocks.

'Tom's got me trust,' he heard Barry say.

'Should not a-be wi' us,' someone else complained, and Tom felt unease creep back.

'He's a guest.' That was Dan's voice, and Tom was reassured to hear it. 'If Barry has his friendness he has mine an' all.'

'What's he been told?'

'Tom's 'ere a-witnessing like the rest of us, is all,' Barry said. 'Don't worry, Mark Blacklocks, your fader himself 'as invited him a'festival.'

'Last Boblight,' another voice spoke up; one that Tom didn't recognise.

'Stay, then, Mr Carey,' Mark's voice said. 'Be a part of our witnessing.'

Tom was angered at being given permission by the obnoxious teenager, but Barry had told him not to speak. He heard the boys shuffling and saw some lanterns placed on the ground. With the night quickly coming in, what little light that was left vaguely showed up ghost-grey faces as Tom ventured closer to the group. Someone was still weeping. Recognising Barry's stocky figure against the thin strip of sunset, Tom stepped up to him.

'Who's crying?' he whispered. Other voices were talking louder than him but, feeling that his presence here was not completely welcome, he thought it best to stay as quiet as possible.

'Young Jacob,' Barry whispered back. 'Only turned thirteen last month. Stay 'ere.'

Barry left him and Tom saw that the figures were shifting to form a line. The weeping boy was the shortest and he held his hands to his face. His head raised now and then to catch glimpses of the sunset but then dropped back to his hands. Barry moved over to him and put an arm around his shoulder.

There were seven young men all standing still, their voices quieting now. Dan was not among them. The lanterns at their feet threw light up to their faces and spilled to the ground in fanned patterns of flickering warmth. Tom, feeling that he was too close, took a few steps back towards the withered trees and met with something solid.

'Hold, you're safe.' It was Dan.

'What is this?' Tom whispered.

Dan made no reply as he took his place with the others.

The dusk was nearly complete; the sky had blackened, and the last of the sunlight was nothing more than a fading sliver of a blade between earth and night.

Now that Barry was with him, the youngest boy had stopped crying. Dan, at the end of the row, was the tallest and they all waited in motley undulation. Their faces, where Tom could make them out them, showed serious, adult, expressions.

One by one, each boy took the hand of the one beside him until they were united, facing the last of the day at the start of the deepest of nights.

Soon they were in total darkness and Tom had only the smell of damp grass for company. The crows had long stopped calling; there were no birds in the trees and there was no breeze to disturb the branches. The countryside was motionless and even with the world open around him the vastness of the marsh was claustrophobic. There was too much emptiness out there, too much loneliness. It seeped through the earth from roots to grass and into the soles of his shoes, into his bones, his blood. It rose through him in channels of despair to reach his heart and flourish. An overwhelming bleakness soaked into him as silent as the ditches, as unstoppable as the sunset.

Tom was not sure how long he stood there. Deprived of senses, with only the unmoving ash-grey faces of the boys, time was of no importance.

Eventually, he heard a quiet mumbling, words that, at first, he could not make out. Heads turned slowly to each other and bowed gently as they spoke, their words knitting together, overlapping, as the boys weaved between themselves in a graceful, unhurried movement. Tom followed Dan through the patchy lantern light with his eyes. He placed a hand on a friend's shoulder, said his words, and moved on. He touched the youngest boy's head, spoke his words, and moved on. He made some kind of contact with each of them, as did the rest to him, until all had met all the others and their voices had died to silence.

Dan came last to Barry. They stood face to face. Tom heard Dan's voice, clear in the silence, 'here for you, friend'. Barry repeated it to him and the two embraced, clinging hold of each other as if it was the last human touch they were ever to feel, treasuring the contact, neither wanting to be the first to let go.

'Last Boblight,' Mark Blacklocks hissed, and the spell began to lift.

Barry and Dan broke apart as the boys bent to collect their lanterns. The lights were shared out and silently, slowly, they began their walk back to the village.

Tom waited and, grateful for the dark, wiped his face dry. The lights abandoned him one by one and he worried that Barry might have left him there. He was afraid to call out in case the strange ritual was not yet over but, as the lights vanished, he felt panic rising. Things unseen waited behind him in the dark. Things he knew nothing of were stalking all about him; a rustle in the hedge, the distant scream of a fox, the brush of an owl's wing on the air, unfamiliar sounds reached him through the crushing darkness, and he was at the mercy of the marshes.

Suddenly, a hand was in his, gripping it tightly, and it brought instant reassurance. It was not Barry's broad and reassuring palm, however; this was smooth and softer.

'You can call me friend an' all,' Dan said, and led Tom towards home.

Twenty-three

By the time Tom and Dan reached the green the other boys had dispersed.

'We'll go in with the back door,' Dan said, letting go of Tom's hand and heading towards the inn. 'Likely there will be many in tonight and though some of us are happy for you to be here not all sit right with strangers.'

Tom nodded once and followed him inside.

'I'll see how ma is doing,' Dan said, and carried on along the passage into the bar.

Tom was keen to warm up and a bath half filled with lukewarm water helped.

Back in his room, he was wondering what he could do about eating when he heard footsteps on the stairs approaching fast. He grabbed for his jeans and had just put them on when the bedroom door flew open and he saw Susan standing there. Her face was red, her hair had come unfastened in places and untidy strands hung around. She didn't seem to care that he was half dressed and doing up his zipper. She glared at him.

'What you been saying to my boy?' she demanded, one hand still on the door handle, the other on her hip. 'And what you still doing here?'

'Do you mind?' Tom replied, turning his back to her and reaching for his clothes.

'I saw you out there. You were touching him.'

'What?'

'I saw you. What have you been saying to Daniel?'

'Would you mind, please?' Tom threw his shirt around his shoulders, hurriedly thrusting one arm at a time into the sleeves. 'What are you talking about?'

'You were at Martin's grave. You got no right to be at the graves.'

'Look, Mrs...' He searched for the name. 'Mrs Vye, I don't know what you're getting at...'

'The boy has enough on his mind tonight without you interfering and leading him along. What you been saying?'

'I've not been saying anything and I've not been leading him on.'

'You been talking about out there?' She threw her head towards the window and more hair came loose. 'You been filling his mind with stupid talk of your places? You can't be telling my boy about that, Out-marsher.'

Tom was struggling with his shirt. 'I don't know what you're raving about,' he said as calmly as he could. 'I've just been looking at my ancestors' graves. Dan was upset so I tried to cheer him up.'

'You leave him lonesome.'

'What?'

'Keep your out-marsh ways to yourself and take them with you. I want you gone.'

'Oh, come on!'

'Out!'

'There's nowhere else to go.'

'And that bothers me not none,' she pitched back at him. 'Take your things. Go...'

'Ma!'

Dan appeared behind her. A touch on her shoulder and she pressed her back to the doorjamb. Her hand flew to her throat.

'You leave him be, Ma.'

'You shouldn't be with him, Daniel.'

'You shouldn't be snouting in my business, woman.'

'And he shouldn't be in ours.'

'Enough.'

It was the first time Tom had seen Dan be anything but sad or quiet and he saw now that he had a strong voice in him. His face had flushed crimson, a vein stood out on his otherwise flawless forehead, and his eyes narrowed. They bore into his mother's and held her stare without blinking. Susan slowly lowered her head. A long, cautious bow took place before she peered sideways at Tom with malice and then slid from the doorway. Dan watched her go as her footsteps died away on the stairs.

'I'm sorry, friend.' Dan said. 'Ma gets like that over me and everyone's tense down there.'

'Yeah, well, she's a bit too tense if you ask me.' Tom reached for his socks, sat on the bed and pulled them on. Dan didn't reply and Tom realised that he'd used a stronger tone that he intended; it was not Dan's fault. He smiled up at the guy still hovering on the edge of the room and all he could think of was the warmth of his hand. 'Want to come in?'

Dan scanned the room and shook his head.

'A drink downstairs?'

Another negative.

'Can I get something to eat?'

'Don't think Ma's cooked tonight. It's a fast night, ahead of...'

'The festival, I get it. What religion are you around here, now?'

'Religion?'

Tom forced his foot into a trainer without undoing the laces.

'Yeah, are you Quaker or something? Amish? One of those things. I noticed the church is pretty unconventional and your graves...'

'What of them?'

'They don't face the right way. Are you some branch of Christianity?'

'No,' Dan replied. 'I don't think so.'

'Don't think...? Whatever.' Tom gave up and wrestled his other foot into the second trainer. Grass stuck to it and he hoped he had not trodden in any whiteback dung. 'What was that all about with your mother? What have I done?' He stood and brushed down the front of his sweatshirt.

There was no reply. Tom glanced up and saw that Dan was still and staring, as if he had been turned to stone in the time it took to put on one shoe.

'There's things I want to tell you,' Dan said, finally.

'But you can't. I know. Look, mate, I'm getting used to your ways and I can even cope with this hand holding thing, and now I'm over that, I reckon there's nothing you could say that would surprise me. Not here.'

'I...' Dan paused. Tom waited while he searched for the words. 'I just want to say...' Another pause. He bit his bottom lip and looked along the corridor, then back to Tom. 'I can't talk about it with no-one from Saddling. It's me and Barry, see.'

Tom dreaded to think what was going to come next but he waited patiently hoping that the revelation wasn't going to be too intimate.

'Me and Barry,' Dan said again. 'We don't want you to see it and think bad of us.'

Tom was about to ask him what he meant when he heard Susan call up from downstairs. 'Dan! Matthew Cole's here to see Out-marsh.'

Dan gave a fragile smile. 'Could be about your book,' he said.

Tom leapt to his feet. 'About time.' He took two steps to the door giving Dan just enough time to move out of his way and then hurried down the corridor to the stairs. He paused at the top and turned back to see Dan entering his own room. 'Dan?' he said, stopping the lad in his tracks. The smile was still there. 'We'll talk later, yeah?'

Dan nodded, and the smile gained strength until it was the first genuine sign of happiness that Tom had seen from him all day.

Cole was waiting at the back door strangling a folded cap. He wore a sheepskin coat, the same design as Tom had seen others wearing, and, although it was cold outside, he was sweating as if he had been running.

'Mr Carey,' he said as Tom reached the bottom step.

Cole opened the back door and slipped outside. Tom followed him into the night.

Barry was waiting for them. Cole checked towards the green and nodded. Barry led Tom a short distance marshward, away from the inn until they were in darkness.

'What's this about?' Tom asked. The night air had leapt on him and taken advantage of the fact that he wasn't wearing his jacket. He wrapped his arms around himself.

Cole came over to them.

'Sorry a-bring you outside,' Cole said, taking off his coat and handing it to Tom. Tom refused. Cole insisted. 'But I don't want a-be seen talking wi' 'e in there.'

'Oh, thanks.'

'Me fader don't mean nothing of it,' Barry explained. 'But a'night's an 'ard night in Saddling, the night afore the festival. Everyone gets... antsy.'

'They skit 'bout like whitebacks at branding,' Cole said, and it took Tom a moment to figure out his meaning. 'Whites are one thing. You can catch 'em and 'old 'em while you tiver 'em, or sheer their wool. But some folks in there get so much in their 'eads a'night they drown in their own bathtub. If you gets my meaning, sir.'

'Sure, yeah.' Tom buttoned up the coat and immediately felt warmer. 'Please, call me Tom. So, what's this about?'

'I've a message.'

Tom noticed the caution with which Cole again checked that they were alone. He looked up at the inn but there were no windows on this gable end, only the door and that was closed.

'Minister Blacklocks,' Cole said when he had reassured himself, 'says 'e's got news on your book. The one I thought 'ad gone up a'Maidstone.'

'Yeah?' Tom felt a rush of excitement. 'It's here?'

'There was three originals, see, but they was taken away a time ago. But there be a copy the Blacklocks ministers done of the olduns, and there it's got records for the last how-many-centuries an' all. The Saddling Diary.'

'Excellent,' Tom said. He reached to shake Cole's hand but the man pulled away. 'When can I see it? Can we go now? I could read it tonight.'

'Well, that be the thing, see,' Cole went on. 'Blacklocks says a'morrow, after festival. 'E's busy with 'is duties 'til then.'

'But where is it? In the crypt? You're the clerk, aren't you? You have a key?'

'Tom, 'old. Slow down, mate,' Barry said. 'Listen a'what me fader 'as a-say.'

Cole took Tom by the arm and pulled him further into the darkness. 'If Blacklocks says a'morrow then that be as it is. But you don't want a-wait 'til then. Come another time again. I can find someone who'll trap-ride you out a'the bridge. The rain's not due in a'night. Take me coat. I'll borrow you a lamp...'

'No, hold on,' Tom took a step back. 'I'm getting sick of people telling me to go. I'll stay for as long as it takes.'

'Tom,' Barry said. 'Listen up.'

'There's things 'appen at Saddling that you don't want a-be no part of. This festival...' Cole said the word with derision, 'it's changed since I were a nipper like this un.' He must have meant Barry but Tom could hardly make out the man's face. 'Forget your books, lad. Now's not the time for digging in your past.'

'Why?'

'Don't ask questions, Tom.'

'That's what I came here to do.'

'You saw Eliza, didn't you?' Cole continued. He must have taken a step closer to Tom as he could now smell his breath. He had been drinking beer.

'That's right,' Tom replied. 'I did, and she wasn't able to tell me anything.'

'Well, that might be a saving of 'er, if Blacklocks believes it. But you saw the eyes.' Cole was slurring his words. He'd apparently drunk a lot of beer.

'Yes, she was blind. So?'

'It were Blacklocks who turned 'er blind. She asked too many questions. Like you.'

'Turned her...?' Tom laughed. 'What are you talking about?'

'She was meddling when Dan's dad was the...' Barry said.

'Careful, sonnie,' his father interrupted. 'Remember the Teaching.'

160

'You knows what I am on the Teaching, Fader.'

'Now ain't the time for that talk, neither. Tell 'im what 'e did but, Mr Carey, you got a-promise me, on me boy's life, on your own, that you don't repeat none a this.'

'I'm not sure what I am supposed not to repeat, but yes. Okay.' Tom was lost, tangled in Cole's veil of secrecy. 'Go on,' he said. 'I won't talk to no-one. Anyone.'

'Well, story is,' Barry said, 'it were twenty year ago, now, Eliza 'ad a run in with Blacklooks...'

'Barry! 'E still be our minister.'

'When 'e 'ad a run in with Blacklocks. Don't know what it was about exactly, no-one does 'part from 'er, but it were a-do with 'er not wanting the festival. Some say she said she'd go off marsh and she weren't a fetcher, so she couldn't 'ave. She made trouble, screaming at Blacklocks. So, on festival night, later, after the... At night. 'E found 'er out and cut 'er from there to there as punishment.' Tom couldn't see if Barry was showing him but he remembered the woman's scar. 'Blade went clean through the eyeballs, sliced them open. He dug deep but not deep enough a-kill.'

'Poor woman. Did he get arrested? Go on trial?'

One of the two of them spat, probably Cole, Tom thought because Barry spoke too soon after.

'No-one gets a trial 'ere,' he said. 'Fixed 'er up 'imself, after. Best 'e could. She'd learnt not a-question the Lore. But she never saw no more.'

'See, son,' Cole said, 'Blacklocks is our law. If 'e says you can see your book a'morrow then you will. But go speak with Eliza more. Ask 'er what she knows, press 'er. Prehaps the blind can make ye see sense. I done my job now. I told you what you 'ave a-know and I told you what you should do. Barry, you coming?'

'Later, Fader. I got a duty wi' Tom.'

'Go tender-footed, lad, and keep the coat,' Cole said as he left them. 'Bloody sister-in-law makes 'undreds of the buggers.'

Tom and Barry sat on the bench in silence. Barry filled his pipe and offered it.

'No thanks, mate. I only smoke stuff that's against the law, if you get my drift.'

'This ain't 'gainst the Lore.' Barry said, and offered it again. 'What comes from nature ain't never 'gainst the Lore. Grows wild all over.'

'What is it?'

'Devil's Choke, be called.'

Tom took the long, thin pipe and the matches that Barry offered. He struck one and lit the small pile of dried leaves in the bowl. Taking a breath, he felt the smoke burn the back of his throat. It tasted of earth and, true to its name, it made him choke.

'Take it slow,' Barry said. 'Takes a-getting.'

Passing the pipe back and recovering his breath, Tom held the smoke and then breathed out. 'Nasty,' he said, and Barry laughed. 'And, by the way, what is this Penit you've all been on about?'

'The seven days afore the festival,' Barry said. 'Used to 'ave something a-do wi' being penitent, so Blacklocks said in school. Now it's more an excuse for us eligible men-folk and boys a-drink, smoke, and get away with things.'

'And older people have to bow to you at the same time?' Tom asked, remembering his first sight of Barry the day before. It already seemed like a week ago. Time hadn't exactly stood still but it did feel like it had melted away.

'Aye, the obediences and addressing is all a part.'

Across the green the shop was closing. Mrs Rolfe was taking in the vegetables while her husband unhooked dead things from the window. It crossed Tom's mind to buy something to eat while he could. A teenage girl left the shop. She wore a floor-length dress, the same design as Susan's. It was old fashioned but somehow not out of place.

'I see where you're looking at,' Barry said. 'They's something what is 'gainst the Lore in Penit.'

'Girls?'

'Aye.'

'I haven't seen many around,' Tom said. Barry offered the pipe again and, already feeling some of the smoke's relaxing properties, Tom took it and dragged deeply.

'Not at this time. They'll be out a'morrow. The women 'ave their own work inside a'night and things a-be getting along on.'

'Sounds a bit old fashioned.'

'It be as it was and is, friend.' He took the pipe back from Tom who was holding in another deep breath. 'Ask you something?'

Tom nodded, not wanting to exhale just yet.

Barry took a quick draw. 'This book so important a'you?'

'Yes,' Tom said letting out the air in one slow breath. 'Very.'

'And Dan?'

'Eh?'

'You cares about 'im. I seen it.'

'I hardly know him.'

'Seen the way you look for 'im. You don't need a-know Dan long a-fall into it. I'd say every girl in the village feels the same.'

'Yeah, well it's not like that.'

'I feel the same, Tom.' Barry took a longer drag on the pipe before handing it back. 'What you say 'bout that?'

Tom knew what Barry was trying to say but he changed the subject.

'I don't like mysteries,' he said before he smoked. 'And there's a lot of them around here.'

'Aye, I can see you feel it an' all. You know what you are?' Barry asked, leaning back and putting his arm on the back of the bench behind Tom.

Preferring silence and the smoke to any kind of answer, Tom said nothing.

'You're a chance for us a-learn what be out there. Beyond Far Field and the North Grazing. Only, you've come the wrong time. The village ain't always tied up tight like this. We got things going on, see.'

'Not exactly sure what's going on.' Tom felt a laugh rising in his chest, but he held it in. 'And what was that sunset trip all about?'

'All part of whatever a'morrow brings.'

'So why was that boy crying?'

'You couldn't understand,' Barry said. 'And I can't talk on it. There's some parts a the Lore I 'ave a-struggle wi' and got a-stay quiet on, else... I got a-think of Ma and me fader, and Daniel. It be just how it be. Always been. Nothing we can do 'bout it, so no point crying if you ask me.' Barry took the pipe once more, drew on it and then tapped it out. 'I like that you care 'bout Dan,' he said. 'Dan be the closest a'me and me a'im. Shame 'e's not a few days older. But, like everything other, that can't be 'elped neither.' Barry lifted both arms and laced his fingers together on the top of his dark hair. 'Aye, you come 'ere the wrong time. 'Like me. Like Dan and them others. Still, this time a'morrow and it be done.'

'You talk some shit, Barry Cole,' Tom said, and couldn't help but laugh.

'Not meant a-use miswords like that in Penit, neither,' Barry said. Smiling, he checked over his shoulder before leaning close in to Tom and saying,

'But who'd give a coot's bugger?'

Tom laughed louder. 'That the best you can do?'

'That be the best there be.' Barry laughed too and dropped his arms. Turning sideways to look at Tom he said, 'Tell us some really rough miswords.'

'No, not if you don't know them already.'

There was something in the back of Tom's mind that told him it would be wrong. There was an innocence about Barry and he should be left that way. He regarded his new friend. From what he could see in the dim light of the anaemic streetlamp, the guy's pupils were huge, his eyes rounder than ever. His grin was as mischievous as usual.

'I like you,' Barry said. 'You're a runagate like me.'

'And, if I understand you, you're not the first person to say that,' Tom replied.

Barry put both hands on Tom's leg and held it with a powerful grip. 'Aye,' he said, smiling. 'Just like me. Alright, friend Tom. You do what you want. Find your buffle-head book. I'm 'ere fur you when needed.' He squeezed and let go.

'You people are so weird.' Tom's head was spinning. His leg ached with an unexpectedly comforting pain. 'This place is weird.' The ground was undulating under his feet.

'Ah,' said Barry, reaching for his pipe. 'Devil take it. Let's burn another. Then I'm going a-see a'you wi' me slip-chin.'

The house was in darkness when Mark Blacklocks returned home. He suspected his father was off at the borders with one of the fetchers bringing in provisions for the festival. He let himself in through the back door and found a note on the kitchen table. Holding it to his lantern, he read, 'Look to your mother.' Having understood the message, he opened the lamp and used the flame to burn the note over the stone sink. That done, he made his way through to the hall and stood under two large framed drawings; his father's wives. He ignored the first woman, he had never met her. She was dead long before his father remarried. Looking at his late mother, though, he felt the same pang of sadness he always felt when seeing her face. The emotion was tinted with distaste, however, because she resembled her brother, Matthew Cole, and his ill-behaved son. He knew he shouldn't harbour hateful thoughts, not on this night, and so he quickly turned his attention to the small table beneath the portraits.

Picking up the leather pouch he found there and feeling its weight, he blew out his lantern and walked through into the front sitting room. The curtains were open and, through the wide window, he saw Barry and the foreigner over on the bench. They would not see him. The night was too dark and the moon had not yet risen, but he had to act quickly.

Using the front door would draw attention and so he felt his way back to the kitchen and let himself out. He reached into the pouch and took out some of the sheep feed. Starting on the verge at the side of the house, and all the time checking that no-one else was about, he dropped pellet after pellet into the grass, pressing them down with his foot and brushing them over with grass. He was especially cautious when he reached the front lawn.

He carefully checked the green. Barry was still smoking with Carey and the two men were too caught up in their laughter to notice him. The shop had closed, no-one else was out, and the inn had its curtains drawn. A solitary candle burned in the window there and he reminded himself that he should light his when this job was done. Until then, he needed the darkness. He felt anger simmer inside when he heard Barry's cheery voice. How could anyone be happy on this night? Anyone apart from himself.

The anger seeped away to be replaced by a confident sneer as he cautiously dropped and planted more pellets. He knew that he and the ancient family of Blacklocks would now be safe when the choosing came.

He was so focused on his task that he failed to notice Matt Cole at the far corner of the church watching him through the gloom and shaking his head.

Twenty-four

Tom climbed the stairs uneasily with one hand on the wall. In the other, he held a bundle of cloth. The low and mumbling voices in the bar faded as he reached the turn at the top and stepped onto the landing.

The gas lamps lit the corridor and he was grateful for the little light they gave as he headed to his room. The short walk seemed longer than before and the light was yellower. His skin tingled and laughter simmered in his chest. The light around Dan's closed door, the memory of his hand, talking with Barry, the smoke, and now the illicit package of bread and cheese Barry had found for him on this fast night, all reminded him that he was welcome here. It's a unique country festival, he told himself; something your ancestors did. You must stay and see what it is.

He reached his door and looked back the way he had come. The corridor was no longer than it had been before, of course, but still, it felt as though he had slid along it in slow motion, taking an age to arrive.

Barry stood at the top of the stairs thumbing silently towards the bathroom.

Tom knew he had to step in there but his mind wasn't telling him why. He lit the lamp and stood facing himself in the mirror. His dirty blonde stubble had become a rough beard. His hair was pressed down and unwashed. He was a mess, but at least the dark circles under his eyes were lightening and there was a glow in his cheeks.

He heard the door close and, soon after, was aware that his coat buttons were being undone. The sensation was strange but he made no objection. Barry was talking to him quietly in the mirror and Tom could see himself nodding in reply. His fingers trailed around the sink and found the tap. He turned it, only half-aware of what he was doing. His back was cold with damp but his face was warm, his eyes half closed. He did as he was told and lifted his sweatshirt over his head. His shirt came with it and he saw his bare chest reflected.

Barry pressed gently on the back of his head and Tom bent to feel warm water poured over his hair. Fingertips worked firmly, massaging his scalp, pulling up strands of hair and knuckling out knots; rough skin on his scalp, a body pressed against him, warm breath in his ear.

'Close your eyes.'

The fingers worked behind darkness and through the scent of soap. The body was firm and moving behind him; leather and sheepskin slid across his back. The voice whispered in the other ear. He heard words but they made no sense. Instead, they lifted him until he could no longer feel the floor. He wanted to float away and was only being held to the earth by the press of the fingers.

More words, more quiet instructions that he obeyed peacefully. The hands wiped his eyes and then set his head free. He lifted it up, breathing deeply, and opened his eyes.

His chin was being held by a rough hand with gentle intentions. Lather was being applied to his face with a soft brush. He saw himself old, a white beard, a tangle of white wrinkles beneath his eyes, his hair pulled back and lost, his expression serious. A blink and the beard was just lather, the wrinkles just soap.

Barry's arm was around his shoulders now and Tom's head was once again gripped. He was being forced to look at the man behind him, meeting his eyes in the mirror, his lips taut in concentration. A long, narrow blade moved across the mirror and came to rest against Tom's cheek.

'Trust me, Tom.' Hushed words on warm breath. 'I be 'ere fur you.'

A gliding sensation, hardly a touch but enough to tingle Tom's skin. A face beside his, an inch away, breath mixing on the mirror, the arm moving, the blade stroking, huge, brown eyes fixed on his. He was still floating, yet he wasn't. He was still confused, except he knew this was meant to happen. He was still alone apart from the buttress behind him, shoring him up against the flood of feelings roused by the Devil's Choke.

The blade vanished but quickly returned, clean and gleaming, wet and ready for his throat. It slid upwards from his Adam's apple, expertly gathering foam to his chin and slipping up and out. Flicked, the foam was gone. The body behind him moved again; he could feel it pressing firmly into him and he pushed back for support as his head spun. He swallowed against the sliding blade. It was under his nose, around his lips; it skimmed over the side of his face and around his neck.

It was gone. It was done. Barry's head rested on Tom's shoulder and he was pressed forwards as Barry scooped up water, his arms pinning Tom's to his sides. Calmly helpless, Tom closed his eyes once more and felt warm hands cup his smooth face. Water ran over his chin, down his neck to his chest, onwards over his belly and into his jeans. He allowed it. He allowed the hands to wash his face again and allowed them to rest there when they finished.

He let Barry's cheek rest against his and, when he slowly opened his eyes, he saw that Barry's were closed.

The next thing he felt was the door latch, cold and solid in his hand. It lifted, the door opened; someone had lit his bedroom lamp, but he was alone. The room was exactly as he had left it, but now he sensed it was larger. Not possible; it was the Devil's Choke, he told himself, and put the wrapped bread and cheese down on the bed.

He came to the window with the distinct feeling that the floor was sloping towards it and peered out at the view. A few dull lanterns, the dark silhouette of the church and a couple of tiny dancing candles in windows. He saw a new one come to life in Blacklocks' house where he could just make out a shadowy figure at the picture window. The shadow was sucked back into the darkness and nothing moved.

He was dressed again. He felt for his cheek and found he was holding a piece of bread in one hand. He turned to look at the bed. The bundle had been unwrapped and the cheese was gone. He no longer felt hungry but he couldn't remember eating. Looking back at the view and expecting blackness, he was confused to find that the moon had risen and was nearly full. Thick grey clouds were sliding past it and every now and then the light dimmed. When the clouds had passed, the fields beyond the church came into light and silver streaks appeared, crisscrossing the dark patches, reflecting the moon. He knew they were the ditches and he could name them, but he didn't know how.

His notebook was open on the desk and, by it, his mobile phone, finally drained of battery. He had no idea what time it was but sensed it was late. No church bell struck, no clock ticked; the only sound was that of his own breathing.

He was sitting at the desk, now, and names and dates were running across his pages. Isaac Carey, Thomas Carey, dead ends, 1895 to 1912; someone had written "For Saddling" beside Isaac Carey's name and he realised it was his own handwriting, but larger. When had he done that? Great-grandparents: Thomas Carey 1899 to... and a blank space, married Elizabeth Edwards, 1916, New Mill, Cornwall. Why? Her parents and beyond. Their under-generations, Matthew Carey, 1918 to 1975—his wife,

Jane Soper. The names shifted, changed position without reason; Matthew Carey slid across the page and rested by Harriet Carey-Smith (great aunt, no children) and then slipped down the page as if it was a piece of a Chinese puzzle. He breathed harder and deeper. Matthew Carey, children: Maud Carey, John, Tom's father, just a name and a number, 1962, and another number, 2005. Another name, Lesley Lawrence, and more dates, 1965, 2005 again, same day; and now the pages were wet and the names were running. Not dripping or leaking ink, but moving around themselves in dance, trotting to the side, bouncing off it, leaping over marriages and deaths to swap places, confusing the tree. His father's name, the wrong dates, 1912, and in the wrong place. His mother's name now joining hands. Hands, names had hands. Barry's hand in his. Dan's, smoother. His parents holding hands and the two of them leaping, laughing, as they fell through history. Landing with a joyous splash in the waves of the pencil-drawn sea at the bottom of the page. They bobbed and floated, waved, and slowly started to drown. The name Lawrence hung above water for the briefest moment before sinking beneath the page to the sound of running water.

Water. It was all to do with water. Blacklocks' words. The damp crypt—I must get in there—but there is water. He heard it; running water, somewhere...

His hands were shaking. On the desk, the notebook was closed. There was no bread but there was running water, and he was thirsty.

He was at the door with no idea how he came to be there but only knowing that he needed to drink. He was in the corridor; there was a light behind the opposite door and on the other side was water. He stepped into the bathroom, a wet mat, cold beneath his feet. When had he taken his shoes off? He saw the tap. No water, only the sound of it. He reached for the tap and it shrank into a small, metal ball that he was unable to turn. The sink bore writing. What did that mean? Nothing. He'd brought no lamp into the bathroom, but there was light. It glowed and curled along the tiled walls behind the curtain.

When Tom saw him, he was standing in the bath, his back to Tom's eyes. His tall, lean body drowning. Water cascaded over his rust coloured hair, running in rivulets between his wide shoulders, down his back, over his strong legs and into the slowly filling tub. His smooth skin glowed in candlelight. Each muscle moved with grace as he lifted an arm, holding out his long-fingered hand to the gush from above. A tuft of soft hair, soaked and dripping, the fold of a shoulder blade, the stretch of the neck, the back narrowing to the waist and the pure, untouchable sound of the voice as the body turned.

The mouth moving. What words? The eyes, smiling through the fountain, rivers running over the soft lips, pink and supple against the carved face, the stream running down over the shaped, smooth chest, further down. But what words?

A hand reaching out, the feel of the skin, the grip of the fingers; it was warm, welcoming, and pulling him towards the candlelight that grew and dazzled behind the halo of flaming hair, lighting up the words that he could now touch.

'Here for you, friend.'

Tom heard something beyond the walls and he was immediately awake. He was on his bed, still dressed, with no idea what time it was. His head numb, he fumbled his way to the window; the gas lamp was out, but something was shining outside. He heard the sound again, felt it, distant and menacing. The moon was up. Had he seen it earlier? If so, it had changed place; time had passed. He reached for his mobile, remembered the dead battery; there was no time in this place. His notebook was open on the desk. The page glowed faintly, caught in the changing moonlight, and he held it up to the window. Scrawled handwriting showed him that he had tried to write when he came to his room last night. Last night or this night? Was morning near? It was pitch black out there save for the moon which, even as he watched, was being extinguished by massing cloud. He could make out one date and some words on the page, "1912 – For Saddling. Why? Remember this!" But he had no recollection of writing it. His eyes were stinging and his mouth was dry.

He was at his bedroom door and had opened it before he caught a flashback of the bathroom.

Looking out into the corridor he could see nothing. All the lights were dead. He reached out, found the bathroom door, opened it as silently as he could and groped his way along to the sink.

His bare foot trod on a wet bathmat. Why was that sensation familiar in this unfamiliar place? The air was damp and held a faint smell of soap that disturbed him for a reason he couldn't fathom. He found the tap and drank from it gratefully before silently returning to his room.

Still dressed against the freeze of the night, he lay on his bed and hoped sleep would come back to him. It did so slowly and reluctantly, but not before he had heard the sound again.

From somewhere far away across the marsh he heard a faint grumble of thunder as if the atmosphere was troubled, complaining and growing impatient with the village that slept below.

Twenty-five

His feet were cold. At some time during the night he had crawled under the covers and tried to wrap them in the blankets, but it had little effect. He had a dull ache behind his eyes and he opened them cautiously to find the room alive with daylight. He was aware of sounds beyond the window and people talking below his room, but his first thought was to undress and wash.

The bathroom mirror showed him his smooth face and his neatly cut hair. The reflection brought with it a half-memory of the night before, but all he could recall were shards; moments in time caught as if by a camera, being shaved, being washed, Barry's eyes closed, Dan's eyes open.

He shook his head in an attempt to return to square one and dispel the night. It helped little so he turned his attention to the shower where he noticed candles on the rim of the bath. They rang a vague bell as did the sight of the shower curtain, wet and clinging.

There was no hot water but, in a strange way, he was grateful for that. The cold shower went some way to clearing his head; the bar of soap cleaned his skin of the smell of sweat and he dried himself on a damp towel that he found hanging beneath the window. He had no choice but to put on the same clothes as he had worn the days before. His thoughts and plans came together as he crossed back to the bedroom and found his trainers. The shoes had been old to start with but now they looked even older, muddied and stained.

The coat that Cole had given him was hanging from the end of the bed and, with that on and reaching to his knees, he, at last, felt warmer. He was finally awake and his head was clear. The sounds from below drew him to the window.

The scene could not have been more different from the view last night and it cheered him. Either the festival started early in Saddling or he had slept in late.

The green had been transformed. Had Tom been awake at dawn he would have seen the sun rise into a clear sky; the thunder and cloud from the night before had moved away. The sun was bright, doing its best to throw down some warmth as village women worked on the decorations. Houses

172

were garlanded with reeds and bulrushes, dried grasses and sprigs of evergreens. Ribbons were hung from guttering and porch roofs, corn dolls, male in form, hung in lines on bale twine between houses, and small flags in earthy colours were strung between the lamp posts.

Stalls had been set up on the green, tables had been brought from houses and cloths laid over them. The small platform was now decorated and, across the back bar, a line of eight wreaths hung, each one a weave of dark brown twigs and deep green grass interlaced with pieces of off-white sheep's wool.

Tom stepped out of the inn. The air was crisp and a few deep breaths cleared his lungs of any remaining Devil's Choke. He searched for Barry but couldn't see him; there were too many people milling around, talking, laughing, and hurrying from one place to the other. He recognised some and he was surprised by the number of villagers.

He wandered into the collection of stalls and tables. People brushed past him, some nodding, some glancing away when he caught their eye, and a few gave him a cheerful 'a'morning' which he returned with a smile. He blended in well in his sheepskin. It was what most others were wearing and he could see that Cole had been right; someone hand-made a lot of them.

He passed a table bowing under the weight of jars of some grey-yellow liquid and the young girl behind it held out one to him, her bright blue eyes sparkling.

'How much is it?' he asked.

She giggled, came around the table and put it in his hand before returning to her station and handing out more jars, taking no money for any of them.

'Thank you.' Tom unscrewed the lid and sniffed before taking a cautious sip. The lemon bit into his tongue, sharp yet sweet and it brought his mouth alive. 'Wow, that's good,' he said to the young girl. She didn't reply. She was busy rearranging her jars to fill the gaps left by those she had given away.

Weaving his way through the crowd, he came to a small group of older men gathered around a piece of downpipe. Iron and black, it rested up against a stepladder at a sharp angle and emptied out onto a bale of straw. One man stood at the top of the ladder with a small cloth bag in his hand. Tom soon picked up that this was some kind of game, a test of speed. As the man dropped the bag into the pipe, another at the bottom waited with a wooden mallet. The idea was to hit the bag as it shot out. The weighted bags flew from the end of the pipe at great speed and none of the men playing the game managed to hit one. No money was charged but competitors paid in laughter as each one smashed away at the 'rat', missed, and bounced his mallet off the hay.

Tom moved on, fascinated at the old-worldliness of it all, and came to a stall offering pies. A woman handed him one absentmindedly while she chatted with someone at the neighbouring stall. She expected no money either. The next table was stacked with cakes. Tom accepted one and again asked how much. The woman stood back quickly and a worried expression paled her face.

'Mr Carey is our guest this year,' came a deep voice from behind. 'Not to concern yourself, Martha.'

The woman curtsied slightly and busied herself with her stall as Tom turned to find Blacklocks standing over him.

'We are honoured that you decided to stay, Mr Carey,' he said, giving a small bow of his own. 'Excuse some of my flock. We are not accustomed to visitors, even with all this.' He indicated the crowd with a sweep of his open palm.

'You do this, what? Every ten years?'

'We celebrate each winter with a meeting but only every ten do we hold a festival like this. You are fortunate to be here at this time.'

Tom, eating, gave a nod of the head. 'I need to talk to you. You know what about.'

'Of course, but, as you can see, we are all rather preoccupied today. When it's over, we shall talk then.'

'When will that be?' Tom said through a mouthful of the best pork pie he had ever tasted; it was even still warm.

'Oh,' Blacklocks scanned the scene, 'late evening, I should think. This is an important day for Saddling. But not to concern yourself. You stay and enjoy. Before tonight I will see that you have what you came for. The excitement really starts at midday. But may I say...' Blacklocks looked him up and down slowly, 'thank you for making an effort. You are well prepared today. We appreciate the younger men being presentable in Penit.' He slipped into the crowd and, despite his height, managed to vanish.

Tom felt his smooth chin and approved of it as he made his way through a maze of tables each with its own collection of items. Knitted caps and woman's bonnets stood alongside tables of vegetables, bread, and biscuits. Some were built up in levels and displayed lace, wooden spoons, hanging baskets, quilts, and all kinds of children's clothes which were all rather dull and very much the same. One section of the green was set aside for farming tools and metal paraphernalia that Tom couldn't figure out a use for and they were lined up beside milk churns and caged chickens. People were taking what they wanted but, it seemed, only what they needed and no-one was exchanging money.

His first impression of Saddling had been one of gloom and inhospitality. Today he saw only goodwill.

He came to the bench and, finding it unoccupied, sat to finish his pie. A woman, bent in a rickety old wheelchair, caught his eye. The chair appeared handmade, and rather well, too. She sat in warm clothes with a blanket over her knees, her head down as though she were asleep. A man stood next to her chatting with some others and then, when they wandered away, he knelt beside the woman with a plate in his hand. He proceeded to feed her and Tom guessed that she had had a stroke. She was able to raise her head and he saw that her face was grey and fixed with an expression of helpless sadness. The man, her husband, perhaps, picked crumbs from her lips and then offered her a jar of lemonade which she drank through a piece of straw. Tom felt tears welling up in his eyes but not because he felt sorry for the couple. This man was caring for her because he loved her. He had made a commitment in the past and was honouring it because he wanted to, despite whatever illness had befallen his wife. Tom wondered if he would ever be lucky enough to find someone who would care for him this way should he suffer the same fate; someone who would tend to him unconditionally, out of love. It seemed impossible.

He swallowed and had to walk away. The scene had altered his perception of Saddling even more. There might be some elusive people here, he thought, but there are those who genuinely care for each other. It was a far cry from anywhere he had been before.

A group of musicians played beside the platform and Tom wandered that way, looking out for Barry or Dan. Although no-one was making him feel unwelcome, he wished he had someone with him so that he would feel less alone. He finished his drink, put the jar down on a table with other empty jars and backed off up the slope towards the east end of the church. From his slightly elevated position he could see that the stalls had been set up so as to allow a line diagonally across the green from the platform to the bridge path and it was there that he saw Blacklocks standing, looking to the sky. The clear morning blue was quickly being taken over by dense cloud. He remembered the thunder that he had heard during the night. There had been something ominous about the sound, as if it was a distant warning announcing that it was going to rain on this rare festival. He pushed the thought from his mind; he didn't want these people to have their fun ruined by the weather. He leant against the corner of the church as the festivities continued.

The music stopped after some time and the gathering fell silent. People parted along the line of tables revealing Blacklocks at the far end. As soon as the way was clear, he processed, followed by a line of young men and Tom recognised them as the group he had seen at sunset the night before. The youngest led the line and Barry and Dan were at the back. As the eight boys followed the minister, people in the crowd held out their hands, touched their clothing and bowed. The lads were all dressed the same, dark trousers and a knitted white jumper, and each one carried a small lantern with a candle burning pointlessly inside.

Their faces were stony, their eyes fixed firmly on the man in front, and no-one spoke. Blacklocks mounted the steps to the platform and the boys lined up beneath, facing him with their backs to the crowd. Still in silence, Blacklocks turned and paced along the line of wreaths hanging from the back bar. He selected one and brought it to the front. He held it up to show the villagers and they, en masse, bowed low. Tom saw couples holding hands, some held children close to them, others stood alone. Everyone was watching the minister.

He moved to the end of the row and stood in front of Dan whose face was stoic, his eyes motionless. He was deep in thought, unaware of what was taking place around him. Blacklocks lowered the wreath onto his head, touched it there and then lifted it. He repeated the same thing with Barry. Barry was also in another place and Tom wondered if he had been smoking his pipe. Blacklocks attended to each boy in the line, having to bend to reach the head of the shortest one, and then returned to centre stage. He held the wreath aloft, faced the church, offered the wreath to it and then stepped down from the platform. He walked calmly to the church and let himself in. At that moment, the villagers took up their talking and returned to their stalls to carry on giving out their crafts and wares. The folk music started up again played on pipes and a guitar. One man beat a drum to keep the rhythm.

The line of boys dispersed. Tom was about to go down and greet his friends when he saw them hurry away. Barry headed for the green and Dan approached the inn. The weasel boy, Blacklocks' son, took a few short steps over to his own house where he brushed his feet across the grass, his hands in his pockets. The others made their way to other houses around the green. One or two of them headed up the rough tracks that led off it and vanished. Tom figured out that each one was returning home, but they didn't go inside; they stood on the patches of grass outside their houses where their parents came to stand with them.

This curious ritual became stranger still when men approached the houses with ladders. Susan carried a wooden one from the back of the inn and brought it to the front where she leant it against the eaves. Cole was doing the same at his house.

Tom was just about to wander over to ask Dan what was going on when he saw Blacklocks leave the church and walk to where his son had also produced a set of steps. Although Tom was dying to know what that was for and what was going to happen next, he noticed that Blacklocks had left the church door open.

Across towards East Sewer, Mick Farrow opened the pen and banged the wooden rail with his crook. The whitebacks inside moved sluggishly towards him at first, their hooves sinking into the mud, their heads down, muzzles close to the ground sniffing for the grass they had been denied for the past few days. The scent of fresh feed attracted them and they trotted faster, jockeying for position. Some leapt, forcing their way through to the front of the flock as they smelt the pasture beyond the pen.

Mick tapped his crook harder and whistled. His dog lay flat on the other side of the gate, its front legs outstretched, its nose close to the earth. The sheep hurried past until the flock of eighty, carefully counted-in two days ago, had all left the pen. Then, with expert precision, the dog leapt into action, rounding them up from the back, running alongside and worrying them into a gallop. Mick worked hard to keep up. He whistled and called as the dog darted about, herding the confused animals together and ensuring they went where the master directed—towards the lope-way.

Two other lookers waited there, studying the approaching flock carefully, watching for stragglers and holding out their crooks so that the whitebacks had nowhere else to go but towards the village. The lookers counted each one as they passed, making sure none broke off and none stopped to graze. There would be plenty of grazing for them shortly. The job now was to get them into the festival as one group.

Mick saw the whitebacks safely on their way and then cut across the field to arrive near the Cole house just before the herd. Here he blocked their path. The two lookers bringing up the rear guided together any last animals and then, when the whole flock was in one place, waited.

Tom decided that the best way to sneak into the church without being noticed was to do it in plain sight. Wearing the sheepskin, his trainers now the same colour as most other people's shoes and his head down, he didn't stand out. He kept one eye on the Blacklocks house and saw the tall man arranging his ladder against the roof, distracted.

Tom took the opportunity. He moved swiftly along the wall, reached the porch and slipped inside.

Hiding behind the door, he peeped out. No-one had noticed. People were now turning one by one to face the lane. Something was about to happen down there and it made for perfect cover. Tom opened the inner door silently.

His trainers squeaked on the stone floor and, although he knew he was safe, he walked on the side of his feet so as to be quiet. In this awkward, bandy-legged fashion, he moved quickly down the aisle, grateful that he could not be seen through any of the high windows. The sound of the festival outside continued, dulled by the stone and brickwork, and he reached the crypt door in seconds.

Something drew his attention and he paused to look at the east window. Its stained glass provided the only colour in the building but, where Tom would normally have expected to see visions of saints or the crucifixion, there was a depiction of a man who clearly was not Jesus. He was a young man with a handsome face. He stared out vividly through sapphire eyes outlined in lead and wore a wreath on his head identical to the ones hanging outside. He also wore a sheepskin, not unlike the one Tom was wearing, and he stood with his feet in water where diamond sparkles of white were picked out on the deep blue, representing small waves. Somehow it appeared that the water was rising and was about to pour from the window to flood the church. He couldn't think what saint or bible story the image was meant to represent.

'Nice artwork,' he said. 'But even I know that's not right.'

If the window was incongruous, the altar was worse. It stood only a couple of feet away between the pulpit and the crypt door on a raised dais. The stone had been covered with a cloth, its edges a blood red colour that faded into the material from a deep crimson at the hem to a sickly pink where it diffused into white. It looked as if it had been dipped in a dye which had been left to spread naturally upwards. Mother tree branches had been laid around its base and some items had been placed on it. A large pewter chalice stood with the wreath lying in front of it and beside this stood the black casket that the minister had been carrying. Towards the corner, a large hourglass stood about two feet high. Sand was running slowly from top to bottom, and it had a way to go before it would need turning.

Making sure that no-one else had entered the church, he stepped up to the altar. He remembered a time at school when he and some friends had stolen into the vestry and drunk some of the communion wine and turned the altar cross upside-down. The adrenaline, the knowledge that he was not only breaking the rules but also being sacrilegious, came back to him and thrilled him. There was no cross here, however, no trappings of the Christian church and he wasn't bothered if God was judging him from above. He lifted the casket and tried to open it. Locked, of course. He felt its weight and could tell that there was no book inside. It was light and, by the sound of it, held something that was made of metal. It clanked against the inside and he put it down. He had been wrong; the casket had nothing to do with his search.

The hourglass reminded him to be quick and he returned to the crypt door. Hoping that it was not locked, he turned the iron ring and felt a bar lift on the other side. He pushed gently. The door opened and he winked at the "Private" sign. 'Yeah, right,' he said, and stepped through.

The sound of revelry grew fainter but he could still hear it coming at him through the ground, the vibration of moving feet a soft rumble in the darkness. He waited for his eyes to adjust to the dark and held the door open slightly, lighting the first few steps. Cautiously, he made his way down. Complete blackness soon enshrouded him and, although there were only a few steps, they turned enough to disorient his direction. He pressed his palms against the cold walls as he spiralled downwards. He knew he had reached the bottom when the walls curved away and his foot tapped out ahead, finding flat ground. His fingers played around the damp stone at the opening but there was no light switch or lamp. All he could sense was dankness, a rough earth floor and the smell of mould.

He stood a while longer, thinking that he would have to find a way to return later with a torch, when he heard hard, fast footsteps on the stone floor above.

'Hell.' He groped desperately for a light. A quick flash would be all he needed to find a place to hide. He followed the wall around with his fingers, but there was nothing. The footsteps approached and then stopped abruptly overhead. Tom stood still. Keeping his breathing shallow and silent, he waited. A new sound joined the hubbub from outside; a constant thumping that sounded like a hundred stamping feet. He couldn't figure out what it might be. The person above him moved again, footsteps clicked back along the aisle.

Abruptly, they stopped and turned back.

Tom felt a cold flush of panic as he remembered the open door.

The light from above intensified and crept down the steps as someone entered. Tom heard a hinge creak and the first footstep of descent. The light increased just enough for him to make out a table a few inches away and, as that was all he could see, he knew it would have to do. He crouched down and cramped himself under it, kneeling on the earth, grateful that his clothes were dark. The footsteps were closer, now, and then he heard the rattle of matches in a box. One was struck. Although still around the turn of the steps it cast light into the crypt enough for Tom to see a small cabinet not far from where he was hiding. A few more paces and whoever this was would be in the room.

He saw the swirl of a black robe. A dark, pointed shoe landed on the next to last step and he crouched lower.

Suddenly, a cheer went up outside, loud enough to be audible through the open crypt door. The pounding of hooves, if that was what they were, increased but it was now less regimented. There was laughter and yelling followed by another huge cheer.

The match was blown out, the crypt plunged back into darkness and Tom heard the door shut. The footsteps faded off down the aisle as the noise from outside died. Having no idea what was going on, Tom concentrated on what he was doing. He kept the placement of the cabinet in his mind as he backed out from under the table and stood, gripping it for a second to let a head rush subside. He reached out his hand and stepped sideways in small movements, his fingers expecting to feel wood at any moment. The silence was unnerving, the darkness was oppressive, and he fought to push childhood thoughts from his mind.

His fingers touched the cabinet just as, out on the green, a woman screamed.

Twenty-six

Tom followed the walls with his hands until he reached the steps. He had no idea what was taking place outside but it sounded bad and he no longer felt safe in the crypt; Blacklocks could return at any moment. He would have to think of another plan.

He mounted the steps, his feet checking each one as he spiralled back up and found the latch. He lifted it cautiously.

A loud cheer from the green covered his footsteps as he hurried to the porch. Another scream ignited his curiosity and he ran the last few paces out into the daylight.

The sight that met his eyes was one of chaos. The green was a melee of confusion. Someone had let a flock of sheep into the circle of houses and they were panicking, running this way and that, knocking over stalls, upsetting tables and tripping people. The villagers seemed more than happy with this and were laughing. Some were calling the sheep to them, others were herding them away towards the houses. Some sheep had stopped on the front grass of some homes but none were being allowed to graze on the green. The band was playing frantically and everyone else was busy whistling at the animals, shouting across to neighbours, and pointing from house to house where the sheep grazed oblivious to the commotion.

Tom inched away from the porch just as another scream sliced through the throng. Some in the crowd watched the sky. Tom followed their gaze and saw a circle of crows overhead. They swooped down and villagers waved their arms, but not to frighten them away; they were trying to attract them. Men hurled their caps in the air and children ran to pick them up before joyfully throwing them at the birds.

Mick Farrow panted his way through the madness and climbed the knoll for a better view.

'What's going on?' Tom shouted over to him.

'The caller birds 'ave come!' Farrow shouted back, and then carried on along the top of the mound, his head bobbing as he looked from one house to the next.

It made no sense. The place was being trashed by sheep, but everyone loved it; everyone but those who screamed.

Tom saw that men were now climbing the ladders leant up against the houses where, if Tom remembered correctly, candles had previously been lit in the windows. They carried small bags with them and threw their contents onto the roofs. Tom couldn't make out exactly what it was; pieces of fruit, perhaps, or feed of some kind. The man throwing his bagful onto the inn held out his palm to the people below. They cheered and Tom caught a glimpse of what he thought were worms before the man made a sweeping arch and landed his handful on the ridge tiles. The things slithered down and came to rest in scattered abandon.

'Over there!' someone shouted, and everyone turned to face the Blacklocks' house where two large crows were circling over the roof.

Tom laughed, marvelling at the lunacy of it all.

The crows landed on Blacklocks' roof to feed and the woman nearest the house let out a scream that chilled Tom. It wasn't a cry of fear; it was more like the howling wail of loss at a deathbed. The crows pecked, their wings flapping to keep balance.

Tom saw the minister by his front door, his face grave, his long arm holding his son close by his side. Loud applause sounded out from over on the far side as everyone there watched a group of men run onto the green bearing one of the sunset boys on their shoulders. The lad waved his arms over his head with his thumbs up and the applause spread through the whole gathering.

Back at the Blacklocks' house, Mark was calling to the crowd, beckoning them all towards him. No-one took any notice and then Tom realised he was calling to the sheep. Mark appeared desperate for them to wander onto his lawn.

More crows came down; some landed on the roof of the shop and again there was a chilling scream almost immediately followed by a cheer.

Someone shouted out, 'whitebacks ain't choosing Jason Rolfe!' and the merriment that followed was as confusing to Tom as the sentence itself.

'Nor Mark Blacklocks!' someone else yelled, and the loudest cheer so far resounded from house to house as everyone applauded. Mark rejoiced with them as a sheep grazed at his feet.

Still dumbfounded, Tom watched the boy strut up onto the platform where the others were waiting. Five of the sunset boys were gathered there, shaking hands, hugging and laughing together. Another group of men came running into the green from behind the shop and the youth they carried was joyfully bundled up onto the platform to join the rest.

James Collins

If there was a connection between the lads last night and what was going on in this comedic nightmare, Tom thought, then only Dan and Barry were missing.

Suddenly, as if someone had pulled the plug on a rock concert, the green fell silent. Crows cawed and sheep crashed about but none of the villagers spoke or cheered. They turned towards the lope-way where Cole, his wife, and Barry stood on their front grass holding each other and looking to the crows on their roof. There were no sheep nearby.

'I get it,' Tom said to himself, crossing his arms and smiling. He couldn't see Dan over at the inn but he saw Susan, her hands to her face, desperately searching the green. 'The race is on,' he said to himself. 'Who's going to be prom king and get the girl.'

He'd figured it out. Some of the village boys were eligible to be chosen as the festival prince, or whatever they would call it. The villagers had tempted the birds to their houses with feed and, if they landed there, the boy was in the running. If a sheep then came to graze, that lad was knocked out of the contest. It was done at random, so it was fair. The last boy randomly selected won the prize, whoever she might be.

Barry's mother was bent forward banging her hands on her thighs, desperately trying to call a sheep while, at the inn, Susan was doing the same. Other people came to help the Cole family. Some men clapped at the whitebacks to persuade them closer to the house but no-one was helping Susan. Then Tom saw Dan standing apart from everyone else, watching with no expression.

A now familiar loud cheer rang out and Tom saw Cole fall to his knees to wrap his arms around a sheep that was grazing on his grass.

But something was wrong.

Something Tom had just figured out didn't make sense. If this was their way to find the lucky lad, the top dog, the one to be celebrated, then, what was the screaming about? And why were the boys on the platform happy to have been eliminated?

It happened again; a loud, piercing wail of the deepest pain, but this scream was tainted with horror. It didn't stop as the others had done. It carried on and multiplied over and over until the woman broke down into sobs.

That woman was Susan, alone on her hands and knees.

The crowd slowly turned to face her, falling still and quiet. The sheep were herded from the village. Evidently, their job was done, the weird event was over.

The last man standing was Daniel.

Tom felt a strange pang of jealousy at that, as if someone had taken a promised gift from him and given it away to someone else and there was nothing he could do to get it back. It was a silent annoyance and forgotten when he saw Barry being led to the platform where he took his place with the others. Susan beat the ground with her fists, sobbing wildly, and the twisted stick that was Blacklocks parted the spectators with his cane to approach the inn.

There, he took hold of Daniel's arm and yanked him. Dan did not want to move at first, but after a silent word from the minister he nodded and began to walk. Susan crawled up onto her feet and reached out to grab at her son, but Blacklocks prevented her with his cane. She hung back, clutching her arms to her stomach, bent at the waist and crying uncontrollably. No-one came near her.

Stunned, Tom couldn't decide what to do, and he looked towards Barry, hoping to catch his eye. Barry was staring blankly ahead as if he was in shock on hearing some dreadful news. Slowly he came to and noticed the scene around him. A realisation hit him and he jumped down from the platform, causing the crowd around it to part and murmur. He shouted and fought his way towards Dan. Men tried to hold him back but his sturdy, stocky body broke through to reach his friend in the centre of the green.

'Leave 'im!' he shouted as he struggled his way to Blacklocks. He was met with a cane-jab to his stomach that sent him to the ground doubled up.

Blacklocks led Dan into the church. Tom couldn't stand back any longer. He raced down the slope and battled his way through the crowd to Barry. He was on all fours, a forest of legs around him shuffling towards the platform.

'What the hell's going on?' he demanded as he helped Barry to his feet.

Barry stared vacantly at him and struggled free before pushing through the crowd to the front.

Tom followed until the crush of people was too thick to penetrate. He saw Barry step back up and take the last remaining wreath from the line. He put it on his head, his face white, his eyes fixed straight ahead, once more focusing on nowhere.

Calm returned as Blacklocks and Dan reappeared from the church
and stood by the porch. The seven boys on the stage then removed their
wreaths and threw them out into the crowd where giggling village girls
jostled for them. The villagers roared approval. The minister led Dan to
the platform where he shook the hand of every other boy as they stepped
down from it. The last to leave was Barry. The two friends faced each other
and Tom saw Barry's lips move as he raised a hand gently to Dan's cheek.
He was about to place it there when the minister's cane came into play
again, lowering Barry's arm. Barry was pushed firmly back into the crowd.

One by one, each villager knelt on the grass until the only people standing
were Tom and Susan. Her shoulders were heaving and her face was ashen.
Dan had raised his expressionless face to the sky and now he raised his
arms. His cheeks were wet.

'For Saddling,' he shouted, sending the crows skywards until every one
of them had flown.

Suddenly, a woman's voice cried out. 'Blacklocks, you got a-stop this!'
Her words soared over the heads of the gathering, attracting the attention
of everyone present. 'You got a-put an end a'this. It's folly! It ain't right.'

The blind woman had one hand at her mouth, the other was supporting
her against the wall of Blacklocks' house. When the minister failed to reply,
she shouted again. 'You got a-stop this.'

'Take this woman away,' Blacklocks ordered, annoyed at the interruption.
Some men pushed their way towards Eliza.

'They got a-know. Out there.' She pointed wildly towards the south
drove-way. 'I got a-tell 'em what you're doing.'

'Stay silent, woman. Do you want a bannocking?' Blacklocks bellowed.
Other villagers booed and jeered at her.

She fell to her knees, her hands searching through the grass, and shouted
up, 'They got a-know what you done.' She found what she was groping for
and stood, holding a small feed pellet in her hand. 'You ain't all as blind as I.'

Eliza sensed that people were coming for her and she backed away, still
protesting. 'Let it be me the one as tells 'em, then. I can't stand for this no
more, none of you should. This time I'll walk beyond Far Field and tell 'em
all, you mark me, Blacklocks.'

Her voice trailed away as she slid out of sight behind the house.

Unsure of what to do, the men turned back to the minister.

'I shall see to that later,' he said, with contempt. His brow was bunched and his eyes narrow, but he slowly untwisted his face to look at Dan. He reached out a long, thin arm and the tips of his fingers touched the youth.

'Again,' he said, with the tone of a loving father.

'For Saddling!' Dan shouted, but this time his voice cracked.

The whole crowd bellowed it back and rose to their feet. Amid much cheering and clapping, shouting, and now singing, Dan was carried around the circle of houses on the shoulders of two burly field-workers. The villagers followed in a jubilant, disorganised procession and broke off to enter their own homes until Dan was gently lowered to the ground in front of his mother. The men bowed low and headed up the slope and around to the back of the church, their faces solemn.

Dan took Susan by the hand and led her into the inn. No words were spoken and Tom could think of nothing to say. His mind was littered with questions just as the now empty green was littered with debris from the festival.

Twenty-seven

He had been there all day breaking off his research hourly to try and reach Tom on his mobile, every time without success. He was on to something that would help his friend in more ways than one. He was sure that there was an answer waiting for him somewhere and he had an uneasy feeling that was not going to be a pleasant one. He couldn't put his finger on why he felt like that, but something, somewhere, didn't add up and that was not the kind of unsettled mystery Dylan could leave alone.

Huddled outside, he tapped on his smartphone and waited for the call to connect. It was answered on the second ring.

'Miss Carey's phone.'

'Hi, right. Can I speak with Miss Maud? I mean...'

'One moment.'

There was a scratching on the line and then Maud's voice.

'Tom?'

'No, it's me, Dylan.'

'Ah, what news?'

'None, really, except I think Tom might be in trouble.'

'When is he not?'

'No, I mean, I think something is going on down at Saddling, but I can't get hold of him. There's no answer from his phone and he's not been online.'

'How very strange,' Maud said.

'I thought I should let you know.'

'What sort of trouble?'

Dylan heard her rough intake of breath but spoke over it. 'I'm not sure. It's just a hunch really. I'm more worried that Tom has not used an electronic device for two days. I'm hoping he hasn't had an accident.'

'Lord! Where?'

'No, I said, I am hoping he hasn't. I'm on my way to find out.'

'How?'

'Well, I'm going to Saddling. I'm half way there.'

The sound of a sharp and painful breath filled the earpiece and Dylan held it away until he heard Maud speak again.

'What time is it?'

'Sorry?'

'Philip!'

'Miss Carey?'

'Philip,' the woman called again, obviously forgetting that she was on the phone. 'Philip, I have an appointment. We shall be late.'

'Hello?' Dylan shouted and received a disapproving look from a man entering the library.

'Yes?' A short breath. 'Oh, Dylan. Yes, thank you for telling me. How soon do you expect to be there?'

'I don't know, a couple of hours?'

'Very well. Call me.'

With that, she ended the conversation.

'Sure thing, no, no bother, thanks for offering me mileage,' Dylan complained to his screen.

Maud put down the mobile and, with a long, rickety finger, pushed it away with distaste. She returned to reading a letter. She studied it quickly once more as Philip swept through the hotel suite clutching a lady's Vuitton Keepall.

'No need for a full sail, Philip, we do have time.'

'My fervour is a matter of weather, Miss Carey. The forecast is for the worst.'

'Indeed.' She folded the paper and slipped it into her jacket pocket. 'But mere bad weather cannot deter me from my Great Matter. Death is a serious business.'

'So I believe,' Philip replied, and wafted from the room.

Maud reached an arthritic hand to her briefcase and lifted it onto her lap. By the time she had double-checked its contents Philip was back and ready to wheel her down to the car.

Back inside, Dylan sat at a wide table in the Kent County Records Office with the Carey family bible on one side, several books and maps on the other, and his laptop open in front of him. He had his theory, hard though it was to believe, and he needed to check his facts before he allowed his concern to become alarm. Without facts, Tom would not listen.

He turned the bible page to the first of the family tree records and compared what was written there with a list of family names and dates

Tom had drawn up on a sheet of paper. Tom's list matched the bible and exceeded it in detail, so it was clear that he had found some information online. The transcript of registers to his right also matched, mostly, what the bible showed. At some point, the Saddling records had been entered into the central county collection and later made available online. So far so good.

What Dylan was worried about, and what he had not yet established, was the reason the Saddling records stopped in the same year as Tom's ancestor fled the village.

He now had a theory.

Late in nineteen-twelve, Thomas Carey left, taking the parish records with him. Why a thirteen-year-old boy should do this was still a mystery. What was clear, though, was that they ended up in the records library as here they were, fully transcribed. An archivist had told Dylan that the originals had been severely water damaged and had long since rotted away. These were the only Saddling records of the village and they pre-dated nineteen-twelve. It was as if the place itself had ceased to exist at that time.

The archivist's words had given him his first clue. Maps of the area showed the changing landscape. Originally, there had been no marshes; just the sea. The marshes had slowly become reclaimed land, with small islands appearing. Villages sprang up as the centuries passed and the land was farmed and irrigated. The coastline had changed, the sea giving way to habitable marshland which, in turn, became lost in the great storms. He saw that a particularly severe storm in 1287 had wiped out some villages. These fierce weather anomalies had returned with uncanny regularity since the thirteenth century and he wondered if there was a connection between that and the water damaged books of which the archivist had spoken.

As he searched, a pattern began to appear. He was still unsure what it meant, but if he could find a connection between the strange weather pattern and 1912, perhaps there would be a reason for Thomas Carey to have fled Saddling.

He had found rolls of microfiche recording local newspapers from nineteen-twelve but had found only one item of interest. It was, however, all he needed.

He checked the wall clock before turning back to reread the only paragraph that mentioned Saddling.

The newspaper had been published on December 23rd, 1912.

TERRIFIC STORM LASHES KENT

ANOTHER VILLAGE FEARED LOST

AT LEAST FIVE PEOPLE KILLED

SEA DEFENCES FAIL FROM SANDGATE TO DUNGENESS

Of all the storms that have affected Romney Marsh and the coastal areas of Kent during the last few years, that which occurred at midnight on Saturday was the most severe, and the disasters which it brought in its train included the unfortunate deaths of five residents whose homes were crushed by falling trees and the ripping off of roofs or who drowned as the sea defences failed and floods surged into the surrounding countryside sweeping away everything in its path.

A number of people caught by the tidal wave of water are thought to have been out celebrating the winter solstice. As the sea defences failed from Sandgate to Dungeness, the low-lying areas of the Romney Marshes disappeared under five feet of water and while most villages have survived, albeit with terrific damage to property and much loss of livestock, it is feared the remote village of Saddling has been altogether lost and claimed by the sea, along with all its inhabitants.

Historians are comparing the storm to the Great Storms of 1287 and 1292 which successively swept the marsh villages of Broomhill and Winchelsea out of existence and which changed the course of the River Rother for ever. As yet, no-one has managed to reach Saddling which may well have suffered the same fate.

He could find no other references to the event or what happened to the village after it, but the timing was too coincidental to ignore.

He spun his chair back to the table and checked the maps. The medieval ones showed the marsh as a series of islands and waterways with the

Rother, having changed its course in 1287, emptying at Rye. Few other places were shown; only the largest towns featured. Later maps showed the same but with more land reclamation and a few more village names, and he was able to locate Saddling from a 17th document. Maps since nineteen-twelve showed nothing in that area apart from fields and the occasional 'ruined church', waterways and dykes. The latest OS map of the area didn't even show footpaths around the area where Saddling once was.

It appeared that the village had been washed away by the storm in nineteen-twelve, or just forgotten about, being so remote as to be of no interest to anyone but those who lived there. It didn't seem possible, even in that day and age, that there would be no record of a destroyed village, the lives lost, the farms and land gone, but that, apparently, was how it was. Although he had scanned aerial photos taken during the Second World War there was still no clear image of that part of the marsh and no listings of Saddling apart from a few references on historical websites; all of which Tom had found before.

Dylan had an eye for computer code, for patterns, symbols, and repetitions and he liked things that ran in sequences; regularity, logic and order all made sense to him and were pleasing to his eye. It wasn't just the 'missing village' mystery that was niggling him, it was also the numbers he had been looking at. He had found patterns in the dates he saw in the family bible and, now that he had access to the dusty old transcriptions of other families from the village, he had noticed several more.

Dylan was sure that what he had seen in the transcripts was the key that would unlock Maud's mystery once and for all. This was the information that Tom had missed. He had been so bent on finding only his Carey ancestors that he had not looked closely enough outside the direct family.

He checked the clock again; time was moving on. He had to get back to the hire car and down to the marsh. It was the shortest day of the year and the weather was turning.

He was as sure as he could be. He had his evidence and, as unlikely as its conclusion was, it was all he had. He scraped his papers and books together, collected a map, switched off the microfiche machine, and returned the film. The last piece of paper he picked up was a list of Carey deaths, listed with other deaths from across the centuries, all at Saddling.

It was while he had been writing these out in chronological order that he had seen the pattern. It was the change in the calendar back in 1751 that alerted him to it. Before 1751 the year started on March 25th but, after that date, on January 1st. This meant that when Tom had been working out ancestors' ages, he had, for this period, sometimes calculated incorrectly, or been uncertain if someone had been born in one year or the next. A bit of sloppy research Dylan had thought at first, but it had opened his eyes to the unchanging Saddling pattern. There were too many entries in the death records that had two things in common. The year of death ended in a two and the date was always December 21st, today. Not only that, there were other similarities between them all which fitted in with the Thomas Carey story and nineteen-twelve. Similarities that Dylan found very unsettling.

And then, or course, there was the postcard that he had discovered hidden in the bible.

Twenty-eight

One by one, the villagers returned from their houses, took down the decorations and carried them to the inn. They leant them against the outside walls in silence, stood for a moment to contemplate them and then returned to tidy up the green. Some men, having nodded to their wives, entered the inn. Tom watched from the bench as villagers walked home, collecting some of the debris and rubbish as they passed him; the bashed 'rats' from the men's game, the knocked over tables, empty lemonade jars, cups and glasses, paper towels, all were methodically and quietly removed.

No-one took any notice of him as he sat in the sea of silent activity waiting to catch sight of Blacklocks, aware that the afternoon would not last much longer. He had just made up his mind to go to the minister's house and bang on the door when he saw him swoop into the green from behind the shop. He took the path, striding towards the church with his head down.

'Got you,' Tom said to himself and stood. He caught up with the minister just as he reached the porch.

'Hey, Blacklocks,' he called with little reverence.

The man lifted his head in one graceful motion that brought with it his distorted smile. 'Mr Carey?'

'Mind telling me what that was all about?' Tom thumbed over his shoulder. He had no doubt that the man would vanish into the church, around the back, into thin air, if he took his eye off him only for a moment.

'Our festival. As I explained. Celebrating the...'

'Yeah, got all that, but the thing with Dan? The sheep, the birds? I mean what kind of festival is that? You Pagans here or something?'

The smile never faltered. 'Pagans? Well, some of the traditions probably come from before this land was Christianised, if that is your interpretation. Ours is a simple celebration of the winter to come, the start of the dark months where the land recovers and the...'

'Not what I was getting at.'

'Then, I fail to understand you, sir. Forgive me. On a day like today my duties are many, my head is alive with subtleties, tasks to remember, jobs to attend to...'

'What happened to Dan?' Tom again cut him off. 'Why was Susan hysterical? Why was Barry crying? Cheering one minute, screaming the next? I mean...' He wasn't sure that he meant anything. Tom was merely confused by everything he had seen and heard.

'Daniel has been chosen as the Saddling, the festival... celebrant,' Blacklocks replied. 'He is very honoured. If you like to look at it this way, it is the same as is celebrated anywhere. A carnival queen in modern festivities might come from the catholic celebrations and represent the Virgin Mary. Here, we simply observe in the masculine. All harmless fun and something the village can prepare for and look forward to over the years. No different than anywhere else.'

'Something tells me it was. Or is,' Tom said. 'Something tells me you've been lying to me too.'

Blacklocks knew how to keep a straight face. He did not appear annoyed or perturbed in any way by the accusation. He just continued to hold Tom's eyes and smile his repulsive slippery smile.

'How so?' he asked.

'Your village diary. Here one minute, not the next, then back again. I've kind of got fed up with the game, now. Know what I mean?'

'No. Now, if you will excuse me...' Blacklocks took a pace towards the door but Tom sidestepped and blocked his path.

For a moment Tom saw a change in the man's eyes, a flash of anger. He felt good about that. At last, he thought, I am getting some kind of reaction from him other than this smarmy wall of politeness; a wall that was rebuilt in a blink.

'There was something else?' the minister asked, his voice betraying no hint of irritation.

'Oh, come on!'

'As I explained previously, there is much to attend to before the culmination of our celebrations this evening. I must prepare the chapel.'

'Good. While you're in there, I'll just sit and look quietly through your records.'

'Sadly, that is not allowed. Until the start of the evening service, no-one but I can enter the church. It is in preparation, you see?'

'Rubbish. Surely I can...'

'Mr Carey, I find your attitude not in the least helpful to your cause.' The tone changed. It was still pleasant, but there was a warning edge to it now;

195

a bitter tang left behind after the taste of a too-sweet wine. 'Please, respect our traditions on this, our most sacred day.'

'I don't see anything sacred about all that.' Tom turned briefly to indicate the green which was still being cleared. When he turned back, Blacklocks already had the key in the lock.

'You will stay for the evening?' Blacklocks asked. 'Afterwards, we can sit down together and I will personally guide you through the texts. It is the least I can do after being so muddle-headed with their whereabouts. I hope you understand my previous confusion now. You have seen how today is such an important one for us all. Distraction is one of the greatest failings of my elderly mind.'

Tom felt somewhat comforted by those words. 'I suppose I could stay another night,' he said. It sounded reasonable and Aunt Maud's promise was all he had left. 'But, if this next part of your... festival involves women screaming like they'd just lost a child, I'm not sure I'll actually come to it.'

'What is a celebration in our village,' Blacklocks said, 'seems unusual to out-marshers, I can see that. But this evening's event is far less dramatic; rather prosaic, I am afraid. But you will appreciate the candlelight and the songs. We have a girl with a charming voice who sings our very oldest folk tunes.'

'Yeah, okay, but...'

'Think of it.' Now it was Blacklocks' turn to interrupt, which he did with good grace. 'These are the same tunes your ancestors would have heard and sung. Who knows? Perhaps they were even written by some very early Careys. You will experience what your forefathers experienced. Now that, surely, must be of great interest to any ancestry researcher.'

'I guess.'

'And so,' the minister continued, stepping into the porch and turning to close the door, 'I look forward to your presence this evening. You will know when we are to start as everyone will gather here. Afterwards, we will browse the records together. Some are in Latin, if you wish to go back that far, but I can translate. The handwriting of my forebears who transcribed the original records was difficult to read at times, but I have persevered. You can sit in one of the pews all through the night if you wish. But not until our little festival has truly finished. Now, does that sound like something you can live with?'

Tom had now all but lost his anger. He gave in.

'Okay, then,' he said, but his tone betrayed his frustration.

'I don't expect you to understand our ways here,' Blacklocks said as he closed the door. 'But I do expect visitors to respect them. Until tonight.' And with that, he winked and shut Tom out. The key grated in the lock.

Tom had had a speech planned in his head that was meant to gain him access to the crypt, but the minister had not kept to it. He'd charmed Tom into doing exactly what he wanted him to do and that angered Tom. As he came to the back of the church to look out onto the marsh, he concluded that he was angrier with himself for letting him.

The air was cold but clammy and he was sweating inside his sheepskin. After the frenetic activity of the past few hours, everything around him was uncomfortably still. It was as if the land was waiting for something it knew was coming; something it feared.

Deciding that he needed a decent drink, he turned from the view, back towards the inn.

The wind picked up as Tom left the knoll. It came in from the east, starting as a warmer breeze. The cloud had been gathering unnoticed in the distance and now began to advance towards the marsh with a stealthy approach. It spread across the hills and reached far out to sea, a high bank of tall cumulonimbus cloud built in the distance on the unstable atmosphere. White at the base with billows of dark grey in places, it rose into columns reaching thousands of feet into the air. They grew gracefully, imperceptibly, fed by water vapour lifted in upward currents from below. They mustered to tower over the land that lay huddled far beneath.

As the clouds grew and darkened many miles away, the sunlight changed. The pastureland became luminescent in the weird light with brighter greens and sharper yellows. The whitebacks, now freed from the green, roamed the fields as moving white shapes that caught stray rays and stood out against the gathering grey.

The mother trees shivered in the changing wind and the high reeds along the ditches rustled together, whispering like nervous children ordered to stay silent. Water voles scurried to the safety of their bankside holes, slipping and scrambling as frogs stroked their way to the banks and sheltered among the rushes. In the dykes, minnows and sticklebacks sought out deeper water with the eels and huddled together, waiting.

Twenty-nine

Tom stepped into the inn where the atmosphere was jovial and warm. The fire was roaring and around it sat several boisterous village men. Beer glasses chinked together, there was laughter, and, to the left of the fireplace, a young man sat playing a small guitar. The music was barely audible over the conversations that jumbled together forming a confused babble punctuated with the occasional laugh. Although there was still daylight outside, some of the lamps had been lit and the room was bathed in a dull yellow glow. Smoke hung in the air like a head-high marsh mist and Tom smelt the tobacco that he and Barry had shared the night before.

He closed the door, slipped off his coat and threw it over his shoulder. He checked around hopefully to see if he could spot Barry or Dan, keen to discover what was to take place that evening. He was disappointed, so, under the sideways glances of the villagers, he moved cautiously among the chairs towards the bar. As he weaved his way through the groups, he became aware that voices were lowered.

'They're saying 'e's tried a-turn Dan,' he heard one voice say as he approached a table. A man knocked the speaker's arm and the guy turned to look. Tom recognised one of the boys from the night before; Aaron, he thought his name was. Tom nodded a hello. The boy glanced at him and then lowered his head to study his pint glass.

A group of older men showed Tom their backs as he inched by. The laughter stopped as the table fell silent. Perhaps he was no longer welcome, but that was not going to keep him from a pint of ale.

He reached the bar and found not Susan, as he had expected, but another woman serving drinks.

'Mrs Cole?' Tom asked, ignoring the eyes that were undoubtedly on him. She nodded to him. 'Is Barry here?'

'No, sir,' she replied. She looked over his shoulder at the men behind him and picked up a glass. 'What'll you be 'aving?'

'A pint, please,' he replied, returning her smile. 'Put it on my bill.'

She turned to a cask and held a glass under the tap where a thick brown liquid frothed up. She knocked the last drops into the glass and put it on the counter.

'Prehaps you should take it in your room as you gather your things,' she said. She leant towards him. 'You might be more comfortable.'

'I know what you mean,' Tom said with a wink.

Irene Cole regarded him for a moment and then flicked her eyes to the bar. The sound of chatter had returned to its usual volume. She blinked at Tom. 'I knows you won't be understanding our ways 'ere,' she said so quietly that Tom had to lean even closer to hear her. He could smell lavender in her perfume. 'Today be an important day. But it ain't one that strangers usually be welcomed at, is all.'

'Oh? But Minister Blacklocks specifically asked me to stay for the evening.'

She pulled her head back and thought for a moment. 'I see,' she said, coming close again. 'Me husband...' She stopped, stood up straight and searched over Tom's shoulder. Tom looked behind but couldn't see Cole. 'Prehaps...' Irene hesitated, 'but then, no. Let me say thank you, Mr Carey. That is all.'

'Thank me? For what?'

'Barry's taken a liking to you.'

'He's very friendly.'

Her face lit up for a moment, her eyes sparkling in the flickering gas lamp. 'Barry be lot of things, aye, and he don't give out 'is friendness easy,' she said.

'His...?'

'Friendness, sir.'

'Oh, friendship. Well, we don't really know each...'

'So, whether you stay or go, or when you do go, or, well, whatever 'appens, I want you to know that your friendness 'as me blessing. As his mother.'

'Well, that's very good of you,' Tom said. 'But we've only chatted.'

Her thanks carried a suggestion of something more intimate and he suddenly flashed back to the bathroom mirror. Did she know? He brushed his hand over the hair at the back of his neck. Where yesterday it had been soft curls, now it bristled under his fingers.

'Take your ale, now, sir, and find some peace upstairs. Best leave the men to their farm talk down 'ere.'

'I will,' Tom said, moving towards the hatch.

She lifted it, closed it behind him, and then ushered him through to the back.

He stood in the passage to take a sip of his beer, sucking off some of the froth so he wouldn't spill it on the way up. He had one foot on the first step when a hand suddenly took a firm grip on his arm. Beer spilt as he tried to pull away but the grip tightened. Someone behind him pressed him into the wall. He caught a whiff of stale alcohol and then felt breath on the back of his neck.

'How many more has to tell you to leave us alone?' It was Susan. He tried to steady his other arm on the bannister so as not to spill more ale. 'Your sort don't belong here.'

'My sort?' he said, trying to turn his head, and then his body. He couldn't, he was trapped.

'See what you've brought? Your interfering.'

'Look, let go of...'

'Get your trappings. Get gone.'

'Oh, please! I tell you what, Mrs Vye,' he said, and his words were short, 'I'm a little more than sick of hearing this ignorance. Get off me.'

'You leave my boy alone. Leave us all alone afore you come to harm.'

She let go of his arm and stepped back.

'It's going to take a bit more than you to keep me from my money,' Tom said, instantly uncomfortable with his own rudeness but unable to stop himself. 'Your threats aren't worth bothering with, woman.' He pointed up the last word insolently because he had heard Dan speak to her that way yesterday and carried on up the stairs.

Turning at the top, he stopped and looked down guiltily to make sure she wasn't following. Susan sat on the bottom step, her face in her hands. He saw Irene Cole come up to her and pull her roughly by the wrist.

'Hold yourself a-gether,' Irene chided. 'Today you are honoured.'

'I can't stand to see it happen again,' Susan wailed with tears behind her voice. Tom was about to leave these strange people to their strange festival but Susan's next words stopped him. 'His fader first and now Daniel. Has Blacklocks made this happen?'

Tom remembered the date on Martin Vye's grave. Today was the anniversary of her husband's death. No wonder she was upset and drowning her sorrows but what did she mean by "now Daniel"?

Sobbing came from below where Irene held Susan against her, comforting her. It would normally be a touching sight but Tom found it unnerving.

'I know, I know,' Irene was saying. 'The Saddling kills the mothers an' all, but we must think of the village.'

Tom pulled back slowly so as not to draw attention. Hoping the floor wouldn't creak and give him away, he took a few steps towards his room, turning over Irene's words in his head.

He saw that Dan's bedroom door was open and, hoping for an explanation, he knocked quietly and looked in.

The room was as sparsely furnished as his own. The single bed was unmade, the covers and sheets neatly folded at the end of the bare mattress. It reminded Tom of the last day of term at boarding school when they'd been ordered to pack up their beds before inspection. There was a school desk under a small window and one chair. Dan had a cupboard in this room, open to show a few clothes. It was the only difference, but it was the desk that caught Tom's eye and, with a glance back to make sure no-one was coming, he crossed over to it.

A dark portfolio lay there, closed and tied with a ribbon, and on it sat, open, a crudely made diary. Someone had gone to the trouble of taking some paper, tearing it into pages, binding them together, and wrapping the whole thing in a piece of leather. Beside it lay a pen and a small bottle of ink. The pages only held a few words each; this was not a personal journal, more of an appointment diary, and Tom wondered what on earth Dan would need to keep one for. The left-hand pages were not sitting flat and it only took a flick of his finger to look back another week.

'Start of Penit,' was written in a careful hand with perfectly formed letters that scrolled both above and below. 'Meeting Barry,' was entered on another day, 'Whitebacks' on another. He flicked to the current week. 'Last Boblight,' was one entry and 'Saddling' was the last, today. Flicking forward, there were no more entries.

'A man of few appointments,' Tom said.

He took a sip of his beer and his eyes strayed to the window. Dan was down in the churchyard again, standing at his father's grave.

'Ah,' he said to himself. 'Now let's go and find out what's going on.'

Thirty

The anvil thunderclouds that had massed together in the east were being driven onwards by the increasing wind. The clouds were swamping the sun, extinguishing it with their six-thousand-meter-high wall of rain. Any light that managed to escape lit the marsh with brilliant clarity but, as the clouds neared, so the light died. Giving up all hope, it fell prey to the massive grey turrets of the advancing storm.

Out at sea, the tide swelled, driving eastwards through the English Channel. The waves rose and broke on each other, confused by the headlong wind. Fishing boats huddled in harbours, tankers turned and braced themselves, lifeboat crews stood on standby along the coast from Hampshire to Essex as severe weather warnings were issued on radio and television.

So far, the storm was still a long way from Saddling.

Blacklocks stepped down from the trap and let the pony graze. It would stay there obediently until he returned. His head down against the rising wind, he glanced sideways at Eliza's shack but saw no light. Now that her nephew had been chosen, he knew what she was going to do. He had to find her before it was too late.

He came to the bridge and considered the planks. They had rotted faster through the autumn and would soon need replacing. He pressed on them with his foot; the bridge would hold his weight for now. Crossing over with deliberate and cautious steps, he regarded the dark water of the wide ditch. The wind was troubling the surface, causing small ripples to lap at the banks and reflect the dying light in broken patterns. The boards beneath his feet creaked and, as he neared the other side, one split, losing a piece to the deek. He hurried to the far side and stepped onto the land beyond the Saddling border. Here he looked to the Moremarsh track and studied the building storm. The cloud was stretching into the south, now, slowly creeping into his line of vision. The wall of the storm was outflanking the land and coming around to push from every direction. He had no doubt that it was also gathering behind him at the hill and he knew it would not be long before it closed in on all sides.

He judged the time from the remaining daylight and peered into the distance. His eyes were still as sharp as a bird of prey and his hearing was acute, but there was nothing to hear except the groan of the rising wind.

A distant flash caught his eye and he set off along the track that led eventually to the road. As he walked, he saw a small, dark movement a long way ahead. It rocked and dipped, approaching slowly with its windscreen catching lost sunbeams and throwing them out like a beacon. He could now relax. Peter Fetcher was bringing in his precious load.

Blacklocks pictured the battered old truck with the door that only half closed, the dashboard overflowing with cigarette butts and the other detritus of Peter's wages. As a fetcher, it was his job to leave the village and bring in anything needed, and Blacklocks knew he used the time to indulge in his out-marsh habits. He allowed them; Peter was loyal and discrete, a necessary emissary between the village and the world out there. This afternoon he was bringing in the most precious load of the past ten years; the second most precious, the minister thought, with a grin. Peter would deliver it to Blacklocks and then return the vehicle to its storage place until it was needed again. As Blacklocks trapped the delivery home, Fetcher would then walk back to the village. He was old but healthy and there was no need for Blacklocks to hold his pony for him.

The vehicle crept closer, followed at a distance by the clouds that were now turning to black as the sun gave up its fight. A dull burst of light lit one of the thunder stacks from deep inside. It was inaudible but it was a sign to Blacklocks that the future of his village could easily be taken from his hands.

His skin prickled and he drew in a sharp breath when he saw a small figure picking its cautious way across the Moremarsh grazing. Her white stick moved quickly from right to left, one hand outstretched. She was on unfamiliar ground, making her way south. She had crossed beyond Far Field, over the deek, left the Saddling land and turned her back on the Teaching. His rage, long smouldering in his chest, boiled to the surface and, carefully judging the speed of the on-coming vehicle against his own pace and hers, he knew he had little time to act. It wasn't only the weather that could take Saddling from him. Eliza had acted on her words and had finally left the village. Like a few before her, she was breaking the Lore and that made her more of a threat than any incoming storm.

Dan saw Tom approaching and hurried away over the graveyard wall and out into the field. He headed towards the sewer at the end of the pasture.

'Hey!' Tom called after him.'Hold up!'

Dan picked up his pace.

Tom ran to catch up with him. 'Hey, Dan!' he called. Panting, he fell in step.

'You leave me alone, now.'

'What's up? What's going on?'

'Leave me be. There's nothing you can do.'

Tom took hold of Dan's arm and stopped him. He could see that Dan had been crying, understandable on this anniversary, but what he couldn't work out was why Dan's face was so pale. His hair blew wildly around it as he stood in the oncoming wind. There were dark circles under his eyes, his cheekbones were more defined than before, but his lips less pink. His eyes were just as powerful, though red at the edges. They bored into Tom with more than their usual intensity.

'Nothing I can do about what?' Tom asked when he had recovered from the shock of Dan's appearance.

'It's how it is,' he said. 'They chose me. I always knew they'd do it.'

'Who chose you? The sheep?'

Dan moved away but, once again, Tom prevented him.

'You saw them,' Dan said. His stare was unsettling even through the tears that ran from his eyes.'You saw they chose me.'

'Those crows? They were enticed to everyone's house, for whatever bizarre reason. So?'

'And the whitebacks?'

'Yes, and?'

'They didn't come to us.' Dan's voice was desperate. 'If only one had come to us.'

Tom released his arm. 'Why are you upset because some sheep didn't come and crap on your lawn? I mean, the whole thing is bullshit, isn't it? May Day in December. What's that all about?'

'You don't understand.' Dan walked on.

Tom kept up with him. 'It's just a festival, mate. I don't know what you've got to do now you're the star, but it can't be that bad, can it?'

'It's more than a festival,' Dan replied. His voice was raised and the wind now struck him from the side. 'That's what you can't understand.'

'More than a festival? What are you talking about?'

'It's the Lore, ain't it? Goes back hundreds of year. It's a big responsibility

I got now. Too much. I didn't think it'd be like this.'

'What have you got to do?' Tom couldn't think what it might be. Making a speech perhaps or being the first to dance.

'It should never have been started.' Dan's eyes were fixed on the ditch ahead. 'It were all a story and just that. I never believed it, but I had to. It's how it is. You got no choice. Now I got chosen. I always knew I would.'

'You're not making any sense.' Tom saw the dyke they were approaching; wide with no bridge.

'We always know,' Dan continued to talk, ignoring Tom, his pace even and quick. 'We always know how it might be. It's what we're learned, what they, he, learn us from when we're down there, small, nippers. We grow up with it and it's for the good, and we know that. And thing is, it's always out there, distant like the hill or far off like the sea. You know it's there but you can't touch it, and it can't touch you. You might think on it at night, you might talk about it when you get to ten, eleven, maybe, but you put it out of mind as there's always more than one of you. It's always a chance there's always someone else, it's never you.'

'I don't know what you are talking about.'

'And it can't be cheated. I can't mess with the Lore.'

'What law?'

'It's in the numbers, ain't it? Thirteen to twenty-two, ten year, every ten year. No-one escapes it, not us boys.' He suddenly stopped and tilted his head back, glaring at the sky. Tom was about to ask him again what he was rambling about when Dan let out a long, deep yell. His voice swelled, pushing back the sound of the wind, a long helpless cry from deep within that peaked and then fell away. It descended into a moan as he crumpled to his knees, his head down, sobbing.

'Jesus...' Tom crouched down and put his arm around the young man. 'Dan. What's going on?'

He nearly stumbled as Dan sprang to his feet and pushed him away.

Dan hurried on faster, the ditch growing nearer.

'It's never you,' he said, and Tom could hear the crying that was rocking the foundations of his voice. 'It's always to be someone else, and then... It's so random!' He shouted to the darkening clouds. 'It's so fair. That's the whole point. It is so fair, so equal, could be any of us and then it's you, and it's so unfair. It ain't right.'

Aware that they were almost at the bank now, Tom tried to stop him but

Dan stepped out of his way, angry.

'They be alright, them others. They missed it, they were lucky.'

He was inches away from the edge and Tom acted. He pulled on Dan's shoulder, jerking him off his step and, with one hand on his chest, moved quickly in front and forced him back. His grey eyes started to focus. It was as if he had just woken up from a long sleep and realised where he was. He looked at the black water of the dyke and shook his head.

'Another few days and I would a-been too old,' he said. 'But I can't cheat it.'

'Too old for what?'

'You don't belong.' As Dan said it, he placed his hand over his heart and banged it. 'You and your kind don't belong here where I want it to be.'

Tom tried to pull Dan around but it was as if he had grown roots and planted himself in the field. 'Come on, Dan,' Tom persisted. 'I just want to...'

'What do you want?' Dan's tone changed in a second and his eyes narrowed. 'What is it you want from us, Tom Carey? What you doing here, really? What you come to do?'

'You know what I...'

'You come to change it, have you?' He was accusing now. 'You think you can come in after all the years and all the festivals and put a stop on it? Bring in your out-marsh ways and change what we do, how we live? Your talk of cars and telephones and trappings we don't never need? You want to change it?'

'No, I don't. I just want to...'

'We're not like you here, Tom Carey.' There was something in the way he said Tom's name that threatened. 'This is our place and this is what I got a-live with.'

'No.'

'And die with.'

'No, you don't. You can walk out of here, cross the bridge and keep walking. You don't have to do what you're told or believe what you're taught.' Tom's anger was rising with the biting wind.

'You don't understand.'

'This is no world for guys like you and Barry. And the others. Even Mark Blacklocks deserves to see what's out there. Get a television, get a radio, hear what's happening in the real world. You shouldn't be living in this kind of backwards, superstitious nowhere. No phone, for Christ's sake? It's the twenty-first century. God knows how you live like this.'

'God knows nothing here.' The wind fought Dan's long coattails and they flapped angrily behind him.

'Well, I do, Dan. And I know that you need to wake up and smell tomorrow.'

Dan's face changed suddenly. He was no longer confused or upset; the colour returned, his eyes widened, and his mouth opened. Before he knew what was happening, Tom felt two strong hands on his shoulders. Long fingers pressed painfully through his sheepskin.

'What good be a'morrow to me, now?' Dan shouted. He pushed himself away and ran back towards the village.

As Dan released him, Tom stepped back and slipped on the ditch-bank. He fell to his knees and grabbed at the grass. Cursing, he tried to pull himself back up but the soles of his trainers found no purchase on the steep slope. He began to slide, slowly at first and then faster, clawing wildly for anything he could. He felt water on his feet, panic in his chest. There was nothing to grip, no reeds to support his feet. The more he tried to scramble up, the further he slipped into the water.

'Dan!'

There was no reply. The sky was piling up and growling, black clouds massed faster in the distance with flashes of lightning within them.

'Dan!' he screamed.

His memories came back to taunt him; echoes and rushing water. He was in up to his knees now. The sucking mud was slithering around his ankles, sneaking in under his jeans, creeping its way up his legs. Any movement only slipped him further into the ditch.

'Someone help me!' he shouted as the water swamped his thighs and his feet sank deeper into the sludge.

A hand grabbed his wrist. A sharp pain shot through his shoulder as a rough palm and a strong arm dragged him against the bank. The mud gave up its grip reluctantly, but in a second he was out of the deek and face down in the field.

'I need a-speak with you, Tom Carey,' Barry said. 'And I need a-talk honest.'

Thirty-one

Dylan leant towards the windscreen and used his sleeve to wipe away the condensation. He clicked the wipers to double speed and slowed the car. The clouds were so dark, now, that it was hard to tell if it was day or night and he had been using headlights since he left Maidstone. Vehicles approached with long, drawn out beams of light reflected on the slippery road surface, driven slowly by cautious drivers intent on reaching their destinations before the storm hit.

He glanced quickly at the map on the passenger seat and then back to the road. He was dropping down from the hill towards the marsh, leaving the heaviest of the storm clouds behind. They had chased him for the last couple of hours, but soon they would be directly overhead. He turned up the radio.

'...on this winter solstice evening as a storm threatens the south coast. Due to the unexpected east-west direction of what some observers are predicting will be a hurricane, the Met Office has issued a severe flood warning from Margate, through the channel to as far as Southampton. With winds gusting up to eighty miles an hour and with a full moon, experts are expecting an unusually high tide in the Dover sea area at ten p.m. Householders are preparing...'

He'd been listening to similar bulletins all afternoon, and he turned the dial to try and find some music.

'... Thames, becoming easterly, eight; heavy rain, 1,000 falling. Dover, easterly, nine; heavy rain, visibility poor, 980 falling. Wight, easterly...'

It seemed that every channel was reporting on the rising storm. He clicked back to the news and turned the volume down. Taking a left and then rounding a wide bend, he slowed the car as he approached the top of a hill. Ahead and below, the marshes stretched out wide and flat. Visibility wasn't so bad down there. He could even see the sun glinting on the sea far away. Tiny black lines moved slowly on the battleship grey water and he was glad he was not on a ship out there right now. They were in for some rough seas if these weather forecasts were correct and, glancing at the chasing storm in his rear-view mirror, they were. He guessed it would be over the marsh in less than an hour.

Downhill, the wide road eventually narrowed and began to twist, lined with high hedges and grassy banks. He was far from the dual carriageways and motorways now and driving into rural countryside. He reached a junction and, checking that there was no-one behind him, picked up the road atlas and studied it. He still had a long way to go and the storm was already tumbling from the crest of the hill to the fields below.

Beside him on the passenger seat, Tom's bible lay open at the family tree. Next to it was the list of names and dates from the Saddling transcripts starting from when the records began. Each date was ten years apart and all of them December 21st or 22nd.

They were all death records.

Tom's socks were caked with foul-smelling mud. His trainers werre lost in the ditch; his feet were freezing.

'You can start by telling me what's going on,' he said, picking his way between the sheep dung and the anthills. 'Where have you two been all day? Why is Dan so upset?'

'I got a-start wi' asking you a question,' Barry replied. He had to trot to keep up with Tom's faster pace.

'Me first. Where will I find Blacklocks?' He glanced up at the sky. Most of what he could see to the east was cloud. The sun was hidden behind a blanket of dull grey to the west.

'You won't get near Blacklocks now, not 'til after... Not 'til later.'

'Then I want the key to the church. Who has it?'

'Only 'im. But let me ask, Tom, what's so important as a-keep you 'ere?'

'You know why I am here.'

'Aye, but that don't mean I understand. What's so important?'

'You wouldn't get it.'

'Give us a try. Prehaps I can 'elp.'

Tom stopped to catch his breath. He saw Barry's ruddy face, wide-eyed and eager. He had a smile of anticipation on his lips.

'I said I got a-talk plain, Tom, and I'll try. Since you come 'ere, you got me, well, 'oping, I s'pose.' Barry took a step back and checked out Tom's face. 'You're looking better. Told you you would.'

Tom had no recollection of being told that but now was not the time to think about it. He was wet and angry and he only wanted to see the diary and get out of this place. He was through being civil with anyone who was keeping him away from his inheritance. Barry's strong grip on his arm stopped him from striding onwards.

'You're a chance fur many a thing, Tom,' Barry said. 'I wants a-tell you that.'

'Great, thanks, now can I...?'

'I see it. I'm not good enough a mate for you, you being from out-marsh, but I wants a-'elp you. Even if you don't speak a-me again nor see me again after a'night. Is all I want. Let me?'

Tom accepted his sincerity and relented. 'Okay. You know about the Saddling Diary. He keeps it in the crypt. He's given me the run-around for it, for some reason. That's what I'm after because when I've seen it I might be closer to finding... You know this.'

'Aye, but why d'you want it?'

'You know. Everyone knows!'

'Will it 'elp you find out who you are, that be it?'

'What?' Tom was not in the mood for more riddles. He started walking.

'Alright,' Barry said as he followed. 'What say I 'elps you find it. What d'you do then?'

'Read it, copy things out, leave.'

'You won't stay fur the rest of the night?'

'You joking?'

'You don't want a-see what comes later?'

'Don't care.'

'You do, Tom Carey. It be in your name.'

There it was again. "Look to your name." Tom stopped and put his hand on Barry's chest. 'What do you mean?'

Barry leant in towards Tom so that their heads were close together.

'I be torn, Tom,' he said. 'You got a-understand 'ow this be 'ard fur me. I been brought up different a-you, we all 'as, but I wants a-'elp you. I wants a-see you find what you come fur and then leave, if that be what you really wants. But I wants you a-stay an' all. I wants you a-...' He looked back to the inn.

Tom followed his gaze, but there was no-one around. He felt Barry take his hand and didn't pull away.

'I...' Barry sighed. He was clearly having trouble expressing himself. 'I wants a-'elp you find your book,' he said. 'After that, well, I got the evening service, I s'ppose.' He stopped again and took a deep breath. He was really struggling. 'Walk on,' he said, and led Tom towards the back of the inn.

'Listen. You seen we 'ave our own ways 'ere in the village. it's 'ow we live, and it works good most times. A'night be different, though, and we all been brought up, us like Dan, Aaron, and me, taught by Blacklocks like our faders were taught by 'is, and that's 'ow it's gone on. So, there's things we learn a-keep in-marsh, in-village, more. We 'ave to. It's 'ow we follow things. So I can't tell you all I wants, but I seen what you got fur Dan, and...'

'Hang on,' Tom let go of his hand; it suddenly felt wrong to be holding it. 'Got for Dan?'

'You got 'is friendness, like you 'ave mine, but I know you got something deeper there fur 'im. Many do.' Barry shook his head as though he were trying to rid it of an impure thought. 'Dan's always been my marker since we was born so close together.'

'What is it with all this "marker" stuff?'

'The dole-stones mark the edge of our land and we need go no further. Like them, Dan keeps me in my boundaries according a the teaching and I keep 'im in 'is. I got the easier job there, I can tell you. Our marker's the one as gives us away on being wed, the one as puts us in our grave, and I got a-do me duty...' He sniffed and then shook his head again. 'We're there for each other,' he said. 'Is all. But I see that you got the same feeling toward 'im and that be difficult fur me, but... Oh, bugger. I wish I'd listened to more schooling. I'd know 'ow a-say things better.' Barry turned away and took a couple of paces marshwards before returning quickly and stepping right up to Tom. 'I'll 'elp you find your book. But I needs a promise from you, Tom Carey. You promise a-do whatever I says. If you can do that, then I'll not only consider you me friend but I'll be your marker.'

'I... I'm not sure...' Tom had no idea what Barry was trying to say, but he was openly offering to help find the thing he came for. 'Okay, deal,' he said. 'You help me and I'll do as I'm told.'

Barry raised his hand and touched Tom's cheek. 'I don't want a-lose you an' all.'

Tom surprised himself; he didn't flinch or take a step back. The hand had been there before and it felt strangely reassuring.

Barry patted his cheek and withdrew his hand. 'We got a-be quick and tender-footed. They'll be gathering at the inn afore long. The church'll be empty, Blacklocks'll be in preparation and so will Daniel.' He checked the sky. 'The weather's fouling in on an easterly, it's... festival day. It always storms fur the Saddling and things 'ave a-be done right. That's all you need

211

a-know. Trust me, friend, and I'll always be there fur you. Trust me?'

'Sure.'

It seemed like the easiest thing to say at the time.

'Right, then I'll go fetch you some bootshoes.' Barry looked at Tom's feet. 'Some dewlaps an' all. And you got no other trousers?' Tom shook his head. 'I'll see what I can find. You get washed, though you're like a-get fair dung-wiped by the time we gets back. You got a torch?' Tom shook his head again. 'You're right in a bad way, ain't you?'

Barry gave a short, quiet laugh. It made Tom realise that no matter what was going on, no matter how strange, dramatic, or odd the last two days had been, this guy was always there with a smile. It, too, was reassuring.

'So, how can you help me get the book?'

'You and your stupid book,' Barry said. 'I'll be back dreckly-minute. Get up a'your room, say nothing a'no-one, keep quiet, wait on me. My fader's got a torch. I can use that.'

Barry scurried away along the back wall of the inn.

'Why do we need a torch?' Tom called as quietly as he could against the wind. 'Where are we going?'

Barry turned and pointed directly at the ground.

Dylan was lost. He had outrun the storm front, though it was still raining hard behind him, and he had arrived close to his destination during a lessening of the weather. He had passed a roundabout, found a sign for Brenzett, and passed a garage. The road that he needed should have been on his right but he could only see a narrow track. Pulled up on the verge, with the car's interior light doing its best, he was convinced that the road atlas was out of date. There was no mention of Saddling anywhere other than the old library maps. The track must be what was left of an earlier road. It was just wide enough to take the car and he decided that he had to try it.

He picked up a sketch that had been tucked away at the back of the family bible. It showed a group of cottages built in a semi-circle facing a small church-like building that sat on a low hill. A man stood outside the church wearing long white robes and other people were kneeling on the ground facing him. A body was being carried from the church on a simple bier and, in the background, the image showed a storm, not unlike the one that was just about to crash down on Dylan's head.

He turned the drawing over. It was mounted on a postcard and a postmark showed the date 1975. It was addressed to Maud Carey and held a cryptic message, "It still goes on. Honour your ancestors." It was signed, "Matthew Carey, your cowardly father." Dylan put it back, checked the time on the car's dashboard and looked at the skies. The hanging storm clouds were rolling down the hills and the brief period of relative calm was coming to an end.

Putting the car in gear, he swung out in an arc across the road, heading for the lane. He had no idea what the message on the postcard meant but it unnerved him. It was the reason he was chasing down his friend and edging his way slowly along a rutted lane with the rain once more pounding the car roof. Something bad was taking place at the end of that track and Tom was unwittingly caught up in it.

Thirty-two

Blacklocks stood at his window, his head down but his eyes raised above the houses. The path-lamps were already lit; dusk would be brief this evening. He held a china cup and saucer in one hand and stirred the black tea with the other. He watched with interest as Barry Cole hurried from behind the inn and ran towards his own house. His curiosity was aroused further when he caught a glimpse of Tom Carey entering the inn through the back door. He smiled to himself, happy that, for all its risks, his plan was falling into place.

The fire was lit in the grate behind him and two large wing-backed chairs faced it. He set the cup and saucer gently on a small table beneath the window.

'Is everything in place?' a young man's voice asked from the other side of a chair back.

'I believe it is,' Blacklocks replied. 'Peter will see to your vehicle and your... other inconvenience.'

'I mean for this evening. We are not convinced that your plan was the most secure,' the man said, his voice quiet and yet confident. 'Can you assure us?'

A light grew in the back bedroom of the inn and Blacklocks saw a vague shadow move across the window. 'Everything necessary has been put in place,' he said. 'Traps baited with curiosity are soon to be sprung by realisation.'

'Are you sure of the outcome?' his second guest asked.

Blacklocks sighed and closed his eyes. 'Of course. Yes,' he replied. 'It is the only way that history can be brought to its conclusion.'

'The Lore is clear.'

Blacklocks opened his eyes. 'The Lore is what I make it. And I have made it thus.'

He heard a rustle from the chairs and then whispered words that, for all his acute hearing, he was unable to catch. Papers were sifted together, more whispering followed, and he waited, picking up his tea and enjoying another sip. As he watched the green, he saw the daylight dim further as though someone was turning down a lamp. The more distant houses shifted into darkness one by one. Lights were lit in others and, by the time his teacup was empty and back on its saucer, he saw Barry Cole return to the inn from his house. He watched him pull on the doors of the barrel chute, only to find them locked. Blacklocks let out a mild laugh.

'There will be no dissent?' his guest asked. 'It will be done freely? Peter Fetcher mentioned some trouble at the choosing today.'

Blacklocks followed Barry with his narrow eyes; the smile had still not left his lips. 'All is taken care of,' he said. 'I assure you. Cards have been played in the correct order.'

'But he has been given trust, we heard.'

'Exactly. And that is to our good.' He saw Barry enter the inn by the back door and, a few moments later, the light in the upstairs room was extinguished. 'Actually, it worked more in our favour than I planned. He will be willing.'

Blacklocks turned to the room. 'Finish your tea. Enjoy it. We have time a-while yet and the hourglass has a way to run.'

There was a raucous atmosphere in the Crow and Whiteback; villagers gathered around the roaring fire, the curtains were drawn against the weather, Mr Seeming was playing melodies on a squeezebox, and Sally Rolfe was singing songs of silly crank-fellows in love with dizzy maidens. Young Jacob Seeming, having tasted his first jug of bathtub, was sleeping soundly, propped up in a corner chair. Other boys had decorated his head with a wreath of dead flowers and left a knife lying on his chest pointing towards his throat so that, when he woke, he would be in for a shock. Mick Farrow sat with a group of cronies banging their glasses together and spilling ale while Aaron Fetcher and his marker, Billy Farrow, played table-cailes, rolling a small ball to knock down skittles; the winner of each round taking a deep slug of burr wine.

Irene Cole, the only woman in the inn, moved carefully between the tables collecting glasses and taking them to the bar. She avoided the pinches and slaps of men falling well into their cups.

'Where you be at?' she called through to the back of the bar. 'Susan Vye? Who's running your establishment?' There was no reply, so she put the glasses by the sink and focused her attention on the waiting customers. 'Who'll be next?'

Several men thrust forward empty tankards and Samuel Tidy tried to push through the hatch to help himself to a keg.

'You stay out a there,' Irene ordered with as much jollity as she could muster. She pushed the bumbling old man back and closed the hatch, bolting it underneath. 'You go orderly or I'll close the taps.' She took a glass and held it under a keg, calling over her shoulder, 'Susan! Where...?'

She stopped and flicked off the beer tap.

Barry was crouched down just beyond the door to the passage, Tom Carey huddled low behind him. She was about to open her mouth when her son lifted a finger to his lips, his face contorted with the need for secrecy. He pointed to the trapdoor on which Irene was standing, then to himself, and then downwards.

'What you at, Mistus Cole?' someone called across the counter. 'You seeing ghosts?'

Irene filled the glass and took a deliberate step to her left to put it down on the bar.

'Don't you be spouting off about ghosts, not a'night,' she said. From the corner of her eye she saw Barry lifting the trapdoor a few inches and sliding through it. Turning to the waiting men, she grabbed a glass in each hand. 'Who's next?' She called across to the room, 'Hey, there, Seeming, shut your squeezing of that old reed-box. Save Sally's voice for when it be needed.' Her own voice was steady but her heart was racing and there was bile in her throat. Some of the customers turned away to look at Seeming who had stopped playing and was now standing.

'What's rotting in you, Irene?' he shouted, cheerfully enough. 'Plenty a time yet and she's got a voice like a sparr.'

'Tell 'er a-use it, then,' Mick Farrow said, and others laughed. 'Sounding like a bar-goose a'me.'

The clatter of skittles on the stone floor accompanied the sound of a glass smashing.

'You go easy over there,' Irene called. 'You boys should be at 'ome, not getting brandy-legged.'

'Ah, play your music, Seeming!' Mick Farrow called out. 'Night's for celebrating, not shouting at Mistus Cole.'

'Pour me ale!'

Other voices added to the heckles that were tinted with merriment but the volume dropped when Mark Blacklocks came in, his long hair bedraggled and dripping.

'Storm's starting,' he announced.

Samuel Tidy banged his glass on the bar. 'Ale, woman!'

Behind him the music picked up. Sally's clear voice sang out, others joined in the song, and the men returned to their talk and their games.

Irene took Samuel's glass from him and moved across to the keg. She saw the trap door closing. 'Right, then,' she said, finding it hard to keep the glass steady in her hand. 'Looker's Crook, was it, Sam?'

Tom followed Barry down into the darkness where Barry's torch picked out stone walls and grey cobwebs, black patches of mould, and a row of shelves laden with clay jugs and bottles. The cellar stank of rot and stagnant water and, once he had closed the trapdoor silently behind him, Tom felt the solid walls of claustrophobia advancing on him. The only other light came from a lantern that was burning in the far corner. The rugged earth floor showed worn tracks between the steps and the bottles, the kegs, and the barrel chute.

He could hear heavy footsteps above him as Irene Cole served the men. This was backed by chattering, music and singing, the words distorted and incoherent through the planked ceiling.

'Where are we going?' he whispered to Barry when they stood side by side at the bottom of the steps.

'Aye. Where are you going?' A shadow moved and a hand picked up the lantern. 'What are you about?'

Thirty-three

The car dipped unevenly from side to side as Dylan struggled to keep it on flat ground. The track was so pitted and unkempt that it was an impossible task. The exhaust scraped on ridges, the wing mirrors scratched through close hedges, and all the time he was bent forwards peering through the driving rain that covered the windscreen as fast as the wipers could dispel it. The headlights picked out nothing ahead apart from close puddles until, after a mile of or so, he saw a glow of orange. Coming closer, he could see that it was the back indicator of a car; his car.

It was parked on a grass verge that widened at the entrance to a field. He pulled up beside it and heaved himself across into the passenger seat. Pressing his face and hands to the window, he strained to see. It was clear that there was no-one there. Back in the driving seat, he tried Tom's mobile number one more futile time.

He carried on his painfully slow journey, arriving several minutes later at a T-junction. Ahead was a gate. Left and right the road was little better than the track he had been on. Another car was parked a little way along but there was no sign of anyone near it. He studied his sketched map again and found his position. If the village of Saddling did exist it was dead ahead a few miles more.

It was madness to be out there at that time of day in worsening weather, but with Tom out of reach and, hard though it was to imagine, in trouble, he knew that the only thing he could do now was walk. Parking the car as far off the road as possible, he killed the engine. He gathered his laptop and the family bible that Tom would need to see to be convinced and climbed out. The rain was persistent, the wind was strong, and he was glad of the hooded mackintosh he had brought with him. An umbrella would be no good, so, pulling up his hood and tucking the bible inside the coat, he locked the car and headed towards the gate.

'Bain't nothing to do with the ceremony, Mistus Vye,' Barry said. 'Nothing for you a-mind 'bout.' Susan didn't reply. 'Mistus Vye?'

She stood as if in a trance with the lantern held close to her chest and her back to the far wall. She was staring at him but not seeing him. Her eyes, flickering in the light, were wet with tears that ran in streams over her pale cheeks and into the corners of her mouth. They trickled on to drop from her chin.

'Mistus Vye?' Barry repeated, and her eyes moved to him.

'There's danger down there,' she said, her voice quiet.

'We'll go careful. You can trust me.'

'Not another one lost,' she said.

'What does she mean?' Tom whispered, but Barry shushed him with a wave of his hand.

'You should be upstairs,' Barry said. 'Dan'll be in preparation. You should be wi''im.'

She shook her head slowly from side to side and tilted it when it came to rest.

'The light has gone from my life,' she said. 'It's been taken from us all.'

'Barry, the book.' Tom hissed.

His words animated Susan a little and her expression chilled him. 'Diaries are for things to come,' she said as more tears dripped from her face. 'There's nothing to come.'

'Go a'Daniel.' Barry aimed his torch towards the steps and Susan nodded.

Silently, she glided across the cellar, pale and upright. Tom and Barry made way for her. She took a bottle from the shelf and clutched it to her chest before putting a foot on the bottom step. She climbed the steps as if the bottle carried the weight of the world and used her shoulder to open the trap door. Some light spilt down and Barry pulled Tom across the room into the darkness where he switched off his torch. The sounds from above amplified briefly until the trap door was closed and the room again fell to black.

It's just like having your eyes closed, Tom told himself. It's just darkness. He heard a latch move and then the torch light was back, giving him something on which to focus. The circle of light showed up a small wooden door about two feet square. Barry pulled it open to reveal more darkness beyond.

'I can't go in there.'

'Bain't no other way, friend.' Barry crouched down and shone the torch into a tunnel.

'No, you don't understand.'

'It be the only other way in a'the church. It'll not take long. Down, along and up. It be easy, Tom. Many 'ave done it afore.'

'My parents...' Tom heard the screams and the rushing water. He felt the river pouring in from above. 'They died...'

'Then I be very sorry fur you. That's not a good thing. We must go quick.'

Barry stepped through the door one leg at a time and the torch light immediately faded.

'No, wait.'

'You want this 'ellish book you come fur, or you want a-stay 'ere?'

'I'll stay. You get it.'

Tom was aware of a hand on his arm as Barry reached back through the entrance and searched for him. He tugged Tom gently a pace further to the door. Tom crouched. 'It's only darkness,' he told himself.

'Trust me, Tom,' Barry said, and took Tom's hand. 'It ain't far.'

The hand in his gave Tom some courage. He focused his eyes on the beam of light as he crouched into the tunnel. The ground fell away from him in a few rough steps until it was soft beneath his feet. The roof was just high enough for him to stand as long as he kept his knees bent.

'Keep me talking,' he said.

'Aye, and you keep a-following.'

Barry let go of his hand and started off along the tunnel. Tom could see, as he followed close, that the walls were planked. When the torch flicked up to the ceiling, he could see that it, too, was wooden. 'It's been built well,' he told himself. 'There's no river above, nothing is leaking in. The floor is solid earth, it's not far, it's only darkness.' But the screams and memories were jostling at the edge of his mind and taunting his imagination. He was thinking both of what had happened before and what could possibly happen now, and he wanted neither in his mind.

'What's this for?' he managed to ask, hoping that talking would occupy his mind-space where the memories wanted to be.

'Goes back a'the smuggling,' Barry replied. His head was slightly bent, his woollen hat touching the roof. With his chin nearly on his chest, his voice was muffled. 'Even Saddling once got in on the smuggle trade, back in some very old days. Some of the fetchers would go far, bring in brandy from out-marsh. They'd keep it in the crypt, I was told, and use this a-get free a'the inn. Not that anyone never said nothing 'bout no-one coming 'ere a-find 'em. No-one came a'Saddling. None does now. I reckon the stories be midden and Blacklocks built this a-visit Mistus Vye secret. You wi' me, Tom?'

'With you all the way, friend.'

'Why, Tom,' Barry said, and there was mirth in his voice, 'you be talking Saddling way, now.'

Tom heard the splash of a footstep in water.

'What's that?' He stopped in his tracks.

'Standing seep, is all,' Barry said.

Tom saw the torch beam lowered to the ground where it showed up a small pool of water in the dip of the tunnel.

'Only where we be,' Barry reassured him, 'just at the middle, lowest point, see? Bain't the flooding coming yet, least, I don't think it be. Walk on, best scuttle.'

Tom felt the ground start to rise; there was more resistance against his shin muscles. He kept thoughts of light in his mind and tried to imagine daytime and sunshine, clean air and open fields, but the walls were close in around him. The tunnel was cloying and black, apart from the torch light that seemed so inadequate. The air was foetid and damp, the humidity was making him sweat. His breathing came in short breaths and he was unable to control his imagination. He pictured the ground shaking, dust and dirt falling, wood splitting, the sides of the tunnel closing in, water rising. He imagined the last gasps of breath as he drowned beneath the earth.

He hit against something solid. It was Barry. He had stopped.

'Keep going,' Tom said, his hands trembling.

'Be steady.' Barry moved again, but this time upwards.

Tom heard another latch click. His feet found steps and, after taking a few of them, he was free from the tunnel. They had come up through the floor of the crypt. All around was darkness but there was more air and, even though they were still below ground, he could stand upright.

'Keep still,' Barry whispered.

They stood in silence until Barry was satisfied that there was no-one in the church above. After some rustling, Tom saw the welcome glow of a hurricane lamp. Barry switched off the torch. He stood on the other side of the table, the lantern between them.

'Get what you come fur and be fast,' Barry said. 'You don't understand what'll 'appen a'me if I gets caught down 'ere.'

Tom nodded and hurried to the wooden cabinet.

He knelt down before it and pulled on the small, round handle. The door would not open.

'It's locked.'

'I would a-guessed that.'

'Will there be a key?'

'I don't know. 'Ow would I know? I never been allowed down 'ere afore.'

'What shall I do?'

'Oh, Tom Carey! You got no idea you 'ave you? Kick the bugger.'

Tom laughed with relief. 'You used a misword.'

'Aye,' Barry replied. 'I reckon I'll be using more if you don't kick it in with me best bootshoe I give you.'

For some reason, the thought of kicking Blacklock's cabinet to pieces appealed to Tom.

'After the bloody run-around he's given me,' he said, more to himself than Barry, 'I don't give a flying...'

He kicked the door and the wood split easily.

'That felt good,' he said as he ripped the splinters and shattered pieces from inside the doorframe.

Now that he was so close to his prize, it all seemed so simple. He reached into the void and felt around. For one horrible second he thought the cabinet was empty but his hand fell on something hard and rectangular. His fingers reached around it and he lifted a thick, weighty, book.

He was so focused on laying his hand on the village diary that he didn't notice the crypt darkening behind him.

Across the Saddling land at East Sewer the rain fell in waves. The ditches boiled in the onslaught. Reeds bent in the wind and voles scrambled from their holes to find higher ground as the dyke water rose. It bubbled; each hard pelt of rain causing ripples that collided with others, tumbled over each other, and combined, massing and pushing towards the banks where frogs clung to the droke-weed, their eyes wide in panic.

At the edge of the level, a wall of thick planks held the sewer closed, forcing the run-off from the hills to take a seaward course. Painted numbers showed the depth and these were fast disappearing beneath the rising tide. The pressure built and the flow found the tiniest of gaps between the hammered-down planks where a steady run fed into the East Sewer. This quickly became a rivulet, the rivulet a stream, and more cracks opened. Rainwater added to the crush from the run-off and the last of the depth markers quickly drowned.

Deep moans of thunder rolled out above the churning ditch, the wind blew through the reeds forcing them to sing their swan songs, and the downpour pummelled the land in a discord of no-rhythm mayhem. A plank creaked as it bowed. Unable to hold back the pounding from behind, a fissure appeared from one side to the other, the agitation of the flow too much for the old wood to hold back. With a last groan, it split, and a wall of cold, dark water poured into Saddling's moat. It kept coming, breaking the lower planks until there was no defence against the onslaught. The banks crumbled around the gate while supports and timber alike were carried away around the village as easily as toy boats over a waterfall.

Dylan had half run, half walked along the side of a long field. His shoes were soaked and muddy, his face was awash. His hand was raw from carrying the laptop case; his chest hurt and his heart pumped with the exertion of the last couple of miles.

The last throws of the dying dusk fought bravely with the approaching storm, and, squinting, he made out the shadow of a ditch. Some planks crossed it and, through the brief pauses in the lash of the squalling rain, he thought he could see dim lights in the distance.

The ditch he had come to was nearly full. Soon it would overflow and the planks would be submerged. He held the bible tighter under his mackintosh, gripped his laptop, and put one foot on the bridge. He felt it shudder beneath him. A second step and all was well. He kept to the centre of it, afraid that a strong blast of wind might throw him over.

Halfway across he was aware of something moving.

He stopped to look, facing directly into the wind and used his free hand to wipe his eyes. What was that? It was coming at him fast, a jumble of white against the inky black of the background. Shielding his eyes, he stepped closer to edge for a better look and saw a wall of water racing towards him. That was one thing, but something was being carried ahead of the flow, turning over on the fast-approaching wave.

A flash of lightning in the near distance froze the image. He saw a woman's body, a white dress, blonde hair tangled across her face and splayed out into the churning ditch. Her dead eyes were staring, her mouth open, and a deep gash across her throat told Dylan this was not a drowning.

He had no more time to think as another figure darted in from the edge of his vision, moving fast towards him.

223

Before he knew what was happening, the wave had reached the bridge, smashing into it with force enough to jolt the planks. He instinctively took a step back and his foot sank ankle deep through rotten wood. The planks gave way on the far side and tipped suddenly. A blow to the back of his head sent him falling forward. The bible slipped from under his coat and his hands reached out to cushion his fall. The laptop dropped as he fell headlong into the ditch. Cold, unstoppable water flooded his mouth as his foot was dragged down by the broken plank. He kicked at it, thrashed with his arms, his mackintosh wrapping around him like a straightjacket. His hood smothered his face, hampering his breathing. He struggled wildly and lashed out until his foot broke free from the rotted plank. He surfaced, pushed the hood away and reached out for what was left of the bridge. He caught a firm hold of one remaining piece of wood and gasped for breath, safe.

He looked up to see a white-haired man draped in a rain cloak gloating down at him; a fat man who, despite the weather, had a cigarette hanging from the corner of his mouth. Dylan reached up to him for help but another blow with a tyre wrench knocked his breath away. He took no more. Eliza's lifeless body crashed into him. One arm stretched out and wrapped around him in welcome, dragging him away on the rushing current. The body turned over, pulling him under, and neither resurfaced again. The bible banged against the bank momentarily before it, too, sank out if sight taking all clues and warnings with it.

Thirty-four

'Tom, we got a-go, now.' Barry was halfway through the trap door, the last of the lamp spill glowing up from below ground as he looked down into the light. 'Tom, quick now.'

'Give me the lamp.' He felt his way towards the glow, his hip bumping painfully into the table. Barry held the light up and Tom tipped the book towards it. The cover simply read, 'Saddling.'

'This must be it.'

'Tom, we got a-leave.'

Barry came back up from the tunnel and put the lantern on the table. He switched on the torch and was about to blow out the light when he said, 'Blacklooks'll know we been in 'ere, so makes no never-mind, leastwise,' and carried it back to the trapdoor. 'You take me torch. Go first and fast.'

With the book firmly in one hand and the torch in the other, Tom began the descent. He was elated that he finally had what Maud had sent him to find.

His elation soon evaporated when the beam of his torch reflected movement onto the walls. He saw water bubbling and rising, soaking up through the ground, and he drew in a breath.

'Aye,' said Barry, so close behind him that Tom could feel the heat from the lantern on his neck. 'And it be coming quick. Flooding's started.'

'Flooding?'

'Just get moving, friend. Straight ahead. Don't be a-feared. I'm right 'ere fur you.'

Tom felt a shove in the small of his back and stepped down into the water. By the time he was on the tunnel floor the level was to his knees.

He pressed his back against the wall and froze. It was like his dream. He was being held; some invisible force was preventing him from moving and yet it forced his eyes open and made him witness the nightmare he was in.

'I can't do this,' he said. 'Go back.'

'Keep on.'

'I can't do this.'

A powerful arm yanked him away from the wall. His head scraped on the wooden ceiling and he stumbled forward.

'You 'ave the word "fast" where you comes from?' Another push from behind set his legs in stumbling motion. 'You're as stubborn as a ram going a-be wethered. Keep on.'

Tom started walking, dragging his feet through the rising tide, keeping his eyes focused directly on the torch beam. It showed the water level rising up the walls and the memories crowded in again. It's only water, he kept telling himself. It's only a tunnel. We'll be out of it in...

A vibration began somewhere deep in the earth around him and the surface of the flooding rippled. An ominous rumble seeped into the cramped space, chilling Tom's skin and restricting his breathing.

'What's that?' He moved on numb legs.

'Keep on.'

Tom felt the ground dip and the water rose to his waist. He tried to wade faster, the beam of light pointing into the darkness where he longed to see the rising steps to the cellar. His head banged against the creaking ceiling where the support planks bowed and scraped his scalp. He bent his neck painfully. He was about to throw up when the ground began to slope upwards, giving him hope that the ordeal was nearly over.

The rumbling intensified and filled the tunnel with a deep tremor that he could feel in his lungs. He held the book out of the water and pushed on as, somewhere behind him, he heard wood split. A loud crack was followed by a muffled splash.

'What the...?' His foot banged against a step. He saw the way out and struggled for it. Stooping, his legs now aching, the book growing heavy in his hand, he took the last two steps on his knees. He crawled from the tunnel door and staggered upright, gasping. The ground was dry, the book was safe. He looked at the cellar steps.

'What if we are seen?' he asked, turning around.

There was no sign of lantern light from within the tunnel.

'Barry!' he hissed, sweeping the torch around.

No answer.

He put the book on the steps and returned to the tunnel door. He shone his light but saw nothing except bubbling water and a few floating planks.

His heart raced, pumping the memories of the accident with each beat. They leapt up, stabbing him with shrieks and cries; the hands of the drowning reaching up for rescue; the shouts of men, the screams of children; the echoes of the hopeless writhing in desperation as tonnes of rubble crushed the helpless. He fought back the bile in his throat and leant into the darkness. The torch showed him nothing. He called again, but again there was no reply, just the churning and the rumbling.

He closed his eyes, told himself that he could do this and crouched back into the tunnel. One step and then two, three, and he was back at the floor level. He opened his eyes; the water was up to his chest, the surface dancing madly around the broken beams and fallen roof wood. Clumps of earth broke away in places but the ground above it held. The surface was so disturbed that he couldn't see beneath it. There was still no sign of Barry.

Tom took a deep breath and dived under.

The Saddling diary waited in near darkness. A few narrow shafts of light shone through split boards in the creaking ceiling as Susan moved about behind the bar above. Voices, the singing and the laughing, sneaked in through the cracks with the clink of glasses and every now and then the rattle of skittles. The dull thump of torrential rain underscored it all and drops leaked through the barrel-chute hatch to drip into a puddle where a mouse drank.

China bottles and jugs, dulled by the years of settling dust, lingered on shelves. Somewhere in a dark corner the mouse moved on to gnaw at wood.

Slowly, the darkness in the room lightened; a brief flash followed by a faint glimmer. The churning in the tunnel eased, the water calmed, and the rumbling died away. A light shone through from beneath, coming closer until Tom broke the surface with a huge gasp. He crawled frantically up the steps, the torch in one hand, the other dragging Barry. He backed himself into the room on all fours and reached back to grab the body. He heaved, once, twice, and it slid into the room face down. Tom scrambled to it, turned it over onto its back and dragged the weight up, throwing his arms around the man and pulling him to his chest. Barry's head flopped back. His eyes were closed. No sign of life. Tom knew what he should do. He shifted to cradled Barry in his arms and opened his mouth. His own was dry and he was breathing fast as he pulled Barry's head towards him. This was too intimate but he had no choice. He drew in a long breath and held it. No matter how much he told himself that he had to do this, when their lips were about to meet he yelled with frustration and let the body go. It fell onto its back, hitting the floor with a thud.

Liquid spurted from Barry's mouth. He choked and gasped, choked again and rolled onto his side, coughing up water that had been knocked from his lungs.

Tom scrambled over to him and shone the torch but still didn't know what to do. He said his name over again, swept his hair away from his face, held his head until Barry finally waved him away and rolled to his knees. The coughing slowly subsided as he knelt facing Tom. He had blood on his face. His hand reached for it, he touched it and then checked his fingers.

'Bloody roof,' he said, and then opened his eyes wide at Tom and grinned. 'Blacklooks couldn't build a barth wi' a beelte. Second time a'day I nearly got chosen,' he said. 'I got a-thank you, Tom Carey.'

'You're okay, mate,' Tom replied, too relieved to ask for any explanations.

'A man's got a-do by right by his friends,' Barry said. 'You're there fur me, I'm 'ere fur you. We did good a-gether, didn't we? It be the right book?'

'I bloody hope so.' Tom reached across and swung the tunnel door shut. 'Is that going to flood?'

'Prehaps,' Barry said. 'But maybe not a while yet. We got a-get dry.' He put one hand to his head. 'Ah, bugger!' He said. 'I lost me wool-cap.'

Tom pointed the torch up to the trapdoor and the increased sounds of laughter on the other side.

'Going to be harder to sneak up there without being seen,' he said, and collected the book.

Barry took the torch from him and shone it towards the barrel-chute. He picked out the bolt. Switching off the light, he put it on a shelf and pulled the bolt back. 'Follow me. You'll be 'right this time, Tom. We're going 'bove ground.'

Upstairs, in his bedroom, Dan sat naked at his table and watched the advancing storm. Distant flashes of lightning showed black clouds blocking out the stars. He would never see them again.

Looking down at the portfolio now open on the desk, his eyes fell on drawings of his parents; Steven Vye at nineteen, a wreath of dead flowers garlanding his head, his white shirt open at his chest, his white trousers, bare feet; an image of simplicity and innocence. Dan wondered what kind of man he had been. He knew that he had worked the inn, the same as Dan's grandfather and others from the family before them. He knew that he loved animals and had kept pigs and hens in a small enclosure on the Cole farm. Matt Cole had leased him the plot of land in return for six glasses of ale each week, a tradition that ran back for as long as anyone who passed down family stories could remember. A simple life, it must have been, and, for his father, a short one.

Another drawing showed his mother, her hair flowing, her dress to the floor, also white and pure; her wedding day, with Dan inside her, almost ready to birth.

The world had treated him well until today. He turned images over in the portfolio to look at his friends. There was his favourite sketch; himself and Barry at an early age standing in the church before the towering figure of a smiling Blacklocks, their hands stretched out before them and a length of gold cloth draped across them, binding them together as markers for life. He wondered where Barry was now and what he was going to do when his turn came to see Dan sleeping. How would he cope without Dan? Who would give him away when he wed? What was going to happen tomorrow? All questions he could not answer; all questions he didn't want to think about.

It was not knowing how others' lives would go on that saddened him the most.

It was not something for him to think on now. He had accepted duties, he had his role. He had been taught the Lore and that was what he must keep to, for everyone's sake. The years of listening and writing, learning and talking, discussing and understanding, had been for a reason, and that reason was this night. He believed the Teaching and abided by it, unlike Barry. He knew he was here by chance and by chance he was chosen. He would follow the Teaching to the end, for the good of the village.

Thoughts of Barry stayed sharp in his mind. He pictured his friend alone in the field where they walked in spring when the none-so-pretty flowers grew wild among the tall and heavy-scented blue bottles. They would pick their dark green leaves and use them as boats on the deeks, racing them under the copse-bridges until after sunset when the boblight, dimming towards night, would signal the time for home. The walk back would be filled with talk of plans for the next day, the day after that, and then, when they were suddenly free of the schooling and working on the land, of the tasks to be done, the earing of the corn, the seed planting, the covering in. They'd make Bo-boys together to scare the caller birds and share glasses of ale in the inn that would one day be Dan's to run.

One day?

There would be no one day.

Dan picked up his drawing of Barry and folded it gently, slipping it into the pocket of a pair of clean white trousers before stepping into them. He would see him before the Saddling started. He had to say goodbye.

He left his room and was about to enter the bathroom to shave when he paused. It was not just Barry that was on his mind; it was not only Barry that he would miss. The door to Tom's room was open and he could see that the room was empty. He stepped inside. Tom's off-marsh clothes were in a heap on the floor, grey with mud. His bags were there; Tom must still be in Saddling.

Dan stood at the window, not to look out but to remember; the moonlight, its warm glow of reflected sun shining on him like so many possibilities; ideas coming to him in the night as his opportunity slept a troubled sleep on the bed beside him. There was so much offered by Tom Carey. There were so many questions Dan wanted to be answered, so many things he knew he could learn. This foreigner who had come to his village and into his life offered something that Dan wanted to believe in. Dan had felt drawn to Tom's possibilities so firmly that he had honoured him with his hand and the foreigner had become a friend. The only other to have that was Barry and he hoped that Tom would help him. Even though it was against the Teaching, Dan knew what Barry wanted; to see what was beyond the dowals. Barry, probably like many before him, was restless in Saddling. Dan felt the same, but, in him, the Teaching had rooted deeper.

It wasn't just the sadness of now having no future that was eating away at him; it was also the missed opportunity, and that opportunity had been Tom Carey. To leave Saddling was forbidden and those who tried were always punished.

To turn your back on the village was against the Lore but to be rescued from it would have been something else.

He stood in the gloom as the rain pelted the roof above him and the wind worried the tiles. The storm was only starting and he saw the distant flashes of lightning that would soon be overhead. He lifted his arms, stretched them out wide, and then brought his right hand to his throat. He felt his skin, warm and vulnerable, and drew a line across his Adam's apple. He wondered how it would feel when the time came.

Thirty-five

Tom and Barry ran back to the Cole's house and entered quietly through the back door. They dropped their boots there and Barry lit a lantern in an empty kitchen before leading Tom towards the stairs. The other downstairs rooms were also empty and the lamplight showed him enough to know that the Coles were expecting the flood. The rain had not let up. If anything, it was falling harder, and, wet and cold, he and Barry made their way upstairs. Beams of light from the lantern showed Tom that one bedroom was packed full of possessions from the rooms below. Barry's room was less cluttered but housed things which would usually be found in a dining room.

Having taken a very quick wash in the bath and dressed in some of Barry's clothes, Tom sat by the window at a small desk. It was like the one in his room at the inn. A mirror to one side reflected the room behind him.

He dived straight into the book, finding transcriptions of Carey births, deaths and marriages in the village dating back hundreds of years. He already knew a lot of this information but there were other sections, some written in Latin with a translation penned in neat italic lettering. Flicking through the pages, he judged the book to be old but not ancient; this was certainly not an original, but it was detailed. It held notes about land and livestock, a list of parish 'teachers' and ministers, all of whom were, in the last hundred years or so, from the Blacklocks family. He found a telling of the founding of the village, just as Blacklocks had told him. He flicked through this as quickly as he had the early parish records; he was searching for nineteen-twelve.

He heard Barry come back into the room; the candles on the desk flickered and the room grew lighter behind him as Barry lit the gas. Looking in the mirror, he saw Barry, a towel around his waist, put out the lantern.

'Found what you're needing?' he asked.

'Not yet.'

Barry dropped his towel and, unbothered by his nakedness, searched through a pile of clothes. At the desk, Tom was once again reminded of boarding school; a cold bedroom, poorly lit, the soap-and-shampoo-scented air of communal bathrooms, the fragrance tainted with bleach, the echoing sounds of water splashing, embarrassed boys, two to a bath, the feel of a hard mattress followed by the interrupted loneliness of the dark.

He realised that Barry was staring back at him through the mirror and, flushing red, he turned his attention back to the book.

'Will you be long 'bout that?'

'I can't really take it with me,' Tom replied. 'I already stole it once.'

Tom leafed through more pages of names, events and lists until he found dates that were nearer to those for which he was searching. Nervousness built in his stomach. This, he knew, was his one chance to find Maud's answer. If there was going to be any information it would be in this book. So far, he had not found anything. He wondered why Blacklocks had given him such a run-around; why he had wanted him to wait to see what was turning out to be a pretty innocuous set of records. He turned another page, and his heart skipped.

'Oh, my God.'

'What you found?'

Barry stood behind him, buttoning up a shirt. The hem touched Tom's shoulder as a bare leg nudged his elbow.

Tom was aware that the young man's groin was only a touch away from his arm and his heart beat faster. He pointed at a paragraph.

'Perfect. Listen to this. "December twenty-first, nineteen-twelve,"' he read. '"Thomas Carey has fled in terror. A coward. Only Isaac remains, but he is unchosen. The storm, however, worsens." Fled from what?'

'The storm, expect,' Barry said, leaning in and pressing closer into Tom. 'More than common fur a storm this time a'year.'

'It always storms for the Saddling, right?' Tom remembered. 'And your festival is always on December twenty-first?' His speeding heart was making his head light.

'Sometimes, prehaps, twenty-second.'

'But always the winter solstice. Why?'

'Always 'as been. As it was, 'ow it's taught, 'ow it be.'

'What does unchosen refer to?'

'Quiet now.'

Barry placed a heavy hand on Tom's arm and the two fell silent. Downstairs a door opened; the sound of the weather grew in intensity before quietening again as the door was closed.

'Best get dressed, go see who that be,' Barry said in a whisper. 'You 'old quiet.'

Barry pulled on some trousers and left the room carrying one of the candles. He moved slowly and quietly as if he was afraid of being caught. Tom was suddenly worried that this was Blacklocks looking for the stolen book. He re-read the entry quickly, just in case, and prepared to hide the diary beneath the desk.

'So,' he said to himself. 'He ran from the winter storm. Fair enough.'

He looked out into the darkness but it was impossible to see how hard it was raining. He heard the wind battering the roof and the rain lashing the tiles. It was bad enough but no reason to run away. At least he had an answer now, and it was a simple one. He had escaped the storm and… Tom remembered the two graves, the same death dates as his great-great uncle, Isaac. He had seen the preparations made in Barry's house.

'Flooding. I bet that couple died in a flood. The storm was bad, it washed them away, Isaac was drowned, and great-grandfather Thomas, young and alone, got out when he could.'

It sounded plausible but also weak.

'No, Dan.' He was distracted by Barry's voice.

Barry stood in the doorway taking a cloak from his friend and throwing it down. Dan wiped his pale face and handed Barry a piece of paper. He was shaking, presumably from the cold.

'I want you to take it,' Dan said, pushing the paper into Barry's hand. 'Keep it with the others. Remember me.'

'Calm yourself, Dan,' Barry said. 'Look, there's Tom. 'E's got 'is book.'

'He's in Saddling,' Dan said. There was something changed about the man. 'So he's one of us.' Dan took two steps and stood beside Tom. His blue-grey eyes bore into him, their edges were still ringed with red. His hands were trembling. 'We can talk to him. Tell him.'

'Tell me what? Are you alright?'

'Too much Devil's Choke,' Barry said, and quickly took Dan by the arm. 'Tom be a good friend, aye,' he said. 'But 'e's still out-marsher. Dan, come on. Calm. You got your duty soon.'

'Sorry about shouting,' Dan said to Tom.

Tom's mind was more on the book than Dan's strange behaviour and he turned back to the diary.

'Barry Cole?'

Barry's father was in the room now. In the mirror, Tom saw him filling the doorway. 'What's 'e doing 'ere? Dan, you in your whites, an'all.'

'No worry, Fader,' Barry said. 'Dan's on 'is way 'ome. Thanks fur the drawing Dan, I'll keep it special. Tom needed a-change, Fader. I 'elped, that be all.'

'Daniel Vye, there'll be folk waiting on you.' Cole said. 'Say your goodbye now, and a'your burdens.'

Tom shook his head and dropped his eyes back to the book. He tried to shut out the scene but something made him glance back. Dan took Barry by the shoulders and pulled him close. Barry took a while to respond but, when he did, the two held each other tight, heads close.

'I'll be there fur you, friend,' Barry said, his voice quiet and breaking. 'You be me marker so damn the Teaching. I wants a-say I love you and I will. I'm angry it be all I can do.'

'It be enough you shout against it,' Dan replied, his voice muffled, his face pressed into Barry's neck. 'I want you to shout against it.'

'But you 'old the Teaching dear.'

'That were yesterday. If I could change it now and change it like you want, I would. But I can't.'

Barry held him tighter. 'I'll shout 'gainst it, Dan. That be my parting promise.'

Cole approached them and gently pulled his son away. Barry immediately turned from him and stood with his back to the room, his head bowed.

'Come on, nipper,' Cole said to Dan. 'I'll see you out. It be nearly your time.'

He led Dan from the room and Tom, knowing that he had witnessed something sad but not knowing what, turned a page. If that couple had died in the storm, then maybe there were more clues as to how bad it was, more evidence to give Maud as to why...

The book was suddenly ripped from under his hand and slammed shut. Barry was leaning in over it, tears on his red face.

'You got your blessed book, now get away,' he said, his voice cracking.

'What?'

'Get, now. You can't be 'ere for a'night. Take your book. Take it, and leave like you promised.'

'In this?'

'We done what we can fur you 'ere, now you got a-go.'

Wind rattled the window and rain seeped in under the frame to trickle down the wall.

'No,' Tom said, fiercely. 'I can't leave in this. What's the matter with you? What's going on?'

'If I could tell you that, I wouldn't be...' Barry dropped to his knees and gripped both of Tom's hands.

A few days ago, Tom's instinct would have been to pull away, but now, somehow, he was able to confront this display of emotion. It was the first time in his life he had felt strong enough to do so.

'What is it?' he asked, gripping back.

'It be so wrong,' Barry said through tears, 'I'm hot-cheeked by it.'

'By what?'

'The Saddling. Us. Tom, why d'you come 'ere now? Last year, next year, any year, but not now. Why d'you find yourself 'ere tonight, wi' me?'

'I... What do you mean? Barry, I don't understand you.'

'And me, neither, and not on this night, and... What you done a'us, Tom Carey? What you done a'me?'

'You tell me!'

'And there be it.' Barry wiped his eyes on his upper arms, unwilling to let go of Tom's hands. 'There be it. I can't tell you, see? It ain't allowed. It ain't right, and yet it be so right it makes me question all I been taught, and that ain't right neither, and...' He stood up sharply and released his grip. 'You got a-go, but you can't. You be right. So you got a-stay, upstairs, away from it all. Don't see what I got a-do. Just let me do it and prehaps a'morrow...' Barry sat heavily on his bed. 'If you can't leave then be a'your room at the inn. Stay there. Read your book and leave us be.'

'Barry?'

'Leave me be.'

'What's going on? Why this? I thought we were...'

'How d'you think that? We not known each other more than two days and you know nothing 'bout me, 'bout us, 'ow it is, what be... We can't be friends.'

'But last night, your... whatever you called it. Trust? You can do that weird stuff but you can't tell me what's wrong with you now?'

'Bain't what's wrong wi' me,' Barry said. 'It be what's wrong wi' all of it. I can't love no-one, be no point, but I do, and now I sees why I can't and the Teaching be right again. I've not been able to be 'appy, say what I wants to, and I can't say why now, not a'you. Oh, what's the blessed point?'

Tom had no idea what to say. He didn't know what Barry was talking

235

about but he could plainly see he was in no mood for company.

'I'll go back to my...'

'Aye, leave me be, Tom Carey.'

Tom collected the book and held it tight. 'I don't understand you,' he said. 'What happened to standing by your mates? What happened to all that, eh? And what's wrong with Dan? Why is he in such a state? And, now, you?'

Barry also stood and he took one long stride towards Tom, who stepped back, the book in his hand ready to strike. There was no need. Barry looked him in the eyes, close, deep and searching. Tom was unnerved by the sudden change.

'I don't mean what I says, Tom. You saved me life,' Barry said. 'If I be cramp-worded it be as tonight's muddling me mind. But now you got a-do what I say, like you promised. You can't go a'night, so you take your book a'the inn. Go in by the back door, up a'your room. You lock yourself in and read your 'istory. You find your answer, and you will find it, I know. The night's heading a'wild, the storm will worse. Go there, stay there, be safe. Promise it.'

'Well, I can't...'

'You 'ave a-trust me, Tom, so follow me words. Please.' Barry's tone had changed again. His outburst was over and now his eyes were pleading.

Tom nodded. He picked up a lantern and his sheepskin jacket and, with a last confused look back, gave up and left the room.

Barry slumped back onto his bed. He took out Dan's drawing and unfolded it; himself and Dan in younger days, the marsh laid out behind them, the mother trees in leaf to one side, his fader's barn to the other. The two boys were leaning on pitchforks at bailing time, the sun was glowing in a clear sky. They were just eighteen. He remembered those happier times and smiled at the other drawings on his wall, all crafted by Dan.

The style matured as the years past. Early ones showed roughly drawn images of the two of them when little. Barry's favourite was the one of them aged six on their first day of Teaching. There was a cartoon of Blacklocks which always made Barry smile. It hung beside a drawing of a terrified young man wearing a Saddling wreath on his dark head as he stood in front of the church. This one was drawn when they were twelve, and Barry remembered that day clearly. He recalled the feeling of anticipation mixed with the awe of seeing the Chosen, the wonder of the spectacle and its meaning. Most of all, he remembered how disappointed he had felt knowing that he was too young to be chosen that year. He also remembered the innocent hope of youth, that how, ten years later, he might be the one to receive the fame and the honour, the adulation, and the wreath.

Now, as the reality of the night ahead sank in, that innocent, youthful pride in the Teaching was washed away. Its absence left room for something that had struggled beneath the surface for many years. He knew what it was but had not been strong enough to accept it, not until Tom appeared. Years of the Teaching had barred what he knew to be true, like a cow-gate against a lamb. Tom Carey had come to open that gate and had shown him the pasture of possibility that lay on the other side.

But it was against the Lore.

He stood up, swiped the drawing of Blacklocks from the wall and ripped it into pieces, anger thumping in his brain. Opening his mouth to yell out, he turned to the door.

His father stood there, watching. The two said nothing while the last pieces of the torn paper drifted to the floor.

Cole watched them fall like dead leaves from an autumn-dying tree and said, 'pack your bag.'

Thirty-six

Susan had just finished dressing when she heard quick and heavy footsteps outside her bedroom. She waited until the spare room door closed before opening her own to step into the corridor. Moving to the stairs, she stood with one hand on the bannister and took three deep breaths. Walking down was like floating on air and she was unaware of what she was touching.

Her thoughts had sought refuge in her heart with all her senses and lay there, huddled, as a battle raged around them. It was a fight she had experienced twenty years before but now it had returned with fierce intensity. She had been younger then. She had had her child to carry her through; a child who grew to be the image of its father with the spirit of its aunt and the faith of its mother. On the day of the last Saddling, she saw him grow from a boy to a man. He entered his thirteenth year knowing what his future might hold and he had braved the responsibility with pride and courage, as did so many of the boys. He was still showing that courage today, although she knew that the burden was impossible to carry.

She reached the bottom of the stairs. Ahead, she could see that the bar was full but no-one was drinking, not now that the time of the ritual was approaching. She walked on, her hair unleashed from its plait and decorated with wind-bibbers from the hawthorn and toar from the fields. Her skin was cold but she felt nothing beyond it.

She was doing as the Lore commanded; she was playing her role, but still the battle raged within her. What she knew must be done fought bitterly against what she knew she would lose. This was not how she expected to feel. She had thought about this moment many times during sleepless nights. She had imagined how it would be if it came. She thought it would be easy because it was the Teaching and what she had been raised to expect. The Lore was right and it was only some primal instinct deep inside her that refused to accept it. How had the mothers before her gone through this? How had they allowed it to happen? They had because it was the Lore. It was her Lore, too, and, for all her doubt and deep regrets, for all her pain, she had no choice. It was to happen and nothing could change it.

Heads turned to her and bowed silently as she made her way into the bar. A path opened, and the men removed their caps. Susan drifted among them on the painful realisation that this was unstoppable and happening to her. She was the mother; this was her duty.

Reaching the door, she saw her hand rise as though through a dream. She was aware that it was touching the latch that she couldn't feel. This was the moment. This was the time when the mother within her screamed out to leave it closed, to turn and climb the stairs, find her son, face the wrath of the men gathered behind her. She could take Daniel by the hand, lead him from the inn, walk out into the fields and keep walking until they reached the dole-stones at the furthest mark, and then... What then? It didn't matter. She knew it would never happen. Daniel was resigned, he followed the Teaching, he would not go with her.

The latch moved and the door swung inwards. Rain lashed in on the wind. The lamplight leapt in panic. Her dress pressed back against her body and her hair streamed out behind her in fear. Some of the haws came loose from it as the rain washed her face but she felt none of it. By opening the door, she had accepted what was to come. She stood back, admitting her acceptance to the men.

They passed her, touching her hand; some kissed it, others bowed, some could not look at her as, one by one, they bent their heads to the wind and shambled towards the church.

Blacklocks stood looking at the smashed cabinet until his laughter subsided. He fought to contain his excitement as he slipped out of the crypt and closed the door behind him. His responsibilities called and he knew he had to let things play out as they must play out, and for as long as possible. Only when it was too late to choose any other course of action would his people see that he was doing right. Until then, the ritual must be as they expected it to be.

He was now dressed entirely in white. His copious black robes had been replaced with a damask vestment trimmed with silk, his hair fell in a waterfall of black beyond his shoulders, and he used the ritual, ebony cane, topped with silver. As he approached the altar, the rising storm rattled the church and reminded him, unnecessarily, of his purpose.

Candles burned on every windowsill, in holders at the end of the box pews, and two had been lit in tall brass stands either side of the altar, shining a light that softly bathed the walls. The east window, backed by the night outside, reflected the flames in vivid colours.

The hourglass was still sifting down the minutes on its pedestal at the side. He watched its lower section slowly fill and knew that, out in the wild night, the ditches would be filling until they overflowed. He picked up the metal casket and held it. He thought of his son, the only love he had known. He thought of grandsons he may never meet, his family name, the ancestors he could sense in the stony air, and he thought of generations still to come. He was calm. He knew his duties, he knew his reason and, with the storm intensifying, he knew that he could bring it all to an end.

Carrying the casket under one arm, he paced the aisle, his cane tapping on the stone. In the porch, he opened the outer door and welcomed the wild elements. They brought hope as he waited for his congregation.

Tom sat in his room with dull gaslight lighting the Saddling Diary. He flicked through the pages, his eyes scanning each one for any mention of the Carey family. So far he had found several references, but all to ancestors long gone and forgotten. It was an incredible record, however, and several times now he had wished he had a camera so he could photograph each page. Tomorrow, he thought, he would start transcribing everything that was relevant. Before then, he had to find Maud's answer and, so far, there had been no further clues to what had happened during the storm in nineteen-twelve.

A flash of light at the window made him raise his head. There was more lightning now among the gusts of wind and the constant beating on the roof. Below, a line of people moved quickly towards the church, lamps swinging in their hands, their heads bent.

'Call that a festival?' he mumbled to himself as he sat again with the book. 'Right, what do we have?' He glanced at his notebook where he had made a few brief entries. 'He flees from the storm, but leaves the brother, Isaac, behind. Possibly already drowned?' He turned a page to where he had noted, "Isaac Carey, 1912, for Saddling," as he had seen on the gravestone. 'Died for the village?' he questioned himself. 'But what did he do?' He sat back and chewed on his pencil, oblivious to the ravings of the storm as he let his mind wander into the puzzle. 'He stayed and helped against the storm?' he said. 'How would you do that? Perhaps the ditches overflowed, and they needed to save their sheep. Thomas ran for higher ground, maybe. Isaac stayed to help, got in trouble out on the marsh somewhere and drowned, most likely. Thomas learnt of it and decided not to come back.'

He checked some notes. 'There were no more Careys, apart from Isaac. We were dying out here anyway. Nice idea but there's no proof to show Maud'

He turned more pages of the diary. He was unaware that the door had opened behind him and someone had entered the room.

'But what about the woman in the shack?' he said, speaking quietly as he skimmed the fastidious entries of the diary. '*Look to your name*. What was that all about? Carey, care? Care about what?' He turned another page. 'Death records transcribed from seventeen...' He fell silent, thought for a second and flicked back two pages. 'From sixteen twelve...' and another two or three. 'Fifteen sixty-two.'

Dylan's voice entered his head. 'It's all about patterns.' Tom tried to shake it from his mind as he wrote down dates and names, turning forwards in time and writing more.

'I come to say my goodbye.'

Tom saw Dan's reflection in the window. He turned briefly to him.

'I'm not away until tomorrow. But I think I've found something here, Dan.' he said, and immediately returned to the book.

'The storm'll quiet soon,' Dan said, advancing towards Tom. 'That'd be your time to go.'

Dan's shoes, trousers, and a long cow-gown smock of fine linen with a low neck, were pure white and hung on him in a perfect fit. His face was drawn, his eyes fixed at his own reflection.

Tom's eyes were fixed on the dates he was scribbling down. 'The years,' he said. 'Dan, there's something odd about the years... Oh, my God, they're all even. Seventeen twenty-two, thirty-two, forty-two... And onwards, look, eighteen sixty-two, seventy-two... Every ten years. But it's more than that. The ages. There's something not right here. This one, Simeon Tidy, eighteen fifty-two, aged thirteen; the next one aged nineteen, and this one, twenty-two. Ten years later and there again, another teenager. Thirty years later, another, at twenty-one.'

'What good's numbers?' Dan asked quietly, approaching Tom from behind. He put a hand into a pocket and drew out a long piece of golden cord. 'Only an hour or so, now. Only a few more breaths.'

'I'm not going anywhere, mate. There's too much in here.' Tom's head was down over the pages.

The cord was all the way out of Dan's pocket and he wrapped one end of it around his hand.

'Eighteen ninety-two, this boy aged fifteen. All boys, every ten years, all between thirteen and...' he checked his list, 'twenty-two. Okay, so people die and some die young, but every ten years? A bit of a coincidence, isn't it?'

'If your family hadn't left,' Dan said, wrapping the other end of the cord around his other hand and now standing directly behind Tom, 'we would a-grown up together.' His voice was quiet, barely audible over the wind that cried at the window and clawed through small gaps around the panes.

'What the hell's been going on here?' Tom was speaking only to himself. Excitement was bubbling inside him; he knew he was on to something and that on the turn of a page he could have his answer.

A crack of thunder vibrated through the room.

Tom ran his finger down a page. '"Nineteen-twelve, Thomas Carey, chosen. Unfulfilled." What does that...?'

Dan put both hands on Tom, near his neck, the cord taut between them. 'It's the solstice storm,' he said. 'It always storms for the Saddling.'

Tom only vaguely felt the touch because the words had stabbed through his thinking and separated them, pushed the coincidences away from the facts and given him a clear way through. He read the death records and his heart rate picked up.

'You brought me hope,' Dan said, his hands spreading so that they could touch as much of Tom's shoulder as the cord would allow. 'You walked in 'ere, at this time, and we saw a way out. But there ain't no way out of the Saddling.'

'And each time, the minister...' Tom rubbed his forehead, 'Blacklocks' family, always the ministers. Every ten years someone, some young person... Male...'

'Is what the Teaching teaches the most when you come to it,' Dan said. 'That it's wrong to love anything but the Teaching. There's no point. You might be chosen, then what's the need of loving someone? There ain't nothing left to love, not after. And who's to love you when you mayn't be there after your thirteenth, or your sixteenth, or your twenty-second? Eleven days more and I would a'been twenty-three and free of it. But there's the trap, see?' He was speaking to no-one; Tom was not listening. 'There's the thing. It don't matter when you're born, not if you're a lad. There's no time to be born when you can't cheat the Choosing.'

'This goes back hundreds of years.' Tom was racing through the pages, ticking off dates and ages. 'One every... This is not right. This is not a

242

coincidence. Maud will die when she sees this.' Back to the nineteen-twelve entry. 'Thomas fled and Isaac...'

'Maybe if it'd been different I would a'been allowed love,' Dan said, and his hands dropped from Tom's shoulders. He backed towards the door, wrapping the cord around his waist and tying it at the front. 'Goodbye, Tom Carey,' he whispered.

'Storms for the Saddling... Every ten years... Festival.'

It hit him as suddenly as a computer crash. Blue screen. There was nothing he could do and yet his mind rebooted immediately. The dates. 'Every December twenty-first, sometimes twenty-second, or... Each one on the winter solstice.'

The boys out on the marsh watching their last boblight; coming together for what might have been their last chance to see the sun go down; to be there for each other because the next day any one of them might be the Chosen; the birds that the boys feared being tempted to the roofs of houses where candles burned for a male child between the ages of thirteen and twenty-two, Barry and Dan among them; the sheep, the chance choosing, the randomness of being born making no difference in the ten-year cycle; the Teaching, the festival, the behaviour; allowing the boys to do what they want in this time of Penit, adults treating them with respect, bowing, addressing and all because any one of them could...

He ground to a halt. It was preposterous. What would happen to them? They would die? They would drown in this meteorological anomaly that came back regularly every ten years on the winter solstice? It was too random; no-one could predict the weather.

Through all this piecing together, through the jumble of thoughts, the slamming of the wind and the ever-growing thunder, there was still one thin voice threading its way to his mind. 'Patterns,' it said. 'It's all about seeing patterns.'

Well, there they were. It was too ordered to be a coincidence.

'It always storms for the Saddling,' Tom repeated to himself with a dry throat.

He turned to the front of the book, flicking fast through pages without care for their fragility. He found the story he was looking for. "1292. The year that the cleric, Di-Kari, killed John, the son of the shepherd with the black locks and, in doing so, appeased the storm and saved the village."

Killed.

He stood. Tripping on the chair, he fell onto the bed and slid from its edge to the floor. Surrounded by his research and history, he knew why his ancestor had left. Thomas Carey had been the Chosen and he had run from his execution. He had stolen the records as proof of what the village had been doing for generations. He had taken the evidence, but the Blacklocks family transcripts were left behind; as was his brother who went in his place to stop the storm from drowning the village.

He died for Saddling.

Even though that was the answer he had been seeking for months now, all he could think about as he staggered up onto weak legs, his heart trembling, was the Saddling Chosen. Dan.

He stumbled his way to the door and pulled on the handle.

The door was locked from the outside.

Thirty-seven

Lightning cracked in cumbersome clouds that heaved and rolled, and the thunder followed at ever shorter intervals. Blacklocks stood in the porch doorway with his hair dancing maniacally around his head and the casket held out in both hands as an offering. Susan stood beside him, staring towards the villagers who had gathered on the green. Everyone held up a lantern, their flames safe behind glass. Each family stood together, their clothes soaked, their faces to the stinging rain. They made an avenue of light, leaving a path free for the young man who stood at the far end.

Daniel's hair panicked about his head like a terrified flame, his tunic billowing white against the black night. He approached the church, his face expressionless, unbothered by his drenched clothes that pressed tight against his body. His steps were slow and measured in a steady rhythm. As he passed each family, they lowered their lanterns and extinguished their lights. All but Barry who, supported by his father, held his flame high and kept it there until his mother pulled at his arm to lower it.

Blacklocks looked sideways and up towards the inn. There was only one light burning in a small window and, behind it, he saw the figure of Tom Carey thumping on the glass, his mouth moving in protest. Blacklocks smiled to himself and bent to whisper to Susan. She showed no sign of acknowledgement but hitched up her skirt and walked down the knoll towards the inn.

Daniel reached the porch and the minister turned him to the side so that they faced each other. The villagers moved forward, the line broke, and they hurried over the muddy ground to press towards the church, each family eager to be the closest. They settled into a silent assembly and Blacklocks raised the casket to the skies.

A great crack of lightning ripped over the far fields and whipped into an ancient mother tree. For a second it illuminated the green and the land beyond where the dykes were already overflowing. The explosion of thunder that followed shook the ground.

Blacklocks lifted the lid of the casket and drew all attention. Offering the open strongbox to Daniel he turned his head to face the village.

'You have been chosen for us all. The duty with which you have been honoured is not a burden. It is for our families, the land and all who now thrive on it, those who have gone before and those who will come after. Saddling will live on if you accept your Choosing willingly.'

'I accept willingly for Saddling,' Daniel replied, his voice almost inaudible. He reached into the casket.

The window was fixed and did not open. It was too small for Tom to climb through even if he could smash the glass. He stopped hammering on it when he saw Dan take out a long-bladed knife and hold it above his head. Through the scream of the wind, Tom thought he could hear cheering. The villagers moved forwards and Blacklocks led Dan into the church.

'This is madness,' he shouted. There was no-one to hear.

The church door closed. The windows were alight with a golden glow and, at the east end, he could clearly see the image of the young man walking through the rising water. The stained glass appeared to move and meld as candlelight glimmered inside. It was as if the blues and greens, the yellow of the boy's hair and the dark purples of the storm were becoming one.

Tom scanned the room, thinking fast. His research lay scattered on the floor with his broken laptop and his useless phone. He saw the parish book on the desk, picked it up and hurled it in anger. It crashed into the door, its pages flapping like a wounded bird. The book lay open to the last entry which read: "The Saddling, Daniel Vye – Chosen."

He kicked it out of the way and was about to throw himself at the door when it opened.

Susan stood there, her clothes dripping.

'Go, now,' she ordered. She took two paces into the room and grabbed Tom by the elbow, pulling him harshly. 'Go.'

'They are going to...' Tom stammered, but the rest of the words stayed lodged behind disbelief.

'I know what they're going to do and it must be done.'

'You have to stop it.' Tom was being dragged across the room with her fingers digging into his arm. He struggled free.

'This is the Lore.'

'They're going to kill him.'

'Aye, like we did his fader afore him, like we will again.'

'You're going to let them?'

'This ain't your business. Here.' She threw the sheepskin jacket at him.

'Blacklocks says you are to go. You've taken his book, you ain't welcome. Cover yourself. Out the front door, follow the lope-way to the bridge and go fast before the flooding takes you.'

She pushed Tom into the corridor.

'Someone has to stop it.'

'None can.'

He realised that she was helping him into the coat and that he was letting her.

'I need to get in there.'

'They don't want you.'

'The police.'

'You do what you think is right, stranger. But be out from my house.'

He was at the top of the stairs. Instinctively he grabbed the bannister as he stumbled downwards. He kept thinking. Run for the police. It's miles. I won't make it. Smash a window. Save Daniel. This is madness.

All thoughts cascaded and churned like the plunge of a waterfall and no clear stream channelled out of it to direct him. His feet slipped on a stair; she was pushing him from behind in short, sharp jabs.

'We started it,' he said, as he stumbled from the bottom step onto the stone floor. 'My ancestors.'

'Aye, so the story says.' She directed him to the bar. 'One of yours killed one of his and that killed the storm. It's the only way.'

Tom resisted. Twisting to face her, he held her at arm's length. 'That's just... ludicrous.'

She pushed back, turned him, and shoved him towards the door.

His foot caught the leg of a chair and he staggered into a table. The wood banged painfully on his shins. He lost his balance and crashed through the chairs. Grabbing at the wall to prevent himself from falling, he dislodged an engraving and it hit the flagstones with a shatter of glass.

'So many boys,' he said, his thoughts tumbling.

'And so many lives saved, so many whitebacks, all our land. One in ten years is worth that.'

'But he is your son.'

'He was chosen.'

Susan pushed him along the wall with hard jabs to his shoulders. Tom struggled to face her and knocked another picture from its hanging. It landed face up and, even though the glass cracked, he made out the image.

247

'But it doesn't, does it?'

He held it up to her. It showed the village submerged by water, a few roofs above the waterline. The church was standing, although some walls had been washed away, the chancel roof was gone. Dead sheep were floating, and men in boats were dragging two bodies from the water. Across the bottom was written, "Saddling – 1912".

'Aye,' Susan said, reaching for his arm again. 'Carey ran from his Choosing, and Cole's people died.'

'They killed his brother instead.'

She was pushing him again and Tom, drowning in what it all meant, let her. He dropped the picture, heard it shatter.

'You go out and straight on, Mr Carey. Blacklocks says he don't want you here no more. You go and let us do what we do.'

He crashed into the door and she reached around him for the latch. The door struck him on the temple as she opened it and the force of the wind blasted into him.

'Go,' she ordered. 'And don't interfere no more. There's nothing you can do. You ain't welcome in that church.' She drew him closer to her and he detected a brief, pleading look in her eyes. She emphasised her words. 'Don't go into the church. They won't open the door to you. Don't go in there.'

He felt the weight of the storm as she forced him outside. He was thrown forward and the impetus continued in staggered steps towards the lope-way. Dazed and confused, his thoughts churned faster as they fought; what he should do clashed with what he wanted to do. Get help, he told himself; get the police and fast.

He ran.

Susan watched him leave, lumbering and weaving his way against the wind until he was out of sight. As she fought her way back across the green, she pictured what was taking place inside; the songs, the minister's talk, the wait for the hourglass, the time slowly trickling away the last moments of her son's life; the ritual that would appease the storm, the culmination in the sacrifice, the long, drawn-out words and music that taunted the Saddling with time as he waited to die. 'Why make it last so long? Spare the child. Do it, and do it fast,' she shouted as she climbed up to the porch. She put her hand on the door and, through the uproar of the storm and the turmoil of her emotions, heard the singing of the first ritual air. Her hand slid down the old wood as she crumpled to the ground. Lashed and battered, she drew up her knees, tipped her head back and howled.

Blacklocks was oblivious to all sound outside. Sally Rolfe was singing. Her pure voice cut through the warm, yellow light and outshone the storm beyond. She stood by the font, facing him in the pulpit. The villagers were seated in the pews between them. Some stood at the back, some were cramped out of sight behind the last rows, and some of the younger children were seated in the aisle.

As he listened to the lyrics of pastures and meadows, cattle and summer hedgerows, of preservation and life renewed, he gloated over the boy beside the altar.

Dan stood with his eyes open, blinking only occasionally. His face was composed, his sweet, untouchable lips were closed and still. His wet cow-gown pressed down on his chest and his muscles showed through. His hands were by his side, palms out, as though he was offering the village everything of himself; nothing was hidden. Blacklocks' eyes slowly travelled the length of the body and saw perfection in every part of the Saddling, a vision of purity and unsullied innocence; the shape of his thighs, the tantalising mound of his groin, his long, soft-skinned fingers and the golden down on his forearms, his slender neck and his strong jaw. He would remember it all. The eyes captured him the most; captured and tortured. They were the stained-glass windows to a soul that Blacklocks knew he would never possess.

The door to the crypt remained closed and it worried him. For the first time in days he wondered if his plan would fall into place. Perhaps he had misjudged Carey. Perhaps he had not fully understood the boy's nature. His gaze travelled to the sacrificial knife that lay on the altar and then on to the hourglass. There was still time.

Sally Rolfe sang the third verse and the sound of the women humming quietly beneath her clarion voice drew his attention back to his congregation. He looked out over them, closing his eyes and smiling down, benevolence falling from him in what he imagined were visible waves.

His eyes snapped open and his back stiffened. He scanned the church thoroughly.

Something was wrong.

As Sally started the fourth verse, she was joined by the eligible boys, Blacklocks' son included. It was then that he realised what was amiss.

The minister raised a long finger and silently signalled to Mick Farrow and his two all-workers. His narrow eyes still searching the church, he descended from the pulpit.

Farrow and the two broad men met him at the foot of the steps, their faces displaying concern.

'The Cole family,' Blacklocks said with menace. 'Find them.'

Thirty-eight

Tom passed the Cole house. Mud clawed at his feet and his body twisted against the wind. There was no way to tell what was path and what was field and he was guided only by the vague shapes of half-lit houses ahead. He would soon pass them and then he would have no guide, no light on the track to the bridge. It was another five miles before he reached the road. Even then there was no hope of finding anyone to help; who would be out on a night like this? The rapidly increasing flashes of lightning gave him split seconds to check his path, but they were not enough.

He stopped. Dan would be dead by the time he even reached the road.

He turned back to the Cole house and saw a small light wavering towards him. He ran to it.

Three people were huddled together, one carrying a hurricane lamp.

'Barry,' Tom shouted. 'We've got to do something.'

'Who's there?' He heard Cole call back.

They met at the front of the house and Cole held the lamp to Tom's face. Behind it, Tom saw Barry supporting his mother. They were both carrying cases.

'They're going to kill him.'

'Come away with us, son,' Cole said, grabbing Tom's arm. 'Bain't safe on your own.'

'Matthew, we must be hurrying,' Irene Cole shouted against the thunder. 'We'll soon be missed.'

'Barry!' Tom pushed Cole away. 'We have to help him.'

'We can't 'elp 'im now,' Barry replied. 'Come wi' us, Tom. Come now.'

'The bridge will be washed away afore long,' Tom heard Irene yell.

A gust of wind caught under Tom's coat and nearly threw him to the ground. He steadied himself against Barry but another squall tore the two of them apart.

Cole's vice-like grip clamped Tom's arm and dragged him to the front door. He kicked it open and pushed Tom inside. Within seconds, as Cole slammed shut the door, the rage of the storm dropped away. Wiping his eyes, Tom saw the family more clearly. Fear was etched on Irene's face; Barry's was a sickly white.

'You won't be understanding this,' Cole said, pushing Tom against the wall. 'Look a'me, son.' He pulled Tom around to face him. 'Look a'me and listen. We can't save poor Dan, but we can save ourselves.'

Tom couldn't believe his calmness. 'You know what's happening?'

'All too well.'

'But someone has to do something. Barry...'

'Leave me boy out of it.'

'Tom.' Barry stepped forward. He whipped his curled fringe back from his face and fixed Tom with stony eyes. 'We said our goodbyes. 'E was chosen. It be 'is time a-save the village and it be an honour. Dan will 'ave gone willing.'

'Then why are you running away?'

Barry looked at his father.

'Just 'cos it 'appens don't mean we agree wi' it no more,' Cole said.

'But you says that aloud and Blacklocks sends you down with a slit of his knife,' Irene said. 'And that's what he'll do to us for running if we ain't gone now.'

'Come wi' us, Tom. Now, afore the waters rise.'

'This place isn't going to flood,' Tom said. 'And killing him won't stop this storm. Jesus Christ!'

'And that won't do you no good neither,' Cole said. 'You want a-stop it? You want a-save 'im?'

'Matthew,' Irene said. 'Don't.'

'Quiet your whimpering, Mistus.' Cole took hold of Tom. 'This is 'ow it be, son,' he said. 'Thing is, you can save 'im.'

'Yes! You said there's a truck. We can drive...'

'Listen.' Cole's voice was firm, his grip stronger. 'Simple truth is, Blacklocks 'as been angling for you a-be put in Dan's place, and there's time yet for that a-be 'appening.'

'What?'

'What you saying, Fader?' Barry pushed in closer.

'Minister wi' 'is lost book and 'is delays, keeping you 'ere for the festival, leading you on, all so you'd be 'ere for a'night. And you are, and I 'ad a part it in, I know.'

Tom couldn't take it in. 'Me?'

'Aye, you. You's who 'e wants on 'is stone. Put *you* there, and there be an end a'the Saddling furever, 'e says. I didn't trust it, I kept it quiet as told.

But you, you got a-go with willing, else it all fails.'

'What are you raving about? What fails?'

'No, Fader,' Barry said, trying to pull his dad away from Tom. 'What you saying? Don't send him back.'

'You 'as a choice, Tom Carey. Aye, you can save young Daniel, but there be a price on it fur you.'

'What's it got to do with me?'

'You're the last Di-Kari, ain't you? The last of your family, the folk what fled 'ere 'undred year back. The last of them as started this whole fear in the Great Storm 'undreds a'years afore that. Blacklocks reasons that if you die for Saddling, then that be the end a'the floods fur good.'

'Madness,' Tom said, and then shock stabbed him in the chest. He pushed himself away from Cole and slid further down the corridor into the darkness. 'You knew about this? You knew he had this plan and you went along with it?'

'Round 'ere,' Cole said, 'it be a case of do or die, kill or be killed, and I ain't joking on that. The Lore be all. The Teaching be all, and Blacklocks be all.'

'Barry.' Tom turned to him. 'You knew about this?'

'No, Tom, honest.' Barry moved towards him and took Tom's hand. 'Not 'til now. Fader...?'

'That be truth an' all,' Cole said. 'Me boy knew nothing of Blacklocks' plan. And I only went along wi' it as I 'ad to, for fear the man would kill me family. Such things 'ave been done afore. But 'e's messing with the Lore now. You're over calling age and you weren't chosen, but that ain't going to stop 'im. Not once 'e saw you in the village; not once 'e learned who you be.'

'But you knew that one of you, one of those boys, was going to be... what, sacrificed?'

'Matthew, the flooding.' Irene insisted.

'Look, son,' Cole was back on him now, the lamp held high to his face. 'If you want a-stop this then you 'ave a-play 'is game. You've 'ad traps laid fur you all the way along, and the last one be that Dan'll be dead if you ain't back there a-stop it. You can do it, or you can come wi' us, but, for my part, I ain't 'aving no more of this and I be taking my family a'safety afore the flood come.'

'It's just a superstition.' Tom's legs were weak beneath him.

'It's saved us now hundreds of years,' Irene said. 'But only if the Saddling boy goes willing.'

'But end it with the last of the Careys, and that be the end of it all. So Blacklocks reckons.' Cole spelt it out, and Tom knew that mad or sane, right or wrong, this was what they believed. He turned to Barry.

'A man's got to do right by his friends, you said? Yeah? Well, we have to do what's right and right now. Come with me.'

'Be right, Fader,' Barry said. 'Someone's got a-shout 'gainst this and running off won't do that. Daniel needs me, and I promised 'im.' He turned Tom to face him. 'I need a-know but one thing,' he said, his voice measured and quiet. He took a deep breath and rubbed his fingertips nervously on the palms of his hands. 'We gets taught that love comes from trust and you said afore that you trust me. Well, then, without asking me no riddles, answer me this. Would you trust me more, with your life?'

Before he had time to ask why, Tom answered, 'Yes.' It came easily and was meant.

'Barry Cole, what you thinking?' Irene pushed her way between the two of them.

'No, you're coming wi' us.' Cole held his son by the arm. 'Now ain't the time a-be a runagate.'

A loud thump on the front door made Irene scream in shock.

'Matthew Cole?' The voice outside was louder than the wind, deeper than the thunder. 'Open up. You're missed at the meeting.'

'Out the back,' Cole hissed, and thrust Tom forward through the darkness into another room. He was pushed until he came up against a door. Cole reached around him. 'Stay or go, Tom Carey. It be your choice.'

'Fader, I'm staying wi' Tom.'

'You're coming wi' me lad and no more on it. Take your ma's hand. She needs you, quick.'

Cole opened the door and threw Tom out into the storm. Tom raised his hand to protect his eyes. Cole was on him again, up close, the lantern swinging franticly in the wind.

'Barry be right,' Cole shouted. 'Someone 'as a-shout 'gainst it, and that someone be you.' He backed away and grabbed Barry by the hand. Barry tried to break free but his father dragged him onwards. Struggling, he vanished into the dark.

Susan drew herself to her feet, shivering from the cold. She knew what she had to witness. She banged twice on the church door and took in a long, slow breath before wiping her eyes. The door opened and immediately the clammy warmth from inside hit her. She stepped into the porch and heard the key turn in the lock. She prepared herself for what she was about to see.

All heads twisted to her as she entered the church and faced the altar. Daniel was now dressed in dry clothes and she was happy that he would be warm. He sat on a decorated chair before the altar, his fingers folded over the ends of the armrests. His head was erect and his expression composed. He showed no fear and she was proud of him for it. Holding back the tears, she advanced slowly towards him and the villagers either side bowed as she passed. The children shuffled out of her way, parting to allow her to walk through them. Some touched her dripping clothes.

Dan showed no signs of recognition and she wondered how much Devil's Choke he had taken to keep him so calm. His hair lay dry and soft beneath the Saddling wreath and his long white robe cascaded down and onto the floor where the candlelight bathed it in warm shades.

Oblivious to the storm, she felt safe inside the church. The community was here for her. She would be revered as the woman who gave up her husband and now her son to protect the village from the flood. This was what she and Daniel were born to do.

The boys and young men made space for her on the end of the front pew and she sat, numb and resigned.

Looking up to the pulpit she saw Blacklocks in his whites. He was staring towards the crypt door as though he was waiting for it to open and it took a cough from his son to bring him back to his duties.

'My friends,' he said, offering out his hands. 'My flock.' He threw another quick glance at the crypt and then at the hourglass. The movement drew Susan's eye. She saw how little time she had left to gaze on her son while he lived and her heart withered. Blacklocks poured benevolence down on her. 'And the mother whom we cherish above all else. What you give tonight you give for Saddling.' He began his ceremony speech. Susan listened, but her eyes stayed on her son as her mind thought of all the things to come that he would never see. Blacklocks' words filtered in but she heard only parts of his sermon. 'For over seven hundred years the solstice storm... to keep our faith... to keep the Lore and protect our community...'

Tom could make out the lights of the church as thunder cracked and tumbled violently among the mass of cloud. Reaching the green, he realised that he was no longer running through mud; he was splashing through water. It was up to his ankles by the time he arrived at the bench. He left it behind as he climbed up to the church door, his chest sore and his body shaking. He couldn't make out if it was because of the cold or the thought of what was going on inside. All he could think about was that he might already be too late.

His frozen fists screamed in pain as they thumped on the wood, each smash jarring his bones. He called out, but no-one came. He kicked the door, but it wouldn't budge. Moving along the side of the church he jumped to slap his hands against the windows, but they were too high. He remembered the window at the west end, but it, too, was out of reach.

He ran into the graveyard and felt his way along the wall; stone, brick, but no glass, although there was a faint glow coming from up ahead. He knew there was no other door but if there was a window lower than the others he might be able to break it. He moved on quickly, bumping into gravestones in the dark.

A great blast of light and sound made him spin. He ducked from the lightning as he blundered on. A spear of light crackled and skated across a vast lake where the field had been, and he felt static course through his body.

Suddenly, the ground disappeared from beneath his feet.

Thirty-nine

Tom thrashed around in the waist-high muddy water that had broken his fall until his feet found firmer ground. Standing, he felt earth walls on all sides and lightning showed that he had fallen into an open grave. He tried to reach the ground above but the pit was too deep. Thinking quickly, he reached for one wall and dug his fingers as far into the sodden earth as they would go. Kicking against the other wall he secured a foothold, albeit an unsound one, and he lifted himself up, kicking out at the other side to establish a second.

He slipped and fell back into the icy water. There was no point in shouting; no-one would hear and nobody was looking for him. His coat was soaked and weighty and he shook it off. His hands searched around the side of the grave but found no roots or rocks, nothing he could pull himself up with. For a second, he considered waiting for the rain to fill the grave and float him to the top but he knew that, even if that could happen, it would take far too long. For all he knew, Blacklocks could be killing Dan right at that moment.

Anger rose within him at the thought and he thumped his fist into one side of the grave. His knuckles met with mud and, twisting his wrist, he buried his hand in deep. He forced another foothold, more secure, and he pulled himself back up onto one foot. This time it held, as did a second. His other hand clawed into the dirt and he wedged it in hard. Painfully, he dragged and pushed himself up a few more inches until his chin was resting on the grass. Loud outbursts of thunder tried to shake him but he held on, his hand now clawing out for something above to hang on to. He clutched at the grass and pulled. Just a few more inches and he would be free.

The village girls left their places in the pews and met in the aisle. They processed towards the front, some dropping hawthorn twigs, others laying down bundles of rushes and sedge. The small, straw boy-dolls that had decorated the daytime festival were offered out to those in the congregation as Sally led the singing of the next ancient poem. This was a joyous one celebrating the dark of winter leading to the calm of spring and the knowledge that ten years would pass before such a storm came again.

Susan heard none of it as she rose to take her place beside her son. She felt the gratitude of the community and its love. She saw Martin's parents. His mother had been put in front of the first pew beyond the pulpit. She was crumpled in the wheelchair she had been confined to since her seizure. It took her on the night she saw her son die and her inability was a reminder to everyone of the mothers' sacrifice. Her head was down as it always was, but she was aware. Her eyes were open and fixed on her grandson.

Susan knew Daniel was standing beside her but she was no longer allowed to touch him. The singing increased in volume and she sensed Daniel moving.

Blacklocks took him by the arm. He led him to stand beside the altar as Andrew White and Aaron Fetcher took the chair away, leaving the stage set for the last few minutes of the ritual. Susan faced east to witness the emptying hourglass. She had only a few more minutes to see her son alive. She was sick to the bottom of her stomach and yet there as something intensely moving about what was happening. She had accepted, she had let the Lore enter her, and it had calmed her. It was the only right thing to do for everyone who stood behind her.

The next verse of the song began and the congregation sang about the sacrifice of the mother; how she, Susan, was the blessed one for bearing the Saddling, raising him up within the Lore so that he would accept his choosing when it came. They sang of the orphan-mothers through the centuries; the women who had given their boys to the storms, those whose lives became barren and twisted, like the mother trees guarding the deeks, as they lived on with a broken heart. They sang of lives praised and thanks given to the orphan-mothers' sacrifices, to women who struggled but who died spiritually fulfilled because they had kept the Lore.

Daniel was kneeling now. The ceremony was entering its final stage but something was troubling the minister. Blacklocks again danced his eyes to the crypt door and then back out to the congregation. He checked the hourglass.

The song came to an end leaving only the sound of the wind battering the windows and the rain hammering on the roof. Candles flickered in drafts and the shadows of everyone present wavered around the walls. Blacklocks took up his place on the far side of the altar and Susan watched him lift the sharp-bladed sacrificial knife.

Tom scrambled from the grave and rolled away. Panting for breath, he stood, momentarily disorientated. He saw the glow of light and, arms outstretched, made his way towards it until he realised that he was, in fact, looking at the corner streetlamp. It lit the side of the inn and he knew what he had to do. He ran to the back door.

He pulled hard on both handles of the barrel chute and they flew open. Clambering down into the blackness of the cellar he fumbled around for the torch that Barry had left behind. His hand collided with bottles which fell to the ground and smashed until one burst of light flashing through the open chute showed up what he was looking for. Switching it on, he shone the beam towards the tunnel.

There was no thought of his past this time. He pulled the door open, thinking only of Dan's face, the figure in the moonlight, the lonely man crying at his father's grave.

Anger drove him on. He didn't flinch as he slipped down the steps into the freezing water. The level had risen leaving only a few inches into which he could twist his head for air as he waded. He pictured Dan sitting against his father's headstone, knowing that he was soon to follow him. With the torch in one hand and checking ahead for falling roof beams with the other, he pushed himself forward. The filthy water lapped at his mouth as he descended and the level rose to reach his nose. A few feet ahead, as the tunnel dipped to its centre point, the breathing space ran out. Taking a deep breath, he closed his eyes and pushed on.

The water was over his head, his hand still guided him along the roof, but there was no air pocket there. His feet moved slowly and pain grew in his chest as he fought against the instinct to breathe. He let out some air, screwed his eyes tighter and dragged himself by his fingertips. He imagined growing up with Blacklocks' Teaching; the boys living a life while saddled with the knowledge that they might one day be the Chosen. He fought back a scream and his hand broke the surface. Tipping his head back, he sucked in air. As the ground rose, so the water level dropped until he met the steps ahead.

Dan lay on the altar. He placed his hands by his side and his feet together, his eyes looking directly up at the roof.

The oldest among the boys came to stand, one at each corner of the altar; Mark Blacklocks at Dan's left shoulder, Jason Rolfe and Matthew

Farrow at his feet. Blacklocks once again eyed the crypt door, frowning. He pointed at Jason's brother Steven, only fifteen and not the strongest boy in the church but, without Barry Cole, this boy was the next in line for the duty. Timidly, Steven stepped up to the altar and stood at Dan's right shoulder. He shivered, either with cold or fear, as the minister continued the ceremony with a nod of his head.

All four boys took hold of Dan, two gripping his ankles and two gripping his wrists. They held them firmly against the stone.

Blacklocks held the knife aloft and the villagers stood. They watched in silence as the hourglass emptied and the knife waited.

'We give for the storm,' Blacklocks chanted. His voice, deep and loud, boomed against the raging elements as though he was challenging it to do its worst. 'What we take from Mother Earth we give back with thanks. To be spared from nature's wrath we offer he who has been called, he who has been chosen. As our village was founded by the call of black-wings and the sheltering of whitebacks, so we remember them and thank them with this life. May it calm the winds and dry the tears of the clouds that wash away the sins of our ancestors. For Saddling.'

The villagers, to a man, repeated earnestly, 'For Saddling.'

Blacklocks admired the boy beneath him. His eyes were open, he showed no fear.

He hesitated, listening intently. He was sure of his plan and there were a few minutes yet to go.

'For Saddling!' he called.

He slashed the knife down and back, swiftly drawing it up over his head in one smooth movement.

He had missed Dan's throat by a hair's breadth.

'We give to the storm,' he chanted, 'one life for all.'

He swooped the knife once more, again purposely missing the throat, and then he placed the knife down on Dan's chest, the blade pointing towards the face as a reminder of what was still to come. He raised both his arms and spoke out to the church.

'He will journey beyond Far Field. He will walk beyond West Ditch with the dole-stones at his back and follow the setting sun.' He paused to look at the door and a diamond of sweat trickled on his forehead. He continued, speaking more slowly this time. 'Daniel Vye, as you travel far from Saddling into the setting sun, you take with you our tempest fear.

You calm the wrath of the flood. You do this for us all...' He broke off and listened. He had heard a dull thud beneath his feet and he smiled. 'And from all, you receive thanks.' He picked up the knife and placed the blade over Daniel's throat before lifting it high over his head, ready to slash one last, fatal time. 'Do you do this willingly, as I do this willingly?'

Dan's voice cut through the rampage of the weather, clear, strong, and unwavering. 'I do this willingly,' he said.

The crypt door burst open and slammed against the wall. Some in the congregation screamed in shock as Tom, wet and filthy, lurched into the church. He took one second to absorb the scene, saw that Dan was still alive and, although he was gasping for breath, he found the strength to shout.

'What the hell are you people doing?'

The villagers immediately started to mumble dissent. Blacklocks lowered the knife, his sick smile cutting a gash through his face. Tom advanced on the altar but Jason Rolfe blocked his path. He shoved the boy to the side, but other men stepped forward to block him.

'You have chosen to join us at last, Mr Carey.' Blacklocks' voice silenced the congregation. They waited on his words. 'You, like your ancestors before you, shall witness the rite of the Saddling, the calming of the great storm.'

'Dan,' Tom called, ignoring him. 'Dan, get up, come with me.'

There were gasps as Daniel wrenched his arms free from the startled boys and sat up. For the first time in the past hour he focused his eyes.

He shook his head.

Tom threw off the two men holding him. He backed away, turned to the villagers but saw only blank faces. Small children blinked at him, holding straw dolls and wondering what was happening. Some men stood up, their expressions turning from shock to anger. Among them, he saw the old man who had given him a lift, the farmer who had brought him to the Saddling path.

'How can you let this happen?' he shouted.

'Get out our church,' Peter Fetcher yelled back, and others raised their voices in agreement.

Tom saw the pulpit and, diving out of the way of the boys who tried to grab him, ran up its steps.

'It's irrational,' he appealed from the top, desperation fracturing his voice.

The height gave him courage. 'Storms happen, floods happen. Killing this man isn't going to stop it.'

'Get back a'your own ways,' a woman shouted. 'Beat 'im down!'

Tom appealed to the boys. 'You can't believe in this. Tell him. Someone must see how wrong this is. It's murder.'

More voices joined in the protest and soon the whole congregation was clamouring against him.

'You can't believe this is going to stop that!' Tom bellowed over them, pointing to the windows. 'You can't believe this killing is going to stop anything.' He tried to shout louder but there were too many voices heckling back. They drowned out the sound of the tempest until Blacklocks stood forward and raised his hands.

Silence fell swiftly.

'Let us be heard,' Blacklocks commanded. He turned calmly to Tom. 'Let me ask you, Mr Carey, what you believe in.'

'I believe you're mad, Blacklooks,' Tom spat back. There was a gasp from the congregation. 'Killing him is not going to stop what's natural.' His heart was pumping hard, his legs were weak with cold. He gripped the sides of the pulpit and took his breath in short gasps. 'These boys shouldn't be growing up believing that it's right to die like this just because of your...' He was going to say religion but there was nothing sacred about this. 'Your superstition. No-one should live a life with this hanging over them.'

A vision of Dylan in his protest T-shirt shivered through him.

'Living a life?' Blacklocks' voice was acidic with derision. 'As you live yours out-marsh? All day with your machines and your screens, your computers, with your addiction to a modernising world bent on destroying itself? Is that a life you would have for these boys? Would you not rather they had freedom and friendship, innocence and purity? As natural a life as we were born to live?'

Tom ignored him and appealed to the villagers. 'And you,' he said. 'You let your sons, your brothers, your nephews, you let them die like this because of his Teaching? Can't you see it? It's only for his own good.'

'It is our belief,' Blacklocks said. 'It is our Lore. And so, I ask again, what do you believe in, Thomas Carey?'

'I believe in facts. And killing Dan will not stop anything. That's a fact.'

'Facts?' Blacklocks winked at his audience. He swished his robes as he turned to the front. 'Every ten years our village floods for winter solstice.

It's in the book, it's a fact. Every ten years we appease the storm in the same way as our ancestors, and I mean yours too, Carey. The first Saddling took place here, on this ground, over seven-hundred years ago. That, too, is a fact. Check the records. One of yours killed one of mine. The ritual was created by your ancestor, Mr Carey, also a fact, and, since then, it has calmed many storms and kept away the waters. All facts.'

A massive crack of thunder shook the building and some of the congregation moved away from the windows.

'And in nineteen-twelve?' Tom fired back. 'When Thomas was chosen but fled? Another went in his place, and what happened then? You flooded, people died. I've seen the graves. I've seen the book. Slaughter did not work. Fact.' He was nearly screaming now.

'Because he did not go willingly,' Blacklocks roared out, louder. 'Because the Carey's were cowards and still are; meddling, murdering cowards who now seek to change hundreds of years of our history, to change our beliefs because they can't understand them.'

The storm outside intensified, the windows rattled, a few panes cracked and several candles were extinguished. Banging on the church door drew Blacklocks' attention. The mumbling and heckling picked up again.

'It's all wrong,' Tom shouted down.

'He was the Chosen. He was one of yours and he fled. The floods came. Lives were lost. All true.'

'Coincidence.'

Mick Farrow dragged in Matt Cole, dishevelled and bleeding.

'The snare gates 'ave all broke, William,' the white-haired farmer bellowed. 'Flooding's up a the knoll. Well underway.'

The two powerful all-workers followed, pushing Irene and Barry into the aisle. Mothers gathered up children and backed away. Irene fell to her knees. Barry tried to help her to her feet but she stayed there, sobbing.

'You see?' Blacklocks shouted up triumphantly. 'The ten-year solstice flood. Out there, now. Fact.'

'William, the hourglass, the Saddling!' a voice called from the back of the church. It was immediately joined by others until the whole congregation were demanding the ritual.

Tom saw Barry standing by his father; both were staring back with helpless expressions. Cole shook his head. He held Tom's gaze for a moment and then slumped to the ground to comfort his wife.

'It's nearly at us!' a woman screamed, and some men closed the doors against the rising water.

'Silence!' Blacklocks raised his head to Tom. 'Tom Carey,' he said slowly, as though this were part of his ritual. 'Thomas Di-Kari of the first clerics of the village. Let me ask you one more question. You think our ways are evil. You think that what we do to protect our way of life is wrong. You shout against our Lore. But tell me, what would you do to end this?'

Tom didn't understand the question. The eyes of the villagers were on him. Susan brought her hands to her mouth. Daniel's face came alive and his mouth opened. Barry turned slowly from his mother as if something was dawning on him.

'What would you give to save Daniel tonight and many others like him in years to come?' Blacklocks persisted. 'What would you give to change our Lore?'

'I don't know what you are getting at,' Tom replied, but the creeping fear that had been eating away at his skin warned him that Matt Cole had told him the truth.

Blacklocks spoke with chilling, calm authority. 'Would you go willingly to our altar in his stead if it would put an end to this ritual forever? One last Saddling to end all to come?'

The storm calmed a little as if was holding its breath, but wind and rain continued to batter on the building.

Tom remembered the grave; had it been dug for Dan or for him? There was no way he could answer, and there was nowhere he could run.

A disturbance at the back of the church caused everyone to turn and see what was happening. Those in the aisle pulled the children to one side.

A tall, young man in a smart suit emerged from the shadows behind the last pew. He pushed a wheelchair. In it sat a withered old woman, barely recognisable as human. Her drawn face was deathly white. Half way down the aisle she raised her head painfully and, with a claw-like hand, removed her oxygen mask.

Maud looked up at Tom through glassy eyes. 'You have to finish this, Tom,' she said.

Forty

Candles flickered madly in the wind that wailed through the window gaps. Tom heard the pandemonium outside and yet he was aware that the congregation was whispering. Some were nodding towards Maud as Blacklocks approached her and bowed.

'Maud?' Tom said, more to himself in shock than to her.

The wizened old woman pushed herself to her feet. Blacklocks and her assistant were there to help her stand.

'You are the last Carey, Tom,' she said. Her thin voice was eerily clear. 'If we don't end this now, more boys will die in the years ahead.'

'You knew about this?' Tom's shock was quickly turning to anger as he pieced it together. 'You knew about the book. You waited until now... Tricked me into coming here... for this?'

'You must do what is right by our ancestors.' Her voice found more strength. 'We started this, you have the power to finish it.'

'It's got nothing to do with me.'

'Innocent young men and children, all dead because of our family.' She tottered towards him on weak legs. 'When I learned of this ritual I had to find a way to end it. And there is only one way.' She gasped for breath, fought back coughing. 'We're stubborn people and I can't leave this legacy behind, knowing that my family was responsible.'

Cole rose and made a sudden movement towards Blacklocks. 'You be messing wi' the Lore, Blacklocks,' he yelled. 'This ain't right. The flood's rising, the Chosen be there, it ain't Tom.'

'That be right,' another voice shouted.

Other voices joined in and Tom felt a rush of hope that he would be able to escape this madness.

An elbow from one of Mick Farrow's men put paid to any more protests from Cole and he crumpled to his knees.

'There will never come another time,' Maud continued, 'when we can end this killing. We must settle the ancestral debt. Let it happen and all these children and generations after them will grow up with no fear of this death. It has to be you.'

'Aye, she be right.'

Tom's face fell in disbelief.

'Minister be right an' all, friend Tom,' Barry said as he slowly approached the altar.

'Barry?' His friend's eyes bore into him, unblinking. 'What are you doing?'

Barry did not reply. He took Steven's place and, with a tip of his head, indicated that Tom should come down from the pulpit.

Tom watched in despair. He was completely on his own.

'A man's got a-do right by 'is friends, eh Tom?' Barry called up. His expression gave nothing away. Was he hinting at something or was he like all the rest? 'I be wi' you all the way,' he said, and laid his hand on the altar stone.

There was something behind Barry's words. There had always been something behind his words; trust, friendship and doing the right thing. Tom thought of Dan; the naked figure in the moonlit dream, the lost, lonesome youth, the eyes that searched, the smooth hand that touched, the unnerving appeal. His eyes flicked back to Barry; the runagate, the loyalty, the things he couldn't speak of, the heavy hand that held tight. The eyes alight with trust.

Tom didn't know what they were saying now, but he had nowhere to run. He was a lone sheep baa-ing against a flock of others dumbed by their faith, and their voice was louder than his. They followed their looker without question as he led them gently towards death.

But he did have somewhere to run.

He saw Barry's calm eyes reflect a flickering candle. He saw his impish smile give a tiny waver. He remembered the tingling glide of the razor across his throat as he stood exposed but safe in a steadying grip. He knew that where Dan exuded mystique, Barry bled loyalty.

Tom finally gave in. He admitted that where Dan had roused lust, Barry had stirred something deeper rooted and far longer lasting.

He came down from the pulpit and the thunder took up its complaining.

'Tom ain't the Chosen,' Cole cried out. 'Remember afore? 'Is kin went unwilling and my people died. Blacklocks...'

This time, one of the henchmen struck Cole on the back of the head and dazed him into silence. Others were mumbling, the congregation growing more uneasy.

'You put your trust in my Lore and me.' Blacklocks spoke with authority. 'So I shall see this through. The hourglass has run its sand. The time is now.'

A panicked yell from the back of the building drew everyone's attention.

Water was seeping in under the door. More was creeping up from the crypt. Villagers pushed forward, but there would be no escape from the rising tide.

As if to seal the fate of all inside, lightning attacked the ground nearby and the whole building shuddered. One of the windows exploded inwards. Women screamed, children cried and pushed towards the door where men held them back.

'Calm!' Blacklocks yelled. 'I will end our anguish. I will put a stop to the Saddling in this one act. Put your faith in me and I will save generations of boys from this fate. Hold faith in the Lore and we will live on. Our way of life as always before but without the need for your sacrifice.'

'Take 'im,' someone shouted. 'Afore we're all drowned.'

Tom saw that Barry had laid his hand by the knife. It was a signal, surely? His way out; grab the knife and run for it. As he stepped up to the altar, he turned and saw his aunt being lowered into her chair. He would process her deception later but, for now, he had a plan forming, and it was going to save his life.

He nodded to Barry and made a lunge for the knife, but the boys were faster. His fingers were on the handle when someone grabbed his arm and held it tight. A second pair of hands took hold of his wrist and pulled the blade away. It was Barry.

'Barry?' Tom was incredulous.

'You got a-do right by your friends, Tom,' Barry whispered back.

The next moments happened too quickly. Rough hands pulled at Tom's legs and turned him. He was dragged onto the stone and wrestled to his back. He kicked out but the two boys holding his feet pressed them down painfully by the ankles. Barry had him pinned by his right arm and, thrashing his head in protest, he saw that now Dan had hold of his left. He struggled, but it was useless.

He heard Cole shouting, 'Tom ain't the Chosen! He's the wrong age.' He heard singing underscored by thunder. His head banged against the altar as he tried to break free.

'It 'as to 'appen this way, Tom,' Barry said. 'Let it be.'

'Dan, please!' Tom yelled out, kicking uselessly against the pressure on his legs.

Blacklocks towered over him, bearing down. His eyes flamed and his hair was wild about his head. His lips parted in a triumphant grin and he lifted the knife, showing Tom the razor-sharp blade.

'Here lies the last of the Carey family,' the minister boomed over the din of the storm and the joyful singing. 'The last of those who brought the Saddling to us, they who began this. So, let them finish it.'

'You fucking murderer!' Tom screamed. 'Dan? Barry?'

It did no good. The hands only held more firmly, the singing only increased in volume.

Blacklocks raised the knife. 'We give for the storm,' he chanted. 'What we take from Mother Earth, so we give back...'

Tom knew the man was speaking but he didn't hear the words. His body froze in realisation. No matter what he did, they were going to kill him.

His right to life was lost to their belief. Their faith was stronger than his reason.

'May it calm the winds and dry the tears of the clouds that wash away our sins from years before. For Saddling.'

The villagers, repeated, 'For Saddling.'

Cole's voice rang out, angry and powerful, 'But 'e ain't going willing.'

'Please!' Tom cried out in desperation, tears in his eyes. 'Aunt Maud, please. Someone!'

'Tom Carey,' the minister boomed. 'Do you do this willingly as I do this willingly?'

'Get the fuck off me.'

'The Chosen 'as a-go willing,' Cole shouted again, but no-one was listening.

In a moment of detached lucidity, Tom felt Barry holding his hand.

'I be 'ere for you, friend,' he said.

A flashback to the last sunset ran through Tom and, for a second, he felt that he was doing the right thing. Perhaps their fanaticism was more than superstition. Maybe he could put an end to this practice once and for all. He could make a difference.

Blacklocks grinned down at him.

'Do you do this willingly as I do this willingly?'

Tom hesitated. He remembered the sound of the youngest boy crying as he watched what could have been his last sunset and said goodbye to his friends. He remembered the touch of Dan's hand in his. He felt Barry's hand now. He had to do something to stop this, to free them all from Blacklocks' horror.

Going willingly to slaughter was not it.

'No, I fucking don't,' he shouted.

Blacklocks' face twisted into an expression of pure hate.

A lightning bolt struck the flood, another window shattered. The congregation sang louder.

Tom knew what was coming. The blade glinted in the candlelight and then he saw it spark as it flashed through the air. Blacklocks brought the knife down and Tom turned his head away, twisting his body. He felt a hot sting as the knife cut through his shoulder.

He'd missed.

'We give to the storm,' Blacklocks chanted. 'One life for many.'

What torture is this? Tom thrashed. Hands gripped tighter as blood ran down his arm.

Blacklocks swooped the knife and Tom screamed.

The knife missed him again. How many times was he going to suffer this before his throat was split? The man was toying with him, exacting his revenge with relish and the worst part of it was that Tom was helpless. This was not his fault. He hadn't chosen to be born as the last of his family.

Following the ceremony that his ancestors had laid down years before, Blacklocks placed the knife on Tom's chest, the blade towards his face.

The minister was lost in the joy of his ritual. He raised his arms ecstatically, called up to the roof as if he were addressing the storm itself. 'He will journey beyond Far Field. He will walk...'

The pressure on Tom's right arm was released.

'Now, Tom!' Barry's voice close by. 'Daniel!'

His left arm was suddenly free.

Tom grabbed the knife but Blacklocks was fast and his great hands wrapped around Tom's immediately. With his legs still pinned, Tom twisted and squirmed, the blade slashing back and forth close to his throat as Blacklocks tried to prise his fingers apart. He heard a cry amid the commotion. The pressure on his legs lifted as Barry and Dan kicked the other boys away from the altar. Cole was on his feet, hurling village men out of his path. Mark Blacklocks leapt on Barry, screaming and bringing his fists down hard on his face. Dan was on him in a second pulling the boy off by his hair and throwing him to the ground where he slid through the water. Cole waded in, pushing and pulling others away from the altar.

Tom was on his side and then on his knees, turning the blade towards Blacklocks, his muscles fuelled by anger.

The minister was stronger. His face contorted in rage as he climbed up onto the altar and forced Tom towards the edge. Tom fought back but his wrists were weakening. His arm twisted as Blacklocks moved behind him. The blade was now under his chin and coming closer. He wrestled to turn it in his hand, to face the sharp edge outwards and away from his throat. He succeeded, but his arm muscles were weakening.

Lightning violently attacked the leaded east window. The glass shattered in a cascade of red and blue, purple and white, raining down shards and lead on the chancel. Singing became euphoric screams of faith as the congregation begged for the Saddling to release them. The wind drove in, billowing out Blacklocks' white robes, his hair writhing like snakes, and, with it, came the rain and the full volume of the storm.

The church shook to its foundations. Floodwater poured in under the doors. People stood on pews, screaming. Others fought to keep Barry and Dan from reaching the altar, hands grabbing to bring them down. Barry smashed the hourglass over Jason's head.

Mark Blacklocks spat and clawed his way through the others and climbed onto the altar. He pushed on his father's hand, forcing the knife to touch Tom's throat as Tom struggled to push back.

He kicked out. The boy fell backwards but Tom's foot slipped on the altar cloth and he stumbled. His elbows cracked hard on the stone as Blacklocks fell on top of him. They rolled and Tom bit down on the man's wrist. He tasted blood in his mouth, heard an animal yell as the grip on the knife weakened. Still pushing against the pressure, Tom forced himself to his knees with his arms taut. He bit harder.

Abruptly, the pressure was gone. His arm flew wide, the blade slicing through the air. He spun and scrambled to his feet, gasping for breath and ready to lunge.

Silence. As instant as it was shocking.

It was all Tom was aware of as he stood on the altar, ready for the next attack. He was tense and prepared but nothing was happening.

Blacklocks lay on his back at Tom's feet, his head to one side, his arm reaching out towards the nave. The drapes of his robes flowed over the edge. Cole was frozen. He had one man by the throat, another trapped beneath his boot. Susan was on her knees, her mouth open in a silent scream. No-one moved. They were all staring at Tom.

Straw dolls floated on the floodwater, spinning in circles. They drifted slowly towards the door. The last remaining candles no longer danced and shadows settled into orderly form around the walls.

No thunder, no lightning, no storm. The only sound Tom heard now was his own breathing.

The water was receding, draining away down the aisle and drawing a pink line with it. The colour intensified to dark red.

Blacklocks slid from the altar in a slow, fluid movement, the altar cloth trailing after him.

One by one the villagers began to move. The doors were thrown open and the realisation hit them.

'It's passing,' a voice called out from the back. 'The flood's drawing off.'

Some climbed on pews to press their faces to the shattered windows. Mick Farrow held a candle into the void at the crypt door. 'Aye,' he called, 'It be leaving below, an' all.'

Villagers moved to the doors to see out but the silence from outside made it clear.

Stunned, Tom dropped the bloodied knife and it clattered onto the altar. Barry quickly picked it up. His lip was bleeding and one eye was already swelling.

Tom was shaking and his arms were trembling as Barry helped him down. He rested Tom against the altar and pressed a heavy hand on his shoulder to keep him there. 'Stay wi' me,' he said.

Barry saw Tom's eyes wide with confusion. 'I didn't want you to see no part of this,' he said. He wasn't sure if Tom was listening. 'That were the only reason we didn't want you 'ere.'

Barry saw a great white thing grow up in front of the altar as the minister rose to his feet. He unwound himself from the floor where he had been crouching and, as he came to his full height, he let out a long, slow wail. It intensified in volume until it was a howl of anguish that chilled Barry's blood.

Blacklocks stood before the altar with his son laid across his arms. Mark's head flopped back at a horrific angle, a thick, dark gash across his neck. The boy's blood fell at the minister's feet and swirled away in the receding tide. Blacklocks screamed out a desperate cry of agony.

'You have killed my son!' he wailed. 'My only son. My boy...'

He took a step forward, tears running from his black eyes and his long gown dragging the swirling red of death behind him.

Cole stepped out to block his path and drew Blacklocks' attention from his son's body.

'The storm...?' Blacklocks asked, his face a deathly pale mask of confusion.

Cole reached into his pocket and lay a handful of whiteback pellets on Mark's body. He glared hard into the minister's eyes. 'You can't cheat the Saddling,' he said.

Villagers gasped. Disbelief ran through the congregation on whispered words, but their horror turned quickly to anger as realisation dawned. Their voices grew louder. Cole threw more sheep pellets to the floor and people backed away from them, their glares rising from the feed to the minister, horror in their eyes.

Blacklocks held his son out to his people as if the body was a peace offering. 'He calmed the storm,' he pleaded. His words did him no favours. Some villagers turned away from him, others took menacing steps towards him.

Barry felt Tom try to lunge forward and he held him back.

'What do I do?' the minister asked, tears flowing freely from his eyes. 'He was all of me.'

'Cheating our Lore,' someone said with spite.

'Offering our boys but his own stays safe.'

'Been playing us all fur stupids,' Farrow growled. 'And you knew 'bout this, Cole?' Others joined the dissent.

'It don't matter,' Barry shouted, and silenced them. 'See? It should never 'ave been Daniel, neither.'

The minister's full deceit dawned icily over his flock.

'Fur 'ow long 'as 'is family been a-cheating the Saddling?'

'But I've saved the village.' Blacklocks wailed, and cradled his dead son tighter to his chest.

'Was 'im.' Cole pointed to Tom. 'Was 'im as saved us.'

'It was he who killed my boy,' Blacklocks yelled.

Faces turned to Tom and Barry's arm moved around his shoulders to hold him back more firmly. Tom was breathing faster; there was a snarl growing in his throat.

'Stay down,' Barry whispered. 'It be done.' He saw his father nod to him, approving.

'You brought it on yourself, Blacklocks,' Cole said.

Blacklocks' legs weakened and he stumbled. 'I gave his life for you all,' he cried, his voice feeble and trembling. 'I gave you all...'

'You gave nothing,' Cole shot back.

The ministers' arms were sagging and, with a great effort, he offered his son up to them once more.

One by one the villagers stepped back from the aisle, clearing a path. Each of them turned their heads away and fell silent until there was nothing for Blacklocks in the church but a frozen wall of hate.

'I'll take him home,' Blacklocks whispered. 'Matthew, you will help me with the burial in the morning.'

'You know well as me what your Teaching say, William,' Cole said.

Barry heard the regret in his father's voice, but there was no regret in his own heart.

'What more would you have me do?' Blacklocks pleaded.

'Find yourself a deep deek,' Cole said, and stood aside.

Blacklocks lowered his head and shuffled towards the door. The only sound was his miserable groaning and the uneven scrape of his footsteps on stone. The last of the floodwater slipped away ahead of him and the villagers followed.

Tom narrowed his eyes to his aunt at the back of the church. She sat defiantly with her assistant kneeling beside her, holding the mask to her face.

He was distracted from his anger when Barry nudged him. 'Told you I'd be there fur you.'

'What the...? What just happened?' he asked, his forehead cramped with confusion.

He was aware that someone else was standing beside him and felt a smooth hand give his own a quick squeeze before letting it go. Dan approached his mother in the front pew. Her head was in her hands and she was sobbing. He put his arms around her and held her.

'Minister's gone mad!' Jason Rolfe was at the door. The remaining congregation pushed past him and Tom saw moonlight streaming in through the windows. He felt a tug on his hand and Barry led him down the aisle.

Tom held back when he reached Maud. She sat, warped in her wheelchair, and removed her mask.

'Your father couldn't do it,' she said. 'He knew of the Saddling and did nothing. Your great uncle ran to save his own life.'

'You knew your answer all the time.' Tom was still filtering her duplicity. 'You...'

'Miss Carey did what had to be done.'

Tom's eyes flashed to the young man beside her.

'Who are you? Are you family?'

'He's nobody,' Maud said.

Philip stood up straight and raised his chin. 'I,' he said, looking down his nose at Tom as though he had no right to be in his sightline, 'am your aunt's assistant. I am the one who has nursed her and helped her, been there for her...'

'He's just a helpful little shit who has been after my money.' Maud dismissed him and clutched at her mask. 'He does what he is told. Unlike you.'

Tom could think of no more words. He took a step away.

'Wait,' Maud croaked. Tom stopped with his back to her. 'You were prepared to do it? For your family?'

Tom watched as Dan led his mother into the porch, her head on his shoulder, his arms supporting her.

'I have no family,' he replied. 'And I'm thankful for that.'

A short pull on his hand from Barry and Tom left her.

Philip drew some legal papers from a briefcase. 'Will you be signing?' he asked, and, raising an eyebrow, waited for a decision. She held his stare for a long time before slowly placing the mask back over her face.

The moon was full. Bright light glinted off the surface as the water receded leaving only a few areas of lower ground still flooded. Wide open spaces of glassy blackness once again became the ordered lines of the deeks, and the fields were revealed. The last of the storm clouds rolled back into the night leaving stars to pinprick the crow-black sky.

The villagers stood among the graves watching a mist that rose from the ground to form meandering shapes that drifted in among the hedgerows.

Tom watched with Barry at his side as the ghostly form of William Blacklocks moved out across the field, the moonlight filling his white robes with an eery glow. He didn't look back and no-one called for him. He was swallowed up by the weird mother trees and the mist until both he and the last of his line were lost to the marsh.

Forty-one

Mick Farrow carried the orphaned lamb to the pen; it was old enough now to fend for itself with the other tegs. He opened the gate and shooed the thing inside, listening to its blarring as it called out to the flock. An old ewe came to give it some attention and Mick turned away knowing the thing would fare fine.

The fields had survived the flood as had most of his flock. Farrow had made sure to pen them on his higher ground and in the coterell barn, as had others, and they had fared fine through the winter and birthed. He surveyed his laid-in field and mopped his brow against the warming day. The heel-weed and horse-knot were well and truly through, and there were buffs of paigle dotted here and there, their yellow flowers moving gently in the breeze. Another few months' fallow and this field would be ready for grazing.

A sound floated over to him and rose in volume. It was a sound he was still not used to and he frowned as he turned to it.

On the far side of the field, coming in from the new bridge, he saw a truck bouncing its slow progress towards the village. He shook his head and sighed as he made his way towards the inn.

The houses around the green stood in spring silence facing the damaged church. The villagers had long since dried their possessions, the shop had restocked as best it could, and what had briefly been mud was now dry earth. The resilient grass was being kept short by grazing sheep. One fed at Barry's feet as he filled his pipe. He stood resting against the back of the bench, facing the church and the Blacklock's house. There were no curtains there now, no lights glowed inside at night; the rooms had been emptied, and the building stood uninhabited. Blacklocks had not been seen or found, and, yet, Barry could feel his presence when he contemplated the church. The shattered windows were boarded and the roof temporarily patched. The village had not used it since that night. All meetings were now called at his father's hay barn. It was warmer, for one thing, and far more welcoming.

Apart from some storm damage that had still to be repaired, the village looked the same as it always had, but now there was a gaping difference.

There was no threat hanging over it. Barry could feel relief in the air. He sensed it in the lads who greeted him in the fields, and saw it on the faces of familes and their young children, especially the families with sons.

At the Crow and Whiteback, Susan dragged a new cask of Philip Tidy's horesebuckle wine from the cellar and closed the hatch. She had cleaned the bar from the night before and was preparing for another lunchtime. With lambing over and the potatoes going in, the men were always hungry for some of her stew. It took away the taste of Andrew White's ravel bread, for one thing.

She heard a fist banging against metal and called out, 'Sally, that ain't how it works.'

Leaning across the bar to see into the corner, she saw Sally Rolfe thumping Dan's new machine.

'Oi!' Susan shouted roughly.

The girl stopped what she was doing. 'Bain't doing nothing,' she complained.

'Hold on.' Susan stepped into the passage and called up the stairs. 'Daniel?'

'Coming, Ma,' he replied, and a few seconds later came bounding down and out through the back door.

He stepped up to the old generator that Nate Rolfe had installed in a new lean-to and checked that the cable was connected. That done, he made sure there was fuel in the tank and then pulled a lever on the side until the thing chugged into life.

Back in the bar, the jukebox lit up and music slowly wound into a tune. A quiet folk song filtered out and, by the time Dan came in, Sally was happily listening to it and reading through the selection of other old tunes. Susan, raising her eyebrows, wove through the bar and opened the door to let in the fresh air.

The truck was parked a little way down the lane at the Cole house. Matt Cole was clambering out of it.

'What is it, Ma?' Dan asked, coming to her hand in hand with Sally. 'About time.' He saw Barry smoking his pipe at the bench and called to him.

'Your fader's back, Barry,' he said when Barry joined them. 'Thought you'd a-gone with him.'

'No, mate.' Barry put his pipe away. 'Went out once, a month past, and that were enough fur now.'

They walked the short distance along the lope-way to the Cole house with Sally trailing after them and reached the truck as Cole was wrestling with the door that barely closed, cursing cheerfully.

'You get 'em, Fader?' Barry asked, his eyes alight with excitement.

'Aye, nipper, I did.' He handed over two small boxes, one each to Barry and Dan.

'What's that when it ain't 'ere?' Sally asked, reading the strange names on the covers.

'Be a telephone,' Barry said. 'Been waiting weeks a'this.'

'Won't do you no good, boy,' Cole said, laughing. 'They say we won't be getting their signal out 'ere come another four month or more.'

'Give me time a-learn you 'ow a-use it,' Barry answered, unpacking one.

'I didn't want a-be learning that,' Cole said, and reached back into the truck. 'What I be wanting a-do with one of 'em? You boys be taking this all too far...' He mumbled on as he yanked the door open, took an envelope from the truck and struggled to close the door again. 'Oh, bugger it.'

'Let me take it, Fader.' Barry saw the envelope and grabbed it from his dad.

'No hurry, nipper,' Cole said. 'There be other things a-tell you, if you want a-hear?'

Barry, at the front door, turned on the step. 'Dan, mate, see you later? We still going 'unting out beyond the west dole-stones? It's growing some great clumps of Devil's-Thread there 'bouts.'

'Sure,' Dan said. 'Come a-calling for me after.'

'Daniel Vye,' Sally protested. 'You said you'd be spending the afternoon with me on the farm helping me fader wi' the dag-wool.'

'Hm,' said Dan with a grin. 'Pulling tags off sheep's arses or hunting out a good smoke. What you reckon, Matthew Cole?'

'There's always time fur women, lad,' Cole replied. 'But when Devil's-Thread's in bloom you won't want a-be missing some good choke.'

Sally stamped her foot and stormed off.

'See you after,' Barry called as Dan followed her, trying to make things better. He waved back and put his arm around her. She shrugged it off. He tried again. Barry laughed and went to speak to his father.

A short while later, Irene hurried from the kitchen with a basket of laundry.

'You two cut your man-clattering, and Barry, come and sort your room.

Soon as you like.' She turned at the stairs and began to climb.

Barry followed his mother up to his bedroom where she knocked once and entered.

Tom sat at the table between the two beds. As usual, he was writing in his books and there were piles of others around him. Irene scanned the room and frowned.

Barry's bed was a riot of tangled sheets, pillows and discarded clothes. Tom's bed, as always, was perfectly made. Barry pushed past her into the room.

'Why can't you keep your lid on your bed nice and tidy, like Tom, 'ere, does?' she asked her son. 'His always looks like it ain't never been slept in.'

Barry blushed and said, 'Aye, Ma.'

She handed him the laundry. 'Have this put away and I don't want none of that telephone thing in my 'ouse. You keep them nasty ways to yourselves. Understood that?'

'Aye, Ma.'

'Tom Carey?'

'Aye, Ma,' Tom said, his head still down over his books.

Irene tutted and left, closing the door behind her.

'Looks like it ain't never been slept in,' Barry mimicked his mother. 'She'll never get it, will she?' He laughed and fell back onto Tom's bed, discarding the laundry to the floor. 'Look what me fader brought in from Romney fur you.' He waved the envelope in the air.

Tom turned to him. He was clean shaven, as was his habit these days, and his hair was kept neat under Barry's scissors. Irene had sewed him trousers that fitted and a few white shirts to wear beneath Cole's old sheepskin. His shirt was open and the scar on his shoulder had almost faded, but it still brought back memories for Barry. Tom sat next to him and took the envelope.

'Go on and open it,' Barry encouraged.

'What news did your fader bring?' Tom asked as he read the return address on the back.

'We'll have a summer festival in time,' Barry said. 'There's talk 'bout a man coming to do something to do wi' God at the church when it be repaired, though 'e don't know where the village will find its money. Don't matter if you ask me as none'll use it. Prehaps, 'e says, there might be others who want a-come fur their weddings and such, and that'd be good fur the inn.

Me aunt can shift some of 'er endless sheepskins an' all. Fader says we's not going a-get swamped by visitors but some'll come in time. Can't stop it no more, 'e says.' He tapped the letter that Tom had taken from the envelope and was now reading. 'It be what you thought?'

Tom dropped the papers to the floor and leant back against the pillow.

'Well?' Barry asked, shifting to lie beside him.

'Aye,' Tom said. 'Her helpful little shit tried to contest it but he got nothing.'

'But you?'

Tom could not repress his broad smile.

Even though Tom winked at him and he had his answer, Barry's cheer left him. He swung his legs off the bed and stood looking down at Tom's books. They were filled with scrawny handwriting telling the story of Tom's ancestors since the founding of the village. He had read it all before.

'That means you can go back 'ome a'London,' he said. 'Get that top-lap you wanted and that car. You'll be away afore long.'

'I could,' Tom said, pulling himself to his feet. He joined Barry at the desk. 'The money's mine, now. I can do what I like.' For the first time in weeks, he saw Barry's face without a smile on it. 'Or,' he added, 'prephaps I'll put in a bid for the Blacklocks house when the auction comes up. It's got room and I can't be living here all the time.'

Barry's concern morphed into his usual grin. 'And me ma wouldn't 'ave to be buffle-'eaded 'bout your bed no more.'

'It's got two upstairs rooms.'

It took Barry a moment to register Tom's implication. 'You mean it, Tom Carey?'

'I do, Barry Cole,' Tom replied. He turned a page in one of his books, pretending to read. 'We can use one for guests.' He looked up to see Barry's grin nearly tear his face in half. 'A man's gotta do well by his mate, as a lompy friend of mine once said.'

Barry elbowed him. 'It ain't lompy,' he said. 'Lompy's when you're thick-stupid. You mean crank.' He smiled and banged his head onto Tom's shoulder. 'I'm crank, I am.'

'I have no idea what you are,' Tom replied, smiling. 'But I'm staying wi' ye.'

In the afternoon, under a blue sky dotted with harmless white clouds, Barry and Tom climbed the knoll to the graves. They approached quietly and came to stand with Susan and Dan at a pair of recently carved headstones.

Tom read one of the inscriptions. "For an unknown, taken by the storm." He knew that Dylan didn't lie there. His body had been found and taken back to his family, but Tom had asked for the stone as a reminder. He was sure that Dylan had been on his way to warn him of his aunt's deception, but there was no way to prove it.

Susan laid some flowers on the grave beside it, the one that remembered "Eliza Seeming, beloved sister and aunt".

There were no graves for Blacklocks or his son. The deeks had never given up their bodies.

'I bet she's giving him hell up there somewhere,' Dan said.

'I doubt he went up,' Susan replied, pondering the grave with her head to one side. 'But she's sleeping well, now.'

Barry put his arm around Dan's shoulder and gave him a brief hug. 'Be 'ere fur you, friend,' he said.

Dan briefly rested his head against Barry's. 'I know. Changes are coming to Saddling, but some things will always be the same.' He turned to his mother. 'She'll be sleeping deep, Ma.'

'That she will, Daniel,' she said. 'Now she knows that Tom put an end to it.'

'Did I?' Tom asked quietly, looking masrshwards.

Sheep grazed in the hedgerow-crossed green fields that rested peacefully beneath the infinite and sheltering sky.

'We won't know that for another ten years.'

They stood in thoughtful silence until Barry said, 'We best be 'eading out if we're a-find any Devil's Thread afore boblight. Come wi' us, Tom?'

'Aye,' Tom replied. 'I'm willing a-walk some miles for some of that.'

Susan kissed her son on the cheek, relishing the moment as she now always did. With her hand resting on her sister's grave, she watched the three lads head down the slope and into the field.

She kept her gaze on them as, arms around shoulders, they strode out towards the deek-bridge and on towards the western mark where the new growth of soft-grass pushed through the old in the spring-weak sunlight. She knew they wouldn't be back until long after dark, but there was no worry.

They were safe; they knew their way and they had each other.

Whiteback flocks moved lazily out of their path as the boys strolled over the tufted fields. They talked freely and made plans along the reeded deek, startling yellow finches into flight. They crossed the bridge where the mother trees watched over them, their new leaves reflecting in the glass-flat water.

A hernshaw raised its broad wings, both greeting and applauding as a murder of crows fled before them in panicked protest. The young men pushed one another, laughing, debating the future and forgetting the past. With arms around shoulders, and warmed by companionship, they finally talked themselves into silence.

They walked on into the distance until they were nothing more than brushstrokes on nature's vast canvas.

19258340R00160

Printed in Poland
by Amazon Fulfillment
Poland Sp. z o.o., Wrocław